ABOUT THE AUTHOR

Daniel Peltz lives in London and is married with four children. He is a fellow of both Kings College and Birkbeck College, London University. He is CEO of London Freeholds Ltd, a property company and also sits on a number of charity boards, including The Anna Freud Centre, The Kings College Campaign Board, The City of London School Bursary Trust, Childhood First, and The Oxford Centre for Jewish Studies. He is an avid cricket follower and is a member of both the MCC Finance and Estates committees.

He has written three previous books published by the Book Guild including *Out of the Blue* which was described by the *Sunday Express* as 'One of the best war stories you'll read.'

He was awarded an OBE in the 2016 New Years Honours list for Charitable and Philanthropic Services.

PREVIOUSLY BY THE AUTHOR

Blood Ties

Out of the Blue

Daffodils before Swallows

THE INDOMITABLE CHIESA DI SANTA MARIA

DANIEL PELTZ

The Book Guild Ltd

First published in Great Britain in 2017 by
The Book Guild Ltd
9 Priory Business Park
Wistow Road, Kibworth
Leicestershire, LE8 0RX
Freephone: 0800 999 2982
www.bookguild.co.uk
Email: info@bookguild.co.uk
Twitter: @bookguild

This work is entirely fictitious and bears no resemblance to any persons living or dead.

Typeset in Minion Pro

Printed and bound in the UK by TJ International, Padstow, Cornwall

ISBN 978 1912083 770

British Library Cataloguing in Publication Data.
A catalogue record for this book is available from the British Library.

To Elizabeth

LIST OF CONTENTS

PART I

PRESENT DAY FLORENCE

I

Molly woke up at eight, her usual time when she was due to take private clients around the museum. That morning she felt both euphoric and fatigued. The previous day she had spent hours at a fourteenth-century convent in Fiesole looking for documents that would help her piece together her doctorate on Humanist Neo-Platonism in the Renaissance. At first, she searched fruitlessly amongst the thousands of volumes on the shelves. She desperately needed source material, and her research had led her here. She looked around the library, and across to the only wall that had no shelves attached to it. In their place hung a beautiful square shaped tapestry, no larger than three foot, of the Virgin Mary. She walked over to the image which, evoked such warmth and empathy that she stood staring at it for some time.

'I could do with some help here,' she muttered under her breath, before returning to her search.

As if the woven image had answered her half-hearted prayer, Molly finally found what she was looking for. Pico della Mirandola was the central historical figure for her thesis, and locating a manuscript written by him, hidden on one of the shelves in the convent library was no ordinary Renaissance discovery. If that was not enough, whilst replacing the manuscript carefully back on the shelf after photocopying it, she saw another loose sheet of parchment lying flat, previously unnoticed.

She had carefully picked up the loose parchment and stared at the image that had been so meticulously drawn on it. The picture, depicting Christ wearing his Crown of Thorns supported by Mary Magdalene and St John Evangelista, had been carried out in pen and ink. Her knowledge of the period immediately enabled her to realise through its technique, that this was a work of the Quattrocento. It was also exquisitely drawn, obviously by a hand of a master, the identity of whom she could not yet tell. Whilst holding the fragile parchment she had noticed a slight shake in her hand, such was the exhilaration that was suddenly streaming through her veins. She immediately knew that she would need to take a copy, and then show it to an expert. She was perversely more excited by the image than the Mirandola discovery. However the condition of the drawing was far more delicate than the written manuscript, and she had been concerned about taking it to the photocopier in case it might literally disintegrate. Since she wouldn't need to work on it because it wasn't directly relevant to her thesis, she had decided to use her phone to take a photograph. At the time, because the library was closing, she was in a slight panic, and in her haste, rather stupidly, didn't think of turning the parchment over to see if it was signed on the back.

Having left the convent at four, she had returned to her apartment in Florence, and spent the rest of the day and evening deciphering the photocopy of the manuscript. Her task had been made even more challenging by the fact that the photocopier at the fifteenth-century convent was of a 1980s vintage, producing a replica of such poor quality that at times during the night she had to hold her phone torch up close to the script to decipher the words in the early Italian script.

She sat up with the sound of the alarm, and reached for the half filled glass of water on the bedside table. It was suffocatingly hot, and even with the courtyard window being wide open there was not a breath of air to be had in the bedroom. She immediately glanced across towards the desk where her work lay. Pausing for a moment, she then walked over, and placed her hands on the edge of the desk, staring at the document and her notes. 'Christ, there's so much to do, and so little time.'

Having showered and got dressed, she snatched her keys from the side table and left the tiny apartment that was all she could afford. Every morning, apart from the weekends, Molly's routine had barely changed. Working part time for the Museo di Santa Maria, located on the south bank of the Arno, her job as personal guide to wealthy tourists was a well paid one for the hours it demanded. The money earned from the position at the museum meant that she was able to pay the rent, and have the means to afford her modest life style with a little to spare.

Molly was well qualified for the position of museum guide, not only because of her obvious knowledge of the Renaissance, but also because she was bilingual. Her mother being Italian meant that she could seamlessly interact with her clients and the public when necessary. There was however another reason why the position was so ideal for the English doctoral student. She had fallen in love with the museum when she had first seen it three years previously whilst on secondment, studying for her undergraduate degree. After returning to the city to continue her doctoral work, she had noticed an advert that appeared on the board in the hallway of her apartment block. Reading that a post for a part time guide was needed, she lost little time in applying. She handed in her application the very same day that the notice had gone up, and Gianni, the curator of the museum, had no hesitation in accepting her. Clever, youthful and very approachable the bilingual Renaissance expert suited the role perfectly.

She was now in her third of a four-year doctorate, and her escape to Florence for that year was something that she had looked forward to ever since she had graduated. Living in the city, where her mother was born and grew up, seemed to have liberated her. She sensed simultaneously a kind of freedom as well as a feeling of being at home whilst in the Tuscan capital. Although she had no surviving relatives living there any more, she had told her father that she had never been happier, and hoped that he would visit her before the summer was over. He said he would, but she knew that it would be unlikely.

2

Life had not come easily for Molly Cavendish. Born in South London, her father was the local priest, whilst her Italian mother worked at the Italian Institute in Central London. She was an only child and therefore had no brothers or sisters with whom she could confide. The mediocrity of her existence was best reflected by the featureless red-bricked terrace house in which the family lived. Her relationship with her father, Simon, was virtually non-existent. He paid more attention to his parishioners than to his only child. It was not that he didn't love her, it was just that his priorities were directed more towards the local community than his own family. As a result, although revered by his congregation, his flock never failed to tell Molly how wonderful he was, his family felt neglected.

The lack of a paternal relationship was more than compensated by the special bond she had had with her mother, Alexandria. Both parent and best friend, she was a vibrant woman who had an inexhaustible passion for life. It was easy to see why they formed such a close bond, and why Molly told her mother everything. Problems relating to boyfriends, friendships, and schoolwork featured in their daily conversations. There was literally nothing that Molly did not confide in with her mother. Likewise, her mother would reciprocate by entrusting her child with things that she could not tell her father. One of those taboo topics that were endlessly discussed was her mother's reminiscence of her home city, Florence, and how she missed not being there. Her father's work meant that they could rarely go away. Every time a holiday to her home city was mentioned, it led to arguments over the difficulties of him leaving his congregants. The result was that she gave up on any hope of going, and rarely mentioned it to him any more for fear of more quarrels.

Alexandria had not been back home for over ten years. Indeed she had only returned twice during her entire marriage, and that was to bury both of her parents. Memories of those last brief visits left her with an unquenchable melancholy. And yet her love for Florence remained undiminished. She could never forgive her husband for the lack of sympathy and empathy that he so clearly exhibited with his parishioners. The marriage suffered from arguments which led to frustration, and then to discontent, but nevertheless held firm, if only as a friendship. It remained loveless. As a result, Alexandria's entire emotional love was directed towards Molly, who was more than a willing recipient.

And yet despite the support she received from her mother, Molly felt a nagging sense of dissatisfaction with her life. At sixteen she achieved modest success at her O Levels, and selected English, History and, naturally, Italian as her A level options. It was during this year, her seventeenth, that Molly suddenly woke up to the dire possibility that her life was destined for under achievement. Something had to change. The dynamic at home showed no signs of readjusting, and thus the transformation would have to come from within.

3

The rewiring of Molly's brain coincided with, although some might say caused by, a sudden love for History and in particular, the Italian Renaissance. One morning, a visiting teacher gave a lecture on the early Renaissance artists. Describing Giotto, and his depiction of St Francis feeding the birds suddenly opened Molly's eyes to the beauty and form that was so much a part of the artist's genius. Seeing a picture displaying such proportion and perspective, and indeed natural harmony, awoke the young student up from her intellectual torpor. The dramatic change to the Byzantine images of earlier years was so pronounced, that she was swamped by a desire to learn more.

It was fortunate that the subject overlapped two of her subjects, History and Italian, and it meant that Molly's entire attitude to the academic challenge that lay ahead of her dramatically changed. Whilst her relationship with her father remained unaltered, the one she had with her mother became almost entirely concentrated on what happened in Florence six hundred years ago. For her mother, this radical change was nothing short of a blessing. Instead of it being a forbidden topic, the two of them could spend hours talking about her birthplace, and the artistic giants that bestrode the Arno.

In her final year at school, three months before sitting her A levels, this halcyon period of Molly's life ended when tragedy struck the Cavendish household. Alexandria, whilst preparing dinner, suffered a catastrophic brain haemorrhage inducing a massive stroke. Collapsing to the floor, bringing down plates and glasses that were laid out on the kitchen table, the resulting crash shocked Molly who was doing her homework. She found her mother lying motionless on the kitchen floor. Molly called for an ambulance, and then tried to call her father. He was at the church, and was uncontactable.

Alexandria was rushed to hospital but Molly knew that the situation was hopeless. When her father was finally reached, he failed to accept what the doctors told him. It was Molly who finally convinced him to turn off the life support machine, and let her mother pass away peacefully. He would never completely recover from the loss of his wife. The guilt Simon felt for not being at the house when Alexandria collapsed, and for not being there for Molly, was something that remained with him for the rest of his life. Despite Molly comforting him, he could not forgive himself.

The nervous breakdown her father suffered after her mother died was a further setback for Molly's young adulthood. And yet, with the help of the parishioners, and indeed from the church, both she and her father weathered the storm. Any resentment Molly might have felt towards her father's neglect disappeared during those first months after her mother's death. In that time she began to recognise how extraordinary her father had been to his congregants. Yes, she knew he was hugely respected in the community, yet the love people showed for him, was nothing short of remarkable. She began to respect, and perhaps love her father, during those awful first few months. Within a year, he was back at the church performing the duties of his priesthood. Although not fully recovered, he managed to recapture something of his old life back, and began to rebuild for the future.

Molly herself met the headwinds face on. She grew in stature, and attained the grades in her A Levels to win a place at Warwick University to read History. Warwick was one of the best universities for History in the country, and yet this was not the only reason why she chose this prestigious Red Brick university. It was the only college at the time offering a six month course in Florence as part of its undergraduate syllabus. Her excitement at finally going to the city of her mother's birth filled her with enormous anticipation. To be able to wander the streets, the same streets that she had discussed so many times with her mother, to visit the places of her childhood, and to be able to speak Italian for the first time in Italy, was almost too much to take in.

Whilst Molly was away at Warwick, she would talk, or write once a week to her father, the pattern of which would remain constant until she returned to London to do her doctorate at King's College in London. The relationship suited both of them. For Molly had immersed herself in her studies, achieving firsts in all of her course work, and indeed in her exams. For Simon, the idea of leaving his beloved community, for any amount of time, filled him with horror. He felt he would be emotionally paralysed without their support. And yet the regular contact with his daughter was a necessary one that he now understood. A complicated man, who never fully comprehended why he could express such love and care for his community and yet found it so difficult to show any real emotion to his own daughter, remained essentially unchanged.

4

Molly's time at Warwick was the best she had experienced in her life. It was not simply her academic success, but also her social activity that made her living so enjoyable. She joined many of the societies, and became editor of the university paper. She had had boyfriends at school, but nothing as serious as the ones she met at university. There were a string of romances in her first year, but in her second year she fell in love with one of her tutors. The relationship lasted over nine months, and increased her enthusiasm for her degree. Impressing him with essays was as important for her as satisfying him in bed. Although ending rather unceremoniously, when he announced to her at the end of one tutorial that he had fallen for another student, the affair had nevertheless given Molly a new level of self confidence.

Molly, at the beginning of her second year left for the six month course in Florence, which was part of her degree course. Her split from her tutor was still fresh in her mind, so the foreign sojourn was well timed. She had matured dramatically during the previous twelve months. Physically she was never regarded the most attractive of the girls at school. However, a late developer in almost all aspects of her life, she had now become a striking looking young twenty year old. She was tall at five feet seven inches; slim with a hint of breast and long auburn hair, almost always tied back into a ponytail. She had full lips, pronounced cheek bones, and large hazel coloured eyes. She felt comfortable with herself, and the confidence that she now exuded enabled her personality to blossom.

Arriving in her mother's city, she spent six months staying in student accommodation. Her outgoing nature meant that she made friends quickly and easily. Speaking fluent Italian played no small part in her becoming extremely popular. She spent some of her time at lectures, but mostly on student visits to the museums and churches that made Florence the greatest Renaissance city in the world. Breathing the cold winter air, speaking the dialect of her mother, and walking the very same streets that she had walked in her youth, was an experience that she wanted to repeat. It was during this trip that she started to think that she would continue with her studies, and do a doctorate on some aspect of the Italian Quattrocento.

During her visit she became familiar with a number of bars and cafes, and yet one became her favourite. Located on the corner of the Piazza Di San Giovanni facing the famous eleventh-century Baptistry, the café was run by an overweight Florentine, Paolo. What drew her to this particular café was not only its position, being located in the beating heart of the city, but also due to the hysterical nature of the eatery. Paolo, who was fifty-five years old, had ran the bar since his father had retired. The family had owned it since before the war. Paolo's management of his staff and his clients was borderline on being psychotic. He shouted at his waiters incessantly, and his attitude to his regulars was not much better.

It was frequently asked why people kept coming back. The location was an obvious factor, but in truth, Paolo exuded a charm that shone through all the hysteria. There was never a moment when an argument would not break out, and yet customers would look on and laugh as they would to a Dario Fo farce. Molly fitted in well in this kind of environment, and Paolo took a shine to the young English student. After a month, they were on first name terms, and after two, Molly got a job as a part time waitress. This was a perfect distraction from her studies, which although she enjoyed, were extremely intense.

Molly did find time to see everything she needed to see, including all of the obvious tourist sites. However, for the discerning historian fascinated by the Renaissance, she wanted in particular to visit the Museo di Santa Maria on the south bank of the Arno before she left. The museum was a well known one for those who knew more about the Renaissance than the average tourist. Located a little distance away from the centre of town, the little museum still attracted many thousands of visitors a year. Booking a time to visit had not been easy since during that part of the year the museum was under refurbishment. She finally attained a slot a week before she was due to leave.

'So you're finally visiting the Santa Maria this morning... you must be excited,' Paolo said, placing the cappuccino on the table in front of her.

'Finally Paolo... Finally. I actually can't wait for the museum to open.'

'I'll miss you when you go, Molly... More for your skill as a waitress, you understand!'

'Of course, Paolo... I wouldn't expect you to miss me for my conversational skills,' Molly replied smiling with a glint in her eye.

'Do you think you'll ever come back... I mean... I need good staff. You know the turnover is catastrophic here!'

'Oh come on, Paolo... you have people working here for decades. They love you despite your terrible man management skills. You wouldn't last a second in an English cafe. I promise you.'

'Yes, yes... I know. We will all be very upset though... Particularly Claudio,' he said referring to a dalliance that Molly had had with one of his waiters, winking at her in an embarrassingly unsubtle way.

'He'll survive… It was great while it lasted. I didn't expect him to fall in love so quickly!' she replied, swallowing the last drop of coffee. 'I have to go, or I'll be late. Now, that would be ironic having waited almost three months for a slot.' Molly laughed.

5

Molly entered the Museo di Santa Maria as the doors opened. Her time for the visit was the first available one that day. There were thirty people with her, the maximum that the museum could hold at any one time. The queue outside had already begun to stretch out along the bank of the river towards the Ponte alla Carraia. The museum was originally a small family chapel that had become derelict through the years after it had been built in the early Quattrocento. In the early 1980s the old church had been reduced to two old walls fronting an open space that was used as a car park. Nobody at that time gave it a second notice. Indeed plans were already being made for their destruction to build apartments. Delays had been incurred due to a potential protection order on the walls, being original Renaissance structures.

The delays were a happy accident, if not for the property developers, most certainly for the entire cultural world. The discovery of what lay hidden behind one of the walls meant that a museum could be built around them and attract hundreds of thousands of tourists from all corners of the globe. Molly had always been fascinated by the story of the discovery, but more importantly, by the fresco that was now its central exhibit. As she walked around the main atrium looking at the photographs that explained how the discovery was made, she then quietly glided through the crowd into the dark room where the fresco was situated. It did not disappoint the young undergraduate. She gasped as she saw the image look down on her.

Having spent almost forty-five minutes staring at one of the finest frescos she had ever seen, she slowly walked away, almost forcing herself to leave. It was at that precise moment as she left the museum, that Molly decided to do a postgraduate thesis, and that that she would have to once again come back and spend more time in her mother's city. Returning to Warwick, she applied to King's College to do a Masters, after which she would go on to do a doctorate. Her choice of college was a natural one. Like Warwick, King's had a very strong History department, particularly in Renaissance studies. She also wanted to come to London, to try and be closer to her father. She rightly felt that time was running out, and one last monumental effort needed to be made in order to form a closer bridge with her last surviving parent.

6

Molly completed her degree, achieving first class honours, a prerequisite for attaining a scholarship to do a doctorate at King's. Returning to London, she lived at home for the first two years of her postgraduate studies. It was a complicated subject that she had chosen; 'Humanist Neo-Platonism' was not a well known topic to graduates, let alone the general reading public. The professors however were excited, and Molly was encouraged with her research continuously. Always, at the back of her mind, was the prospect of spending her third year in Florence. Indeed she had made preparations for her stay well in advance, finding a small flat to rent, which was advertised on the Internet. Ideally located on the Via Martelli close to the Duomo, it being very near to the beating heart of the city. She knew that she would need a job when she was there to help her pay for outgoings, since her scholarship funding would not cover all of her living costs.

The time spent at home during those two years prior to leaving, were ones in which Molly tried to improve her relationship with her father. They went out more, to the theatre or to restaurants. Although not at all religious, despite both her parents being devout Catholics, she even went to church to spend more time with him. It was to little avail. It was not that he didn't enjoy being with his daughter; it was just that he was unable to open up to her in any meaningful way. The guilt of not being present when Alexandria died had remained with him. This made matters even worse. As a result the relationship remained stunted, with lots of conversation, but with no real feeling. In a perverse way, Molly's leaving to Florence came as a relief to her father, as he was now able to drop the pretence of trying to be someone he could not be.

For Molly, her departure filled her with regret that she was unable to achieve a proper, and full relationship with him. She loved her father, but like him, knew that there was nothing she could do to bridge the chasm that lay between them. Her regret in regards to this failure was however more than cancelled out by the excitement of returning to the Tuscan capital. She couldn't wait to see her friends again whom she met and had stayed in contact with, three years previous. Some of them had come to London during the intervening period, but most of them had kept in contact on Facebook. But the moment she was most looking forward to, was the morning taste of that first cappuccino at Paolo's café.

7

Molly had spent nine months in Florence working furiously on her PhD thesis' as well as earning her small living as a museum guide, when she finally found the precious document written by Pico in the convent in Fiesole. She left her apartment that warm morning, anxious that there was still so much to do in the months before she would leave the city to complete her doctorate. It would take a long time to fully translate and understand the notes written by the Florentine humanist. She also wanted to find someone to examine the photo of the drawing she had found the previous afternoon. Although unrelated to the thesis, if the picture was indeed drawn by a master, and if it was connected to Pico in some way, it might provide an interesting vignette to tie in to her project.

She walked the short distance down the Via Martelli to Paolo's café on the corner of the Piazza Di San Giovanni. She managed, as usual, to find a table, unoccupied facing the famous Baptistry. She just had enough time to briefly look at the notes on the clients she was about to meet in forty five minutes, and have a coffee. However, service was particularly slow that morning. Molly was about to get up to see if she could get some attention when she heard shouting at the back of the café. She sighed and then smiled. Things would never change. From the noise, she could make out that the bread delivery was late, and that Paolo was not at all happy. Suddenly, the familiar rotund figure of the owner came running out with her cappuccino, having seen her sit down earlier.

'Good morning, Molly... I'm sorry its been slow this morning... One cappuccino.' He placed the coffee cup on the table.

'Thank you... Problems with the bread delivery I hear,' Molly replied, trying to concentrate on her notes.

'Who told you that?' Paolo asked, alarmed that people would know that he would be unable to serve any bread for at least another hour.

'A deaf man could hear you, Paolo,' Molly replied not looking up.

'I was no louder than usual... Was I?'

'Not really.' She looked up and smiled at him. 'Paolo, I wouldn't worry, everyone is so used to the noise coming from the café that nobody ever listens to what's actually being said.'

'I hope you're right, Molly... Who are you seeing today? Americans, Japanese, English...'

'English in the morning, and Americans in the afternoon... Thankfully I begin with a small family of three.' She looked at the photograph of the Jameson family, which had been sent to her. 'I know it sounds strange but I've always found smaller groups so much more satisfying to take round than larger parties.' She glanced at her watch. 'I haven't got much time, Paulo, so I'm going to have to rush.' She gulped down the last of her coffee, and pushed the table away from her so as to get out. Paolo obliged in helping her. 'I'll probably see you later, Paolo, sorry for being a little abrupt.'

'No problem, Molly... Have a good day.' Paolo turned around and walked back towards the door of his café. Seeing Molly, as usual, lifted his feelings. Her presence and poise always made him feel better. Admittedly, the bread truck arriving at the same time also somewhat helped his demeanour.

She walked briskly across the square. It was 9am, and

she could hardly see Ghiberti's *Gates of Paradise* through the throng of tourists that were gathered around them. This morning, as far as she could see, it appeared that it was mostly young Japanese students holding either their iPhones or cameras high up above their heads to obtain the images they all craved. Molly glimpsed the top two golden panels still visible above the crowd. She was always relieved when seeing so many people around the *Gates of Paradise*. Even though copies, the doors somehow still possessed the magical qualities of the real ones. It seemed to make no difference to their appeal that the original doors were locked away for preservation at the Museo dell'Opera del Duomo.

8

Walking briskly through the old streets of Florence, she crossed the Arno over the Ponte alla Carria, finally reached her destination. Surveying the large crowd that had already started to queue outside the main entrance to the museum she looked for her clients. This was no easy task given the numbers of tourists milling around the museum. They were meant to be waiting at the side of the main building, just under the private tour sign nailed on the wall twenty metres away from the ticket kiosk. She stopped and checked her notes again. The photograph she had was not a clear one, but gave a good enough impression from which she could recognise them when she saw them. Finally she spotted a mother and son who indeed closely resembled her photograph, but there was no sign of the father. She slowly walked towards them.

'Hello, I'm Molly... You must be the Jamesons?' Molly thrust out her hand towards the mother, smiling reassuringly.

'Yes, hello I'm Juliet, and this is my son, Sam. My husband, Dan, has just gone to get us some water. It's getting awfully hot. He should be back any minute... Ah! There he is. Dan!' she shouted and waved at the distant figure walking towards them. He quickened his step, almost losing control of the three bottles of water and the city guide of Florence he was carrying. Molly saw that the guide in his hand was an old green Michelin Italy guide, a more intellectually demanding handbook, which catered for the more discerning tourist. From this, she immediately assumed that the father was well informed, and that she would probably have to be on her toes with him. So many times in the past, when taking knowledgeable clients around the museum, she was asked questions that tested her own knowledge on the Renaissance.

As he came closer, she also spotted in his pocket another travel book, which Molly assumed was for his son Sam. Filled with pictures, it was the most common guide for sightseers.

Molly took two of the bottles from him, and gave them to Juliet.

'Hi, I'm Molly,' she said taking his hand.

'Oh hello… I'm Dan… It's very nice to meet you, Molly. I'm really looking forward to this.' Keeping hold of her hand, he gently ushered Molly to one side, out of earshot from both his wife and son. 'You ought to know before we start that my son suffers from a mild form of Asperger, and can be quite difficult. But he does engage…' He paused. 'He can be quite demanding, especially in this sort of environment. You will find that he might ask lots of questions, or he might just as easily walk away and not be interested… But please don't worry, my wife is brilliant with him.'

'No problem Mr Jameson.' Molly smiled hesitantly. In the months that she had been a guide for the Museo di Santa Maria, she had surprisingly never had to deal with children who had behavioural difficulties. She walked ahead. 'Come along, let's go, shall we.' Molly took them through the main entrance, walking past the queue for the museum that had now lengthened and had stretched out towards the Ponte alla Carraia.

'I can't believe the crowds. I mean I know my husband is an obsessive bore about the Renaissance… And he's been going on about coming to see the museum, but I had no idea that there were so many people around like him! I'm afraid I don't know much about Masaccio, and have hardly heard of the Museo di

24

Santa Maria. How do people know about the museum? Its not exactly in the middle of town.' Juliet looked at Molly, laughing disarmingly at her own ignorance.

'Don't worry Mrs Jameson. There are tens of thousands of tourists who visit Florence but never come here. You have to have a proper knowledge about the period to want to visit this museum. It is rarely on the 'must do list' for a first time visitor... Although it really ought to be. When you see it, you'll understand why the crowds are here... I promise.'

They entered through the door carved out of the unfinished Quattrocento front façade, a wall made up of rough, seemingly crumbling, giant brown bricked slabs, and entered the glass covered atrium. The floor was of modern white stone, and the walls were covered with photographs dating from the late twentieth century, revealing the history of the restoration and refurbishment of what was now the museum. Molly stopped in the middle of the area, and turned around to face her three guests. She had realised that she would speed up the opening of the tour by trying to engage Sam as quickly as possible. Fortunately, the origin of the museum was a story that should excite a thirteen-year-old boy.

'Welcome to the Museo di Santa Maria.' She paused and smiled. 'I'm going to briefly talk to you a little about the museum itself before we go next door. The building that we are now in, less than thirty years ago was a derelict open space, with only two walls of the original structure existing.' She stretched her arms out pointing to the north and south facades. 'Originally a chapel, it had fallen into such a state of disrepair, that people had forgotten it had existed... Literally for hundreds of years. That all changed on July 5th 1982, because of a football match.'

'What? A football match? Really?' Sam shouted out, his attention now captured.

'Yes Sam, a football match was the reason for the

restoration of the chapel, and in turn led to arguably the greatest Renaissance discovery in recent times.'

'Wow! But… I don't understand…'

'Let me show you.' Molly ushered Sam towards the wall, followed closely by Juliet and Dan, where black and white photographs depicting the Santa Maria restoration, were displayed. She pointed to the first picture. 'This is Gianni Vannini. He was two years older than you in 1982… Fifteen. He knew nothing about the Renaissance, or even art for that matter. But with one kick of a football, he and his family became very much part of the Florentine Renaissance.'

PART 2

FLORENCE
JULY 5TH 1982

I

It had been a long day at school for Gianni Vannini. From the moment he got out of bed, he had started to think about the match that afternoon. He was not the only pupil at school that day who was crippled academically by the obsession with that afternoon's game. The papers had clearly laid out what lay ahead for the Squadra Azzurra. It was a crucial one for the Italian team. They had drawn their first three games in the World Cup that year, but had suddenly awoken from its lethargy with a much-needed victory over Diego Maradona's Argentina. The obstacle facing the national side that day was Brazil. The unbeaten South Americans had dominated the tournament with their exhibition style football. They were overwhelming favourites to win the competition, and only needed a draw that afternoon to qualify for the semi finals whilst the Italians needed a victory.

People throughout the world had fallen in love with the Brazilian football team of that year. Gianni was no exception. He was obsessed with the giant midfielder Socrates, a qualified doctor, who captained this team of footballing magicians; footballers including Zico, Eder, Junior and Falcao to name but a few had become heroes during the last two weeks to every school boy across the land, who liked the sport. Under Tele Santana's management, the side played unrelenting attacking football. It appeared that the beautiful game was about to be crowned with champions that befitted its description. It was a small wonder that Gianni amongst millions of others was fixated by the anticipation of the afternoon spectacle.

The day had started at school before lessons had begun, with Gianni and his friends playing their version of the game to be played that afternoon. Gianni was a gifted footballer and was always the star of their playground games. Even when the bells rang, all the boys could not stop talking about the afternoon event. Morning break, followed by lunch, were the only times the boys could release their pent up excitement about events happening later. The afternoon lessons were an exercise in testing one's endurance. However even the teachers, most of whom were young men, appreciated the momentous occasion, and wanted to go home as soon as the bell rang. The lessons were filled with anticipation and excitement. Little was taught and nothing was learnt. All of them, teachers and pupils alike, expected defeat, and yet there was still a perverse air of expectation that something special was about to happen.

By the time the final bell rang at 4:30pm, Gianni Vannini's patience had run dry, as he raced out of the school gates and ran the two miles back home. He arrived at the family apartment located above a delicatessen on the Borgo San Frediano. Gianni's father, Ludovico, and his twin brother Giovanni were already watching the coverage prior to the game. His mother, Maria was in the kitchen preparing dinner. As soon as Gianni closed the door behind him, he heard his mother call him.

'Your father and uncle are glued to the television. I know you want to watch, but you must promise to do your homework straight after the game. I mean it Gianni. The school has warned me that you're slipping. The world is not just about football you know.'

'Yes Mama…' He grabbed an apple from the bowl, and ran into the living room.

'Hi Papa… Hi zio'. He kissed them both and sat down on the floor in front of them.

'My God, Gianni, you left it late… I thought you might have missed the start!' Ludovico said, quite surprised that his son hadn't come earlier to watch the build up to the match.

'Oh Papa, you know lessons end later today, and the headmaster hates football and issued an instruction at the beginning of the week that nobody could leave early. My teachers were really annoyed, but I'm here now!' He barely looked at them since both sets of players were being led out onto the pitch.

'What an idiot… He must be the only Italian in the country who doesn't care,' Giovanni muttered.

It was now 5pm, and the world's attention would be focussed on the Estadio Sarria in Barcelona for the next two hours. The Vannini household represented the vast majority of most Italian households that July afternoon. The country literally came to a standstill as the game kicked off. One could sense the pent up atmosphere in the city. The roads outside were deserted, and all public transport had ground to a halt.

'Well son… This is it. Bearzot must be mad to be playing Rossi. I would have played Altobelli. We haven't got a chance.' His uncle nodded, clearly agreeing with his father.

'I don't agree. Anyway we have Antognoni and Graziani playing, and the team looks ok. We have to be positive.' Gianni glanced at the two men on the sofa. They both smiled back. It was no coincidence that Gianni had only mentioned those two players, being that they played for Fiorentina.

The game started at 5:15, but it was really set alight by Paolo Rossi, who opened the scoring with a fine header after only five minutes. The noise that greeted the goal, in every Italian family was deafening. The Vannini apartment was no exception. Gianni leapt up and danced around the room. They were still celebrating when Socrates, literally out of the blue, scored a stunning equaliser seven minutes later. The silence that greeted the Brazilian goal was just as dramatic as the screaming that accompanied Rossi's opener. All three Vanninis sat stunned not quite believing that the Brazilians had equalised so quickly. However the silence in the Vannini sitting room did not last very long as Ludovico unleashed a torrent of abuse at the hapless Dino Zoff, the Italian goalkeeper.

'Hopeless; he's just too old. I never liked him.' Gianni's father was continuing to criticise the Juventus player, when inexplicably the Brazilian defender, Cerezo, gave the ball away to Rossi in front of his own goal. The Italian forward skipped past Junior and drilled his shot home. The Azzurri were once again in the lead, and after twenty-five minutes of football mayhem, the Vannini family returned to a euphoric state of excitement.

'Ah Papa… You are always so negative. I really think we could win this game. The Brazilians are not comfortable… You can see it in their passing.' Gianni reacted to his father's endless pessimism.

'I don't know son… They'll never hold on… There's still over sixty minutes of football to play.' It was Giovanni this time who was grumbling; when it came to football analysis, he was similar to his brother. They were both doomsayers, the glass always being half empty rather than half full. This pessimism had been given new life during the regular club season when the family's beloved Fiorentina had lost out to Juventus for the Scudetta on the last match of the season. Although despising the 'Old Lady' of Italian football, both Ludovico and Giovanni had put aside their club feelings and embraced the six Juventus players who made up the Italian team that hot afternoon.

The game remained 2-1 in favour of the Italians until the sixty-eighth minute, when the Azzurri defence was finally breached through a spectacular strike from outside the box by Falcao. The Brazilians had finally gained parity, and for most of those who were watching, the game was as good as over. However, six minutes later, the Brazilians failed to clear the ball, and for the third time in the match, Paolo Rossi stabbed it home to recapture Italy's lead. Pandemonium erupted all around the city's flats and houses. The noise reverberated across its streets and squares. It was no different in the Vannini flat. There were only sixteen minutes left, and with the Italians' renowned defensive qualities, the dream had now become a reality.

'They won't be able to do it… I know Brazil will score. We need another one.' Ludovico's prayers were nearly answered when the family's beloved Giancarlo Antognoni, the Florentine midfielder scored, only for the goal to be wrongly disallowed for off side. 'I knew it… Brazil will definitely score now. The Gods are against us.' His words appeared to be prophetic as Oscar at that moment, in the last minute, rose above the defence and head towards home only to be denied by a miraculous save by the much-maligned Zoff.

'I told you… He's the best goalkeeper in the world. The first name when picking the side…' Ludovico screamed. He looked at Giovanni and Gianni. 'What? A man can't change his mind?' he shouted at his brother and son.

Gianni had not said much during the game. It was almost impossible, given the tension, and the continuous moaning, and depressing commentary from his father and uncle. But when the Israeli referee Abraham Klein blew the final whistle he jumped up and ran to the two older men. He had never seen his country go so far in a world cup before. They hugged, kissed and jumped together in rapturous delight. Gianni had never seen them cry with such happiness. The victory meant everything to Gianni Vannini. His national side, against all the odds had beaten the one of the greatest football teams ever assembled.

'I'm going to play football in the square against the old chapel walls… Is that ok, Papa?' Gianni grabbed the old leather ball lying by the front door.

'No you don't, young man. You promised you would do your

homework after the match,' his mother Maria shouted, coming out of the kitchen, drying her hands with her apron.

'Oh Maria, let him play. It's a special day. He can do his work later.' Ludovico was never one to push his son. As a father, he doted on his only child. It was left to his mother to instil discipline and a proper school ethic into the young boy. Forever chasing him, to read, and to study, it was a thankless task for Maria Vannini. She was given no help or support in this area of the child's upbringing. Not surprising then, was her reaction to Ludovico's latest contribution to his son's development.

'Well done, Ludovico. You saw the boy's report. He has to work… What chance have I got with you around? You only have to see what happened to you… Your family's attitude to education is beyond belief. It was a major failing of your mother that she never pushed you after the war to work harder. All these years you keep telling me of your proud Florentine tradition… but where has it got you?' Maria shouted.

'Well… It's true. The Vanninis are one of the very few families that can say that they have continuously lived in this city from just after the Black Death in the early fourteenth century. I admit, we haven't really become, what you would call, pillars of society, but we have been part of this city for over six hundred and fifty years. And Maria… Don't forget my mother, and what she achieved. There are not many like her around.'

'This is not about Francesca… I'm talking about you and your attitude towards your son. He needs to buckle down. He's not working hard enough… You saw his report.'

'Not everyone can be clever at school. Not everyone can go to university. Not everyone can get a job as chief Renaissance restorer at the Uffizi. It doesn't make you any better you know. The city needs bus drivers.' He responded to the sound of slammed doors. One of which was the kitchen, where Maria was preparing supper, the other was the front entrance where Gianni had already left, not waiting for the argument to finish. He knew that his mother would prevail in the end, and he had to leave at the first opportunity. The chance of replaying the game he had just seen, and re-enacting all the goals was something he could not, and would not miss.

2

Gianni lobbed the ball forward and started dribbling with it around the cars, mopeds and bicycles that had hastily been parked by people in a rush to see the game earlier in the afternoon. The Borgo San Frediano was a narrow street, and with people now leaving their homes to go and celebrate their nation's victory, it meant that Gianni's skill at controlling the ball was severely tested. Some of the crowd shouted at him to pass the ball. It wasn't surprising since everyone wanted to play football at that moment. Gianni ignored them, and even having to tackle some of them when they tried to get the ball from him. He turned right into a quiet cobbled lane away from the crowd, which led out onto the square where the derelict remains of the old Chiesa di Santa Maria stood.

The square, in recent times, had been used as a temporary car park, but the city authorities, pending a decision on its redevelopment, had now cordoned it off. The council had wanted to sell the site to residential developers, but had been hampered by its own planning department over a potential listing of the two chapel walls. This was particularly frustrating to some city councillors who could see the vast potential value in the site, given the uninterrupted views over the Arno. For Gianni of course, the potential of a residential site was unwelcome to say the least.

As long as the site was quarantined from development, it meant that his football game was played out on open relatively flat ground, bordered by two chapel walls, which in Gianni's mind were two goals. The outer facades consisted of rough brown brick slabs that appeared to look like large crumbling rusks. The inner walls had become so decayed through a mixture of time and pollution, that they were almost black. The southern wall was slightly, but noticeably thicker than the other. Throughout the years some observers had questioned why the southern wall was thicker, but nobody had ever followed this up. Nevertheless, it was a good enough reason for Gianni to make it the 'home end'. He had even painted lines on the facades to delineate goalposts. Although not quite the Stadio Comunale, it was more than enough for a sixteen-year-old Florentine boy wanting to imagine he was playing for the 'Viola'.

That late afternoon, he wasn't wearing the purple shirt of his local football club, but the blue shirt worn by the Azzurri. He kicked the ball into the square and scrambled underneath the flimsy temporary metal fencing. Already people were beginning to come out of their homes, milling around the city; the sense of celebration was beginning to feed through the streets of the Tuscan capital. Gianni was oblivious to the swelling crowds, even when some sat down by the fencing and began drinking. None of his friends, who frequently played with him, were out that night. They were almost certainly being kept at home to do their homework. Gianni was pleased. He could now be Paolo Rossi, Francesco Graziani, and Bruno Conti at various moments in his make believe football world.

Breathing heavily, sounding like an ecstatic crowd, and then commentating in a barely audible voice, Gianni Vannini played out the whole Estadio Sarria spectacle that had taken place that afternoon over a thousand kilometres away. He suddenly stopped, approximately fifteen metres away from the southern wall. He stood motionless, as if waiting for the imaginary tackle. He then effortlessly glided the ball away from him before striking it low and hard with the outside of his right foot. As soon as he kicked it, he knew that it was a perfect strike. The ball flew towards the top corner of painted goal. As soon as it hit the wall, Gianni turned around, and ran towards the fence in mock celebration, re-enacting the second of Paolo Rossi's goals.

The ball rebounded off the wall, making a crunching sound, followed by an unstable but violent crumbling of that section of the facade. Gianni was still celebrating, as he saw the onlookers beginning to stare at the disintegration of the wall. He rather presumptuously assumed that their look of shock was an expression of his spectacular strike. He glanced behind him, and saw that where the ball had struck, the once grey featureless structure, a kaleidoscope of rich colours had suddenly become visible. He turned to face the image, and slowly walked towards it. People in the crowd who were drinking and revelling, suddenly stopped what they were doing and looked at the disintegration that was occurring in front of them. An eerie silence had replaced the convivial celebratory atmosphere around the piazza.

As Gianni followed by others in the crowd approached the structure, an enormous fissure developed, from the small area of colour at the bottom left of the wall. Everyone stopped in their tracks, as the grey polluted veneer of the old facade, became fragmented by giant cracks. Dark powder started to form at each crack, and as if in slow motion the whole outer skin of the structure came crashing down. The noise was thunderous, and the entire area was blanketed in a dark cloud of dust. For a few moments, nobody could see anything such was the filth and pollution that had finally been unleashed from the wall that had been decaying for over five hundred years.

More people gathered at the sight. And slowly, the dust began to dissipate. The sun began to break through, as people stared transfixed, holding on to their friends and partners. Laughter from relief, that the noise had stopped and that the dust had disappeared into the atmosphere, was soon replaced with gasps of awe, at what they now saw in front of them.

'Gianni... Gianni!' Where are you? Are you all right?' Maria had heard the crash and had come running down to see where her son was.

'Yes Mama, I'm fine... But look... Look what happened... Look what I've done.' He pointed to the wall. She looked up behind her son, and remained motionless.

'My God.' Maria muttered under her breath. 'I've never seen anything like...' she paused, 'this.' She walked closer to the giant fresco. She looked at the image in front of her, gesturing to the crowd to move back. 'Excuse me... Please give me some space... I am a restorer at the Uffizi... This is very fragile.' She put her hand in her back pocket, and pulled out her work identification card proving her position. The crowd started to ease back, giving Maria room to fully take in what was in front of her. In her time she had seen the greatest creations in western art, but she had never witnessed anything as beautiful as this. A six-hundred-year-old fresco revealed in pristine condition.

It was as if it had just been painted. She touched it ever so lightly, to sense the gilding, the aqua marine, and indeed all of the rich fine colours. 'Maybe... No it can't be...' She walked along the breadth of the wall, stopping to look at various aspects of the image. The symmetry of the image, the various sweeps of the figures, the blue robes of the Madonna, the folds in the drapery, the feet of the baby Christ, the angels at the back of the throne revealing the depth of the composition. She gestured to the main image on the wall. 'This is... Masaccio,' she muttered to herself as she gazed upwards and stared at the fresco in front of her. 'So this was why the wall was thicker...' She laughed at the spectacle in front of her. 'Someone wanted to protect... or perhaps... hide this treasure... My God...' She paused and then whispered, 'Thank God.'

PART 3

PRESENT DAY FLORENCE

I

Sam listened to Molly's story, mouth half open, staring at the photographs of Gianni, and the images of the old site where the relics of Santa Maria stood. Molly led Sam towards the entrance to where the giant fresco was located.

'But, then what happened?' Sam asked, pulling on Molly's arm as they walked towards the room where the fresco awaited them. Juliet and Dan followed across the large atrium, which was now bathed in sunlight, stopping suddenly as Molly began to answer Sam's question.

'Sam, I don't think it's that important. Come on, let's go and see the fresco. I've been waiting years to see it,' his father interrupted.

'Dan, a few moments more won't hurt.' Juliet answered back, clearly indicating to Molly that she should continue responding to Sam and ignore her impatient husband. Dan shrugged and walked ahead towards the room where the fresco was.

Molly smiled, and looked down at Sam. 'Well then... What immediately happened, Sam, was complete confusion and chaos. The city authorities suddenly made decisions that they had been delaying for years. They issued orders to protect the wall. It was immediately cordoned off and covered. From that moment, every art restorer, historian and expert from around the world tried to become involved with the future of the Chiesa di Santa Maria. The outcome led to this magnificent museum, which we are now standing in. Both the north and the south walls are completely restored to their original condition. They are now linked by the glass roof and the modern walls either side. The floor is obviously not the original stone.'

'Yes, but who painted the wall? What was it originally? I don't understand?' Sam asked, desperately wanting quick answers.

'Sam, for those answers we have to go back six hundred years.' Molly paused. Dan had been right. His son was different. Fully engaged, and exhibiting a thirst for knowledge that she rarely came across during her year as a museum guide, she was inspired by him. Usually teenagers showed no interest at all, either hiding behind their parents saying nothing, gormlessly playing games on their iPhones, or simply behaving in a surly manner. And yet he was only thirteen years old. She couldn't simply talk about Burckhardt, Stellar and Panofsky without killing his interest in seconds. She would have to try and take him back in time, and tell him briefly about the age when the church was first built.

'You see, Sam, something in the art world, and we are still not quite sure what, began to change in the thirteenth century, and then set in during the fourteenth and fifteenth centuries. To put it simply, Sam, despite what some modern historians might now be saying, there was, I believe a cultural break from the period before, known as the Mediaeval Age... or the Middle Ages. Building and painting, and even creating sculptures fundamentally changed in their visual representation of line and colour.'

'What?' Sam asked, with a look of bewilderment, clearly not understanding Molly.

'Oh... I'm sorry Sam. It's difficult to explain...' She paused, and tried to relate to a thirteen year old. 'Sam, you've heard of the word 'Renaissance'?'

'Yes... We've been taught it at school. And Dad keeps going on about it. He did a degree in it.' He nodded.

'Oh good... that makes it easier then. Well you know then that it is a French word meaning rebirth. In this context it referred to the rebirth of classical art from Greece and Rome. This is effectively what happened between, approximately, the years 1250 and 1550. People rediscovered techniques and ideas that they thought had been lost thousands of years previously. Something occurred... Here on Italian soil, whether it was due to curiosity or individuality... we just don't know for sure. It represented art that was more like what was achieved in the ancient world. Paintings became more realistic and natural.' Molly knew that such an interpretation would not have sat easily with her professors from Warwick or London, some of whom did not even regard the Renaissance as a definitive separate period at all. However this was by no means a universal view, and she felt more comfortable presenting the more traditional, and indeed simplistic interpretation of the age to Sam. She certainly didn't want him to get bogged down by the prevailing historiography of the era.

'Did you go to the same university as my dad... You sound just like him.' Sam laughed.

'Oh God, Sam, am I boring you already? We haven't even seen the fresco yet!'

'Oh it's ok. Dad goes on for much longer. I must admit I preferred the football story!'

'Well that's pretty normal,' Molly replied smiling.

'Did this Renaissance painting only happen here?' he asked.

'Well it started in Northern Italy, but mainly in Tuscany... whether it was Florence, or Sienna or even Mantua, we just don't know. Places such as Padua and Assisi were also infected with this spirit, but Florence was the beating heart of the age. There was an atmosphere here that was so febrile as well as creative. The city was constantly changing. Families wanted to do things in their own names. There were competitions all over the city; some started by the city council, others by the working

associations known as guilds or special works committees…
and finally several, by rich patrons, all of whom vying to see
which or who could produce the greatest creations.

The story of the family, who remain unknown to us to this
very day, and who built this church was probably no exception.
They were rich and powerful, and they wanted to build a family
chapel, which would be a symbol of their wealth and prestige.
They wanted the finest architect and painters for this project. We
are now standing in what was their church, the Chiesa di Santa
Maria.'

'Ah… I think I now understand everything. In there,' he
pointed to the room with the fresco, 'is one of the two remaining
walls, which Gianni kicked his football against, of an old family
chapel where a giant sized Renaissance fresco is painted?'

'Yes,' Molly smiled, sensing that she had managed to convey
at least something of the greatness of the subject to the boy,
although she was still not convinced that he would appreciate it,
until he saw it. 'In there, Sam, is a fresco painted by one of the
pioneers of this age… Masaccio.'

Juliet and Sam followed Molly into the room where Masaccio's
fresco was. Dan was already in there gazing at the magical image.
The pristine vivid colours always shocked the audience when
first seeing it. Nobody was used to seeing an image painted over
six hundred years previously in such remarkable condition.

2

Molly took the Jamesons around the fresco, explaining the image in as much detail as she could without letting Sam become too bored. However with Dan asking the most taxing questions on Renaissance painting techniques, it became a juggling act between catering the needs of both father and son. As they left the fresco behind, and came out to the atrium, Molly saw the very person she needed to talk to that morning. He was standing at the entrance, talking to tourists, trying to organise the queuing, which at times became unruly. The slots for visiting the fresco were tight, and invariably, people came late. This in turn led to arguments, and people demanding to see the person in charge. That person was Gianni Vannini.

Socially warm and humorous, he was also conversely, very cool under pressure. He was also an excellent communicator, and an ideal person to deal with the crowds that visited the museum. Gianni had worked at the museum since he left university, as a trainee curator. He climbed up the ladder, to become the managing director of the museum much to the delight of his mother, Maria. Being so heavily involved in the city's art, by having a son who would continue that tradition, filled her with immense pride. The fact that it was Gianni who discovered the fresco over thirty years previously, continuing the extraordinary family connection with the history of the church, added to the irony of the situation.

At that moment, when Molly caught sight of him, Gianni was dealing with an angry Dutch family, who had lost their position in the queue due to one of the children being ill earlier in the morning. Having seen the penalty of not being on time, the queue now stretched towards the Ponte alla Carraia, the father of the family was extremely unhappy. As usual, Gianni had been called, and whilst there was little he could do, he did offer refreshments, and if anyone else before them were late, they would be the first replacements. The family walked slowly back, half satisfied with the outcome.

'Mrs Jameson, can you wait here. I have to speak to that man over there. I will be back very soon,' Molly said.

'Yes of course Molly… Where are the loos?' She asked.

'Over there, just behind the ticket kiosk.' She pointed to the other side of the atrium. 'I'll meet you here in five minutes.'

'Ok, then. Come on Sam… Dan, what about you?'

'No… You go… I'll be over here looking at the photographs.'

Molly nodded and then walked over to Gianni. She shook his hand, kissing both cheeks at the same time.

'Gianni, how are you?'

'I'm well, Molly… Just the usual crowd trouble… Nothing too serious,' he said.

'You're a saint… I don't know how you have the patience.'

'Sometimes, Molly nor do I!' He laughed. 'Tell me, did your clients enjoy their morning? Were they impressed?'

'Yes… actually they were all really good. The boy, a thirteen year old called Sam, was particularly engaged. Would you mind seeing him, and having a chat about that day in 1982? I know you must be bored of telling it, but he seems a really great kid.'

'Molly when have I ever said no… You should have just brought him along.'

'Well, actually before you see him, I also need a personal favour.'

'Name it,' he replied, smiling.

'Gianni, I was in Fiesole yesterday afternoon doing some research for my PhD, when I came across a drawing that I believe is a mini Renaissance masterpiece. However I need to have someone look at it for me. Unfortunately I only have a photo of it on my phone, and I don't know if the identity of the artist can be gleaned from the image. I was wondering whether your mother might have time? I wouldn't normally ask someone as important, but I really believe...'

'Molly...' Gianni interrupted. 'Stop!' He raised his finger towards her mouth. 'I will call her, and get back to you. She will be happy to see you. Any friend of mine she will see. I'll call you on your mobile when I've spoken to her, and then you can get in touch direct.'

'Thank you Gianni... Really, thank you.' Molly turned around and beckoned over the Jamesons. 'Now, Sam, can you recognise this man, bearing in mind he is over thirty years older than the photographs on the wall?'

Sam did not have a clue being unable to link the photographs on the walls he had seen an hour earlier, to the forty-five-year old face that was looking at him.

'No... Sorry, Molly, I don't,' Sam replied.

'This is Gianni Vannini, the man who struck that football at the wall all those years ago.'

'Wow! Really?' Sam was flabbergasted.

'Yes,' replied Gianni, as he crouched down to talk the young boy.

Molly said goodbye to the Jamesons, leaving Gianni to chat about the events of that July afternoon in 1982. She left the museum, and walked towards the Ponte alla Carraia a few hundred meters away. She turned around and looked at the crowds of tourists, and then at the museum itself. She stopped and thought how beautiful it must have been, when it had just been completed in 1417. She tried to think about the mind set of those involved in the building, most importantly, the architect, financier, and, of course, the artists. It must have been such a remarkable project having the great leaders of the age being involved in its construction.

PART 4

FLORENCE
MARCH 28TH 1417

I

The clouds had gathered that late March afternoon when Bardo Giovanni rose from his chair and walked over to the window, which looked directly south across the river towards his family chapel, the Santa Maria. The dome had not yet been completed despite what Francesco Vannini, the stonemason had promised him. Although the chapel had only taken two years to physically build, the toll on the seventy-year-old Bardo Giovanni was far greater than that. He was exhausted, and he now sensed the dark shadow of his own demise creeping up on him. The construction of the church had been far from easy. His architect, Filippo Brunelleschi, was one of the most temperamental geniuses of the age. His design was indeed revolutionary, however the added expenditure in providing him with the right engineers and equipment was exorbitant. In addition to this, the enormous gamble of letting Filippo pick two unknown artists to paint the interior, filled Bardo with such anxiety that at times he would wake up in the middle of the night with cold sweats. What was meant to be an enjoyable project to fill his autumn days had become an extremely stressful one, both emotionally and materially.

His life had been an immensely successful one in the world of banking. He was a part of that great Florentine banking era from which the names of various families still resonate today with wealth and splendour. Banking houses such as those of the Medicis, Peruzzi, Scali, Strozzi and Bardi, not to mention those from across Europe such as the fast rising Fuggers, were incredibly powerful and had begun to influence everyday life at the end of the fourteenth and beginning of the fifteenth centuries. Bardo enjoyed the power and wealth; indeed he had accumulated riches that he could never have imagined when he arrived in the city, at the age of twenty, shipwrecked and penniless.

But now, the family and the bank were on the brink of eclipsing all of the success that he had already achieved. They were about to cash in on a vast fortune that he believed would catapult him to not only to being one of the richest men in Florence, but also potentially enable him to become Gonfaloniere, the leader of the city's ruling council. He could not believe his good fortune, in having a son such as Tito who would carry on the family name and run the Giovanni Bank for years to come. It was his son who had taken over the bank two years previously in 1415, when he himself had decided to retire and concentrate on building the family chapel. He reflected on his son's apparent success, not quite believing how fortunate he was.

He gazed at the chapel, which was still some way from being fully built. Inside, the work was nearly finished with Masaccio's fresco of the *Madonna and her Son with Angels* on the southern wall being the only artwork that had been completed. Uccello's panels were still very much works in progress and were nowhere near being the finished product. At least the young artist was hard at work now, having been delayed due to other commissions. With regard to the exterior, the brickwork was still not completed, and the columns and arches that were so much part of Brunelleschi's experiment, representing both classical antiquity as well as the art of the future, had yet to be built. He remained unsure when Brunelleschi would be able to finalise the structure now that his dome had almost been completed. The city's interest in the architectural genius and his revolutionary ideas on the construction of the dome for the city's main cathedral, the Santa Maria del Fiore, had been fuelled by the apparent success of his one at Santa Maria.

Suddenly the house bell rang, and a small commotion could be heard on the ground floor of the palace. Bardo turned around to face the doors of his vast salon. He was not expecting any one that afternoon. Announcements were made, and the doors suddenly swung open.

'Signor Bratti Ferravecchi is here to see you, sire!' The doorman then turned, and gestured for the gentleman to come in.

'What? What's he doing here?' Bardo shouted as Bratti entered the room.

2

The extraordinary life of Bardo Giovanni only really began forty-five years previously in a chance meeting with Margherita Bondi, the eldest daughter of a notable banking family, in the Piazza della Signoria, the day after he had arrived. The extraordinary encounter dramatically changed the trajectory of his life for ever. The twenty-year-old heiress was wearing a dazzling gold ring encrusted with the finest jewels recently discovered in the East. Her father had bought it for her only a week previously for her birthday, and the whole of aristocratic Florentine society was talking about its extravagant beauty. Margherita, whilst walking with her friends, suddenly screamed as she realised the ring was no longer on her finger. She looked frantically along the cobbled street and gutter to see where it had landed. People, knowing who she was, and realising what she was looking for, joined in the search with the hope of a reward if the ring was found. Such was the commotion in the square that the young Bardo, thinking nobody was watching a random fruit stall one hundred yards away, decided to seize the opportunity to steal an apple unnoticed.

Unfortunately Nello, the local barber who was watching events sitting outside his shop, spotted him.

'Thief! Quickly, he's over there,' he loudly shouted out, as he got up from his chair to chase Bardo. Suddenly there were two public commotions in the same square. One was looking for a gold ring, the other for a vagrant with a bright green apple. As incongruous as they might seem, they converged, as if they were two circles in a Venn diagram. The scramble for the ring and the apple inexplicably became one, involving hundreds of people. Bardo managed to extricate himself from the melee, albeit without the apple. However at that precise moment he spotted something glint from two badly cobbled together stones. Realising that this could be his chance, he swiftly, and deftly, freed the gold ring from the crack in the stonework.

It was in moments such as these when one has to weigh up the situation in a split second. Bardo, in that moment, made the right decision. Instead of fleeing for his life, he screamed, 'Whose ring is this?' From utter turmoil, the noise hushed, and a gradual silence descended upon that part of the Piazza della Signoria. Margherita looked up, and with her cortege pushed her way through the crowds towards Bardo.

'Oh my God... Thank you... I owe you so much, how can I ever repay you?' the Florentine heiress asked the tall handsome young man.

'It was nothing, my lady...' Bardo said, but then heard shouting in the background and turned around. 'Although there might be a small problem from...' He looked over in the direction of a number of well built men running towards him from the fruit stall on the other side of the square, located in front of Nello's barber shop.

'He stole my fruit... that beggar over there... Nello saw him with his very own eyes!' Girolamo Calvo, the stall owner pointed to Bardo. 'Bring him here,' he shouted.

Girolamo was a well known Florentine, not just because of his string of fruit stalls, but also due to his physical appearance, being six foot five inches tall. His huge girth sat comfortably with his height. He was quite literally the largest man in the city, and his stature exuded a threatening violence, which intimidated almost everybody, not least Bardo Giovanni.

'Please Girolamo!' Margherita said calmly. 'I'm sure we can settle any outstanding debts that Signor…?'

'Oh… Bardo, Bardo Giovanni, my lady,' he introduced himself, bowing yet again obsequiously.

'That Signor Giovanni has with you. I am quite sure it's a case of mistaken identity, do you not agree?' Margherita calmly looked at both Nello and Girolamo in the eyes. The giant Florentine fruit seller certainly did not intimidate her.

'Of course, my lady, it must have been a misunderstanding. I had no idea that this… Uh… Man was an acquaintance of yours.' Girolamo looked at Bardo with contempt. 'Nello obviously saw someone very similar to you… Nello?' he said through gritted teeth, visibly trying to control his frustration.

'Yes, yes… Now I think about it, he looks a bit taller than the scoundrel who stole your fruit, Girolamo,' The barber said, shrinking away from the dispute.

The giant fruit seller realised that he could do nothing about the situation now. He was a rich man, owning some of the most sought-after fruit stall locations all around the city, but his wealth did not compare on any level to the Bondi family. He bowed to Margherita, and walked back with his friend Nello, to his stall, cursing his luck under his breath.

Margherita, smiled at her new acquaintance. He himself was over six feet tall, a well defined face with green eyes that glinted in the sunlight, and long jet-black hair that fell on his shoulders. There was not an ounce of fat on him, which was hardly surprising given his travails over the previous few days.

'Now then, you must come back with me to my family's palazzo. I would like to repay you properly and introduce you to my father, Piero Bondi, who will be most grateful to you.'

'No, it's quite all right my lady. I mean, he won't know what has just happened, and if you want to repay me in any way… a small gesture might help,' Bardo replied, frightened over the prospect of meeting someone as powerful and famous as Piero

Bondi. Even a man from an island as far away as Capri, had heard of the great bankers of the day. Bondi was no exception.

'Unfortunately my father would have heard about this incident already. He has ears all around the city who report to him on every step I take. If he doesn't actually know now, he will do very soon. He will be angry that a ring costing a thousand florins could have fallen off my finger so easily. In fact you would be doing me another favour if you did come to meet him… His attention to you might deflect his undoubted anger away from me!'

'As you wish, my lady.' Bardo nodded and reluctantly followed Margherita's entourage towards the Bondi residence in the Piazza San Firenze.

3

The walk was a short one, and barely gave enough time for the young survivor of a shipwreck the chance to regain his composure. He had arrived in the city barely four hours earlier. The boat had foundered on the rocks off the coast of Pisa. He had managed to swim ashore, and climbed on the back of a cart arriving in Florence that morning. He was starving, and his first thought, when seeing the bright green apple detached from the basket of others on the fruit stall, was to steal it. It would not be an exaggeration to say that it had been an extremely eventful morning for young Bardo Giovanni.

Although, highly unusual for an heiress of one of the great banking families, to befriend a stranger who was nothing short of being a beggar, it was understandable in this particular situation. Margherita's father had an explosive temper, that whilst serving him well in the cut and thrust dealings of his business world, was a fearsome and destructive weapon at home. Even his beloved daughter would have felt the full force of his anger if he had found out that she had lost the ring. She knew how much he had paid, and how the Florentine aristocratic classes were already chattering about his extraordinary gift to his daughter. Bardo's more than fortuitous find, saved Margherita from untold misery. She was also determined to reward him since in addition to her being rescued, she found him not unattractive despite his obvious low birth.

They entered the palazzo, and went directly through the colonnaded loggias to the grand central staircase that led to the main meeting rooms and apartments. Bardo felt extremely self aware, in his torn clothes and unclean state, surrounded by such magnificence. He had never seen anything like this in his life. Standing at the entrance of the great meeting room where the scion of the banking family met with all his advisors and employees during his working day, he watched in a state of bewilderment at the activity that was being carried out before him.

Unbeknown to him, the activity that was taking place in the great hall was an exemplar of the city's growing intricate banking transactional business that was happening in Florence at that time. Hundreds of men were talking to each other, negotiating and signing contracts between themselves. Many were clutching the famous bills of exchange, which were the cornerstone of the Florentine banking system.

Piero Bondi sat in the middle of the great room, behind an enormous wooden desk, upon which huge piles of parchment were stacked. The old, grey, bearded man listened intently to one of his most senior lawyers, Baldassarre Calvo, a man in his early thirties who would later become a very important advisor to Bardo himself. Baldassarre was the family consiglieri who looked after not only Piero's business dealings, but also any personal disputes that occurred within the family. His skill in diplomacy was at times known to be breathtaking. When Baldassarre had finally finished informing Piero of what had happened in the Piazza della Signoria that morning, he beckoned Bardo into the room.

Bardo felt the piercing gaze of onlookers as he walked towards the old man. He sensed the shakiness in his legs with each step he took towards the desk situated in the middle of the room. He was then finally introduced to, the now informed and very grateful Piero.

'So then... Uhm.' He looked up at Baldassarre.

'Bardo Giovanni,' the lawyer helpfully interjected.

'Yes... Signor Giovanni... Thank you for finding my daughter's ring. No doubt you would like some reward.'

'Well... Uh... Yes... Thank you... I'm sorry, I'm a little nervous.' He coughed.

'Bring him some water... Quickly!' shouted Piero. The old man might have had a temper, but he was also capable of kindness. He had mellowed over the years after losing his much younger wife to the plague soon after Margherita's birth. His life, after becoming a widowers was concentrated on both bringing up his daughter and expanding the bank.

'Oh... Thank you sir.' He gulped down the fluid and continued. 'Of course a reward would be most welcome, sir... But a...'

'Well, what else would you want?' he snapped, already running out of patience, and looking across to Baldassarre.

'I have just arrived in the city from Capri where I grew up. My father is a farmer, and I have three brothers and two sisters. I had to leave; he could no longer support all of us, and I went to find my fortune. The boat was shipwrecked and I lost everything.' Bardo was beginning find both his legs and voice, speaking now with composure. 'My letters of reference, and what little money I had, were lost. I have not slept for forty-eight hours. I have nothing, and I desperately need employment.' There was silence amongst those standing around Piero. Bardo waited for a reply.

'Do you have any skills? Languages, for instance?'

'Not really sir... But I can run.'

'Yes I heard...' Piero smiled, his demeanour softening. He had been informed of the whole story, including the part about Bardo's dash with the apple. He looked up at Baldassarre, who shook his head slowly. He then looked towards Margherita, who's implored expression on her face led the old man to weaken. 'Do we need messengers and runners, Baldassarre?'

'Not really sir, but...' He too looked towards Margherita, and relented. It was always difficult to go against Margherita's gentle, but persuasive facial expression. 'But I hear that he's fast on his feet!'

'Really?' Piero asked.

'Yes sir... I believe like the wind'.

4

Bardo Giovanni's rise in the House of Bondi was nothing short of meteoric. As a runner he proved invaluable, performing his duties flawlessly. He was certainly the fastest and most reliable messenger the bank had ever had. However, it would have been unlikely that he would have risen from messenger, to clerk and then senior administrator for the bank in the space of twelve months had it not been for his relationship, and the pending marriage to Margherita. She had fallen in love with Bardo at first sight. He too was attracted to her, but he wrestled with his feelings over whether they were based on who she was rather than what she was. Coming from a simple hard working family with strong moral values, he had not been tainted by the lure of the modern city attractions. His innocence was now inexorably being eroded by the worldly life that surrounded him. He did not however have much time to settle this emotional struggle, since Margherita was beautiful and extremely rich, making her one of the most sought-after women in the whole of Tuscany.

Pressure on Bardo, not only from Margherita, but also from the competition of a procession of men wanting to marry her, made his mind up and forced the young man from Capri to ask Piero for his daughter's hand in marriage. Although the old banker was not at all thrilled by the prospect of his only daughter marrying a man of precious little breeding, it was difficult for him to go against her will. Although powerful, and was able to control most situations, this was different. She loved him, and Bardo appeared to be sincere.

Piero's recent strategy had been to avoid Bardo at all costs so as to prevent him from asking for his permission. This was not a very difficult task since the old man was extremely busy working very long hours surrounded by his minions. These included not only his advisors and employees on the payroll, but also notaries, and administrators, as well as doctors, bakers and spice traders. However, whenever he was free to speak he would feign illness so as not to let the young suitor near him. The situation was fast becoming comical, if not upsetting, for both Margherita and Bardo.

He realised that he could not put off the inevitable forever, and Bardo managed to seize a moment when the unsuspecting Piero was alone at his desk. Shaking with fear, Bardo summoned up the courage to ask the question only to be met with silence. Piero hardly averted his gaze from his papers.

'Write to me, explaining why you want to marry my daughter,' he said in a quiet undertone.

Bardo remained silent, standing on the spot without moving. He stared down at his master, totally speechless, and unable to respond. Piero looked up and then smiled. Another few weeks' delay suited the old man well. Not only was he extremely busy, with the bank executing the largest deal in its history, but also it might give him one last chance of persuading Margherita to wait a little while longer and perhaps meet other young men more suited. Bardo suddenly turned around and left the room hurriedly. Piero then shouted for Baldassarre Calvo, his consiglieri to come in and help with the 'matter' at hand.

5

The 'matter' at hand was the largest loan that the Bondi family bank had ever made. King Edward III of England had been borrowing from the Florentines for most of his reign, and his debts had resulted in the bankruptcy and downfall of two of the greatest banking families, the Scali and the Amieri. The sovereign, now in his last years was desperate for more money to finance his unsuccessful war against France. Piero Bondi knew how high the risks were, but the interest rate charged meant that the rewards were enormous. Baldassarre was against him making the loan on his own, and had managed to persuade the Peruzzi family to come in as senior partners. The 400,000 florins lent by the two families was the equivalent of the entire English annual budget. Locally, such a sum could have financed the entire payroll of workers in the Florentine cloth industry. The intended collateral for the loan was perhaps one of Europe's most attractive markets: English wool.

As time went on, it was clear that the debt was in fact unsecured and was not going to be paid. The vicissitudes of late mediaeval markets put the entire Bondi bank on the precipice of bankruptcy. It was Baldassarre and the young Bardo who kept the ship afloat, whilst Piero panicked, hesitated and then lost his authority at the bank. In such an atmosphere Bardo, who had suddenly been thrust into the front line of Florentine finance, found it difficult to have the time to deliver his letter of intent, much to the frustration of his lover. Never had Margherita missed not having a mother as she did then.

Indeed Bardo would never be able to deliver his letter. Piero Bondi, a month after Giovanni's initial approach, suffered a massive stroke and became paralysed and unable to speak. The family consiglieri, Baldassarre Calvo, assumed control of the House of Bondi. Giovanni Bardo became his aiutante di campo, accompanying him everywhere. With the help from other Florentine banks, they managed to recapitalise, and reposition its business towards the Orient and concentrate on the lucrative trade in silks, spices and luxury goods. The two men worked closely together throughout this transition, drawing up the complicated contracts with new partners, and providing the bills of exchange necessary with such a radical change of direction. It was an instant success with the bank recouping half of its losses within twelve months. It would take a further two years for it to recover all of its capital in real terms.

Piero, in his will, had left everything to his daughter, but with the proviso that Baldassarre would take operational control until the latter believed he could pass it on to a suitable heir. Piero had originally assumed that his daughter would marry a gentleman from the correct social standing. Initially he thought that Baldassarre might have been the ideal suitor, yet when his chief advisor got one of the maid servants pregnant, he did the honourable thing and married her. Baldassarre had never entertained marrying Margherita anyway. He was much older than her, and had known her since she was a child. The thought of her as a potential wife never crossed his mind.

Now that Piero was incapacitated, Baldassarre stepped into his shoes, and acted as a guardian in overseeing his daughter's future. He obviously knew of Piero's reservations about Bardo, particularly about him not being a member of the Florentine nobility. And yet in Baldassarre's mind Bardo was a man who had proved himself more than suitable. His help during the last number of weeks had been invaluable, without which Baldassarre might not have been able to save the bank. He also understood that despite Piero's original silence over an approval, Bardo's devotion for Margherita was sincere and realised that the old man's days were coming to an end. It was only a matter of time before Bardo married Piero's only child, with or without approval, and would almost certainly be the new patriarch of the family. Baldassarre understood that his fate would be inextricably tied with the young suitor, and was content to hand over the reins to Bardo in the future. He was sure that Bardo Giovanni would be more than a worthy successor to Piero.

6

The House of Bondi became the House of Giovanni following the death of Piero a year later, and then the marriage between Bardo and Margherita soon after. It was a smooth transition with both Bardo and Baldassarre forming a formidable partnership. Although there were fifteen years between them, the partnership became a long and close one. Bardo assumed the trappings of his new found wealth and position. Yet he never forgot where he came from. It was at this time, that he persuaded his family to come to Florence, where he bought them a beautiful house in the hills of Fiesole. He found jobs for his brothers in the family bank, and ensured that his parents were provided with an income to keep them living in comfort during their retirement.

He looked at his peers across the city and began to follow their example by entering politics, and becoming a patron of the arts. The new works being created at that time, and indeed the new buildings being built in Florence captivated him. He was determined to become involved and aided by an immensely powerful and influential banking society, he won seats on various administrative bodies that controlled the city's development. This was a clear break from the Bondi family past. Piero, his father in law had shown no interest in the new art of the age. The city was delighted to have Giovanni involved in its rapid development, given his wealth and power.

One of those who helped him was Bicci de Medici, known at the time as simply Bicci, a particularly astute businessman who had already become one of the richest men in Italy. He had transferred his business to Florence from Rome just before the turn of the century. Whilst maintaining an important presence in the Eternal City where he could play the role of the Pope's banker, his business activity now spread across Europe, laying the foundations of what was to become the greatest banking dynasty in the Renaissance era. He hoped that Bardo might prove very useful in the future, and introduced him to the Arte del Cambio, the Bankers Guild. Piero had been an established member of the guild, and Bardo's membership was never in question.

However, having the enormously influential Medici acting as his sponsor was crucial and Bardo knew this. Slightly wary over the cost of such support from Bicci, Bardo was nevertheless extremely grateful, and looked to Bicci for further advice on all municipal matters where he was involved. Bicci also was instrumental in encouraging Bardo to take a more proactive lead on the committees that were directing the extraordinary building developments of the city. Florence, at times, looked like a development site with sandstone quarries inside the city walls, which provided the building material together with the gravel dredged from the riverbeds, to produce the new churches and palaces that had begun to spring up all over the city. The Palazzo Vecchio was of course, a prime example of this building boom, which reflected Florence's growing stature as a major city in Europe. With a population of fifty thousand, it already rivalled London as a commercial centre.

One of these committees, where Bicci de Medici crucially managed to get him elected to, was the powerful Arte di Calimala, the Cloth's Importers Guild. His appointment on to the latter, in 1401 was auspicious, even providential. The Plague had once again revisited Florence the year before, and as many as twelve thousand Florentines, a fifth of the entire population, had perished from the Black Death. In addition to this, Giangaleazzo Visconti, the Duke of Milan was encamped with his army, about to storm the city walls. In order to assuage the anger of the Almighty, a competition by the guild to design the second set of bronze doors for the Battistero di San Giovanni had been recently announced.

The Baptistry was one of the most important buildings in Florence where every citizen was baptised. The aim of the commission was to create a new set to accompany the doors designed by Andrea Pisano eighty years earlier. Bardo had walked past Pisano's gates many times, and even though they had fallen into poor condition, he had never forgotten the impression they made on him when he first saw them as a messenger some years back. Touching the engravings, and feeling the images on the panels, even then, captivated him. Seeing such beauty and creative genius made an indelible impression on the young man from Capri.

For Bardo, to now come into contact with the great young artists and be involved in the planning of a new set of doors was therefore very exciting. His love for the new art that was now being created at that period had captured Bardo's imagination for some time. Now being amongst the thirty-four judges, he was at the very heart of the decision making process, which was nothing short of a dream coming true. The competition attracted some of the brightest young stars in the world of art. Lorenzo Ghiberti, Filippo Brunelleschi, Donatello and Jacopo della Quercia were among the seven semi finalists. The contest was narrowed down from seven to two, Ghiberti and Brunelleschi. Each would have to provide one bronze panel depicting the sacrifice of Isaac as their final presentation.

The professional rivalry between the two goldsmiths that arose from this competition became a lifelong one. Ghiberti's approach was an inclusive one whereby he brought in the judges and the public to look at his work, and take their advice. Brunelleschi, on the other hand, worked in isolation and secrecy. Picking a winner was almost impossible given the quality of the work, and the judges, including Bardo, were leaning towards a joint assignment. This was not surprising given the scale of the commission, and also due to the fact that both artists were still very young in their early twenties. The debate on who should win was a heated one, but their job was made easier when Brunelleschi refused to share the prize. He would not consider working with Lorenzo, and would never contemplate giving up control. Vowing never to work on sculpture again, he and Donatello, his fellow competitor and friend, left immediately together for Rome, to study classical architecture through its ancient ruins.

Ghiberti's artistic genius, and indeed his superior technical skill, particularly in regard to bronze casting, meant that his twenty-eight bronze gilded panels on the Baptistry Doors became one of the wonders of the fifteenth century. Lorenzo, it was reported, had said that he won the competition unanimously, but Bardo, and indeed Bicci, knew that this was not the case. Both panels by Ghiberti and Brunelleschi were the subjects of intense debate, and no clear winner had been decided on until Brunelleschi had made the decision for them. Ghiberti's victory ultimately resulted him in not only making this second set of bronze doors, but also twenty-five years later, a third set, which eventually became known in the words of Michelangelo as the *Gates of Paradise*.

Brunelleschi, having abruptly decided to depart, was on his way out of the city, before bumping into Bardo, who was on his way back to the bank.

'Filippo, if it's any consolation, I would have voted for you alone... It's just that he cast the panel as a single piece... And he showed it to the public as well as the council. He kept everyone informed... He was clever you know. He played the politics... You didn't... You must have realised all of this. We all liked your panel very much. Why didn't you accept a joint commission?'

'Ah! Bardo... Thank you, my friend. Call me 'Pippo', everyone else does. Listen, I know you were keen on my work, but let Lorenzo get on with it. I can't give up control of a project. It would be a disaster. I know that my relief was better... But I think the judges liked the fact that he used less bronze than I did!' Brunelleschi clearly felt that the judges had one eye on the costs. He paused. 'Maybe it's for the best... His workshop will be very well set up for the designing and casting. He will employ the best young artists. He's a good choice... but having said that of course I would have been a better one!'

'I can't help but feel that you've made a big mistake, Pippo.'

Bardo could sense that the twenty-four-year old artist's pride had been severely wounded, even though he seemed relatively good humoured about the result.

'Maybe I have... Anyway, I must go to Rome. I'm taking Donatello... You know he's only fifteen! It's a new age, my friend. The world of art is changing and it all started here with Cimabue, and then really with Giotto... Look at this Campanile.' Brunelleschi pointed to Florence's great bell tower. 'Giotto's creation, you know... Pisano constructed it to the letter of his design... It's magnificent, don't you think?' He paused. 'You've been to Padua... I assume?' the artist asked.

'Yes... But I didn't have time to see the... Oh... I've forgotten the name...'

'Scrovegni Chapel,' Brunelleschi interrupted.

'Yes... That's right, the Scrovegni...' Bardo responded, feeling rather stupid at his loss of memory.

'Go back and see what Giotto did. He changed everything.' He paused. 'I need to get to Rome. We have to find out more of what the ancients were doing. I will come back, I promise, with new ideas and creations.'

'When you do come back, be sure to remember me... I might want you to build something for my family and myself. A chapel dedicated to our beloved Virgin Mary,' Bardo replied, shaking the artist's hand.

'Don't worry, Bardo... I won't forget.'

7

Bardo Giovanni did not see Filippo Brunelleschi for another ten years. He was a very busy man, intensely involved in the bank, active on the building committee of the council, and also being a father. He and Margherita had wanted a large family with lots of children, and when she gave birth to a son named Tito, they both thought that their dreams would be fulfilled. However, tragedy struck the Giovanni family, not once but twice, when two of her next issue, died very young of the plague. The effect on Margherita was profound, as she gradually withdrew from public life, and refused to go to any social engagements. She eventually turned to her faith, and prayed constantly at the city's half built main cathedral, Santa Maria del Fiore.

At first, Bardo thought that the idea of building a private family chapel would serve two purposes. The first being that it would now provide his wife with a private place for prayer, whilst the second one, his initial plan, was that it would exhibit the family's growing power and wealth as well as show off the new art of the age. However as time moved on Margherita hardly came home, spending all of her time at the cathedral. She lost interest in her surviving son, even questioning why he was allowed to live and why the others were not. These were questions that Bardo could never answer. He worried that she might be a harmful influence on Tito, and when she asked her husband whether she could retreat to a convent in Fiesole, Bardo agreed and became Tito's sole parent.

Bardo's life began to change. He had realised that Margherita's involvement with her son had become negligible over the recent years, but he had relied on the servants to fulfil the maternal duties that his wife had failed to perform. However, with Margherita now away, he took more interest in his only son. He doted on him and was a proud father. Tito, himself was no ordinary child. He excelled in his studies, and was taught by young teachers who were well versed in the developing humanism of the age. When he reached his eighteenth birthday, the decision had to be made whether he would go to university. Tito was an ambitious young man who idolised his father. He frequently watched him transacting in business in the great room of the palazzo where they lived. He watched carefully, from the sidelines when his father, with Baldassarre, would negotiate terms with other bankers. Tito had no doubts what he wanted to do, but the decision was not entirely his.

'I think you would benefit from going to Bologna… It's one of the best universities in Europe. I think it would be a shame to come into the business when you show such promise in your studies,' Bardo told his son.

'Father, I know you have these ambitions for me but I want to help you. I am more interested in the affairs of the bank. Baldassarre has been educating me on most of the aspects of the bank.'

Bardo looked across at Baldassarre who was standing by, looking slightly embarrassed. 'Has he indeed… Is that true, Baldassarre? I thought you were on my side!'

'He's very persuasive, Bardo. The boy is extremely clever. I did suggest as a compromise that he might study to become a lawyer. That way he would satisfy your wishes by continuing his studying, but would also nourish his desire for doing something practical.'

'Oh come on, Baldassarre... I don't want to read law...
Father, please let me help you. Apart from Baldassarre, there is
no one here you can completely trust.' Tito desperately wanted
his father's approval.

Bardo knew that Baldassarre was right in that his son was
extremely persuasive. He found it difficult at the best of times
to deny his son anything, but when he was in this mood it was
almost impossible.

'All right then, but there is one condition you have to abide
by.'

'Of course... What is it?

'You have to stay close to Baldassarre... Shadow him and
learn from him. You, in fact will work for him directly.' He
looked across to his partner, who nodded.

'That's all? Oh... Thank you, Father. I cannot wait to start. I
won't let you down... I promise.'

8

Baldassarre began taking him on his business trips, teaching him the intricacies of the banking world. Tito showed that he was a natural, and adapted to the world of finance with ease. So much so that Baldassarre felt that he could retire soon knowing that the bank was in safe hands. Indeed he told Bardo that the time was right for him to now take the lead with his son. It was important for the outside world to see the heir apparent. This he believed would be best served by Tito joining his father on his travels in Italy.

It was during one of these business journeys in 1403 that Bardo took Tito to Padua. Bardo had a number of meetings whilst in the city, but had managed to leave some free time for him and his son to visit the now famous Scrovegni Chapel. Unlike his father, Tito was not interested in architecture, sculpture and art, notwithstanding what was being created at that time in Tuscany. Despite his brilliance, his cultural aestheticism paled in comparison to his father's. However Tito realised that to keep his father happy he would have to endure the odd visit, now and then to various new creations that were either being built or painted. It was a small price to pay.

For Bardo, every journey would be carefully prepared, ensuring that some time was left to one side in order for him to see the new work that was being carried out in each particular city. It was early days in the Italian Renaissance, but the trail blazed by Giotto was burning ever more brightly. The Scrovegni chapel, commissioned by the financier Enrico degli Scrovegni, was one such work. The plain pink brick building that sat on the site of the old Roman Arena was built next to the grander Scrovegni Palace that had just been restored. Enrico had built the chapel for family worship, and as a burial space. It was rumoured at the time, though it was never confirmed, that he commissioned the chapel to gain forgiveness for his father, himself and his family from the sin of usury. Although Bardo felt no guilt over his business, which of course was based on charging interest, he was obviously aware that to many, he too was guilty of usury. The Scrovegni visit was important to him on more than one level.

Bardo, ever since his brief conversation with Brunelleschi was desperate to see the fresco cycles painted by Giotto. As he walked into the chapel with his son, he was immediately struck by the beauty of the chapel. He immediately went before the altar to pray, leaving Tito to stand at the doorway. Bardo was an observant man from a religious family, who felt he owed much to God for his fortune and well-being. Whenever visiting churches, primarily for their artistic splendour, he never forgot his roots, and the debt he owed to the Almighty. After rising from his devotion, he wandered around the open space, looking at the brilliant ultramarine blue paint on the ceiling that was so striking surrounding the fresco cycle. Other colours such as gold, red and pink were also used in abundance, producing a kaleidoscope of richness that was difficult to imagine. Bardo studied each one of the thirty-seven scenes, depicting the lives of the Virgin and Christ. The last Judgement took up one entire façade.

He at last understood what Brunelleschi had meant when he insisted that he should go back to the chapel. Giotto had moved away from the elongated Byzantine style of his master Cimabue and others, such as Duccio from Sienna, to produce

79

three-dimensional figures. They all had faces with expressions and emotions, and were clothed in robes that hung and folded naturally revealing a reality not seen in painting before. Hands for example, at the end of arms, making gestures that were life like. The artist, crucially had started the process of foreshortening through chiaroscuro, enabling the light and the shade of the painting appear to have perspective. Spectators could look at the works, and follow the narratives, immersing themselves in the scene, not just as an onlooker, but also as a participant. It was both magical, and more importantly revolutionary.

'Look Tito... look at this one.' Bardo called to his son, pointing to the panel illustrating the *Massacre of the Innocents*. Look at the soldiers dragging that baby... Look at his embarrassment, his shame... Look at the expressions. It's so real.' He knew his son was perhaps a lost cause in the realm of art, but he never gave up on the opportunity of trying to make him understand beauty when he saw it. He hoped that one day he would understand it, and appreciate it. He was desperate for Tito to not just take over the bank, but also to perform his civic duties in Florence, and participate, as he himself had done, in helping Florence continue as a centre of cultural greatness.

Tito looked at the fresco, but was unmoved. He was not a devout person, and was always slightly irritated that a man like his father, urbane and sophisticated in so many walks of life, was so convinced by the dogma of Rome. He felt that it was a weakness in his father, and indeed the devotion he exhibited at times was a source of disappointment to him. The pictures, of various biblical images as a result meant very little to Tito. The style failed to interest him. His mind was fixed on returning to Florence as soon as possible. His patience was wearing thin. 'Yes Father... It's very beautiful... Have you had enough time now?' He asked in a somewhat desperate voice. 'We've been here for two hours now. We really ought to go.'

'I haven't finished yet,' Bardo replied, gazing up at the work. The Scrovegni family had generously allowed him to visit their chapel, a privilege that was quite rare. He was not going to waste this opportunity due to an impatient eighteen year old. 'Don't you understand, Tito,' Bardo continued, 'this is what I want for my family.'

9

From the moment Bardo left the Scrovegni Chapel, his mind was now made up. He too would have a chapel built for his family to worship, and be buried there. He too would have it constructed by a great architect, and have the interiors painted by the greatest artists of the age. He would dedicate the chapel to the Virgin Mary. He did not like the personalisation that was so prevalent at the time when naming private chapels. He believed that the 'Giovanni Chapel' would be too ostentatious for him. His humble background kept him firmly on the ground when it came to excessive displays of wealth. He preferred to have the Virgin's name than his own, and in the event of it actually being built, the chapel would be known as the Chiesa di Santa Maria. Arriving in Florence, a week later, he spent the next twelve months, during his spare time, walking around the city looking at the architecture. At the same time he travelled around Tuscany searching for artists, and talking to aficionados, including the judges from the Baptistry Door competition, hoping to find the right men for his project.

The bank meanwhile was growing at a rapid rate, not only vastly expanding its own headquarters in Florence, but also establishing satellite offices all around Europe. Over the next five years, Bardo devolved even more responsibility on to the broad shoulders of the ever reliable Baldassarre, and then later on to those of Tito. Margherita, when visited by Bardo, was concerned that it would be too much for her son to cope with at such a young age. However her husband assured her that Baldassarre would be there, looking after him, and that he himself was still around in any case of emergency. But in reality, Bardo's interests became increasingly focussed on painting, sculpture and architecture. All the time, he was thinking of how he would proceed with his project of building the family chapel.

In 1412, he managed to purchase a plot of land on the south bank of the Arno. It was an open space of about half an acre, located between the Borgo San Frediano and Lungarno Soderini, close to the Ponte alla Carraia. It was not as close to the city centre as Bardo wanted, but even with his position on the city council, not to mention his influence with the guilds, he was unable to secure anything better. However in its favour, he liked the site being close to the river, and also because he could see it from his office window of his palazzo. His ambition to build a chapel was at last beginning to take shape. He had one man in mind to fill the post of architect for the project. Although staying in Rome, Brunelleschi did return to Florence intermittently, and Bardo had heard from other artists about his work on the Roman ruins, and indeed on architecture.

'Filippo!' Bardo shouted across the Piazza della Signoria at the top of his voice. 'Pippo, over here… Please!'

'Signor Giovanni… How are you?' Brunelleschi replied graciously.

'Ha… It used to be Bardo… Now you call me Signor Giovanni… Am I that much more important these days, Pippo?' Bardo knew the answer. He was now one of the richest men in the city. 'I am well, Pippo, and you?'

'Busy, my friend… Very busy. Come this way… Come with me now… I hope you still have the same passion for art as you had when I last saw you?' he asked as he placed his hand on Bardo's arm, guiding him through the crowds.

'Yes, yes of course… But where are you taking me?' he asked the artist.

'To the Cathedral Santa Maria del Fiore in San Giovanni. The cathedral works are gathering pace. I want to show you something that my friend Donatello is sculpting.'

The two, well known, and indeed respected men, walked through the crowds towards the cathedral where Donatello was working with his assistants. Bardo knew about the works Donatello was executing, one of which being a sculpture of the *Seated St John Evengelista*, which was four arms' length tall and located in a niche on the corner of the façade of the cathedral. However, he could never get near the sculpture due to the number of workmen and barriers surrounding the church. Even important men such as Bardo Giovanni had problems when it came to artists and accessibility to their work, especially when it was work in progress.

'Niccolo!' Brunelleschi shouted as he simultaneously pushed the workmen aside whilst tugging on Bardo's sleeve.

'Pippo… You look well… Careful!' Donatello shouted to Bardo as he brushed by a lose piece of marble.

'You remember Signor Bardo Giovanni… The banker. He was on the Guild council when it awarded Lorenzo the Baptistry doors,' Brunelleschi said, patting Bardo on the back. 'Of course they would never have made their minds up had I not walked out!' He laughed and turned to the workmen beside him.

'Of course I remember… Signor Giovanni.' He smiled. 'Oh don't worry about Filippo. He's always trying to score points over everyone… He's very competitive! If the truth be known, we all just started off as simple goldsmiths you know. There will always be some sort of rivalry between all of us. Tell me is there any truth in that the discussions in vaulting the dome here at Santa Maria del Fiore are finally reaching a decision?' Donatello pointed above to the cathedral.

'Yes… The Capomaestro and The Opera del Duomo have a number of good ideas but are still some way away from making a decision.' Bardo was referring to the works office and architect in chief who ran the Santa Maria del Fiore project.

'The difficulty is that by adopting Neri di Fioaventi's seventy-year-old design to the letter, has meant that the dome might well be impossible to build.' Bardo knew from his membership on the Wool Guild which controlled the Opera del Duomo, how exasperated things were getting. Neri's model of 1367 had become an obsession amongst engineers and architects, wanting to build the dome. They believed it could be done even if it meant no buttresses, the traditional Gothic method of support for such a structure, would be allowed.

'The problems with Neri's double shell and pointed shape are enormous, not to mention the costs involved. If it's ever completed it will be the widest and the highest cupola ever built. Since Arnolfo di Cambio died nobody has come forward with any sensible idea of how to vault it without buttresses… I'm sure in the end there will be a competition, but not yet,' Bardo continued, shaking his head.

'Well… I think if there's a competition, he will win it.' Donatello nodded towards Brunelleschi, who was negotiating with the six foot five inch Girolamo Calvo over the price of an apple. Bardo smiled to himself. The giant no longer looked at all intimidating to him anymore. Over the years the fruit stall owner had unsurprisingly become much more friendly to Bardo.

'What makes you say that?' he asked the young sculptor, his attention now returning to their discussion.

'Whilst we were in Rome, Pippo spent hours – no, days –at the Pantheon. He made endless notes on the huge structure of the cupola. I never could read what he had written… It was all so cryptic. But one morning he did say to me quietly that the Pantheon was proof to him that Santa Maria del Fiore could be built without support. He now knew it was possible, and that he could achieve it.'

'Interesting, Donatello… Very interesting…' Bardo paused. 'Listen I will bear it in mind when there are more discussions at the Opera.'

Donatello's words struck a chord, and remained in Bardo's memory for a future time. He knew that the members of Wool Guild were under pressure in regards to the cathedral's dome. It was fast becoming an obsession for the city's ruling bodies. Many were saying that Neri's ideas were impossible to achieve, and that the expenditure was far too great. A decision would indeed have to be made soon. The rumours were now spreading that a competition would indeed be announced to invite engineers, carpenters and masons to produce models that would solve Neri's problem of the vaulting. When, and if it came to that point, Bardo would champion his friend, Filippo Brunelleschi.

'Come let me show you St John, I've nearly finished it.' Donatello took both men, pulling Filippo away from the apple stall, under the sheets protecting the area and revealed the immense statue. Bardo immediately recognised the new art of the age; the realism of the hands, the legs, and the folds in the clothes. The magisterial sweep that illustrated the natural lines of the sculpture were all too clear to see. Brunelleschi nodded and smiled.

'You've surpassed yourself, my friend,' Brunelleschi said, admiring the seated statue.

'Are you staying in Florence?' Bardo asked Donatello.

'Yes… I've been asked to do some sculptures for this bell tower over the next two years,' Donatello replied, looking up at Giotto's giant structure. 'You know… Pisano's work on the campanile is an architectural wonder. I know its Giotto's design, but just like his doors over there, Andrea knew how to create and build. He was a master in his own right.' He paused and looked across at Brunelleschi. 'What about you, Pippo?' Donatello asked poking his chisel into architect's stomach.

'I'm working on my architecture, my geometry and mathematics, and of course my linear perspective. I must try and get people to view the space behind the narrative... In the past everyone has simply been concerned with space in the front of the painting,' he responded in animated fashion.

'Ah then... You must show Signor Giovanni, if of course he hasn't seen it, your experiment on the vanishing point, Pippo,' Donatello said to Brunelleschi, genuinely impressed by his friend's groundbreaking rediscovery of what had been lost since antiquity. The importance of Brunelleschi's mathematical invention was only just being realised.

'I don't think he will be interested,' Brunelleschi responded, knowing full well that Bardo was desperate to know what they were talking about.

'No... No, I'm very interested... Show me, Pippo,' Bardo said excitedly.

'Ok then... Here it is.' Brunelleschi took his panel depicting the Baptistry from his sack, and led Bardo and Donatello to the gateway of the cathedral on the exact point from where he had painted his panel. He placed the panel in front of Bardo so that the banker looked through the pinhole at the centre of the painting. In his other hand Brunelleschi held the mirror, making it impossible for Bardo to work out which image was reality. The one he could see through the aperture, or the reflection of the panel from the mirror.

'My God that's amazing... And this is what you call linear perspective? Can I buy this panel from you, Pippo?'

'No Bardo... Sorry... I have promised it to the Medici family. But now that you have seen it, you can tell them how brilliant I am.'

The three men laughed, even though Bardo Giovanni was still dumbstruck by what he had just seen. At that point the two older men left Donatello to work.

'Filippo, I need to talk to you about some plans I have. I

want to build my own family chapel.' Bardo was now more than ever convinced that Brunelleschi had to build his family chapel. 'Come to my palazzo where we can talk.' This time it was the banker leading the artist through the crowds.

10

Bardo Giovanni discussed his ambition at length with Brunelleschi that afternoon to build a family chapel. The Scrovegni Chapel was the template for his plans. Brunelleschi fired questions at Bardo, about size and proportions that the former envisaged. For the artist it would provide a brilliant opportunity to build a structure that would represent classical antiquity in its purest forms. He wanted it to be sober and formal. There was to be no marble or decoration. The only decorative elements would be the pillars and the arches. He was extremely eager to try and include the three architectural orders that he himself had classified: Doric, Ionic, and Corinthian all in one structure. The building would be mathematically precise reflecting perfect proportions, and representing the ancient past and the immediate future. It would be unique. The commission was an ideal one for Brunelleschi. He could develop everything he had learnt in Rome, and show everyone his mastery in not just architecture, but in at the same time, mathematics and geometry. He would want to start immediately.

It was Bardo's intention, to commence the project as soon as possible. However, a tragic and unforeseen event changed everything, and delayed the project by another three years. Baldassarre Calvo had been feeling less than well for a number of months. Bardo had told him to take some time away from the bank and spend it with his family, or at the very least take some rest from the hectic schedule that the bank was forcing on him. This was not the reality since he was committed to the well-being of the bank much more than to his own well-being. Having taught Tito everything he knew in the world of finance, he initially thought that his obligations were coming to an end. However with Tito's rising ascendency, the bank was starting to embark on an ever more expansionist cycle. He was constantly travelling around Europe, visiting the bank's offices in the major cities. He was also setting up new agreements with other banking families, one of whom was the new and increasingly influential Fugger family in Augsburg.

One evening, whilst in that German city, Baldassarre Calvo had gone to bed feeling unwell, complaining of severe chest pains and an acid reflux in his throat. During the night he suffered a massive heart attack and suddenly gasped his last breath in his bed. Tito, who was sleeping next door, heard the anguished scream of the old man, his mentor. Jumping out of bed, he ran out and pushed in the adjoining door. By the time he reached Baldassarre, the old man was already dead. Tito immediately sent for his father, who dropped everything and travelled as fast as he could to be with his son.

It took Bardo over a week to reach Augsburg. It was always a difficult journey across the Alps, and this time proved more problematic than before. The weather was atrocious, and the conditions of the route, at times, were equally bad. The tolls, that were very much part of the Empire's patchwork of estates, delayed the journey even further. Bardo therefore had plenty of time to think about the future. Could his son take over the bank, or was it too early? He knew the answers, but did not want to face the truth, since it would mean delaying his ultimate desire of building his family chapel. He realised during those wretched days of travelling over the rocky Tyrolean passes, and through the Bavarian mud, that he would be sucked into the bank's affairs, given its recent rate of expansion, for at least five years, if not more.

Having reached the German city, he arrived at the church where the embalmed body of Baldassarre lay in its coffin. 'Father... He's in here.' Tito beckoned his exhausted father over. Bardo walked slowly towards his son, accompanied by a number of other men who stood over the casket. Bardo looked down at Baldassarre. A wave of sadness washed over him. He had been there at the very beginning, and had been instrumental in achieving the success that had come the bank's way. This was the man who not only taught him all he knew about the world of banking, but had also been such an extraordinary loyal supporter from the very outset. Without Baldassarre's willing support, Bardo would never have been able to marry Margherita, and in turn take control of the bank. It was Baldassarre who had been a brother to him, and also a father to his son.

'I don't know what we are to do now... Everything is...' He paused, as tears rolled down the old man's cheeks. The full force of the tragedy began to now hit him. Thinking about him, and remembering all of what they had done in the past over the previous seven days, was not enough to blunt the horror of seeing his old friend motionless before him.

'Father... Everything is what?' Tito asked Bardo.

'I don't know, Tito... He did everything... He was the bank. Without him, we would not be where we are...' He looked up, and now noticed the men who were on the other side of the coffin. 'Who are these people?'

'Signor Giovanni... I am Andreas Fugger, son of Johann. These are two of my young sons.'

'Ah, yes I know your name... And you?' Bardo asked, looking at the fourth man standing at the end of the coffin.

'Signor... I am Lucas Welser. I represent the Welser family in honour of Signor Calvo.'

Bardo nodded, losing interest immediately, and looked back at the embalmed body of his great friend. He then turned around, gestured to Tito to follow, and left the church.

11

Bardo and Tito had much to discuss after their return to the inn where they would spend much of the next few weeks. The grief that both of them suffered had to be compartmentalised as quickly as possible, given the feverish activity that the bank was currently going through. Of immediate attention was the need to make arrangements for Baldassarre's body to be transported back to Florence where he would be given the appropriate funeral. Bardo would let Tito remain in Augsburg to continue the continental business of the bank. The old man would take up the reins once more in Florence after his friend's funeral.

'I know the bank has grown, but the Fuggers... Can we trust them?'

'Father, they are growing in importance. They are transacting all around central Europe. They have interests in in wool, copper and luxury goods. We can join them in making syndicated loans at vast interest rates. I promise you father, when you come back, you will see. You will like them.'

'And... This Welser?'

'Ah... Don't worry about him. He's clever... From a very good family, but his house is just beginning to become involved in banking. Baldassarre liked him, and wanted to include him in some of our business. They are relatively very small, but also very hungry. We can benefit from their enthusiasm.'

Bardo nodded, and smiled. His son had been taught well, and had come a long way in the world of finance. He showed maturity well beyond his years. However he knew that he had to take back control of the bank, and his worst fears were realised in that it meant shelving his plans for his family chapel for a number of years. The day after his return to Florence he would have to let his architect Brunelleschi, receive the bad news. This was not something that Bardo was looking forward to, but he had no choice. The bank was his livelihood, and his son had to be protected. The latter was not yet ready yet to take control without his help. Indeed, nowhere near ready.

12

'I'm sorry, Filippo, but I have no option. I am going to be in Augsburg a great deal over the next few years, since the bank is becoming more involved in central Europe. I have no choice... I can't let Tito do everything.'

Brunelleschi was not impressed. He had drawn up plans for the chapel that included eight metre columns and arches, with a dome that resembled a miniature of the one that he would eventually build for Santa Maria del Fiore. It was sober and dignified.

'You'll have to pay me for the work I have completed, Bardo... I'm not a charity you know!'

'Of course, Filippo... Come on... Did you think I would short change you?'

Brunelleschi smiled; he was not too disheartened. In a way it suited him since he wanted to continue his studies in architecture. He believed that he could surpass Ghiberti, and keep Donatello at bay as well, since in his mind, building was more important than sculpture and painting. He never grew tired of the grandeur of the buildings in Rome. Their perfection in proportion and structure never ceased to amaze him. Although the air there frequently made him ill, he knew he had to return to the Eternal City.

'Alright then... I understand, Bardo... But I might not be available when you're ready. I'm returning to Rome.'

Brunelleschi's burgeoning reputation would enable him to be employed in the ancient city whilst he continued to learn about the techniques of the ancient masters. 'It's actually not so bad for me, Bardo. I have lots to do there... Studying for one thing... I will return once again to the Pantheon and its extraordinary vaulting, without the use of any type of external support or scaffolding. You know, Bardo, I think I know how they built it. One day I might let you know... But until then...'

'I hope you do, since if you can work that out, I will put pressure on the Works Department of the Santa del Fiore and the Wool Guild to give you the commission to finally vault the Fiore dome! But for now, you'll have to wait for that. I, on the other hand, will have to gamble on you being able to build my church when I am ready to employ you,' Bardo replied.

13

Over the next three years the bank grew at an exponential rate. Bardo almost commuted between Augsburg and Florence, his son remaining in Germany. By 1415, Bardo was mainly transacting with Bicci de Medici, unquestionably by now the most influential man in Florence. Even though The Medici family had not yet reached its apogee, the Strozzi family was still the richest in Florence, it would not take long for them to gain supremacy not just in that city, but in all of Italy. The Medici bank's zenith would come over the next one hundred and fifty years, when through marriage, political intrigue, and extraordinary business acumen, the family would become one of the major dynasties in Europe. At present, it was some way off that summit, and the relationship between the Medici and Giovanni banks was a productive one. Bardo felt that it was impossible to be best friends with Bicci since they were rivals, but he remained grateful to Medici's advice he had received earlier on in his career.

Bardo was now in his late sixties, and his dream of a family chapel was starting to disappear. His ambition of building a family chapel that would represent the finest art of the city, as well as provide the family with a house of prayer, was becoming a fantasy. His relationship with his wife was virtually non existent, although he still loved her. He frequently made trips to the convent, dedicated to the Virgin Mary, located in Fiesole.

He told her about Tito, and how well he was doing. Even that failed to gain her interest. He desperately searched in her eyes to see if there was any of the old sparkle left in them, to no avail. How he adored her when she was young and vibrant. His loss of that young woman was a tragedy for Bardo. Margherita had detached herself completely from the real world, and had immersed herself in the scriptures.

The glimmer of hope for Bardo suddenly presented itself one morning during one of those visits to his wife. He told her that had reached a critical point in his life. He had to let go, and allow Tito to take over. This would mean he could finally devote himself to building the family chapel. When he mentioned this, Margherita's eyes lit up. She started to engage with her husband in a meaningful way, asking him about the church, and who would build it. She became interested in its design and its lay out. However when Bardo said he was thinking about dedicating it to Mary, she immediately knelt down before him.

'Bardo, my love… If you do that, I will be forever grateful… Look I must show you this.' Margherita took her husband to the convent library.

'What do you think, Bardo? I did it myself… It has taken me over two years.' She pointed to the most exquisite tapestry of the Virgin Mary, which hung on the wall.

'My God, Margherita, its beautiful… How did you learn this craft?'

'The nuns here showed me the techniques… And I seemed to have some talent. They encouraged me to continue… And this was the result,' she said, staring at the one metre squared tapestry.

'Extraordinary… Maybe you might continue when you return home?'

'Of course I will… I will immerse myself in good works,' she said smiling.

'Yes… But will you be my wife again? Can you be a mother to Tito? What is the point otherwise?'

'I will try, my darling.'

Bardo embraced her for the first time in years. A tear rolled down his cheek. His Margherita was returning. All he needed to do was to find Filippo Brunelleschi.

14

Bardo was leaning towards letting Tito take over the reins of the bank before seeing Margherita. However after seeing his wife, his mind was made up. His mother would provide added support at home, and he felt now that his son was more than ready to assume control and happy to take responsibility. He had already over the years, developed a number of his own contacts, but his growing relationship with Bicci ensured that the bank became even more closely involved with the Medicis. Tito was confident that he would make his father proud, and the close association with the Medici family provided impressive results almost immediately. Bardo was extremely pleased over how things were panning out, but he continued to keep a watchful eye over what was happening particularly on the major transactions.

The old man knew he could finally make that approach to Filippo knowing that nothing would now distract him. He put out feelers as to the whereabouts of the great artist. Unexpectedly, one of his employees told him that he had returned from Rome and was amusing himself in Florence, joking with fellow artists, designing models and mechanisms for the planned new dome for the cathedral, and most surprisingly helping Ghiberti with his doors that were now causing a stir all around northern Italy.

Bardo went directly to Ghiberti's workshop, the centre of artistic creativity in the whole of Europe, where indeed he found Filippo polishing one of the panels of the second set of doors being created for the Baptistry. 'Pippo, my God... What is the world coming to? What are you doing?' You... Here... With Lorenzo?

'Ah Bardo... I've buried the hatchet with Lorenzo, for the time being anyway. I'm just teaching him how to polish gilded bronze sculpture in the best possible manner...' He replied laughing, even forcing Ghiberti to smile.

'They are magnificent,' Bardo exclaimed looking around at the other panels, some of the twenty-eight had now been completed. 'I've never quite seen anything like them before. They are unbelievable.'

'Come, Signor Giovanni... Here, these eight panels are now complete and make up the lower section of the doors. You see the four Evangelists... And here the four Fathers, Ambrose, Augustine, Jerome, and Gregory.' Ghiberti showed Bardo his mastery. It was hard for the banker to fully appreciate the incredible beauty of the work.

'Lorenzo, each panel is a miracle... Of course you have me and the Wool Guild Council to thank!' Bardo said jokingly. He then turned, and took Brunelleschi's arm. 'I'm ready for you to start work, Filippo.'

'Not before time, Bardo. I hear there might be competition soon for the building of dome for Santa Maria del Fiore. Have you heard anything yet? If they are going to make a decision they must listen to me. I can do it you know... I can be faithful to Neri and Arnolfo, and still build it without the expense of buttresses, beams or scaffolding. I don't need any reinforcements... I can prove it to them. I worked out how they did it in Rome with the Pantheon, and it is possible.'

'Filippo, you know I have influence with the Wool Guild, and they are not yet ready. I promise that when they are, I will put pressure on them. But in return, you must promise me that you will design my chapel before anything else.'

Brunelleschi looked straight into Bardo's eyes. The great

man had aged. His once dark jet black hair was now silver, and brushed back. His tall frame had been reduced by a pronounced stoop. And his face, which when he first met him, was unlined and well defined, was now aged with wrinkles. His green eyes had retained their sparkle and he remained a fine looking man, but the years had taken their toll on Bardo Giovanni.

Brunelleschi was arrogant enough to know that he didn't really need Bardo's help, or indeed influence, if it came to a competition or a straight forward commission, over the vaulting of the dome since he was the only one who knew how to do it. He hadn't even told Donatello. However he liked the idea of building a private chapel, and it would actually be his first commission for a major Florentine family. He suspected it would not take longer than a year, by which time, his plans for the dome would be even more advanced, and the Opera del Duomo might have finally made up their minds. The Giovanni project, indeed, suited him perfectly.

'Bardo… If you are certain that any decision by the Wool Guild, whether it's a straightforward commission or even a competition for Santa Maria del Fiore is still more than a year away I will find my original designs I drew a few years back, and will be happy to start.'

15

Bardo Giovanni was taken aback by the speed that Brunelleschi embarked on the building. He had told the architect of his desire to dedicate the chapel to Mary, and Brunelleschi in turn, said that the main artwork inside should therefore be a fresco of the Virgin painted on the southern wall. The structure had already been agreed previously. The chapel would be sober and formal, decorated only by columns and arches including all of antiquity's architectural orders. The dome would be for Brunelleschi, a miniature of what he planned for the cathedral. The only thing that needed to be discussed was, who would paint the fresco inside.

'Listen Bardo, I have two very young painters for you. The first you might have seen in Lorenzo's workshop. He apprenticed for him since he was ten. He's now eighteen, and has already done some exquisite work. He is one of the leading exponents in perspective and foreshortening. He works endlessly on geometry and is already an expert on Euclid... Yes, I know, Bardo... Your face is one of bewilderment that a teenager would be so immersed in mathematical puzzles, but that's what happens when you're trying to understand perspective. I know him through Donatello, he's one of his closest friends.'

'His name?' Bardo asked.

'Paolo di Dono... But everyone knows him as Uccello... You

understand… Its because he loves birds! Actually he loves all animals but he's so poor, the wretch, that he keeps hundreds of pictures of them at his home. Anyway Bardo, that is all besides the point… Most importantly for you, he paints as he sees. Whether its ploughed fields, ditches, animals or whatever, he draws them so naturally, it's exquisite.'

'He sounds perfect… What will he paint? The northern wall, around the main entrance, and the side facades between the columns?'

'I suggest he paints the sidewalls. They are smaller panels, and he is already in demand. He won't have time to complete the main fresco that the southern wall demands… The northern wall I might leave for a later time… We have to consider the entrance and how it all fits… Let's just concentrate on the southern wall and the sides.'

'Any ideas on the narrative of these panels, Pippo?'

Not yet… I will chat to him… Obviously a biblical one… But maybe you should really discuss it with him.'

'Fine… What about the main fresco then? Who do you suggest?'

'Look, I know you might one someone more famous maybe like Donatello or even Jacopo della Quercia from Siena, but believe me I have found someone who is more gifted than anyone I have ever seen.' Filippo waited for Bardo to respond, but the banker simply waited for the painter to continue.

'His name is Tommaso di Ser Giovanni di Simone… He's better known as Masaccio, since he is so unkempt. He's only sixteen years old… Very amiable… But don't be fooled by his manner or appearance… He is a genius.' Bardo listened intently, unable to form a judgement. He wanted someone more established, but clearly Filippo was in charge. There was very little chance of him having any real say in the project now that he had given away control to the temperamental master.

'I can see that you're unsure, Bardo. But look at these

drawings.' Brunelleschi showed his employer some sketches that the young Masaccio had recently done.

Bardo looked at the drawings. He had never seen anything quite like them before. The images of angels, and humans were of such beauty that he visibly shook whilst looking at them. The expressions, the gestures, the boldness and vitality gave the figures a natural and appropriate beauty. 'My God, they are exquisite… The foreshortening on this one,' he was looking at a young girl standing on tiptoe, 'is perfect… Pippo we must ask him. He knows that the image must be of the Virgin. He must understand that there will be no compromise on the south wall. Will he do it?'

'Of course, Bardo, he will do anything for me… And naturally for money! But we have to start building. I have the stone masons already contracted.'

'What about scaffolding?' Bardo asked innocently.

'I have already told you that I can build it without any buttresses or support. It will show the Santa Maria Del Fiore Works committee, once and for all that I can construct the dome without any support.'

'But it hardly compares in size.'

'I know that, but the technique I will use will prove mathematically that the dome can be built this way, whatever its dimensions.' The two men laughed and shook hands. For Bardo, his dream of a family chapel which would adorn this golden age with a rare magical beauty, and which would stand in the future as a testament to his greatness and good taste, was becoming a reality. For Brunelleschi, it would be a building that would exhibit his genius as an architect, as well as show the city that he had rediscovered the classical methods of constructing a dome without scaffolding. A real break from the Mediaeval Gothic past, that the city wanted so much.

16

Three months later, towards the end of November 1415, the chapel's construction was beginning to take shape. Bardo went to the building site to discuss with Filippo the artwork for the walls. He knew that the young artists had now completed their designs, and was anxious to see what they had produced. He was of course particularly interested in Masaccio's drawings.

'Filippo… Good morning.' Bardo spotted the architect in heated debate with some of the masons. Short, overweight, now balding, and bedraggled, Brunelleschi looked more like a street fighter than an architect. There was little sign in his physical demeanour that would suggest him being one of the greatest cultural polymaths of his age.

'Ah! Just the man I was waiting to see… Come, come.' He pulled the very well built middle aged man standing next to him towards Bardo. 'Let me introduce you to our chief stonemason. Francesco Vannini, this is Signor Giovanni.' Brunelleschi paused. 'Bardo, Francesco Vannini is the best stonemason in Europe. He is in charge of your chapel… He's also in responsible for all of these men.' Bardo looked across at the hundred or so men, an army of masons and stonecutters, blacksmiths, carpenters, water carriers, and other craftsmen. It was indeed a very impressive sight.

'Very nice to meet you Francesco… You're from the city?' Bardo asked.

'The Vanninis have been here for over a hundred years… Since the great plague.'

'Excellent… And I trust you know Signor Brunelleschi, and what a temperamental, and obstinate man he is!' he said, taking the stonemason to one side.

'I know Pippo very well, Signor. But I must admit his plans for your building are a little strange. Apart from having me build a three-speed hoist with an intricate gear and pulley system to lift the stone and bricks to the top of the building, he's also making us construct a double skinned cupola with giant wooden rings, employing what can only be described as a herringbone pattern with the bricks themselves. Your dome will be the first to be built in the city without support. I don't quite understand why he's so obsessed about the dome. It's going to cost you a fortune.'

Bardo immediately knew what Vannini was talking about. He had discussed ad nauseam with Brunelleschi about the latter's plans for the city cathedral, Santa Maria del Fiore. He also was aware that Brunelleschi would be showing off some of his new techniques on the chapel, but he hardly thought it necessary to have the architect carry out a complete practice run on his much smaller building. At the same time he was slightly flattered that the genius was adopting his revolutionary ideas on his hitherto insignificant plot of land. After all, to build a double skinned dome, using a hoist and supported by giant timber rings around the circumference was incredible in its own right. However in addition to this, by using this ingenious herringbone system of brickwork, thus simultaneously redirecting the structure's weight outwards which in turn meant supporting the dome without scaffolding, was an extraordinary concept. If it worked it would add enormous prestige to his chapel.

'Filippo… I know what you are doing here. This is not the Santa Maria del Fiore. This is the Santa Maria Chapel. Tell me why I should let you put your theories into practice at my expense?' Bardo shouted at his master architect, having been informed by Vannini of his plans for the cupola. 'Surely you can show off your skills, when needed, by producing a model… Such as Neri's.' Bardo, referring to Neri del Fioraventi's prototype, was becoming exasperated.

'Of course a model would be enough but I thought, Bardo, by actually designing a real building this way, you will attain great fame and glory. You are already a wealthy man, but you have not yet gained the prestige that you so rightly deserve. This here will provide you with such esteem that people will be talking about you and your family for years to come. I realise the structure is small, but the principles I have for the building and the dome hold true for all sizes. It may not be necessary, but it works… But if you want me to resign…'

'No, no of course not Filippo. Just don't let all this engineering stuff slow it down. I want it finished by spring of 1417.'

'Do not worry, my friend… Oh! Before you leave, come here.' Brunelleschi led Bardo to the side, which led to a flight of stairs going underground. There the architect showed his employer the family crypt, where the Giovanni family would be buried.

'Excellent Pippo. At least one part of the chapel is complete… Now for God's sake hurry up and complete the rest of the project.'

With that brief conversation Bardo Giovanni had just consented to a building that would be a prototype for one of the greatest engineering and architectural feats in Renaissance history. Brunelleschi would now be released from his shackles, and be able to put into practice his ideas on building a dome without any kind of support structure. A feat that had not been achieved by anyone for over a thousand years.

17

There was little chance that the chapel would be complete in the sixteen months that Bardo had demanded. Although the marble and the stones had been delivered on time, inclement weather, and contractual disputes inevitably delayed the building work. Brunelleschi was a very difficult taskmaster, but his relationship with Vannini remained resilient. By the summer of 1416, a year before the deadline and despite the incessant delays, the external stone and brickwork with the tiled roof had been built. Apart from the area where the dome was to be constructed, the shape of the chapel was there for everyone to see. The marble columns and arches had yet to be designed and inserted in relief, but Bardo knew that Brunelleschi's classical fantasy would be years away from completion. He would be satisfied if the chapel with its dome in place would be water tight and that the frescos inside be completed. He was desperate for his wife, and not to mention his powerful friends, to come and join him for the first mass.

The construction of the dome proceeded exactly as Brunelleschi had expected. Vannini worked tirelessly to carry out the architect's designs, and much to his amazement Filippo had been correct with his designs. The inner skin of the dome enabled the church to be water tight, to enable the two young artists to start their work. Masaccio had already drawn his cartoon of the Virgin Mary with Christ sitting on her lap, surrounded by angels looking up at her. The image's exquisite harmony and softness; it's naturalness composed of subtle colours would not yet be apparent until the fresco had been painted. However Brunelleschi could already envisage what the image would look like, and wanted the young genius to start as soon as possible.

'Come on, Tommaso... Its time...' Brunelleschi thrust the drawing into the young man's hand and took him inside the chapel. 'That is where you're going to paint your Madonna. The whole southern wall, above the altar will contain your fresco. Paolo will paint the sides, but his frescos will be much smaller. He is going to paint a cycle of panels depicting the life of Christ according to Senior Giovanni's wishes.'

'He's doing both sides? You have to be joking... He'll never finish, Filippo. You know that he takes ages over his work.'

'That is not your concern, Tommaso... You concentrate on your Madonna, and I'll get Uccello up to speed on his panels.'

He marched off and left Masaccio inside. The latter walked around the beautifully proportioned chapel. It's classical dimensions, and pure simplicity encouraged him to produce a fresco that would be unsurpassed in technique. He would introduce a realism, a subtlety in colour, and a perspective that would exhibit foreshortening to perfection. People would be dazzled by its beauty and harmony.

'There... I will start there...' He pointed to the top left hand corner of the wall, where the highest point of Mary's throne would reach. 'Giorgio, Sergio... Luciano... Come where are you? We need to start with the intonaco immediately,' he shouted to his workmen.

18

The young artist, he was more of a boy, climbed the ladder, which was held firmly in place by his assistants. He touched the stone wall with the tops of his fingers, feeling the texture of the cold stone. He was already picturing in his mind the image he would paint. He breathed in the warm still air of the newly built chapel, calculating the timing of the technical process that he was about to embark. For many artists planning such a fresco would take days, if not weeks to plan. For Masaccio it would be a few minutes. He smiled, and started to laugh loudly.

'What is it, Masaccio?' Luciano asked, worried about his master's present state of mind.

'Oh nothing... Nothing at all. It's just that the space, and the sunlight when the doors are open, will produce the perfect setting for my idea.' He paused. 'Well, what are you waiting for? Three of you... Climb up here with the plaster!' He shouted.

At breath taking speed, Masaccio applied the wet lime plaster to the wall, a process known as intonaco. The water was used as a medium for the paint to be absorbed into the plaster, and as it dried the pigment becomes embedded into the structure of the wall itself. The buon fresco technique meant that the images were durable, resilient and stood the test of time. The problems were manifold, not least of which was the limited time to apply the paint, and produce a composition, whilst the plaster dried. The artist could not make any changes once the paint had been applied to his original outline, his sinopia. However for a man of Masaccio's brilliance, changes were never necessary. Each day the intonaco was applied, and each day an area of the painting, the giornata, was completed.

Bardo visited the chapel every day, and stood gazing at the unfolding work of art. The sheer splendour rendered him speechless. He felt enormous comfort in the fact that when he died he would be laid to rest here, just as Enrico Scrovegni was laid in Padua, surrounded by such majesty. He brought Margherita on one occasion, but when she saw the fresco, and the young genius working on the image of the Virgin, it was too much for her to bear. She collapsed, overcome with devotional emotion. He sensibly decided to wait until the chapel was complete before bringing her again. However, he himself never missed the opportunity to pray at the altar table that was now in situ at the south end. Kneeling, clasping his hands together, the old banker lost himself in devotional thoughts, whilst all around him was a hive of activity. It was an incongruous site, but there was something beautiful in seeing the old figure in unearthly solitude, undisturbed by the chaos surrounding him.

Whilst the southern wall was now being taken care of, the sidewalls remained untouched. Bardo was disturbed by the lack of progress.

'What about the panels? How is... Or should I say, where is, Paolo di Dono?' he asked Brunelleschi, who in turn was screaming at Francesco Vannini over some technical problem on the wooden rings that wrapped around the inner skin of the dome.

'Ah... Bardo, forgive the shouting. That Vannini is so stupid. The timber hasn't been placed in the right way.'

'I thought you said he was the best?'

'You should see the others... Anyway... Ah yes! Uccello, Uccello, Uccello... He's elusive, but he has promised me his drawings. I'm not worried, Paolo takes his time because he's very meticulous.'

'Alright then, Pippo... I must say... It is absolutely magnificent.' Bardo pointed at the seated Mary with Christ on her lap. The angels, and background, had not been painted yet.

'I told you he was a genius... Am I also not a genius for suggesting him!' He shouted.

'Yes... But the colour... the folds in her blue robes... The sweep of the figures... the symmetry can be seen with the Madonna's face being at the very centre of the fresco... and of course the perspective... Look, is that what you artists call the vanishing point?' He pointed to Christ's foot, which was pointed into the gown of the mother.

'Bardo... Yes... My God, you really are learning.' He paused and smiled at his employer. 'Now then you must leave and let us geniuses carry on our work.' Brunelleschi stepped away. 'I'm going to kill Uccello, where the hell has he got to?' he muttered under his breath.

19

It was the last time Bardo Giovanni visited the chapel for some months. When he returned, Masaccio's fresco, *The Madonna and Her Son with Angels* would be complete, and Uccello's cycle of Christ would be work in progress. The old man was once again drawn back into the affairs of the family bank due to the unquenchable ambition of his son Tito. The latter had ensured that the bank's growth continued. It's business now involved the affairs of the expanding force of the Fugger family in central Europe. Tito spent as much time in the Swabian Free City of Augsburg, practising commerce with both Johannes Fugger, and his son Andreas, taking increasingly large positions in the wool trade, as he did in his hometown of Florence. The larger these positions became, naturally meant that the risk to the bank became greater.

Tito was desperate to gain the approval and respect from his father, not realising that he already had it. Europe was always in a state of flux, particularly in the northwest where the kings of England and France were seemingly in a state of permanent war. It was here that Tito saw his greatest opportunity. Andreas, his contemporary, was similarly convinced that vast sums of money could be made, especially now that the newly crowned Henry V of England was so intent on securing the old dynastic claim of the French throne, first claimed by Edward III. Both the Giovanni and Fugger Banks made enormous sums of capital available, secured on export licences they obtained in the wool trade, to the young king of England. Henry was only too delighted to accept the money, which was vital for his 1415 campaign. However, the king, not fully understanding the cost of debt, and the enormity of the sums involved, did not have, and as it turned out would never have, sufficient funds to repay the banking houses. The export licences for the wool were indeed extremely valuable, and taxes raised on the nobility of his kingdom were vital, but the sums simply did not add up.

Obviously even with the amount of debt Henry took on, his stunning victory at Agincourt in the previous October 1415 meant that the financiers were more than happy to continue backing the winning horse. However, one director of the Giovanni Bank exhibited a somewhat more cautious approach. Bardo remembered what had happened to his father in law forty-five years earlier when the then King of England, Edward III had not only almost bankrupted him, but bought down two major banking houses in Florence.

'Father, it was different then. Henry is clearly a military genius, and to date has paid the interest on the loans. What I have done is to double our exposure, and quadruple the interest rate. The revenues from the wool trade and the guarantee of a share of Henry's war booty, will more than cover our costs.' Tito was still young, but his banking expertise was that of an experienced mature businessman.

'I know Tito. And I am very proud of what you've achieved to date, but you cannot trust these rulers, particularly from that kingdom. The risks are enormous. I heard that the English garrison at Harfleur is under siege. The French are not yet beaten.' He was worried that his son was falling into the trap of avarice. He understood that all things being equal the business probably made sense, but his experience was telling him otherwise. He looked at his son, who's exuberance and enthusiasm reminded him of himself when he was that age, and smiled.

'Yes, but, Father that is old news,' he replied approaching him close up with the documents of the loan. 'We have now adopted new messaging systems. We receive the news much quicker now. Even before some of our rivals. Times have moved on… This is why you should just relax and concentrate on building your church. John Lancaster, the Duke of Bedford, and the King's brother has just defeated the Franco Genoese fleet off the coast, and has liberated the town. A feat made possible by the debt secured from our family, and the banking syndicate of course.'

'So you have Bicci de Medici, Andreas Fugger, Lucas Welser, Rinaldo Degli Albizzi and Paolo Strozzi, all standing with you on this loan of three million florins. And what is our exposure in that debt?' Bardo was reading the contracts and the bills of exchange that Tito had handed over to him to look over.

'I had to take the lead in this, Father. Our bank is the only one to have a branch in London. That is where we obtained the export licences, and negotiated with the king on our delegated share of taxes raised, and the plunder gained from war. Medici and the two Germans, Fugger and Welser have pledged to take fifty percent in the next few weeks, whilst Strozzi and Albizzi have already provided the king with five hundred thousand florins… I understand that two and a half million florins is more than we have, but when the others come in, the exposure is down to one and a quarter million. The interest alone will return us two hundred thousand florins in the first year.'

'And what happens if the Medicis and the Germans renege… Or Henry fails to pay because his ambitions are not satisfied? Or more importantly the price of wool collapses due to political instability caused by the war? What then, Tito… What then?' His father, turned his back, and walked away towards the giant sized window in his office, and looked out across the Arno.

'I know but look at the other side of the coin, which I think is much more likely… If the price of wool goes up… And Medici and the Germans are true to their word... And Henry keeps on winning? You will be the richest man in Florence. Don't worry, Father... Please trust me. I know what I am doing.'

'I trust you, Tito... It's just that one cannot trust Bicci... I've done business with him for many years.'

'But he is your friend... He helped you when you were young... He introduced you to all the civic authorities and the guilds.'

'I know... But in business, he's ruthless and unscrupulous, and will do anything to gain an advantage. As for the Germans... Well you know them better than me. We have a debt exposure at this moment, greater than the gross assets of our bank. If things go against us, we could go bankrupt, Tito.'

20

Bardo from that moment, although not fully returning to the bank, paid much more attention to the business. He was excited at the vast fortune that the bank was on the brink of making, but anxious about what might happen if things went wrong. In the early months of 1417 things were looking positive on all fronts. In France, with the Genoese being defeated and Harfleur being relieved, Henry struck another blow against the French by successfully forming an alliance with the Holy Roman Emperor Sigismund. It seemed that Tito had indeed backed the right horse.

In late February 1417, Bardo visited Brunelleschi at the chapel for the first time since the autumn of the previous year. He pushed open the doors of the northern entrance, and he then saw for the first time Masaccio's now completed fresco of *The Madonna and Her Son with Angels*.

'My God... its magnificent. It's a monument to modern art. As he walked towards the giant fresco, he marvelled at its extraordinary beauty. He noticed two Franciscan monks standing by the painting, trying to push their hands into the wall.

'What are they doing, Pippo?' Bardo asked quizzically.

'Ha... I'm not sure,' Brunelleschi replied, as they walked towards the monks clad in their brown robes. 'Ah, yes I understand now... Bardo... They don't understand the foreshortening... The depth. They cannot comprehend the vanishing point. They don't believe that the fresco had been painted on a flat surface!'

'Breathtaking... Its just incredible... Everything is so realistic. Christ... He looks like a real baby... The angels in the background... No wonder these fellows,' he pointed to the monks, 'don't understand the depth.' He wandered across the giant image and stared at the central figure of Mary. Her body was wrapped in the blue magisterial robe. Her feet flat on the floor, not on tip toe as previously painted, added to the realism and weight of the image. The folds in the garment were so natural and true. He looked closely at the small angels playing their lutes... The movement in the putti, and more generally at the pictorial space. The gentleness of the colours combined with the symmetry and balance of the picture was awe-inspiring.

'You see Christ eating the grapes, Bardo... You like the symbolism there... The blood of communion. He is aware of his own death. Tommaso wanted you to understand this.'

'Tell Tommaso that I understand, and that just because I'm a businessman, and a very rich one, does not mean that I'm artistically ignorant... Now, Filippo, if you don't mind I would like to pray.'

'Of course Bardo.' Brunelleschi bowed to his master, and walked away as Bardo knelt down at the altar, and gave thanks to the Lord for everything. As he finished praying, he looked up at the fresco, the beauty of which enveloped him, transporting him to another level of emotional spirituality. It was a sublime moment for Bardo. He immediately thought of Margherita, and how she would love this chapel. He smiled as he rose, blessed with a feeling of tranquillity, and walked away towards the eastern wall of the chapel where Uccello was now working on the panels depicting the life of Christ.

'Paolo! I don't think you've met our patron, Signor Giovanni,' Brunelleschi introduced the two men.

'It is a pleasure to meet you, Signor. Come let me show you what I have done.' Uccello proceeded with Brunelleschi to take Bardo through the six completed panels. There were still ten more to undertake. The work was of stunning beauty, with rich colours and life-like figures that were exquisitely drawn. The wild life in particular caught Bardo's attention. 'Why are there so many animals, Paolo? Here... and there... Are they fighting here?' Not waiting for an answer, he continued to the panel representing the Baptism of Christ. 'I like this a great deal. The landscape... Here.' He pointed to the background. 'And the river... And the dove. Yes, this is good... You were right about him as well, Filippo.'

Despite enjoying what Uccello had so far achieved, particularly the Nativity panel where the most exquisite birds and animals were represented at Christ's birth, Bardo was slightly underwhelmed at the slightly more idealised approach taken compared to that of Masaccio's more natural one. It was certainly not due to a lack of perspective in the panels, or even a lack of talent in the artist that Bardo questioned. Uccello had worked hard and was obsessed with the intricacies attached to foreshortening. Indeed there were few in the city who could match his understanding of perspective. It was just that Masaccio was a genius, and had perfected linear perspective, and made everything else seem dated and unnatural.

21

After an hour of walking around, Bardo said farewell to Uccello, and then pulled Brunelleschi to one side. 'It's February, Filippo, and you are nowhere near completing.' Bardo looked up at the dome. 'You're still constructing the second skin... It's going to take you at least six months.' Bardo then looked across at the walls. 'And what about the columns, and arches that were going to make this such a unique structure?'

'I know, I know. I admit I've been distracted by the rumours about the Opera del Duomo of Santa Maria del Fiore and the Wool Makers Guild. I hear that there is, after all, going to be a competition for the building of the Del Fiore dome. One of the members told me they were going to invite applicants to provide models. I told them to come here and see the real thing for themselves, but they're just not interested. They thought it unfair! Ghiberti has already told people that he has already been invited to design some models. Quite unbelievable.'

'Pippo... It's far too early. I don't know who you've been speaking to, but the guild is two years away from making a decision. You promised me that you would concentrate on my chapel and complete it. Believe me, when the time comes, the Opera del Duomo will be interested in real buildings, and not just models. I will make sure of it.

'You promise? How can I trust you? How can I trust anyone? You just want your church built... I still have a career ahead of me.'

Bardo looked into Filippo's eyes, and placed his hands on his shoulders. 'You have my word, Pippo... Now I want the chapel finished... And finished as soon as possible. You have to hurry young Uccello up. He's way behind schedule as well.'

'Ok Bardo... I believe you... And don't worry about Uccello. Actually he is also going to help me with the vaulting of the arches and in the construction of the columns. He knows he will have hurry things along... He has experience in this. We will finish sooner than you think.' Brunelleschi was lying, and Bardo knew it. But there was little he could do.

'Is everything up to date in regard to payments?'

'Yes, you have paid for everything... I think no more money will be needed until the end of March.'

'I will come back then... Goodbye, Pippo... And by the way... Do not let anyone see inside. Monks and nuns of course are fine, but no one can see the interior until everything is complete. I want the shock of the new to hit Florence like a thunderbolt from the sky!' With that, Bardo left to return to his palazzo. He did not know it then, but he would never enter the Chiesa di Santa Maria again.

The joy of building his own chapel had been replaced by fatigue. He was awe struck by Masaccio's fresco, and he liked Uccello's work very much, but Brunelleschi had tired him. He knew that artists, particularly geniuses were difficult, but this man had taken mood volatility to a new level. He slowly walked over the Ponte alla Carria back to his palazzo. For the first time Bardo Giovanni felt old. He was relieved that his son was now in charge of business. He was pleased for him, even if more than a little worried about the enormous deal that he had made with the English crown, in concert with the finest names in European banking. He would be relieved when Medici and the Germans put up their share of the exposure. The Giovanni Bank would be under pressure, theoretically insolvent, if things did go unexpectedly wrong.

22

March 1417 would see the Giovanni Bank rise rapidly to become the most important bank in Europe, but at the same time clouds were looming along the horizon. Tito Giovanni at the beginning of the month, sensed that the delays from Bicci de Medici, Andreas Fugger and Lucas Welser in investing their share of the one and a quarter million gold florins. The pressure was being felt particularly in London, where demands for margin were being put on the bank's local branch. Neither the income from the promised taxes, nor the revenue from the wool export licences was forthcoming. Wool prices had plummeted due to the ferocity of the war in Northern Europe. It had an exponential impact. Without the money from the others, the Giovanni bank was suddenly in an extremely perilous position. Tito had to go to London himself to try and resolve the deadlock. The urgency for such a visit dramatically increased when he heard that Bicci, Andreas and Lucas had been seen in Windsor at the court of the ambitious young king.

Without telling his father Tito left Florence on the 3rd, and arrived in London a week later. His burgeoning reputation was now under threat. Over the last two years, Tito had dazzled the banking world. He showed remarkable maturity and poise for a person so young. He was not only popular within the bank, but also with his competitors. People spoke of him as the future ruler of Florence. The gifted young entrepreneur was also the favourite of society with young women from all over the region, keen to become his wife.

It was not surprising. Standing over six feet tall, he resembled his father, in looks, many years ago when he first arrived from Capri. His black hair was tied behind his head. His green eyes, aquiline nose, full lips and strong chin, with a pronounced cheek structure, gave him a formidable presence that few could rival. His physical appearance coupled with his huge apparent wealth made him one of the most eligible men in Europe. He however had no time for women, since business occupied his thoughts night and day. He would now need all his skills that had been honed from the teaching of his father and the late Baldassarre Calvo, to extricate himself from the potential problems of this latest transaction. Women could not have been further away from his mind at that precise time.

23

Exhausted from the journey, he nevertheless went directly to the bank to find out what news there was.

'Hello Signor Tito... Welcome to our office. Do you need some refreshment?' Bratti Ferravecchi, the London branch manager ushered him into the office.

'Yes some water... And some meat and bread... Tell me, Bratti, what is going on?'

'Signor Tito... We have enormous problems. The king... Well I mean the English government has acted duplicitously. They have hardly any tax revenue. All the figures that they gave us for collateral were untrue. Any taxes the king does garner from his nobles, appears to be going directly towards his new campaign in France.'

'How long is this new campaign going to last? What are his aims? Do we know anything?' Tito asked, bewildered by the king's behaviour.

'We know very little, but it appears to be a much larger campaign than previous ones. King Henry has a ferocious reputation, and his quest for glory appears insatiable... But, Signor, that is only part of the problem.'

'I know,' Tito whispered under his breath. 'The price of wool has collapsed on the continent... Our capital is being eroded before our very eyes. Bratti, we have real problems.' He paused to think, whilst pacing the room. 'What about

Medici, Fugger and Welser... What are they doing. Why are they here?'

'Rumours abound... But I think the king wants more money, and they are here to provide it.'

'But what about our deal... They are committed to us first... Look I have it in writing,' Tito was now shouting. He knew deep down that there were no morals or ethics in the world they traded. He also knew that pieces of manuscript were worth nothing when placed against a monarch's desire for fresh funds at more lucrative rates.

Tito, bolted out of the door, and made his way to the Thames, where he boarded a boat to take him to Windsor where the king was in residence. Henry V had taken control of his kingdom in 1413, and had stamped out any hint of rebellion, in this once unstable realm. He had acted ruthlessly in dealing with the Southampton Plot in 1415, and acted similarly two years later when the Lollards threatened revolt. He even had his old friend, Sir John Oldcastle, burnt at the stake to ensure that the movement had no future. His reputation was fearsome, but even more so, when at war. His merciless cruelty at Agincourt with the murder of French prisoners had already been well recorded.

Tito was no stranger to the young king. Two years earlier he had had an audience with him, accompanied by Medici, Fugger and Welser to orchestrate the initial funding of his war effort. The four bankers conversed with the young king in French, a language they could all understand without any need for interpreters. He thought Henry was unlike his predecessors who had brought down Florentine financial houses in the past with their dishonesty; he thought he was different and that he could trust him. He was, after all, a contemporary, and like him, he was ambitious and wanted desperately to succeed. Tito believed that there was an understanding between them.

On the long trip up the Thames, negative thoughts kept invading his brain. Questions about the king's honesty and integrity dominated his mind. But it wasn't just the king that Tito was thinking about. He had been friendly with Fugger, and to a lesser extent Welser for a long time. It was Tito who had introduced Andreas and Simon to Bicci de Medici, and had been the architect of the international lending that was now taking place between the Florentine and German banks across the continent. It had been highly lucrative for everyone. It was unthinkable that they would be involved in a betrayal that could result in his, and his family's, downfall. He also spared a thought for Strozzi and Albizzi, the other partners, but their losses would be manageable. The former was indeed the richest man in Florence. They would have no trouble surviving even if what he was now beginning to suspect, and fear, had taken place.

24

Tito entered the castle, and showed his papers to the attending courtiers. He was left waiting for over an hour, until finally he was shown through to the king's private chambers. The king was sitting at his desk, surrounded by advisors and courtiers. Tito recognised, from his previous meeting two years earlier, Dukes of Exeter, Gloucester, and Bedford. He also saw Thomas, Duke of Clarence, the king's younger brother, and also in this instance the conduit of the deal between the bankers and the king. There were others in the room, such as the Earls of Salisbury, Warwick and Westmoreland, who were looking at maps of France, preparing for a new invasion.

'Ah… Tito Giovanni… I remember you… Vaguely! My brother Clarence has informed me of your predicament. I still don't quite know why you're here… I have had discussions with your friends and I now have the funds needed for my new invasion into Normandy.' The king asked in French to Tito to rise from his prostrate position.

'Sire… With respect I have no idea what you have agreed with my so called partners. I assume you mean Medici, Fugger and Welser?' Tito looked at the king. He was a fine looking charismatic man whose presence could be felt, and not simply seen, when in a room. His nose was long and straight, his cheekbones and chin made more pronounced by the unshaven stubble. His brow was high, revealing an unexpected intelligence in his expression. His hair was cut very short which was the prevailing style for military men of that age.

'That is correct, Signor Giovanni,' Clarence responded. 'I understand that your position might be somewhat exposed, but there is very little we can do about it. The price of wool has been predictably weak due to the war. Taxes at home have been insufficient to cover our expenditure. The campaign in France, which we are now planning, is vital. We have to take advantage of the situation there. John, the Duke of Burgundy, our ally, has taken Troyes and will march on Paris. We are concerned that if we do not intervene, he might no longer be an ally... Do you understand? We have to invade on a massive scale and secure Normandy, as a base... And then march on. This requires enormous credit. I have explained all of this to my brother.'

'I have no doubt of this, Your Highness, but... Their funds were meant to repay half of my loan to you. Without it... My credit is worthless. My bank will not, or cannot meet its funding requirements. The collateral, which we have, is not sufficient. The price of wool, as you correctly said has collapsed, and the revenues you promised, which again you admit to, have not materialised.' Tito's tone was becoming desperate. 'Do you not see my problem? The Medicis and Fuggers will betray you as they have me.'

'But we now have their money. We have spent yours, and we also have a further fresh line of credit from your friends. It really isn't our problem,' Richard Beauchamp, the Earl of Warwick interjected sneeringly. The military commander had no time for moneylenders, even though they were his lifeblood. 'We are all very sorry for your loss, Signor Giovanni... I am sure you will be able to recoup your losses elsewhere,' he added.

Tito stared at the group of royal advisors and the king. 'One last thing, my lords... What terms did you offer them?' he asked.

'Oh, uhr... Similar ones to the original agreement, but a

bigger percentage of the plunder, and a slightly higher interest rate of course… That's all I can say,' Clarence replied.

'You'll never repay it, will you? You seem to be so indifferent to the consequences of your actions.'

'No… I mean you're right, Signor Giovanni, that we are uninterested in the fate of your banking houses, but your friends also have been granted some of the king's real estate in Normandy, as extra security. They seemed delighted,' Clarence continued.

Tito stood transfixed to the floor. In a split second he could feel the ground beneath him disappear. His young life was about to be ruined by the duplicity of these men. All of his achievements were about to be undone, and all he could feel was a sense of helplessness. How could he let the situation get so out of control? He had let himself down, and worst of all, his father. He couldn't move, paralysed by a kaleidoscope of emotions, primarily laced with fear and anger. His father had been right all along about England. He should have listened. An English king had once again reneged on a loan, leaving the debtor in financial ruin.

The councillors meanwhile returned to their preparations, all of them leaning over the maps that were spread over the table, no longer noticing Tito's presence. The only person who was sitting was the king. All of his advisors were putting forward their advice on the military strategy that was about to be adopted. Not one of them looked up to see if Tito had left. At that moment, he fully understood the dire position that he was now in. There was only one thing left to do. He had to confront Medici, Fugger and Welser before they left the country.

25

Returning to London in the middle of the night, he was determined to sort matters out as speedily as possible. He told Bratti that it was imperative for him to find his former partners. The bank must locate them, if they were still in the city. Bratti Ferravecchi was a man who could deliver when asked to. The bank employed many men who acted as spies, watching competitors transact their business. Bratti now directed them all over London, searching for the duplicitous bankers, but it was to no avail. The only information he had managed to obtain, and in the event proved to be crucial, was that three foreign gentlemen had left the city for the coast. Medici, Fugger and Welser, their business now complete, had indeed left London and were on their way to Dover to take a boat across the Channel.

'Bratti... It must be them... I will follow them. If I can catch them before they set sail, I might be able to make some sense of this mess. I want you to stay here. If you don't hear from me in the next twenty four hours, I want you to travel to Florence and explain fully the catastrophe that we now are in.'

'Yes sir... Let one of my men go with you, and show you the way. There are fresh horses at the back,' Bratti replied.

Tito stormed out of the office, screaming, 'Damn Medici... Damn all of them... I will have my revenge.'

Tito and his companion had ridden their horses into near exhaustion when they arrived at Dover in the middle of the night. Tito told his companion that he should return to London and let Bratti know that he had arrived at Dover. He then searched around the port alone, trying to glean information. A number of boatmen were aware of some foreigners in town and one of them informed him that he indeed was taking an Italian, and two Germans to Calais the following morning. He told Tito that they were staying at the castle, under the hospitality of the king. Tito thanked the boatman, giving him some coins as a reward. Little did he realise that the loose change he placed in the hands of the boatman was all that he was now worth.

He wandered around the town tortured with thoughts about how to resolve this dilemma. He was racked with doubt about how to approach the men he thought were both his friends and business partners. He also felt enormous guilt about letting his father down so badly, when the latter had placed such trust in him. Although it was mid March and there was hardly a breath of wind, it was bitterly cold that night. Finally Tito lay down on a stone wall near the outer wall of the castle, wrapped his coat around his body, and closed his eyes. He would wait for them here, and then confront them. He was prepared to die for what he believed was right.

26

The sound of Italian and German voices woke Tito from his restless slumber. It was still very early in the morning, and the sun had not yet risen.

'Well, I see that you are making a quick departure then, my friends,' Tito shouted at his three former partners.

'Tito, I did not expect to see you here. What are you doing?' Medici responded, taken aback with some surprise at his friend's presence.

'Oh… Please show me some respect. I do not understand how you could betray me… Particularly you, Fugger… And you, Welser. I brought you into our network, and gave you your first major start in banking. Now you have the resources to expand all over Europe… And this is all due to me.' He stared at Fugger, who knew he was right. But he also knew in the cut and thrust world of banking that all opportunities must be grasped, and moral efficacy played very little part in decision making.

'Listen Tito, the risks in your deal were far too great, and by the time we were going to invest, things had moved on… Low wheat prices meant our collateral was compromised even before we entered the deal… The king was planning a new venture… One with far more opportunity… What can I say?' Fugger's tone was steady, and cold.

Tito looked at the German, and glanced across to Welser who was silent. He was the youngest, and least to blame for the treachery since his individual stake was minimal. However he expected much more from both Fugger and Medici.

'You know this will… Or, has already ruined me, and my family. I hear that there have been margin calls on our exchange bills. We are facing bankruptcy. 'I should have known better, and especially from you, Medici. My father warned me about you from the very start. This has got your fingerprints all over it. Your betrayal is even worse than Fugger's. You are a Florentine… A brother…' Tito lunged across at the Florentine taking his sword out of its sheath.

'What are you doing?' cried Fugger, as he tried to hold Tito back from thrusting his sword into Bicci de Medici. However, Medici was older and a much more experienced swordsman than the young impetuous Tito. His speed was more than sufficient, in managing to parry Tito's lunge, and with a riposte, slice into the young Florentine's arm, causing it to bleed profusely.

Tito withdrew, clutching his arm. But the injury was not enough to quell his rage, and he lunged once again. This time, Fugger and Welser held him back, fearing that Medici would seriously injure him. 'Go back home… I will try and help your family bank when I too return from Augsburg. I will speak to Bardo… Don't worry, Tito,' Medici responded. By no means ashamed at his actions, Medici was however slightly remorseful. He wished no harm to Tito, or indeed to his father, but business came first. The opportunity was too advantageous to let slip.

'I would rather die than accept your help… Or yours…' He glanced at Fugger and grappled free of the German's clutches. Once again he thrust his sword at Bicci, but this time he slipped and fell onto the Medici blade that was raised on guard in defence. Tito stared into the Florentine's eyes, as his life drained away from him, onto the wet cobbled stones and gutters of the road that lay between him and the port below.

Bicci de Medici pulled his sword clear of Tito's body. Tito fell face downwards onto the road, lying prostrate and motionless. The house of Giovanni had lost its beating heart. The bank's extraordinary rise to the pinnacle of success had met an abrupt and dramatic end. Tito's star had illuminated the European banking system. His demise would send shock waves across the continent. Bicci de Medici saw the other side of the tragedy, immediately realising that one of his few rivals for supremacy in Florence was effectively removed by this unfortunate accident. Although guilty, with Fugger and Welser, of betrayal and duplicity, he was certainly innocent of Tito's murder. However, he and his partners knew that they had to be quick on their feet.

'Nothing shall ever be said of this. I will ensure that your businesses will be protected. All financial transactions which the Medici bank needs to carry out in Central Europe will involve you, Andreas... And you, Welser.' Medici's ruthlessness and quick thinking, so much a part of the meteoric ascendancy of his family bank over the next hundred and fifty years, was clear for all to see. There was no doubt that he was shocked by Tito's death, but he had to remain calm. The Germans, frightened, nodded in agreement. After which the three hurried down to the port where their boat was ready to take them across the channel.

27

Bratti Ferravecchi arrived in Dover later that day, having been informed by one of his messengers that Tito had disappeared. Finding the body laid out and drenched in blood was a horrifying sight for the young banker. His own family had been friends of the Giovannis for many years. His father, who had worked for Bardo in Florence, groomed his son to work for the Giovannis during the bank's expansion. Bratti was sent away, to be taught languages including French, English and Flemish, so that he could serve in the newly established overseas offices. He started in Germany, reflecting the new relationship with Welser and Fugger, but had settled in London for two years to keep watch over the main transactions with the king. He now reported directly to Tito. The latter trusted him, not only for his ability, but also as a loyal family friend.

When he saw Tito, Bratti fell to the ground next to his friend, and burst into tears. He held the bloodied hand that once held the sword, placing it against his lips. He then let it go, and stroked the bearded skin of his dead face. After a while, Bratti regained his composure.

'Yes... I can confirm that it is Tito Giovanni. He is the son of Bardo Giovanni, the owner of the Giovanni Bank in Florence,' Bratti Ferravecchi said quietly to the soldier who had found the body early that morning, and had reported it to the town authorities. Tito's identification papers, in order for his return to

Europe, were found in his clothing, along with some jewellery around his neck.

'It was no robber... Look at all this money... And this jewellery. His sword... Christ his clothes are worth a fortune,' the soldier replied. 'We don't know who did it... There was nobody around, apart from three foreigners who were rushing to depart early. But they were men of noble birth it seems.'

'Where were these men going after Calais?' Bratti asked, now realising what might have happened.

'We don't know for certain, but I heard from one of the sailors here that they were going to make their way to Augsburg, and then later to somewhere in Italy.'

'I thought so.' Bratti suspected the worst. The bankers had murdered his master when he had confronted them. 'I must take this body to Florence to be buried, sir... Can I take him?'

'Of course... We have no suspects... And he's a foreigner... Best to be shot of him,' he replied, quite relieved that this matter was going away.

Bratti made the arrangements for the transport, and started the long journey with Tito Giovanni's body back to Florence, which would take him almost three weeks. Fortunately, spring had come early, and most of the roads were passable. By the time he arrived at the city walls, Medici had been back for over a week. The latter had kept his presence in Florence a secret, and had avoided meeting Giovanni, in the hope that he could consolidate his position with other banking houses in the city. He hoped that the news of Tito's demise would take some time to filter back home, so that when Bardo did find out, financial matters would be settled, and the situation would be irretrievable for the old man. Medici was determined to ensure that the ascendancy of his family bank would be untouchable.

28

The Florentine weather had been particularly wet in March that year, and today was to be no exception as the grey clouds that had gathered, finally produced a steady rainfall. Bardo immediately thought of building delays as he walked away from the window cursing the wretched weather. And yet he had no reason to be ill tempered. Almost everything in his life was going according to his wishes. His wife Margherita had finally returned from the convent. She seemed composed, and looking forward to being reunited with her son, Tito. The family church was, incredibly, now close to completion, and Easter Mass would be a wonderful celebration for them and the many notables of the city. He had arranged for the Archbishop to take the service. There was however one blot on the horizon that the seventy year old had not told his wife about, and one that he was becoming anxious about. He had not heard from his son for weeks, however he was generally confident in his Tito's ability to recover the situation, which was by no means out of control. The riches that were to be gained, if the deal was successful, were unbelievable. He was hoping that it would enable him to achieve political status to accompany his wealth. The office of Gonfaloniere was in his grasp.

He slowly became aware of the noise below him in the palace's hall on the ground floor. The doors swung open. 'Signor Bratti Ferravecchi is here to see you, sire!'

'What? What's he doing here?' Tito shouted as Bratti entered the room.

'Signor Giovanni...' Bratti knelt down before his master and began to weep. 'I bring shocking news to you.'

'What... What is it, Bratti?' Bardo knelt down opposite him, grabbing his robe by the collar, trying to get his employee to speak.

'It's your son... Your son Tito... He's dead,' he whispered

'Bratti you're not making any sense... I can't hear you... Where's Tito?'

'He's dead, Signor... He was murdered in Dover... Some three weeks ago.'

'You're lying!' Bardo shouted. 'Get out of here and never show your face again in my home.' Bardo turned around and walked towards the window. The rain was pouring down onto the streets.

'Signor Bardo... Here is your proof,' Bratti shouted back and handed Bardo Tito's possessions, including his jewellery and his identification papers. 'His body is downstairs.'

Bardo stared at him. He seemed to be lost in a trance. He was in a state of confusion. 'How... How did this happen?'

'I don't know for certain... But our transaction with King Henry collapsed. We were ruined. Tito went to see the king, and then he rushed to Dover to confront Medici, Fugger and Welser. They... With the king's collusion, were responsible for our demise... And Tito was going to...'

'What was he going to do, Bratti? Tell me!' Bardo screamed.

'Sir... He wanted to... I don't know... He was so angry. He wanted to recover his position. He had been betrayed. He... Wanted revenge...' He paused. 'We are not sure what happened, but I was told that all three of them were in Dover, and left that same morning when Tito was killed. He was found clothed, with all his possessions. I assume that they must be involved but...'

Bardo walked past Bratti, and then rushed down the stairs to where his son's coffin lay. As he reached the landing, he could hear the wails of crying. It was Margherita. She was draped over the coffin, sobbing hysterically. Bardo approached her and put his arm around her. He then began to weep, uncontrollably.

29

That evening Bratti Ferravecchi explained to Bardo the timetable of events and told him that it was still unclear what had happened to Tito, but his conjecture was that who else would have wanted to kill him except the men who betrayed him. He also said that apart from the personal tragedy he had suffered, the bank was now in ruins. The London office had closed, and the ones in Northern Europe, where the messaging services had been much quicker, being closer to the unfolding events, were in the act of shutting down. Hundreds of people had lost their livelihoods as a result of the catastrophe. It would not be long before the headquarters in Florence would suffer the same fate. He begged his employer, after he had buried his son, to leave the city with as many possessions he could take, to a safer place in the country. Creditors would be everywhere now that Tito's body had returned. Gossip was already becoming rife in the city.

Bratti's words fell on deaf ears. Bardo failed to respond. A mixture of emotions raced through his mind: the torment for his dead son, the anguish for his wife, and the rage at the duplicitous murdering bankers, and most importantly, his hatred of Medici. That name and the image of Bicci remained crystal clear in his mind. Everything else had become a confused muddle in his head. He knew what he had to do. Bratti was right. He had to leave town. All his ambitions lay in tatters; his life was finished including his beloved dream of his chapel, the Chiesa di Santa Maria. The problem for Bardo was that the right thing to do did not correspond with the thing he wanted to do. He was now bent on killing Medici, and having accomplished that, he would then kill the two Germans. Nothing else made any sense. If he were to flee with his wife and his possessions, his remaining life would be tormented by the regret of not gaining revenge for his son.

Sitting there motionless, Bratti gained no response from the old man. He got up to leave.

'Is Medici in the city? I have not seen him,' Bardo asked quietly, but with a steeliness that Bratti did not recognise.

'Word has it that he arrived a week ago... Signor Giovanni, please do not do anything stupid. Please!' Bratti begged Bardo as the old man brushed past him towards the door.

Bardo walked calmly out of his home, and walked the short distance to the Medici residence. He started to run, as he got closer. The rain had now stopped but the roads were still wet and therefore treacherous. One hundred yards away from Medici's house in Via Larga, he stepped out onto the road, without watching and was hit by a horse, unable to stop due to the treacherous conditions under foot. He lay on the road, motionless. A number of passers-by, with candles and lamps, came over to help him.

'It's Bardo Giovanni... Quickly call for help.' People were now milling around the scene of the accident. Bardo was a very well known man. He had spoken at many of the city's council meetings, and his face had been at public places all around the city throughout his later life. The gossip about his son and the failure of the family bank was already spreading across the city like wild fire.

'Please... Get me up,' Bardo whispered to the people around him.

'No... Signor... You must wait for help,' one of the men crouching by him, holding his head, said.

'You don't understand... I must get up... I have to go... I have urgent business to attend to...' Bardo wrestled himself free, and managed to stand up. He started to limp the last few remaining yards to Medici's house. He would not be cheated by the weather, the crowds, the horse, or even by his own death.

30

Arriving at Via Larga, Bardo made his way into the house, brushing past the doormen, and where he had been a guest many times before. A stabbing pain in his stomach suddenly began to take hold. He put his hand inside his tunic, and felt the warm wet moisture of his blood seeping into his clothes. Not only was his leg fractured, but the horse's hoof had also torn his stomach apart. The old man immediately realised he had very little time. He shouted as best he could for his erstwhile friend Medici.

'Bicci... Come down... You... Murderer... Have you no courage... ?' Bardo collapsed on one knee.

'Bardo... My God what happened... You're hurt. Quickly get some help for this man,' Bicci shouted at his servants as he came down the stairs.

'Don't touch me... You have my son's blood on your hands. You're a liar and a traitor as well. After all these years, I thought that we were friends...' Bardo was breathing very heavily.

'I did not kill your son... He tried to kill me but fell on my sword. He was in a terrible rage...' He looked at the dying Bardo Giovanni, knowing that he would never receive his forgiveness. 'Your boy was too impetuous. The deal he made would have brought us all down...' Medici wasn't sure if Bardo could hear him. His eyes were glazed and fixed, staring upwards. 'I would have made things right between us, Bardo, if the boy had just kept his head. It was an accident, Bardo... I promise.'

'I don't believe you, Bicci… I don't believe you… You should have done more. You reneged on our deal without telling him. You ruined us. Damn you, and damn your house.' Bardo then slowly exhaled his last breath, and died in the arms of his family's nemesis.

31

The news of Bardo Giovanni's death shook Florence, and it's banking system to the core. With his, and his son's death, the bank was vulnerable to attack from its growing number of creditors. Ironically Bicci de Medici immediately saw that there were still assets in the Giovanni house, and that by incorporating them into his bank, an enormous marriage value would be created. The takeover was one of the many reasons of how Bicci was able to create a colossal financial institution, that provided funding for three successive generations of rulers, Cosimo, Piero and Lorenzo, who governed Florence throughout the fifteenth century. This same family produced four Popes, two Queens of France, not to mention successive hereditary Dukes of Florence.

The bodies of Bardo and Tito Giovanni were taken away in an open top cart to a public cemetery where they were buried in unmarked graves. Their burial, just like the fate of their bank, lay in direct contrast to Bicci's funeral. He died ten years later, and was interred in the Old Sacristy in a sarcophagus made by Donatello himself. Margherita returned to the convent in Fiesole, where she lived out the rest of her life in penitential prayer. The Giovanni Palazzo was sold to pay off any remaining family debts. The tragedy of the Giovanni family was the mirror opposite to the extraordinary success of the Medicis.

The construction of the Chiesa di Santa Maria was never completed. Uccello's panels remained unfinished, the artist leaving the project since he was no longer being paid. Brunelleschi was never able to build the columns outside the facades, and thus create a structure that represented his architectural orders. The church however still possessed an aesthetic beauty that was symptomatic of the age. It was simple as well as being harmonious. Its dome had been completed without any type of support, the first of its kind, and sat perfectly balanced on the roof of the church. The interior, dominated by the finest fresco of its time, was spatial as well as intimate. Uccello's completed panels, were exquisitely painted, and held their own even when placed next to Masaccio's Virgin.

When Brunelleschi heard of Bardo's demise, and of the collapse of the Giovanni bank, he went straight to Bicci de Medici, with whom he had been friends, and asked for advice.

'Filippo, if I was you, I would lock the place up and move on. You know that I am close to those on the Arte della Lanna, who are in charge of the commissioning of the new Cupola for the city's Duomo. There will be a competition, and I am sure it will be between you and Lorenzo again, just like before with the doors.'

'Is that really true, Bicci? I mean I've waited seventeen years to get my revenge over Lorenzo... I have radical ideas over how we can build the dome without scaffolding. I mean the Chiesa di Santa Maria is proof!'

'Yes, yes I know, Filippo. But no one is interested in that building. It's not even finished, although I hear that the fresco by Masaccio inside is breathtaking.'

'It is... Do you want me to show you?'

'No... I don't have time Filippo.' He paused. 'As I said, don't get delayed by fussing over that church. Concentrate your mind on the Cathedral Santa Maria del Fiore. Get your designs ready. Produce a model. I'm sure that when it comes to the decision, I will be able to help you.'

Medici walked away, leaving Brunelleschi to ponder his future. It was true that he desperately wanted to win the competition to construct the dome for the Duomo. If he was to be triumphant, he would be remembered for ever. It was also true that he was no longer being paid for his work on the Chiesa di Santa Maria. Added to this, he was Vannini's contractor, and he had to settle the outstanding debt on the building with the stonemason, which was a major problem since he was short of money himself.

32

The following day, Brunelleschi met up with Vannini at a local bar in the Piazza della Signoria. The architect explained to the stonemason, that due to the demise of the Giovannis, he obviously could no longer be responsible for paying him the outstanding moneys owed to him.

'Listen Filippo... I know Giovanni is dead... Christ the whole world knows about what happened. But I thought that you had been paid for my work. After all you were the project manager as well as the architect.'

'Francesco, you know how things are... I've had my own expenses, and I think I paid the artists too much. I've over extended myself, and am unable to settle with you.'

'What about all of my workers... It's not just me who is going to be out of pocket,' Vannini shouted, having now lost his temper with Brunelleschi.

'I understand you are upset, Francesco. I feel terrible... And I will pay you back.'

'Not good enough, Filippo, I will notify the authorities of your dishonesty, unless you can settle the account within the week.' Vannini got up to leave, but not before Brunelleschi pulled him back into his seat.

'Shhhhsh... You're creating a scene, Francesco. I have an idea,' Brunelleschi said, trying to calm the stonemason down. 'What about I give you these...' Brunelleschi took the keys of the

Chiesa di Santa Maria out of his pocket, and placed them on the table. 'The church can be yours… I will make no claim on it, and the Giovannis certainly won't!'

Vannini stared at the keys on the table. He knew he would never get the money out of the architect. The church was a good asset, located in a prominent part of the city. He placed his hands on the keys, and felt their iron corners.

'This might work, Filippo, but I don't have any title documents, or proof of ownership.'

'Vannini… If you were to obtain those, you would owe me money. The building is effectively owned by the creditors to the bank… The city being one of them. But, no one needs to know that you have the keys. And you know as well as I do, that in time, people forget and die. In the end, there will be nobody alive who can make a claim… So de facto it will be yours.'

It did not take long for Vannini to agree to the deal. The connection between the Vanninis and the Chiesa di Santa Maria had begun. Although not the legal owner of the church, the family held on to the keys of the building for generations. It was rarely opened, and the art inside the church became forgotten. This was not because the family did not want people to see the magnificent frescos, but more to the fact that they were worried that if the church became a popular visiting place they might lose their control. Questions might have been asked about their ownership. As a result the building was left, slightly decaying, unvisited by anyone outside the Vannini household for almost four hundred years. It was only when a young French officer stumbled upon it, that the Chiesa di Santa Maria opened its doors once again to unwelcome eyes.

PART 5

PRESENT DAY FLORENCE

I

Molly took a crumpled piece of paper out of her bag which had Maria Vannini's telephone number written on it. She hesitated before ringing her. Dr Vannini was after all one of the leading Renaissance art specialists in Florence, and Molly did not want to waste her time with an image that might be of no interest. However, bearing in mind what Gianni had told her that morning, namely that she was easy to talk to and always approachable, she decided to call.

'Hello? Is that Dr Vannini?

'Yes... Who is this?'

'My name is Molly Cavendish. I work at the Museo di Santa Maria, and your son...'

'Ah... Molly! Gianni told me that you would be calling. He speaks about you a lot. He tells me what a fantastic guide you are, and how well you get on with all the staff at the museum.'

'Oh that's very kind of him. I must say that he has been wonderful to me. He is so understanding. Honestly, the number of times I have changed appointment times with the clients he sends me due to the work on my thesis, cannot be counted.'

'He's a lovely man. He's done a great job at the museum. His handling of the visitors, and his control over the numbers is extraordinary. It's such a small place, and yet he manages to somehow get everyone in.'

153

'I know.'

'How can I help you, Molly?' Maria asked, after a slight pause.

'I was at the convent in Fiesole, looking for a document written by Pico della Mirandola, which I found after a great deal of rummaging around.'

'Yes.'

'Well, when I finally located the manuscript, I came across another piece of parchment, lying flat, that had clearly not been seen for a very long time. It was in pristine condition and contained an ink drawing of Christ wearing his Crown of Thorns supported by, I assume Mary Magdalene and St John Evangelista. It was exquisitely drawn, and having had some experience at looking at images of the period I immediately realised it was a Quattrocento drawing,' Molly said, speaking so quickly that even her Italian came under severe pressure.

'Slow down, Molly! It sounds very interesting. You shouldn't be so modest. I'm sure that you are correct in your analysis. Do you have an image that I can look at?'

'Yes I do, but it's a desperately poor one since I wasn't allowed to turn the phone flash on in the convent library.' Molly said apologetically.

'Don't worry. Listen, why don't we meet up for a coffee. I would like very much to meet you after hearing so much about you anyway. If you can, print off the image you have on your phone, and we can examine it together.'

'That would be wonderful. That is so kind of you, Dr Vannini.' Molly was overwhelmed at the warmth and the generosity of the celebrated restorer.

'It's Maria… Only the staff at the Uffizi call me Dr Vannini… Where shall we meet?'

'Well I know an extremely good café on the corner of the Piazza San Giovanni, opposite the Baptistry.'

'Oh… Paolo's… Yes I know it. I haven't been there for years. The service was terrible.'

'I know but Paolo has been so kind to me during my year here... Do you mind going there?'

'Not at all, Molly... It will have to be early in the morning, or after six in the evening. Take your pick.'

'Evening is better for me... Do you mind seeing me this week. I know it's an imposition, with you being so busy, but...'

'Is tomorrow soon enough?'

'Wow! Yes of course. See you tomorrow at six... And thank you, Maria.'

2

Molly arrived at Paolo's Café at 5:45. She had forgotten to ask Maria, what she looked like, and as a result looked furtively around for a seventy-year-old woman sitting on her own. There was no one there who remotely fitted that description. She started to relax, and sat back and enjoyed the view of the eleventh-century Romanesque Baptistry in front of her. She never grew tired of looking at this exquisite building, particularly the three sets of bronze doors that acted as gates to the building. Obviously Ghiberti's *Gates of Paradise* attracted most attention, where tourists flocked from all around the world to see and take pictures. However for Molly, she preferred Pisano's doors on the southern side of the building. Almost ignored, in comparison to Ghiberti's gates, Andrea Pisano's story of John the Baptist sculpted in bronze on twenty eight quatrefoils provided the informed historian with a magnificent example of the very early, or what is known as the Proto Renaissance.

As she began to lose herself in her thoughts about Pisano, and how he worked on those doors for over six years during the first half of the Trecento she was interrupted by a soft voice.

'And you must be Molly!'

'Oh! Yes… and you of course must be Maria Vannini!' Molly replied excitedly, getting up from her chair and shaking the lady's hand. 'How did you know it was me? I was worried about not recognising you!'

'Gianni gave me an excellent description of you. It was easy.'

'Well I am glad he did, because you certainly don't look like a woman in her seventies.'

'Thank you, Molly.' She momentarily paused. 'I must say, your accent is perfect. Where did you learn your Italian?' Maria asked.

'Well I am half Italian… My mother was born and raised here. She spoke Italian at home… So I guess I should speak it well!' Molly laughed. She loved being complimented on her Italian. It made her feel even more at home in the Tuscan capital. It also validated her mother's efforts in forcing her to speak in her tongue, which made Molly feel warm inside.

'Well then, what would you like to drink? I haven't been here for years,' Maria said, looking at the menu.

'Professore! Professore! Welcome back… Its been so long.' Paolo was almost running, bumping into the tables, disturbing some people drinking their cocktails, to come and embrace Maria.

'Bounaserra Paolo… I'm happy you remember your old clients. I hope the service is better than it was five years ago,' Maria said kissing the owner on both cheeks, but not as enthusiastically as he might have wished for.

'Professore… Please… You know I have problems with staff here, but it's much better now… Is that not right, Molly?'

'Oh, of course you're right, Paolo,' Molly said, glancing at Maria revealing that the opposite was true.

'Well, we will see… I would like…'

'A crisp cold glass of Suave?' Paolo interrupted, exhibiting an excellent memory. 'And for you, Molly? A Pironi? Or a soft drink?'

'A beer would be great, Paolo.'

As the owner walked away, Molly shook her head smiling. 'How did he remember you, let alone your drink?'

'Oh the Vannini family used to come here for years. But it became impossible in the end… It was too popular, and Paolo couldn't cope. In the end, we just stopped coming… Well I did. I think my husband and his brother still pop in now and again. Anyway, Molly, what have you got to show me?'

Molly opened her bag that was lying on the floor next to her. She took the image that she had printed off from her phone, and showed it to Maria.

'Ah yes! It's the *Lamentation of Christ*… It's a beautiful, yet haunting image, and the style is recognisable,' Maria said holding the image close to her face.

'Definitely Quattrocento don't you think?' Molly said.

'Yes… Quattrocento… I assume you know the artist?' Maria placed the image on the table, still looking at the three figures depicted. Her work worn fingers lightly stroked the outlines of Christ, Mary Magdalene and St John Evangelista, as she waited for Molly to answer.

'I'm afraid I need your help here,' she said almost apologetically, waiting for Maria to reply. However there was a period of silence as the old woman looked at the ink drawing before replying.

Molly looked at the old woman facing her. She seemed to have such poise. Everything around her in the café appeared chaotic, whilst she remained an oasis of calm. Her face was bronzed and lined. Her auburn hair was brushed back, revealing a high forehead. She had pronounced cheekbones, and light blue eyes. Her nose was straight, and she had delicate, but at the same time full, lips that were perhaps her softest facial characteristic. She exuded not only elegance and class, but also intellectual weight. Molly felt inferior, and yet this was self inflicted. It would have been the last thing that Maria would have wanted her to feel.

'Molly this could be an extremely rare work. The narrative of course is Renaissance trope, repeated everywhere during that period. But you were right to bring it to me. The technique of the artist is superb, and the image itself is exquisite. It should be in a museum. Would it be possible to ask permission to borrow it from the convent, so that I can see the original? If not I can always come with you.'

'I don't think the convent is aware of its existence,' Molly said. 'I could put it in an envelope and slip it into my bag!'

Maria burst out laughing, just as Paolo arrived with the drinks.

'There you go... That didn't take too long, did it!' Paolo said as he placed the drinks on the table.

'It was only drinks, Paolo... But yes. Service was satisfactory. Greatly improved since we last met,' Maria said jokingly, as Paolo made a bow and walked away.

'You cannot steal it, Molly! Are you mad?' Maria was so shocked that laughter was the only reasonable reaction.

'Well perhaps you ought to come with then.'

'Yes, perhaps I ought to. We don't want a drawing by Andrea Mantegna to suddenly go missing, do we!'

'Mantegna! Seriously?' Molly looked down at the drawing. 'I have discovered a Mantegna?' Molly felt a rush of blood and her heart begin to palpitate.

'It could well be... Now arrange a meeting for us as soon as possible. It should be fun.' Maria said as she sat back and drank her wine. 'This could be quite a discovery.' She said under her breath.

'I will speak to Sister Anastasia at the convent. She's very sweet, and is always willing to help. What days are you free?' Molly asked trying to contain her excitement.

'I can make time for this. Perhaps the day after tomorrow... In the morning,' Maria replied.

3

Molly could hardly contain herself once Sister Anastasia had given her a time that was convenient. She left a message for Maria at the Uffizi providing her with details of the proposed visit.

'That's fine, Molly. I shall pick you up from your apartment, and we will drive there. It's not far. I know how to get to Fiesole... You'll have to show me the direction when we arrive... I think I know the convent... But it's been a long time since I was a student searching for manuscripts!' Maria replaced the receiver, and turned around to the window in her office. 'God... These monasteries and convents... They never let you down when looking for treasures. Times never change,' she whispered referring to her student days, when she was looking for her own Renaissance discoveries.

'Great... I can't wait!' Molly replied, so excited that she hadn't realised Maria had already hung up. That night she hardly slept. Going to a convent with one of the finest art restorers of the day, and potentially discovering a drawing by Andrea Mantegna was a dream come true. It might not be in the same league as Gianni Vannini's discovery thirty-four years earlier, but if the drawing was original, it would be a highly impressive find.

The following morning Maria's pale blue Cinquecento arrived on time. Molly was waiting for her.

'Good morning. How are you, Maria?'

'I'm fine... Here,' she said passing her a coffee. 'Maria said in a business like manner. 'How are you?' she then asked.

'Tired, but excited. I didn't sleep a wink last night! I need this.' She took a slug of the hot brown liquid. 'I can't quite believe that we are on the brink of a Renaissance discovery!'

'Don't get too excited, Molly. We are a long way from being at that point.' Maria said smiling to the young student.

They drove off, out of the city. As they climbed the hills leading to Fiesole, Maria gesticulated to her companion. 'Look Molly, to your right.'

Molly looked out of her window seeing a view of Florence that she had seen many times before. 'I know Maria... It is just so beautiful... Even sublime. I could never get tired of the view from here.'

'Well the city survived its turbulent history... and has retained its beauty and character... Rather like Venice I suppose.'

'I prefer it here,' Molly said, staring out of the window.

'We have had some close shaves... War, plague, floods... And occupation. It wasn't just the Germans who tried to steal everything.'

'Who else occupied the city? My history is really bad now. Having to concentrate and study on one particularly period, leads you to forget the rest! I'm slightly embarrassed over what I have forgotten from school, and from university as an undergraduate,' Molly replied apologetically.

'The French of course... Napoleon. He tried to take everything. I often wonder why he, or rather his Arts Commission never said anything about the fresco at the Chiesa di Santa Maria.'

'They might not have known about it...' Molly said, still more interested in the view.

'No... I don't believe that. The Arts Commission set up by Napoleon, and his main advisor Vivant Denon, never missed anything. They stole everything they could, and

161

it's inconceivable to believe that they did not know about Masaccio's fresco.' She paused. 'We have some evidence that they were aware of it, but it's unsubstantiated... Perhaps we will never know.' She looked across at Molly and smiled.

PART 6

FLORENCE
1ST JULY 1796

I

It was almost four hundred years since Filippo Brunelleschi handed the keys of the Chiesa di Santa Maria to Francesco Vannini. The stonemason did nothing with the building, except keep it locked up. He left instructions in his will that the family should not open it to the public for fear of an old claim being presented against them. As time went on, the fear of a claim being made disappeared. As each generation followed, interest in the building waned to such an extent that by the seventeenth century, members of the family had little idea about which building the keys related to. Indeed the keys became an object of fascination by the eighteenth century, and efforts were made to discover the doors to which they would open. However towards the end of that century, not only had the church been forgotten but so had the keys. It was not until four years before the end of that century that the discovery was made by the most unlikely of Vannini beneficiaries.

Marco Vannini was the last of his particular generation of Vanninis. He was now sixty years old, and had lived an unfortunate life. Deformed at birth with a severe hunchback, he was the third and last son of his family. He had lived alone after his parents died, remaining in their small apartment not far from the Chiesa di Santa Maria on the south side of the city in the San Frediano district. He was bullied by his friends at school, and teased by his family at home. His life had been a continuum of abject misery. He managed to find work as a blacksmith, enabling him to receive a small income to pay for his limited existence.

Not surprisingly, given his deformity, he never married, or even had an intimate relationship with either sex, and remained alone after his parents died. After his brothers had passed away, their children hardly kept in contact, apart from the odd cursory note at birthdays or at Christmas. They were aware that the small apartment would be passed on to them once Marco, himself was gone. There was therefore always a reason to keep in contact, even if it was rare. Marco had long since cared. His habitual routine, after retiring five years previously, was to wake up, read the news leaflets that were normally strewn across the cafes and bars, and spend the afternoon getting drunk, before hobbling off back home to sleep. Unloved, and almost unknown, this miserable wretch was perversely now finally relatively happy with his lot. He was content to be left alone, and enjoyed the peace that he now had.

This routine that he had acquired, changed one morning two months back, when he managed to climb the steps leading from the apartment on to the roof of the building. He had not been up there for years, but he was now looking for his old tools that he knew had been stored there when he had retired. He now needed the tools to repair some loose floorboards that creaked unbearably every time he hobbled over them. The Vanninis had kept a shed on the roof to keep their old family chattels and belongings. Marco, due to his infirmity, had not been up there due to a not unreasonable fear of falling down the steps. On reaching the flat terrace, he breathed a sigh of relief, and slowly shuffled over towards the shed.

Unlocking the shed, he was shocked by the mountain of articles that were stacked in front of him. The toolbox was not visible at first, hidden behind boxes of useless objects and old clothes. Marco, despite his physical condition, was a strong man, and had no trouble in moving the obstacles in front of him. Finally seeing the toolbox, he bent over and wrenched it clear from the other miscellanea that were in its way. Whilst pulling the box clear, Marco noticed a small wooden chest that had been exposed by the disturbance he had caused, and by the removal of the tools. He dropped the toolbox, and bent over to pick up the small chest. He then turned and took it outside, where he opened it.

Inside the small chest lay a very large set of iron keys. They were clearly very old, and had not been disturbed for many years given the cobwebs and general decay of the interior of the container. He sat down on the floor and took the set of keys out, examining each one. He was curious to know why they were there, and what they related to. He continued to fumble around with the metal objects, his fingers massaging the curves of the keys. For a grotesquely deformed man, he had an extraordinary gentle touch. He unexpectedly noticed a small indent in one of the shafts of the keys. He placed the keys down, and went back to the shed to fetch the toolbox.

Sitting himself down once more, he took the pointed screwdriver out and, pushed it carefully against the small hollow in the key. Suddenly, the pressure of the screwdriver released an extra blade. It was quite small, but not only did it reveal that there would be an extra lock, but also in tiny engraved handwriting, the address of the building where the doors for these keys were located. Marco had discovered the secret that generations of Vanninis had lost. The location, the Chiesa di Santa Maria, he knew very well. It was only a stone throw from where he lived. Nobody alive remembered how long the building had been locked up, but nobody much cared including Marco Vannini.

That early evening, when, by chance, it was even quieter than usual, Marco hobbled across from his apartment to the old church. He put each key, there were four in total, in their appropriate keyways including the one with the secret blade,

167

and unlocked the doors with little difficulty. The doors creaked open, allowing the setting sunlight to bathe the nave for the first time in hundreds of years. He then saw the magnificent spectacle of Masaccio's fresco in front of him. Even to untrained eye the majesty and beauty of the work could be seen if not truly appreciated. He gasped at the fresco, and limped slowly towards it. Touching the work gently, he had never seen anything like this. He turned around and saw the panels painted by Uccello, some of which were of course unfinished. Although paling in comparison to Masaccio's genius, the sublime touch of this young artist could easily be understood. He had no idea who had painted these masterpieces but their beauty and grandeur was undeniable.

He stopped in the centre of the church, and tried to gather his thoughts. He really did not know what to do. His immediate reaction was to leave and lock the building up and throw away the keys. He had heard vague rumours of some church that the family had some hold over, but they had long been forgotten. Now that those stories had been proven, he certainly did not want the responsibility of looking after such a treasure. He had nobody to talk to on this dilemma. He, Marco Vannini had to work out what to do on his own. Questions ran through his mind, such as whether he should tell his nephews, or speak to the local council, seek advice from a parish priest, or even try and sell the building to a businessman. Each day, he would come to the church, and sit on a nearby wall, across the piazza in order to find some inspiration to help him reach a final decision. It would have helped had he known who the artists were, but even that information eluded him. He was still pondering these ideas, when the decision was suddenly taken out of his hands on the 1st July.

2

The young General Bonaparte was unusually in a carriage, and not on his horse, that morning, on the road to Florence. He looked out of the window as the carriage passed through the lush green countryside of Tuscany. Glancing at a letter in his hand, which he had read at least six times already, he smiled to himself. 'She's pregnant... A son I'm sure... Everything is going perfectly to plan.' He laughed out loud. It had been an extraordinary nine months for the twenty-six-year-old general who was in command of the French Army of Italy. His meteoric rise had begun in October the previous year when he crushed the Paris Mob on the 13th Vendemaire with a 'whiff of grapeshot', thus ensuring the Directory would survive and continue to rule the young revolutionary republic.

Within months of his triumph he had met the undeniably sensual Marie Josephe Rose, better now known as Josephine, and fell in love with her at first sight. She was five years older than the Corsican and was not only socially far more sophisticated, but also sexually much more experienced. Napoleon failed to be deterred from his pursuit of her, despite it being common knowledge that she carried a dubious reputation with a string of lovers including Paul Barras, the leader of the Directory. He insisted on marrying this femme fatal notwithstanding that she did not seem to love him as much as he, her. However age and the numerous debts that were creeping up on her, meant marriage ironically suited her perhaps more than him.

Married in March, and awarded the Generalship of the lethargic Army of Italy, Napoleon was climbing the social and military ladder at electrifying speed. The Directory, the new government of Revolutionary France, was happy to send Napoleon to Italy, not only to revitalise the army there, but also to remove him from Paris. His popularity had already started to grow in the French capital. Although a side show to the Army of the Rhine, the new position for the Corsican was not an inconsequential reward for one so young.

Leaving his love behind in Paris, where she would continue her affairs, most notably with Hippolyte Charles, Bonaparte now concentrated on the campaign in northern Italy. He immediately made an innovative impact by employing a chief of staff, Alexandre Berthier, who was to stay with him until 1814. Blessed with a prodigious memory, and with a tireless work rate Berthier was indispensable to the young General. Napoleon was also incredibly fortuitous in having a number of extraordinarily talented commanders including men such as Augereau, Marmont, Massena, Murat, Lannes and Kellerman, all of whom would become household names over the following fifteen years. They, with others would form the Grand Arme Marshalate that would conquer Europe with breath taking speed and skill.

His first major victory in Italy, and the one that became legendary, came in May when the French stormed the bridge at Lodi. From that moment the men named him 'Le Petit Caporal'. The victory opened up Milan and Central Italy, where he spent the next two months, mopping up city after city. His entry into Milan was widely celebrated by the French government. Bonaparte was now in control of events, and was eager to take dramatic steps to establish his mastery. One of these centred on his interest in the spoils of war. Helped in this by the instructions he had received from the Directory, telling him to take what he could from the cities of Italy, Napoleon began the process of robbing her, and later the rest of Europe, of its art treasures.

Every ruler, when making peace with Napoleon in Italy to date, had to give up his art treasures to the Muse Central des Art in Paris. Napoleon had set up a Commission of Arts and Sciences, specifically to control these confiscations. Although the young general knew little about art, officers such as Jean Baptiste Wicar, and envoys such as Jean Guillaume Moitte, monitored the commission's work scrupulously, and who ensured that the most valuable art was taken. Men like these had enormous power in this sphere, and were rarely questioned. In the course of their work, they naturally enriched themselves by creating vast personal collections in their own estates.

During the first few months of 1796, Napoleon had managed to collect art and sculptures from Milan, Piacenza, Modena, Ravenna, Rimini and Bologna. From Parma the Duke had to give up works by Michelangelo, Correggio, and an exquisite manuscript by Petrarch on Virgil. From Venice Napoleon took the four bronze horses that the Venetians had stolen from Constantinople in 1204. In June he had signed the treaty with Pope Pius VI, which included a clause that the Pope was to give up one hundred pictures, busts, vases or statues selected by the commission. The Vatican and Capitoline museums were virtually stripped of their most admired works, including busts of both, Junius and Marcus Brutus, the *Apollo Belvedere*, and Raphael's *Transfiguration*. And if that was not enough, more was to follow: the theft reached its apogee with the confiscation of Italian Renaissance paintings, in particular, Veronese's gigantic *Wedding Feast at Canna*.

3

The Petit Caporal was in a good frame of mind that morning, even though this particular trip had taken him out of his way and hence delaying seeing his wife. Approaching Florence in his relatively non descript carriage, he wanted to see what he could take from the greatest Renaissance city of them all. He was meeting Grand Duke Ferdinand III of Tuscany, the brother of the last Holy Roman Emperor, at the Pitti Palace that afternoon after taking a tour of the city. 'More art for the Directory... I must remember to keep more for myself... My wife will want our house to be adorned with greatest paintings.' His mind wondered back to the love of his life. He couldn't stop thinking about her. He knew that she had finally arrived in Milan, where he would meet her in three days. He could not wait. He would not hang around or overstay his welcome. He would perform his duties, speak to his Art Commission experts on what to confiscate, and then race back on his horse to the Serbelloni Palace in Milan.

Finally arriving at his destination, he opened the door of his carriage.

'Good afternoon, your grace.' Bonaparte nodded to his host the Grand Duke of Tuscany, Ferdinand III.

'Welcome, General... Please come in,' Ferdinand replied in French to the general, and gestured to enter his palace that was located in the picturesque Boboli Gardens. The crowds were standing all around the piazza outside the palace, cheering as the two men entered the building.

'It's suffocatingly hot this time of year, your grace, but I am pleased to be here. Your hospitality is most welcome. However I haven't got long... Unfortunately I have to race back to see my wife, who has just arrived in Milan. She's pregnant you know... It will be our first!' Napoleon said, making no effort to speak in Italian, trying to be as unaccommodating and as intimidating as possible to his host.

'I am very pleased for you, General. I hadn't heard that news. If you are in such a hurry, we should eat presently, and then perhaps maybe take a short walk in the gardens before your departure.'

The duke was socially very much more at ease than his guest. The former was not at all intimidated, and did not mind speaking in French since he was an extremely well educated man. He was also comfortable in this somewhat awkward situation being a member of the Habsburg family and had having been bought up in court politics all of his life. An upstart parvenu such as Napoleon Bonaparte did not fill him with any trepidation. The latter's reputation as a military man did not impress him either. Ferdinand himself had been anxious to stay out of the war, and remain neutral despite his brother Francis' predicament, being Emperor, and having to defend the oldest European Empire against the revolutionary state of France. The meeting today was merely a formal gesture, and one that had to be made for public appearances.

'Perfect... Come let us eat, your grace!' Walking through the staterooms, his hand resting on the duke's back, Napoleon immediately eyed the artwork in the palace, and saw the magnificent Cortona frescos on the ceilings. His knowledge on art was limited, but he immediately realised the frescos could not be moved from this location. However the paintings that Ferdinand showed him by Rubens, Titian and Rembrandt and the numerous Raphaels were indeed, easily transportable. He made a mental note as they sat down to eat.

'I am happy that you like our masterpieces Monsieur Bonaparte... They are our national treasures.' Ferdinand, dropping the more formal address to his guest, was seeking to gain an advantage at the lunch. He knew that he would have to pay compensation to the French, and he also knew that it would not just be money, having seen what had happened recently in other cities in Italy over the past few months.

'Yes your grace... Your art is quite remarkable. We have now, in Paris, the Musee Central des Arts, where we send all the treasures that we are given. There they are protected, and indeed cared for in an extremely professional way. However most importantly, it now means that these treasures will belong to the masses... The general public... Not to just a handful of privileged rulers,' Napoleon explained, justifying the confiscations with familiar republican trope. He displayed very little subtlety, or indeed embarrassment. Waving his arms around, gesticulating in an exaggerated way, he continued.

'The winds of war have now meant that such treasures are not safe in some areas. You must understand, Duke Ferdinand, we are only trying to protect your masterpieces!' Napoleon was repeating another well versed justification hitherto used by the Arts Commission he had set up.

'I fully understand, but I do hope that the fact that I have been more than reasonable with you... Indeed I have hardly been an active ally of my brother throughout the conflict. I am sure it will cost me dear, but I just would like to stay out and rule a peaceful kingdom.'

'I shall bear that in mind, your grace... But I have people to report to... Perhaps your councillors can speak to Citizen Wicar here, and agree to what should be taken.' He could sense the excruciating embarrassment at the mention of a 'Citizen', amongst his Austrian hosts as he pointed to Wicar who was

174

sitting at the other end of the table. He smiled, enjoying the uncomfortable situation. It didn't matter that he was born a poor Corsican, or that his breeding was of relatively low birth. His substantial power that had come from a cocktail of timing, opportunism, talent and of course, pure chance, meant that he could negotiate at any level.

'Of course… Now let us eat.' Ferdinand looked down at his food, his appetite having suddenly disappeared.

4

For Napoleon lunch became an excruciating bore. He had no interest in formal extravagant performances of etiquette, but meals such as these were dominated by such shows. The food was rarely to his taste and his routinely bad table manners merely added to the embarrassment of the situation. All Napoleon wanted, was to leave as quickly as possible, and return to Milan to see his beloved pregnant wife. His desire was more than shared by Ferdinand who wanted to be rid of the uncouth barbarian slobbering opposite him. He felt a wave of despair at the thought of the reality of his situation, and the imminent loss of his family's masterpieces that adorned the walls of his palace. As they finished dining, Ferdinand asked the general if he wanted to come and see the gardens. It came as a great relief when his guest excused himself, saying that he had to leave.

'Have a safe journey, General… And please send my wishes to your wife. I hope all goes well during the pregnancy.'

'Thank you, your grace. I will indeed do that.' He walked briskly with Berthier to his horse. He then paused and turned around. 'Please ensure that your people are not obstructive to my Arts Commission. Citizen Wicar is extremely efficient and…' he paused, 'reasonable.' He laughed loudly as he walked away.

'Of course… I will be as helpful as possible.' Ferdinand

grimaced as he returned towards his palace, a tear forming in his eye and rolling down his cheek. The gravity of his situation had become clear. He was about to lose his kingdom's greatest treasures. Perhaps he should have been more supportive to his brother Francis after all, against these wretched savages.

'Come on, Berthier!' Napoleon shouted at his friend.

The French entourage had hardly exited from the palace piazza, when one of Napoleon's close confidents, Guillaume Charles Faipoult galloped towards them stopping them in their tracks.

'General!... General!' Faipoult screamed as he saw Napoleon about to ride off towards Milan.

Napoleon peered out of the window of his carriage, and recognising the man who was calling him, told his driver to wait. Opening his door he stepped out and nodded at Faipoult, who had indeed been extremely useful to him in a number of ways during the recent months. As a minister who exercised independent power in Genoa he had arranged very quietly, a valuable, and much needed loan of over three million francs from the resident Jews for Napoleon's much undernourished army. Whilst in the Ligurian port, he had also effectively destroyed the Austrian and English agency network, disabling their information channels. And finally, and indeed only very recently, he had been instrumental in making up the lists of available art to be purloined from the Italian cities recently taken, and in turn had helped the Arts Commission enormously. Faipoult was the type of man that the General would have to stop and listen to.

'Christ Faipoult... What is it? Why are you here?' Napoleon asked in an irritable manner.

'Sir... You have to see something. It's not far... A stone throw away if that.'

'I haven't got time. My wife is in Milan waiting for me. I need to get back. Berthier can go with you.' He looked across at his chief of staff, who was not at all happy at the sudden thought of having to go with Faipoult. He too wanted to leave and get back to Milan.

'Sir... I know that you are in a hurry, but I implore you to come with me. I think the Directory will be very appreciative if you do come with me...'

'Stop talking in riddles...' He paused. Napoleon was always anxious to please his superiors, and it was true that Faipoult had delivered in the past. He knew it must be something special, otherwise why would he waste his time. 'Aaagh... All right then... Show me this thing. But it better be close by.'

Napoleon followed Faipoult with Berthier towards the Borgo San Frediano. They arrived at the Chiesa Santa Maria two minutes later.

'Well what am I looking at... It looks like a decrepit old church that hasn't been open for hundreds of years,' Napoleon shouted out of his window, beginning to lose faith in his erstwhile productive servant.

'It looks like a pile of shit... He's wasting our time, sir.' Berthier interjected unhelpfully.

'Please sir... Wait.' Faipoult dismounted, and walked around the old church. To a trained eye, even though it was incomplete and in a state of disrepair, the church was an exquisite example of early Renaissance architecture. Faipoult knew that neither of his superiors would understand its beauty and restrained splendour.

He continued to walk around the church desperate to find the man he had met earlier that morning who had the keys.

'Ah! There he is!' Faipoult exclaimed much relieved. 'Marco! Marco Vannini... Please come... Come, don't be scared.'

5

Earlier that morning Guillaume Charles Faipoult had been wandering around the city of Florence, seeing if there were any treasures or masterpieces that the Arts Commission might like to confiscate. He was also on the lookout for artefacts that he could steal for his own pleasure at the same time. He had not found anything of note that the commission had not already earmarked for the Musee des Arts. Crossing over the Ponte alla Carria he walked along the Lungarno Soderini next to the Arno, where he came across a man with a hunchback who was sitting on the steps of an old dilapidated church. Faipoult stopped and looked at the man who was one of the ugliest people he had ever seen. But before long his gaze was averted to the church itself. Being an educated man he immediately saw that this was an exceptionally designed building; a beautiful example of early Fifteenth Century architecture.

He approached Marco Vannini and made polite conversation in his rudimentary Italian, asking if it was possible to go inside.

'Why do you want to go in? Nobody comes around here... You can see how quiet it is,' Vannini replied, tightly holding on to the keys, which were attached to a thick metal bracelet around his wrist.

'Pray sir... I am a lover of Italian art, and would very much like to see inside.' Faipoult was making little progress. 'What is your name?' he asked in a gentle manner.

'Marco. Marco Vannini. I am in charge. My ancestors were the builders of this place, and for generations my family has been responsible for its upkeep. And that is how it's going to stay,' Vannini said firmly to the foreigner.

'I do not want to do anything or take anything, Marco… Perhaps a gift… Or a donation, might persuade you to open the door?' Faipoult placed a gold coin into the palm of Marco's hand.

Vannini stared at the gold coin, calculating how much food and wine he could buy with it. At least a week's worth, he pondered.

'Oh… All right then… But don't touch anything, will you.' Marco hadn't quite grasped the fact that the French were now his masters, and he was in a powerless position to prevent Faipoult from doing anything he wished. However Faipoult himself sensed that the old hunchback would have been a very difficult nut to crack if he had not adopted a diplomatic approach. He certainly did not want to harm him.

Vannini opened the door, and walked across the church, lighting the candles, which allowed Faipoult to follow. The Frenchman was speechless as he finally looked up at the south wall. 'My God… Is that Masaccio?' he whispered, looking at the magnificent fresco in front of him.

'How do I know… Whoever it was, he was quite good at it! There are other pictures… Here.' He pointed to Uccello's panels. 'They're probably done by someone else… They're not all complete, and the condition of them unlike the main fresco is getting worse… Look.' Vannini went over to the panels, and picked off a corner of the gilding that was lying loose.

'What the hell are you doing, man… leave them alone!' Faipoult rushed towards the hunchback and pulled back his hand. 'You'll do more damage,' he said, astounded that the old man could be so ignorant.

Vannini himself had no idea about the history of the church, or about the painters and the architect that made it so unique in Renaissance history. The decayed panels were more of a nuisance to him, and whilst the fresco was nice to look at, he couldn't fully appreciate its beauty. This was certainly not the case for Faipoult, to whom the structure and images were all too recognisable. He immediately saw their greatness.

'The panels are almost certainly by Uccello... and if I'm right about the fresco, which I am sure I am... Then we are looking at something special here.' Faipoult remained there for approximately an hour, appreciating the building itself, which he now saw as a perfect Renaissance structure. He then told Vannini to stay there until he returned in half an hour, so that he could reopen the church for someone else.

'I am going to bring General Napoleon Bonaparte to see this... I can introduce you to him... One of the most famous people in Europe, and the most charismatic man you will ever meet. Would you like that, Marco?'

'Well I don't know... I'm very busy, you know... Beside what does your Monsieur Bonaparte want with this church? I probably won't be able...'

'Now now, Marco... You will be here.' Faipoult placed another gold coin in the hunchback's hand, and left. Marco, himself realised that he was not going anywhere.

Faipoult mounted his horse and rode straight to the Pitti Palace. He knew that lunch would be finished and the General probably would be leaving very soon. He had to get there before he left for Milan.

6

Marco Vannini walked slowly up to the carriage housing the most powerful man in Northern Italy. He had heard of him, as had everybody in Europe, but he now recognised him from drawings that had appeared on leaflets and posters around the city. Ignoring Faipoult, and to his amazement, he walked straight up to the window from which the General was looking out, and graciously bowed his head.

'Welcome sir… To the Chiesa di Santa Maria.' He straightened up as best he could and reached out his hand to Napoleon.

'Thank you,' Napoleon, replied in Italian making more of an effort for Vannini than he had earlier to his Habsburg host, and opened the door stepping out of his carriage and taking the hunchback's hand, slightly bewildered by the bizarre situation. 'Faipoult… This better be worth my while,' he said staring at his compatriot.

'Yes Faipoult… He's in a foul mood, and just wants to get back to Milan to fuck his wife. This indeed better be good,' Berthier said quietly in Faipoult's ear as Vannini led Napoleon to the church entrance.

'Don't worry… He will realise why it was important when he sees inside,' Faipoult responded to Berthier.

As the four men entered the church, the candles were already lit, making their entry a far easier task than the one Faipoult made an hour earlier. At first Napoleon looked right and saw the incomplete panels by Uccello. Although five of the panels were stunning, it was true that the condition due to them never having been fully completed, was not good. Napoleon grunted his dissatisfaction, oblivious to the south wall, not quite understanding why Faipoult had brought him here to see these pictures.

'They're very nice, Faipoult... But I hardly think it was worth my while to see these panels. My personal knowledge on art is limited, as you know... Besides... It will be difficult to transport the panels, since they are intrinsically part of the wall. I suppose we might cut them out... But some of them are not even finished. For Christ sake man... What a waste of time.' Napoleon quickly turned around to face Faipoult, but not quick enough to miss a glancing snapshot of the image on the south façade. He turned his head back more slowly and deliberately. He then took in the image of Masaccio's fresco of the *Madonna and her Son with Angels*. He stood motionless on the spot. He then moved slowly towards the painting.

'My God, Faipoult... I am not a religious man but... Have you ever seen anything like this?' He stared at the image. It appeared so clean, the colours almost shone from the wall. The harmony of the image, and indeed its splendour gave off an aura that captured his imagination.

'No General... I thought this one might even interest you.'

'Interest me? Interest me? This is the finest thing I have ever seen. Who is it by?'

'Almost certainly Masaccio... One of his earliest works I assume... Hardly anybody knows about it... This church has been completely forgotten,' Faipoult said rather smugly, certain that he was right, looking across at Berthier. 'The Vannini family... That is... His family.' Faipoult nodded in the direction of Marco. 'Keep it a closely guarded secret... I'm not quite sure whether by design or by accident. Anyway, it appears he's in charge,' Faipoult said, pointing to Marco.

'Who did you say?' Bonaparte muttered.

'Vannini... Apparently the family built it, and got left with the keys. It was never completed. The benefactor ran out of money... According to legend... Well, that's what Marco here tells me!' He pointed to the hunchback, who immediately realised they were talking about him. He suddenly interjected without understanding what Napoleon and Faipoult were discussing, but realising that he should state his family claim anyway.

'Yes... It's the truth you know. My family have been in charge of the building for hundreds of years. We have looked after it though war, plague and famine!' Vannini was now embellishing his family's role as church guardians in no small measure. He was ignorant of the history but realised quickly that the place must be very important or why else would someone as important as Napoleon Bonaparte be looking at it. There could be a lot of money in this, he thought.

'What did he say?' Berthier asked.

'He said his family have been the guardians of this place for generations,' Faipoult replied, translating the hunchback's Italian into French.

'How did you find it?' Berthier asked.

'Well... I was wandering around the city, looking for anything the Commission might have missed... And literally stumbled upon this exquisite church, with its dome that seems to be a miniature replica of the Duomo... It might have been a forerunner... We have no way of knowing. I mean, it is not beyond the realms of possibility that it was Brunelleschi who designed it, but again, we simply don't know... I thought the Commission might want to have a look.'

'Well Faipoult... Thank you for bringing me here... But there is no way at this time... With Mantua still under siege, that we have the manpower or indeed the wherewithal to take an entire wall back to Paris!' Napoleon said with an air of real disappointment. It was true that his knowledge on art and its history was poor, but it was impossible not to see such sublime beauty when confronted with it. He didn't practise the rituals of his religion, and was only really interested in Catholicism as a potential organ of power and control. But such was the exquisiteness of the image of the Madonna and the infant Jesus, that even he couldn't escape its spiritual intensity.

'I understand sir, but I thought you should see it anyway… We might in the future, when the war is over in these parts, think of a way to bring it to our capital.' Faipoult was very pleased with himself. He saw that the general was impressed. Berthier's irritation merely added to his delight.

'Yes… I agree.' Napoleon was still walking back and forth across the church, looking at every part of the fresco. This was something he would not forget. When the time was right he would make sure it would end up in Paris. 'Tell your man here, Faipoult, that he must look after this place and not let anybody in… Unless sent by me.' He then took a small pouch of gold coins and placed in Faipoult's hand to give to the hunchback. Faipoult in turn whispered to Vannini the general's instructions.

'Thank you sir… I will make sure nobody comes in,' Vannini bowed, realising that he was being asked to do nothing more than he did anyway. He stepped back.

Napoleon nodded, and the three Frenchmen left the church. Napoleon stepped onto his carriage followed by Berthier.

'Faipoult… Thank you… You continue to be of good service. I will neither forget your loyalty…' He looked at the church 'Nor that fresco.' He nodded and gave the order to his driver to leave. For the first time in weeks, the general of the Army of Italy stopped thinking about his wife, Josephine, and concentrated on how he was going to bring that fresco to France.

7

Napoleon's thoughts were rarely focussed on one thing for long, and as such the fresco at the Chiesa di Santa Maria soon drifted away from his memory. However, without him realising it, the beauty and brilliance of the image would eventually force its way back into his mind when the circumstances demanded it. Shortly after the signing of the Treaty of Campo Formio in 1797, which effectively signalled the beginning of the end of the Holy Roman Empire, Napoleon returned to the French capital with his thoughts now firmly fixed on an invasion of England. He understood that to embark on such a mission would be impossible in the short term, and therefore the Directory offered him the chance to invade Egypt, which would directly affect Britain's trading routes instead. He accepted the task, excited by the opportunity of hitting his future nemesis' economic interests hard.

There was another reason for Napoleon's enthusiasm in accepting the new plan. The young general of the recently formed Army of Egypt was an avid historian, and the historical element to this expedition would be significant. He planned to take with him a library of books that included those written by Plutarch, Tacitus, Caesar and Herodotus. He also, following in the footsteps of Alexander the Great, prepared to take scholars and local men who would record all the details of the expedition. This was going to be a cultural event as well as a military invasion.

Archaeologists, historians, botanists, printers, mathematicians, antiquaries and members of the Arts and Science Commission, all known as 'savants', would record for posterity this somewhat great, but implausible expedition.

One evening in April 1798, a month prior to the May invasion date, Napoleon was at Josephine's house for a soiree where he happened to meet a man named Dominique Vivant Denon. The latter had been a friend of Josephine since his return from Venice, where he had lived in exile during the early years of the Revolution. His return to France was extremely risky being an émigré, yet the protection afforded him by the painter Jacques Louis David proved crucial for his survival. A member of France's Royal Academy of Art and Sculpture, he was himself an artist, chronicler and novelist. With a particular expertise in Italian primitive artists, a description then used for those painters who created such extraordinary work in fourteenth century Italy, his conversation during drinks that evening triggered Bonaparte's memory of his time in northern Italy.

'So you spent time there, Denon... in Florence?'

'Well I was mostly in Venice with my wife... Isabella... She's now talking to your wife, General.' Denon pointed to the two women by the window.

'Ah yes... Tell me... Have we met before?

'Yes we have... At the home of Foreign Minister Talleyrand. You were thirsty, and I had just taken the last glass of lemonade. I offered it to you instead of drinking it myself... We talked a lot about Corsica, Italy and Sardinia. I'm surprised you don't' recall the moment,' Denon said, not quite understanding Napoleon's reticence.

'That's right... You were my saviour... I was desperate for a drink!' The frozen demeanour of the general melted away as he suddenly remembered Denon, and the conversation he had had with him.

The two men then discussed at length a number of topics

including his collaboration with Saint Non on the latter's sumptuous book, *The Voyage*, and his own book, *The Voyage en Sicile*. It was clear to Napoleon that this impressive fount of knowledge would be a vital addition to his army of 'savants' embarking on his expedition to Egypt.

'You must come with us!' Napoleon insisted after a long diatribe of persuasion.

'I am over fifty years old sir... I am surely too old. I will be a burden.'

'Nonsense... You are coming, Denon... I insist!' Napoleon turned around and joined the party. Nobody refused an order from the general, and Denon was no exception. He embarked on the frigate Juno on May 1798, and arrived in Egypt, early July in time to witness the Battle of the Pyramids.

8

One of the results of Denon's participation in Egypt was the extraordinary *Voyage dans la Basse et la Haute Egypte pendant les campagnes du general Bonaparte*. His account of the expedition which, included the author's engravings, was received with great acclaim. However the other, and perhaps more important outcome of Denon's presence on the expedition was that Napoleon would never forget this man again. After returning to France, and having gained complete control of the country through his coup on 19th Brumaire, Napoleon now needed someone to organise and preserve the planned systematic looting of art from Western Europe. After each battle over the next fifteen years, the treaties that ensued would almost always specify what art would be confiscated. Denon would be faced with the enormous task of organising its transport, and its location in Paris.

On the 19th November 1802 Napoleon, now First Consul, appointed him Directeur General des Musees Imperiaux, which crucially meant that he was in charge of the Musee Central des Arts. In the following year it became known as the Musee Napoleon, a name it retained until 1815, when it was renamed the Musee du Louvre. Denon remained a devoted servant to Napoleon, but his true dedication was to the incredible accumulation of art treasures that arrived in Paris.

The relationship between the future Emperor and his advisor became an extremely close one. The latter's extraordinary mastery in collecting was made even more apparent given the fact that Napoleon himself knew virtually nothing about art.

'It's quite embarrassing you know, my dear,' Denon said to his beloved mistress, Isabella Teotochi. 'He is quite ignorant on anything aesthetic. After seeing Veronese's *Wedding at Canna*, he simply remarked that he thought the Pyramids in Egypt were much more impressive! He wasn't at all interested in the painting. To put this in perspective, my dear, the work is so vast that we had to cut it in half so it could be transported from Italy, and then stitch it back together again, here in Paris. It's all very sad, and yet his ignorance does have its advantages. He allows me to decide where these masterpieces can go. He rarely questions me. Veronese's masterpiece is one of the highlights of the museum.'

'Dominique, be careful you don't get ahead of yourself... One day he might surprise you.'

'I doubt that, Isabella, my love. His most consistent questions to me are either...' Who painted that?'... Or 'Who was he?'

'Don't underestimate him, Dominique... Don't underestimate him, my love.'

9

Isabella's words would eventually prove to be prophetic. During the halcyon days of the French Empire, Napoleon's stunning victories, particularly against the Prussians at Jena in 1806 and against the Austrian coalition at Ratisbond in 1809, thousands of pieces of art were seized, resulting in the exponential growth of the collection in the Musee Napoleon under Denon's directorship. The director ensured that his master's victories were celebrated and commemorated with columns erected in the Place Vendome, fountains built in the Place La Bastille, and sculptures sculpted on the Pont de la Concorde and Pont d'Iena.

It was in 1810, after the gradual suppression of the monasteries in the Kingdom of Italy, including most importantly Tuscany that Denon was provided with the chance to satisfy his thirst for, what he called, Primitive Italian art. Having entertained the Pontiff who was interned at Fontainebleau after protesting against Napoleon's decision in crowning his own infant son King of Italy, he immediately became aware that there were still vast numbers of paintings ready to be taken. When approaching the Emperor the next day, telling him that he intended to make a sweep through Italy to secure more treasures the following year, Napoleon barely looked up.

'Your Highness... the churches and monasteries are full of art... Men like Cimabue, Giotto, Fra Angelico, Piero della

Francesca, Pisano, and I think even Masaccio… Their paintings will adorn the museum. It will be…' Denon suddenly stopped talking as the Emperor looked up from his work and stared at him. 'What is it Your Highness?'

'What did you say? I mean who was the last name you mentioned?'

'I don't know… Cimabue… Giotto… Masaccio…'

'That's the one!' Napoleon got up from his desk, threw his quill on to the stack of papers before him, and strolled around the room. 'I had forgotten about that church… It was Josephine's fault you know. She had lied to me about being pregnant, and I was so angry that I totally forgot to speak to the Commission about the church.' He was now talking clearly to himself, but making no sense to Denon.

'Your Highness… I'm sorry but I don't know what you are talking about. What church are you referring to?'

'Denon… Listen to me. I know you think I'm an ignorant Corsican when it comes to appreciating art, but I saw something in Florence almost fifteen years ago that was extraordinary. I cannot believe what I fool I have been to have forgotten it.'

'Your Highness… I certainly never thought that you were ignorant on art… On the contrary you show great aesthetic awareness…' Denon was being his most unctuous, but was still in the dark over what Napoleon was talking about.

'Oh do shut up Denon… And just listen. This church was located on the south side of the Arno near the Pitti Palace.' He paused, and then shouted out towards one of his servants. 'Get me a map of Florence… Come on!' He shouted impatiently.

Opening the map across his desk, Napoleon, with his quill, pointed to the precise location of the church. 'There it is…' The Chiesa di Santa Maria… that's the name, the old hunchback told me.'

'Hunchback? And what's in the church?'

'The hunchback will let you in, if he's still alive. When you enter, there is a painting... A fresco by that fellow you just mentioned.'

'Masaccio,' Denon said quietly, immediately realising how important this could be. Not only were paintings by Masaccio rare, but he was also regarded by connoisseurs including Denon himself, to be the finest artist in living memory.

'Yes... Masaccio! That's him! Ha!' Napoleon had become quite excited. 'It was quite exceptional. I want you to get it... And bring it to Paris. I think it was called the *Madonna and her Child and Angels*... Or something like that. It might be problematic... You might even have to transport the wall!'

'We have transported far bigger things than walls of churches... Remember the Bronze Horses from Venice!' Denon replied, never seeing the Emperor so excited by a piece of art before.

'Yes, but the condition is perfect... It will be fragile. But I want it here.' He turned away and walked towards the window.

'I will try my best, Your Highness.' Denon left the room. He paused outside, after shutting the door. He shook his head, remembering what Isabella had said some years back. He smiled, and although not really trusting his master's memory, he left. 'Well I'll be damned!' he muttered under his breath.

10

Vivant Denon's confiscatory sweep throughout northern Italy coincided with Napoleon's decision to invade Russia in 1812. The Emperor had neither the time nor the luxury to think about art during those months resulting in Denon having a free reign to do as he pleased, and take what he wanted. Arriving in Florence in mid-June just as the Grand Arme was crossing the Niemen, Denon went directly to his hotel. He had much to do, not least preparing for meetings with the Arts Commission to discuss what artefacts to confiscate, and from where. The list was enormous, brimming with some of the most famous masterpieces ever painted. Success in bringing them to Paris would be for Denon, the crowning achievement of his career.

A list of places was discussed and those that were to be looted were immediately assigned a number of men who would carry out the process. Nothing that was of real value, and that could be easily transported, would be left behind. The procedure would take weeks, even months, but for Vivant Denon it was the most enjoyable experience of his life. Every artefact was carefully documented, checked and cross checked. Transportation was carried out in an extraordinarily detailed manner. Denon knew that his reputation would depend on the success of the entire operation.

He wrote to his mistress Isabella Teotochi, who was now back living in Venice.

'If it wasn't so stiflingly hot, my work here would be perfect. I was at the Santa Croce this morning. Cimabue's *Crucifixion* was so beautiful it brought tears to my eyes. Knowing that it will be in the Musee within months filled me with such joy. Later we went to the Santa Maria Novella where I stood literally transfixed facing Masaccio's *Trinity*. Alas, we cannot remove the fresco. The condition is far too fragile, and if we tried to cut the image out, we might destroy the masterpiece itself. Apart from this setback, I am so happy with what we have achieved. I am almost finished here in Florence. I will miss this place.'

He then added as a postscript, 'By the way... I shall be back with you in Venice in four days. The delay is primarily due to having to go to an obscure church that the Emperor insisted that I see. He said that there was a magnificent Madonna painting by Masaccio, guarded by a hunchback that nobody knew about. I expressed surprise and wonder at the time since it was the first time the Emperor had shown any real aesthetic interest in art, but in truth, I really can't believe it's existence. How would no one know of such a painting except an old hunchback. It's laughable but I have little choice except to go and see.'

11

After packing his cases, making sure that a number of beautiful manuscripts written by, amongst others, Francesco Petrarch, Poggio Bracciolini and Leon Battista Alberti were kept under his direct control since they were too fragile and far too valuable to be left with anyone else, he finally left his hotel. His final journey was to the Chiesa di Santa Maria to carry out the emperor's extraordinary order. He would take a short detour to the Pitti Palace where Duke Ferdinand III, some sixteen years earlier, had hosted Napoleon for lunch. Denon walked through the very same rooms where the paintings by Titian, Rubens, Rembrandt and of course, those by Raphael, used to hang. Now the walls were bare, stripped of their masterpieces. Denon felt like a burglar returning in broad day light to the scene of his crime.

'Baron Denon... I assume.' Ferdinand walked towards him.

'Yes that is me... and you are?' Denon asked, not quite believing that it was indeed the duke.

'I am Duke Ferdinand III...' He gestured to Denon to walk with him.

'Your Grace!' Denon bowed. 'I am sorry. I had no idea you were here. I thought you were away on vacation. I would never have come unannounced.'

'Don't worry, Baron. You can now see for yourself what you have taken.' He pointed to the walls of the palace. 'Our most prized and loved paintings. Citizen Wicar, as the general said, proved to be extremely efficient. I am only relieved that Cortona's frescos were not transportable.' He half smiled and then walked on.

'Well, we tried...' Denon joked, but he now felt extremely awkward, and, not surprisingly, very unwelcome. The duke's tone betrayed a bitterness that was only too apparent.

'Since there is very little left to see in the palace, let us take a stroll through the gardens. Something your master had no time for some years ago.'

The two men, in the mid afternoon heat, walked through the Boboli Gardens, a place that symbolised Renaissance landscaping like nowhere else. The views over the city were quite magnificent, forcing the Frenchman to stop and look out across the patchwork of terracotta tiled roofs dwarfed by Brunelleschi's giant dome of the Duomo. The duke was careful to steer Denon away from the Bacchus, Neptune and Oceanus Fountains, in case the French connoisseur's covetous instincts would result in them being taken away to Paris. Indeed, he also kept Denon away from the rare plants grown in a special area of the gardens. He had read that a certain French botanist, Andre Thouin, was particularly talented at spotting rare and exotic plants, and successfully seizing them for the French public. He did however show Denon the amphitheatre and the Grotte Grande, confident that even he would have no intention of moving these actual building structures.

Walking down the Viottolone, a delightful avenue of Cypress trees, Denon decided to ask Ferdinand about the Chiesa di Santa Maria.

'Have you even heard of it, Your Grace?'

'No... I'm afraid I haven't. Why? Is there another painting in there that you perhaps want to steal?' Ferdinand's tone had now shifted away from being unwelcoming, to outright hostility.

'No... No... Of course not... I just heard that it was a very interesting building and wondered if you knew of it. Please think nothing of it,' Denon replied, now even more doubtful of the Emperor's story.

Denon was glad to leave Ferdinand's residence. It was a stupid indulgence he had afforded himself, before leaving the city. He would never have visited the palace had he known the duke had been there. The whole episode was extremely embarrassing and one that he wished to forget. He entered his carriage, followed by a small entourage, the last remaining art experts in Florence. Andre Dutertre and Henri Joseph Redoute both artists and Jean Baptiste Lepere, the architect, had stayed behind with Denon to oversee the last remaining objects to go to France. Denon, now in his carriage looked at his notes.

'Alright… we have to get to the Borgo San Frediano or the Lugarno Soderini… There's a small church we have to find. It's very close and I won't be there long… And then we will make our way to Venice,' he shouted angrily at his coachman to leave. Denon's humour was getting worse by the minute. Longing to be with his wife in Venice, similar to how Napoleon had felt wanting to see Josephine fifteen years earlier, he still had to embark on this seemingly fruitless mission to satisfy the whim of his master.

12

The carriage came to a halt, three minutes later, outside the building where Denon had instructed his coachman to go. He pulled back the white linen blind that was down to protect the passengers from the sun. Looking across the piazza, he caught sight of the Chiesa di Santa Maria. His look turned into a stare, as the exquisite beauty of the building captured his imagination. Here was the connoisseur's dream. Although incomplete, Denon could see its beauty. A Quattrocento structure revealing perfect proportion, obviously built by a master. They all disembarked the carriage.

'Astonishing... Why has nobody seen this... Or even spoken of it? I suppose it is rather out of the way and it's a very quiet part of town, but even so...' He looked around at his fellow art experts in the carriage. What do you think, Lepere... It's unbelievable?'

'I've have never heard of this place, sir...'

'Look at the structure. Clearly the architect would have built some form of arches there... And there... You can see the brickwork is not complete. But...' He pointed to the dome. 'Look at that! It's...'

'Almost a miniature replica of the Duomo in Santa Maria del Fiore,' Lepere interrupted him.

Denon nodded and walked around the church, concentrating on the dome. 'I wonder if there is a double skin... My God,

I wonder if Brunelleschi was the architect. The building is so classical and symmetrical. It has his fingerprints all over it.'

'It's almost uncanny... It would not surprise me if Brunelleschi was the architect.' Denon stopped walking and Lepere stood still with him looking up at the brown tiled dome for a moment. They both realised that Napoleon would not have even noticed the architecture. All he could remember was the fresco inside.

'Come... Let us go inside.' Denon's mood had dramatically improved. Maybe the emperor's memory was accurate. Maybe Isabella was right in that he should never have underestimated him. He would soon find out. He looked across to both Dutertre and Redoute. They tried to open the doors, but they were locked. 'I have been told to look for an old hunchback... He will have the keys,' Denon said to Redoute. 'Find him... Quickly. If the outside is anything to go by... inside will be magical.' He impatiently looked around but could see nobody.

Thirty minutes went by, and Denon was now thinking of more practical solutions to enter the church. However, just as he about to order his men to break down the doors, a disfigured shape of an old man appeared from around the corner.

'Ah! There he is. Please sir... Are you in charge of this church?' Denon shouted in his best Italian.

'I am... My name is Marco Vannini. What is your business here?'

'I come in the name of the emperor. We would like to enter the church please. Will you open the doors?' Denon was visibly excited.

'Aaagh... That Bonaparte fellow... He's seen it already. Years ago! Why do you want to go in? I thought you lot had forgotten about it... Well I kept my word... You can tell your emperor. I haven't let anyone near the place... I can't believe he still remembers this place.'

'Not at all... On the contrary. He was so impressed by what

he saw, he has asked me… My name is Baron Dominique Vivant Denon… I am the director of all the museums in France… To see it.'

'Oh… If you must… I wasn't expecting anyone to show up from you lot… It's been at least fifteen years!' Marco Vannini was unimpressed, not only by the length of time but also by Denon's lofty manner.

After finding the keys all those years ago, he had taken a more 'active' role in looking after the church. His routine had now changed, which meant him coming to the building every day with a bottle of wine and a stool, and slowly getting drunk. Nobody was in the slightest bit interested in the Santa Maria, particularly with the grotesquely deformed Marco Vannini sitting near it. Dirty and unshaven, he was an effective deterrent from a visitor showing any type of curiosity. His world of solitude and inebriation however was now going to be turned upside down by this haughty man from Paris. Reluctantly, he now agreed to open the church up. He hated doing it. Unlocking the locks was laborious, and lighting the candles inside was also somewhat time consuming and tedious. But he realised he had no choice.

The five men entered the dark interior. Vannini started lighting the candles, one by one. Unfortunately the doors never remained open, so illumination of the interior was a gradual process. Denon's attention was immediately captured by the cupola. He could not only see the architect's mastery in its design, but also the fact that there were two skins forming the dome. Although watertight, a number of bricks had fallen away over time through neglect at certain areas where one could notice the dual layers.

'Brunelleschi… it was Filippo… He probably worked on this, proving himself before starting on the Duomo. My God its beautiful.' He laughed with Lepere. They immediately knew what a discovery this was.

'Most people look at that… Not the bloody roof!' Vannini pointed to the south wall.

Denon looked at Marco Vannini with utter contempt. He hated ignorant people, but when coupled with such an ugly appearance, he could not bear to be in their company. He looked across to the wall where Vannini was pointing to, and where his two art experts, Dutertre and Redoute, were already standing.

13

Vivant Denon walked slowly towards the Masaccio fresco. He then stood still and looked at the glorious image in front of him. It was the most beautiful thing he had ever seen. The colours, the forms, the lines and the perspective all seemed in perfect harmony.

'The emperor had been right. Even a barbarian like him, recognised beauty of this magnitude when he saw it,' he muttered under his breath.

'How long do you want here? I mean I don't want people starting to come in and poke their noses around here!' Vannini moaned. He was after all a creature of habit. He enjoyed his lazy squalid life. The church had, over the last fifteen years given him a sense of self importance. After all he was now a guardian of a holy place. He did not want to lose it, but he suddenly felt his position was in real danger.

'Quiet, man...' Denon barked back. He did not want to be disturbed. He needed to immerse himself in the lavish beauty, and indeed the religiosity of the *Madonna and her Son with Angels* that dominated the fresco. 'Unbelievable... It is Masaccio... And yet, still nobody knows about this place.' Denon could not believe his good fortune. He was already thinking of how he was going to transport the masterpiece back to France. Indeed, wild thoughts of taking the entire building back to Paris entered his mind. He was still thinking about logistics, when he turned towards Uccello's panels.

'Andre... Henri Joseph... Come... Come here and look at these. I don't know whom they are by. Do you have any idea?' Denon asked.

'The colours... And the landscape with animals... Look here at the *Baptism* panel. Again the same narrative. I think they are by Uccello, but I need more time,' Andre Dutertre said, intensely studying the art.

'Your friend said they were by Uccino... Or whatever his name was!' Vannini interjected.

'Thank you for that,' Denon replied sneeringly. 'Uccello is the name you're looking for.' He looked back at the panels, whilst Vannini shuffled away towards the entrance, making sure nobody else was snooping around.

'The condition here is much worse than that of the Masaccio fresco. Only six of them seem to be complete, but even those ones are fragile to say the least. We will have to be careful when removing all this,' Denon said, examining the art and the condition carefully. 'Tell me... Do you have any plans, or drawings that would show how the church was built? A survey might be too much I suppose?' he called out to Vannini.

'No... Nothing.' He paused. The hunchback might have looked like a pitiful excuse for humanity, but he was no fool. 'Wait a minute! You're not taking anything away... I am in charge of this building,' Marco shouted, suddenly realising that his position of church guardian was now in jeopardy.

'Sir, a period of silence from you would be most welcome.' Denon then turned to his colleagues. 'What do you think?'

'It will be difficult to remove any of it, sir. I mean we would have to dismantle the building. What do you suggest?' Redoute asked his employer.

'Well we will have to stay here in Florence much longer than we thought. You two must bring reinforcements. We need engineers, stonemasons, builders and art restorers. By the way, gentlemen, when I said remove it... I meant the whole building.

The structure and the art. It is the finest example of Quattrocento beauty that I have ever seen.' Denon walked around tapping the walls, trying to assess the structural stability, whilst the other three began making notes.

'Oy! What's going on? Vannini asked. 'Nothing's going anywhere, as far as I'm concerned,' he screamed, hobbling after Denon.

Denon looked at his colleagues. 'Get rid of him, in the nicest possible way, and secure the building. I need to contact the emperor, wherever he might be,' Denon quietly told his assistants, and then turned and left the church. Climbing into his carriage, he shouted to the coachman.

'Back to my hotel… Now!'

14

Communications between Baron Vivant Denon and Napoleon were at best difficult during this period. It was obviously nothing personal, since the emperor was leading the Grande Arme across Russia. Denon was however keen to receive instructions from his master. The fresco by Masaccio was the finest he had ever seen. He himself was an expert in Italian art, particularly that produced by those artists of the early Renaissance, whom he called, the Primitives. He knew how important the painting was. But what he also knew was that the building itself was of great value, notwithstanding the panels by Uccello. He needed men, even soldiers, to bring the structure back to Paris. The undertaking, which was extremely complicated in engineering terms, meant that he would have to employ hundreds of bodies. However, Denon believed that it was vital for the capital of Europe to have this magnificent exhibit in its metropolis. The prestige of having a structure such as this, in the heart of the city, perhaps even in the Tuilleries, would establish Paris as the cultural centre of the world.

He wrote at the end of August for the fourth time. 'Your Highness... The church could be placed in the Tuilleries gardens, in front of the Musee Napoleon. I cannot tell you how wonderful it would look. It will be the centrepiece for the whole of cultural Europe. However I need men. It will be impossible to move the church without soldiers, and of course engineers.

Can you spare anyone? Please respond. I have not received any replies from my previous correspondence. Your dedicated and most loyal servant, Denon.'

It was unusual to hear nothing. The Emperor was always eager to have trophies of great value brought back to Paris. France's prestige and glory was never far from his heart. However if Denon had realised the situation that Napoleon and the Grande Arme were in at the time, he might not have wasted his time bothering the Emperor with his requests over transporting a church from Florence to Paris. The Battle of Borodino was the bloodiest of all the Napoleonic wars, and although it was victorious for the Grande Arme, it was a pyrrhic one. The road to Moscow lay open, and the French arrived in the now burning abandoned Russian capital in the second week of September.

Napoleon received Denon's letter the day after the battle had been won. He took a cursory glance at Denon's scrawl. He almost threw it away, its content seeming so trivial when standing on the blood soaked turf of the battlefield. However he had the presence of mind, to push the letter into his coat pocket, and to reply to it later. When he did respond, he was sitting in an office in the Kremlin surrounded by his advisers and courtiers.

'My dear Denon… I am pleased that you found the church, and agree with my observation of the fresco. I cannot spare you any troops for obvious reasons. I have however contacted people in Paris. I can send you twenty engineers… All of them were in Egypt, so you will be familiar with them. I suggest you concentrate on the fresco. Transporting a building sounds too difficult. I would be amazed, even with our engineers and technical expertise that it can be done. Anyway, there is a limit to what I can do for you in current circumstances. Don't let me down, Denon.'

Denon received the letter in October, by which time most of the engineers promised by Napoleon had already arrived in

Florence. Plans began on how to successfully transport an entire building intact from Florence to Paris. The difficulties of such a scheme did not weigh on the Denon. All he could see was the image of the church sitting in front of the Musee, at the edge of the Tuilleries gardens facing the Place de la Concorde. The irony of having such beauty located near the site of such horrors sixteen years previously during the reign of terror, was not lost on Denon. The exercise of transporting a building, to everyone except the baron, seemed fantastical. However nobody had the courage to stand up to him. As a result, his folly, as it soon became known, was set in motion.

15

At the outset, the French cordoned off the whole area around the church, allowing none of the local population near the church. This included Marco Vannini, whose relatively short tenure as guardian of the church had been abruptly terminated. Banned from even approaching the building, he was at least handsomely paid in gold coins by Denon, and was also given twenty crates of Bordeaux wine, the quality of which was lost on the hunchback. Marco initially was happy with his lot, despite the change in his routine. However, having heard of the plans to move the entire building to Paris, he could not help but feel, even if ignorant in such matters, that it was doomed to failure. He only hoped that the structure would survive so that he could return to his old ways.

The folly, indeed, suffered setback after setback. The first stumbling blocks were Uccello's panels. Denon wanted to remove the panels before transporting the church. He believed that by removing them from the wall, and sending them to Paris separately, would prove to be an excellent insurance policy in case anything went wrong with his grander plan of transporting the church. At least the emperor would have six exquisite panels to see in the museum. However Denon's strategy went against the advice of his assistants and engineers.

As Dutertre and Redoute suspected, the condition of the frescos was terribly fragile. The wall was not thick enough for the panels to be extracted without compromising the very structure of the walls themselves. Because of this, they tried to chisel out the frescos, making only shallow indents into the walls. The result was that Uccello's masterpieces crumbled away as soon as they were dismantled. Only the *Baptism* panel retained any semblance of its original beauty. Denon sent it to Paris immediately, so that when Napoleon returned to the French capital, at least he would see something tangible from his efforts.

The east wall was now void of any artistic value; it was now simply a supporting edifice for the dome. Denon realised that the stakes had now increased. He carefully examined the Masaccio fresco on the south wall. He could not now afford to damage the masterpiece. Transporting the entire building with its remarkable dome was now the only option left open to him. Given the disastrous outcome for the Uccello panels, he knew that his whole reputation and life's work depended on him not destroying the fresco. He spent hours with his advisors over how they should proceed,

'It will be impossible to move the entire building,' Jean-Marie Joseph Coutelle explained, finally speaking out against the folly. 'The foundations are very shallow. The dome is already in a state of disrepair, and any excavation will seriously compromise the structure.'

Denon listened carefully to the colonel. He had no option in the matter. Colonel Coutelle was the genius who, during the expedition to Egypt, successfully transported one of the ancient obelisks from Luxor to Paris.

'Yes, but if we dig deep enough...' Denon was desperate.

'If you dig deep enough... It still might collapse. Your precious dome will be the first to implode,' Coutelle said firmly to the doubting Denon.

'You are being too cautious, Coutelle. I say we dig deeply around the church. Create a type of trench, and then place rafters underneath. Then slowly...'

'Aaagh… You're insane, Baron. I will have no part of this. Your desire to impress the emperor has distorted your senses man! For God sake, this will not succeed. It's a complete folly. I want nothing to do with it.' Coutelle knew what he was talking about, and although Denon, himself recognised it, he was unable to follow his advice. His ambition was overriding all rationality. He was blinded by the thought that he could achieve something that would be remembered by the people of France for eternity.

'Well Coutelle… You have to follow my instructions… You know that the emperor has put me in charge. I say we start… And take each day as it comes.' Denon was not going to be swayed by anyone, especially not a career army officer who he had little respect for despite his proven record in the transport of artefacts.

16

The digging took four weeks. Rafts were placed under the foundations. Vast pulleys were located at various points around the church. Denon managed to reinforce his army of engineers, by paying two hundred locals to help in the enterprise. It was important to begin the transport before the end of October. The weather had been kind to date; there had been very little rain, and the ground was still firm. Coutelle walked endlessly, and menacingly around the site, giving advice on the structural engineering aspects, but knew deep down it would prove to be a fruitless enterprise. When the day arrived, to test the strength of the transport, Denon stood with the colonel from a raised platform fifty yards away.

'I've done my best, Baron. You know how I feel about all of this. But just for the sake of the record. As soon as you hoist the church up, the dome will be first to collapse.' Coutelle looked Denon in the eye.

'I understand... But you are being a little too pessimistic, Coutelle. Brunelleschi who built this chapel was a brilliant architect. The structure is balanced and I believe will withstand the movement, as long as the hoists and men move perfectly in tandem. All I need from you is that you can achieve this part of the exercise.' Denon was trying to protect himself from any blame in the event of a collapse. He had managed to convince himself that the transport was going to be a success.

'The hoists are all in position, and will be perfectly aligned...

Yet you fail to understand that it is all irrelevant,' Coutelle said with an air of fatalism.

'Wait and see,' Denon replied confident that Coutelle was being overly circumspect.

'Let us start please!' Denon shouted across to the army of men waiting to participate in the lifting of the Chiesa di Santa Maria.

At first it was the noise from the groans of the men pulling the ropes coupled with the grinding noise of the giant hoists and pulleys that could be heard. However, nothing seemed to be moving. And then after two minutes, in what seemed like two hours to Denon, a loud crack was heard as the church started to be raised away from the ground. It was painfully slow, but a smile began to appear on Denon's face as Brunelleschi's miniature dome rose towards the sun.

'You see, Coutelle... I was right!' He then laughed, looking straight into the half profile of the engineer. As soon as Denon uttered those fateful words, there was a long crushing sound that was not one that he welcomed.

'I don't think you were, Baron... Look.' Coutelle's face had not moved; his expression remained unchanged. Denon turned away from him to face the site, only to see the men dropping the ropes and running for cover. The dome was no longer to be seen. The fragile double-skinned prototype that Brunelleschi had constructed had imploded into the nave of the church. All that could now be seen from Denon's position were four walls that had now sunken back into their original position, and a plume of dusk arising from within.

'It's a miracle...' Coutelle muttered.

'What are you talking about?' Denon screamed.

'That the four walls remained upright,' Coutelle replied. Satisfied that his professional expertise had not been compromised, he smugly smiled to himself and walked towards what was left of the church. Denon followed him, crestfallen, his dreams in tatters.

17

Denon, followed by Dutertre and Redoute, entered the four walls to be confronted by dust and rubble that had amassed in front of them. Placing handkerchiefs over their mouths and noses they stared at the wreckage. The pile of debris was over seven feet, and covered the entire nave. The three men gingerly climbed around the rubble towards the altar. The dust had begun to settle, and they uncovered their faces, and began to breathe the clear air.

'Thank God!' Dutertre exclaimed seeing that Masaccio's *Madonna and her Son with Angels* was relatively untouched by the catastrophe.

'It's unbelievable... Look, Baron... Even the borders of the mural are still in perfect condition,' Redoute said, weeping with gratitude. Despite the destruction, the serene and holy image of the Madonna and Jesus remained in tacto. The incongruity between the ruinous greed of the French and the moral message of the fresco was palpable. It would not be the last time that someone inside the church would defile her message.

Denon looked up towards the sky. His dream was shattered. However he still had the presence of mind to realise that he needed to replace the roof of the church. The fresco would not easily survive a storm if open to the elements.

'Where is that blasted Coutelle?' Denon shouted.

'I am right behind you… And I know what you are thinking, Baron. I can make the building weather proof in a matter of days,' the engineer said calmly.

'Good… Well let's get on with that first,' Denon said, walking towards the fresco. 'Tell me, Andre… And you Henri Joseph… Do you think we can extract the fresco away from this wall?' Denon would not be denied. He was so desperate to please the emperor, and promote his own prestige that moving the fresco was now an obsession.

'I don't think so, Baron.' Andre Dutertre responded. 'You remember what a disaster extracting the Uccello panel was.'

'Yes… Yes I know but… We could…'

'Do not even think about it, Baron,' Coutelle shouted. The wall is not thick enough. It has to stay… And you have to take my advice now.'

Denon nodded. He fell back on to the piled rubble of stones that once made up the double-skinned cupola built by Florence's master Renaissance architect. His ambition had led to the destruction of one of the most beautiful buildings of the period. He would never be able to forgive himself. He, now for the first time realised his ambition had been finally defeated. There was no way the *Madonna and her Son with Angels* was ever going to reach Paris. He wearily got up, helped by his assistants and walked out of the church, ordering the men to clear the rubble inside. He called to Coutelle, to tell him to start immediately on replacing the dome with a roof. 'You can take the cordon away… allow the local population to come back… And I suppose we will have to give the keys back to the hunchback Vannini. I won't be needing them anymore,' he said softly. He had no anger left in him. He then climbed into his carriage to return to his hotel. He had letters to write. The first to the emperor; the second to Isabella. They would not be easy letters to compose. He looked to the heavens. There was not a cloud in sight. He prayed that it would stay that way over the next few days.

18

The response Denon received from Isabella was a sympathetic one.

'My darling Vivant.

Please do not worry about all that has gone on in Florence. You acted with the best intentions. I am sure that the emperor will understand your frustration and anger. He knows how much you have contributed to his, and the Empire's prestige. All I care about is that you come home, here to Venice, as quickly and safely as possible. I miss you terribly.'

Isabella in her mind was not at all sure how Napoleon would react, but she was honest in her desire for her husband to come home. However she knew that would be impossible until he had received instructions from the emperor. The latter had received Denon's note during the excruciatingly desperate retreat from Moscow back to Paris. The fate of Masaccio's fresco was now furthest from his mind. Despite winning battles, Napoleon had lost hundreds of thousands of men, and any victories were merely meaningless. His own position was now perilous. Not only did he know it, but the Grande Arme and the French people were also aware of it. A failed coup d'état in Paris, during the autumn, gave a tangible reality to the situation. Napoleon's presence in the capital had become more critical than ever. He finally arrived back at the Tuilleries in December, where he began to put things back in order. One of the matters he wanted to address was Denon's letter.

'My dear Denon… I am sorry that you have failed in what you promised. You should never have gone against the advice of Colonel Marie-Joseph Coutelle. He is a fine engineer and officer… However your failures can be put into perspective with those of my Marshalate who have at times disgraced themselves during the retreat from Moscow. You must understand I have had little time to think about, let alone deal with, the administrative or cultural affairs of state. I knew that the fresco was a fine one! You must have been shocked that I recognised its beauty. I can just see your face! From what you tell me, you have no choice but to come home. At least it remained dry whilst you managed to construct the temporary roof.

I have now been told that most of the artefacts have arrived in Paris, and people at the Musee are running around trying to organise the new collections. Worry not, my friend. I need you to oversee things here… Hurry back. Napoleon, Emperor of France.'

Denon received the letter the week before Christmas. He was astonished at the emperor's tone. The retreat from Moscow had clearly exhausted him, and as a result had drained him of all anger. But for Denon, leaving the fresco in Florence was problematic. He could not bear the thought of others enjoying his discovery. He viewed it as his discovery in the sense that nobody else would have understood the fresco's historical importance. He had conveniently forgotten Guillaume Charles Faipoult's contribution in locating it and telling Napoleon about its existence.

All but one of the experts had now left Florence. Only Henri Joseph Redoute remained to help him transport the documents that he did not trust others to keep. It appeared that Denon had nothing left to do in Tuscany. He told Redoute that he would leave the next day.

'Inform old Vannini that I want a final look before I leave town,' he said in a melancholic tone.

Vannini, the old hunchback had done rather well out of the whole fiasco. Much richer than ever before, he had moved into a bigger apartment in the same block. He also still had many bottles of French wine to drink. His only worry was that he would not have enough days left in him to drink the amount of wine he now owned.

'He will be pleased to see the back of us, I'm sure!' Redoute said.

'Yes… I'm sure he will. I feel terribly foolish about the whole thing… I heard people call the fiasco 'Denon's folly'… They're right. The church is now just another building in the city with its wonderful dome destroyed, and with one of its walls ruined by my stupid ambition… Well, it wasn't just ambition, Redoute… I had this vision for Paris… God what a mess. We shall have to just let the Masaccio remain here. Perhaps that's the way it was meant to be.'

'I think so, Baron.'

'We will take a final look at it tomorrow before leaving.' Utterly defeated, he bid good night to his loyal assistant, and retired to his bedroom for one last night in Florence.

19

That late December of 1812, Florence was blessed with a spell of crystal clear days. The 22nd was no exception as Denon made his way to the Chiesa di Santa Maria. Marco Vannini was waiting for him. Denon could sense the satisfaction felt by the hunchback. He had defeated them in their attempts to steal the fresco. Yes, his church had suffered terrible damage, but the *Madonna and her Son with Angels* remained in its original place on the southern wall.

'Redoute has told you that we are leaving, Vannini... I'm sure that you are delighted. All that gold, and not to mention, French wine. You probably won't miss the dome, will you? Ha! You probably didn't even think about the roof, did you?' Denon said, shaking his head with utter contempt. This ghastly, deformed urchin had seemingly got the better of the great Denon, he thought.

'Now then, I am going to take a final look inside and we shall then leave.'

Vannini, said nothing, and unlocked the doors, and proceeded to light the candles in side. Denon, entered the church and gazed at the fresco one final time. The artist, archaeologist, writer, diplomat, author, and Tsar of French culture could never hide his emotions when looking at the spectacular colours and harmony of the painting. After ten minutes he suddenly turned around and walked out. He left the church with Redoute scuttling along behind him, and entered his carriage.

'Au revoir!' shouted Vannini in French, virtually the only French expression he knew, affording himself a loud sneering laugh as the carriage left. He was now happy looking after the church with its magnificent fresco as his ancestors had done, deliberately or by accident, for hundreds of years. He sat back down on his stool, and slugged a huge gulp of the full bodied claret from the bottle. He looked across at his church and laughed again. It was the best kept family secret in the city, and it was going to remain that way as long as he lived. It was a laugh that he would immediately regret.

After five minutes, the carriage reached the city walls, and Baron Dominique Vivant Denon could not stop the anger and frustration from flooding his thoughts. The Vannini laugh was the tipping point.

'That little shit… Coachman!' he shouted. 'Take us back to the church.' At which point the carriage abruptly stopped.

'Are you sure, sir?'

'I have never been so certain in my life,' Denon said. He looked at Redoute. 'If I can't see it again, why should he or any of these bastards who live here have the chance? It will also teach that old hunchback a good lesson. He'll end up being in charge of nothing. His family secret will be worthless.'

Vannini had just finished locking up when Denon's vehicle returned. He almost fell off his stool, when he saw the vision, now blurred by alcohol, of the French aristocrat disembark from his carriage.

'Vannini, open the place up again,' Denon shouted at the hunchback. 'And after you have done so, find me a dozen local artisans.

'Why?' he asked, still unsure why the Frenchman was back.

'Just go and do what I say… Get me the men.' Denon turned to Redoute. Giving him a list of materials needed for the work he

220

wanted completed. The list primarily consisted of stone, plaster of paris, some canvas, and building equipment. 'I want the stone to be cut as thin as possible, and constructed against the fresco. It must not touch the work… I suggest we put some fabric between the two skins. The thickness of the double skin should not be too obvious. I intend to come back at some later time to see if we can devise a way to finally remove it. But for now just cover it, and then plaster over the new stonework… Nobody in the future, entering the church will notice it.' He paused… And make sure you keep Vannini away… Cordon the place off until the work is finished. Pay everyone double the rate on condition that their work remains secret. When we give Vannini back the keys, give him some money… Not too much… By the look of him, he won't be around for much longer.'

Denon's plan was simple but effective. The local builders were happy for the work, and knew little about the art. The stonework could be cut very thin, and then rendered by the plaster. A fine piece of canvas would separate the fresco from the new façade. The work would take no longer than two days, and nobody would be the wiser. The irony of a new double skin, so much an integral part of the old church's dome, was not lost on Denon.

20

The work indeed lasted forty-eight hours. The local builders toiled around the clock. The canvas was placed against the fresco, and nailed to it, so that it sat tightly against the mural. The stones were cut to a very fine width, to the extent that one could hardly notice that there was indeed a double skin on the south wall. When the stonework was complete, the artisans rendered the wall in a matching white to the rest of the church. To the untrained eye, one could not see that the thickness was enhanced in any way.

When finished, Denon stood at the altar alone, knowing that if he did not return, the fresco might never reveal itself again to the outside world. However it was the price he would happily pay. If he could not have it for France's, and more importantly his own glory, then nobody could have it. Arguably the greatest image painted during that golden age for western art would be removed entirely from history. Its existence expunged from living memory.

Denon returned to Venice on Christmas eve to spend the holiday period with his beloved Isabella. He would never again return to Florence. Indeed he would never speak about the *Madonna and her Son with Angels* with anyone. The secret cover up of the fresco remained with him, Redoute, and twelve local artisans. As for Vannini, when having the keys returned to him, he was at a loss to know what had happened. He assumed that the fresco had been painted over, and thus irretrievable. At first he was very angry at the loss of the splendour, but over time, and after many bottles of French wine, he managed to forget. He never realised what had actually taken place and that the fresco was protected and hidden. Denon's desire to keep Masaccio's fresco a secret, as well as to punish the old hunchback, had seemingly been achieved.

Napoleon, in Paris, had himself forgotten about the fresco, and even failed to mention it to Denon on his return to the French capital. He had other, more pressing concerns on his mind. France's survival being one of them. As for Denon, he had more than enough to do, organising all the art that he had been stolen from Europe. His official task was enormous. When Napoleon fell and the Bourbons were restored, Denon lost his position as the man in charge of all art in France. He however managed to keep himself occupied. He assembled a magnificent collection of paintings, drawings, prints and books for himself. He never had the time to return to Florence.

Marco Vannini remained looking after the Chiesa di Santa Maria, and after his death passed on the responsibility to his distant heirs, some of whom Marco never knew, and who suddenly had come out from the woodwork. In its present state, it did not appear to be such a treasure to protect. In the past, the unique Renaissance structure with its magnificent dome and its beautiful painted interior was a secret worth coveting. Now it was a rather mundane, empty square structure with a flat roof and bare walls inside. Leaking inside, the building slowly began to deteriorate. The process of inheritance became not very appealing to the future generations of the Vannini family.

Viewed more as a liability than an asset, with the threat of repairs always on the horizon, there were times when the family thought about selling it to the city. However, there was always one member of the family that would object to a sale.

The problem of having no proof of title, a crucial flaw in the Vannini claim, meant that it was very unlikely that they would be believed, or that they would receive any money. However, the attraction that one day the family might be able to somehow get around the issues attached to ownership, and profit from a redevelopment of the area resulted in them keeping the keys. The result was, that the church would remain with the Vanninis over the next one hundred and thirty years until a far greater threat than had hitherto been experienced, appeared over the horizon. The spectre of the Grande Arme paled into insignificance when compared to the grey might of the German Wehrmacht.

PART 7

PRESENT DAY FLORENCE

I

Arriving at the convent in Fiesole, Maria and Molly got out of the car, and pulled the metal chain which hung outside the large wooden doors. Given the weight of the chain, a rather disappointing noise rang from the bell. Molly looked at Maria, and smiled.

'I know... You'd think you that the bells were the size of Notre Dame looking at the chain! Now, you have to be patient Maria, because last time I was here, it took them ten minutes to open the door,' Molly said, sensing Maria's irritation at waiting.

Molly was right in that they waited for fifteen minutes until they heard activity from within the halls of the building. The door slowly opened, and an old lady dressed in the habit, appeared.

'Can I help you?' she asked, looking at the visitors.

'Yes we have an appointment to see the library. I spoke to Sister Anastasia on the phone... I was here earlier in the week, if you remember? My name is Molly Cavendish... And this is Maria Vannini, from the Uffizi.'

'Please come in... Yes, I now remember you from earlier, and Sister Anastasia did mention that we would have visitors, but she forgot to tell me who...' She welcomed them in.

'Follow me please. As you have been here before, I assume you don't need me to show you where the library is.'

'No, that's fine, Sister. Will it be possible to use your

photocopying machine? I will of course give a small donation to the convent,' Molly asked.

'Yes of course you can... Here are the keys.' The sister gave Molly the keys to the room. 'How long will you be here?'

'Well I don't know,' Molly replied, not wishing to commit herself. She looked at Maria.

'Oh no longer than two hours... Can I ask you, your name Sister, just in case we need someone.' Maria asked.

'Claudia... Sister Claudia. I am on duty today, so I will be around for any assistance you need.

'Thank you,' Maria said, having taken the keys, and already walking towards the library.

2

'They are so helpful here... Isn't she so lovely?' Molly said innocently to Maria as she unlocked the library door.

'Yes, she seemed very nice... For the moment.' Maria replied. 'But I have spent a great deal of my life in monasteries and convents, finding paintings and drawings that have been hidden for centuries. The monks and nuns are very pleasant people, but they are clever, and are not so obliging when you ask them to loan their treasures to the museums.' Maria looked at Molly as a teacher would when advising a student.

'Oh, I had no idea... All right then I'll be a little more cynical in future!' Molly smiled, not really believing her. 'Let me show you where I was earlier... Come... The drawing is on that stack over there.' Molly pointed to the shelves next to the window. She went straight to the shelf where she had placed the drawing, neatly behind the binding that contained the Mirandola manuscript.

'It's an absolute gold mine here. I'm sure that if we delved more deeply into the shelves... For instance at the back there,' she pointed to a dark recess of the library, 'we would find more stuff.'

'Molly, I know. The number of unfound masterpieces that are hidden away in places like these, must be enormous, but I haven't much time, and I need to get back to town. Now then hurry up... Have you found it?' Maria asked, looking up at

Molly who was now on a small stepladder rummaging behind the relevant bindings.

'Yes! Here it is... It's lose, just as I had left it.' She took the parchment off the shelf and gave it to Maria. The latter took it and gently placed it on the table, next to the window, through which the morning sun lit up the room.

Maria examined the drawing. It was an image of the 'Lamentation' with the tortured body of Christ being supported by Mary Magdalene and St John Evangelista. The crown of thorns was placed on his head. The drawing was in immaculate condition, penned in ink, with each figure exhibiting sublime balance and harmony. The body of Christ was strong, physically powerful, and yet at the same time presented as crumpled and weak, only standing upright due to the hands of Mary and John supporting him. Maria spent at least fifteen minutes looking at the details. She even examined the reverse side, something Molly had failed to do when first seeing the drawing, which had Latin script written on it. Molly watched, but grew impatient.

'I love that tapestry over there, on the wall... Don't you?' Molly asked, feeling uncomfortable at the long period of silence whilst Maria examined the drawing.

'What?... Oh, you mean there... Yes... There are a number of tapestries of the Virgin hanging in convents all around the country. It is beautiful... But let me concentrate on the drawing, Molly.' Maria returned to her work.

'Yes of course... Sorry.' Molly walked over to the sewn image on the wall, and wondered who was its creator. She would never find out that the tapestry was the labour of a mother who was grieving her lost children some six hundred years ago. After another ten minutes, Molly could not resist breaking the silence again.

'Well? What do you think? Is it Mantegna? Or is it...'

'Molly... This is an exquisite drawing. It's in beautiful condition. This is probably its first exposure to sunlight in over

230

six hundred years. We will need to ask permission to bring it back to the Uffizi. It can't be left here anymore. Now that it's been discovered, word will get out, and the convent will be under pressure. Also, you see here on the edges, and there.' She pointed to a brownish area above the figures. 'It needs a little bit of restoration… Which I can carry out.'

'Yes, but who do you think drew it?'

'Mantegna of course,' Maria replied without hesitation.

'How do you know? How can you be sure?'

'Look!' Maria turned the sheet over, and pointed to the Latin script, which Molly immediately translated. Her Latin was excellent. It was a prerequisite, as with her Italian, for pursuing a doctorate in Italian Renaissance.

'I feel like an idiot,' she said smiling after reading the inscription. *"For my friend Pico. Andrea Mantegna 1485"*.

'Do you think they will let us take it?' Molly asked.

'I don't know… I suspect they will.'

'Why would they?'

'Because, as you rightly suggested earlier, there are probably many more treasures hidden away here, and the nuns are not stupid. They will probably make a fuss, but let us have it, delaying more prying eyes returning here and finding other masterpieces, which are probably much more valuable.'

'Really… You are more cynical than I ever thought.'

'I am… And I can guess that this place will be no different to others that I have visited. Now, who is in charge here? Did Sister Claudia mention who the Mother Superior was?'

3

Maria and Molly, left the drawing on the table in the library, and after much discussion with Sister Claudia and Sister Anastasia, both of whom became very emotional at the thought of someone taking a drawing away from the convent, they were directed to a small room to wait for Mother Lucia. When the latter arrived, both Maria and Molly were surprised how young the Mother Superior was.

'Hello Dr Vannini... And you must be Molly... Welcome to our convent. Poor Sister Claudia is a little demonstrative, particularly when people like yourselves... I mean academics of course want to take away our possessions that have been part of our heritage for hundreds of years,' Mother Lucia said calmly.

'I understand, Mother... But the picture does need restoration... And it would be nice for the public to have a chance to see this beautiful work. After all, it is not as if you knew of its existence. It was tucked away behind books on a shelf that was not easily accessed, even with the stepladder!' She paused, noticing that Mother Lucia's expression had not changed. 'We would of course compensate the convent...' Maria continued, hoping that as in many similar conversations like this one during her career, Mother Lucia would in the end concede. She had no doubt that there were many artefacts, even more beautiful than the one discovered by Molly, hidden in the library, or in the vaults of the convent. By giving way here, it would prevent further intrusions by scholars and public bodies.

'If Dr Vannini, I let you take this picture, I trust you and Miss Cavendish will leave us in peace... And perhaps confirm how helpful we have been,' Mother Lucia said, before continuing without Maria having the chance to respond. 'A gift would be most welcome to the convent finances.'

'Of course Mother Lucia. I will speak to the relevant authorities. I am sure the city would be happy to compensate you handsomely for the drawing.'

'Very well... I will ensure that the relevant papers will be signed,' Mother Lucia responded, in a most surprisingly commercial way. She was obviously a pragmatic woman, and realising, as usual, that there were limited options available to her, chose the most practical one; that being to sell the asset the convent was unaware of ever owning, and to try and get these guests away out of the convent before they start looking for other treasures hidden on the shelves, like others previously.

'You have lawyers?' Maria asked, astonished. She had never experienced anything a quick as this before.

'Of course we do, Dr Vannini. We have to make compromises all the time. For example, the number of books that have been recently found here, that scholars have wanted to take, has forced us to protect our collection. We not only have lawyers, but also valuation experts. When we negotiate our compensation, we do not want to be taken advantage of, would we?' Lucia responded with a smile. Her cold steeliness, matched her ice blue eyes.

'Fine then... Of course... Can we take the picture now? I have a special case in my car that will hold the picture and protect it.' Maria couldn't believe how easy this had been.

'Yes as you like... You can sign a release form. They're number of them that have been drawn up.'

'Of course there are,' Maria replied, her astonishment at the nun's commercial expertise turning into expectation.

'Mother Lucia... Would it be possible for me to take the manuscript that Pico wrote, which I photocopied earlier in the week. It would be so much easier for me to work from the original. The photocopy is very poor,' Molly asked, much to the chagrin of both Mother Lucia and Maria.

'I think one treasure is enough for today!' Mother Lucia responded curtly.

'Quite right... I'm sorry... We shall be getting out of your way,' Maria said, pulling Molly away from the meeting, preventing Molly from further upsetting Mother Lucia.

4

Maria and Molly left the convent, packing the picture by Andrea Mantegna carefully into the special case that Maria had brought with her. As soon as they got into the car, Maria reprimanded Molly.

'Are you mad? We nearly lost the picture. Were you being serious?'

'Yes I was actually... I don't know why she didn't let me take it.' Molly looked across at Maria, and the two of them burst out laughing.

'Have you ever met a devout religious person... A nun no less... Who has such commercial expertise... It's just unbelievable!'

'It was amazing. She was so cold... And methodical. Did you notice those blue eyes... And her skin... It was like porcelain, it was so smooth. She was quite scary,' Molly said, continuing to laugh.

'I know... I was surprised how young she was... She could not have been over forty.'

'No... The whole conversation was slightly surreal.'

'I don't blame them you know,' Maria said, driving out of the town towards Florence. 'Renaissance scholars come here, and are constantly trying to find documents, books, drawings and paintings... Anything. The monasteries and convents are repositories for these artefacts, and they are under enormous pressure to let people in. I sort of admire her for protecting her house.'

'I suppose so… God the views Maria.' Molly exhaled, looking across once again at the city that lay below them. 'I am never tired of looking at this city. When you think of Europe's history, it's a miracle that it wasn't destroyed like Dresden for example.'

'Well it nearly was. The Germans declared it an open city, but they still bombed the bridges before retreating. Don't you know about Florence during the war?'

'No not really… My history is fairly rubbish when it comes to the twentieth century,' Molly said apologetically.

'Oh Molly… You should meet my mother in law, Francesca. She was a resistance member who saved countless people's lives.'

'Really? How interesting… Gianni's grandmother… He never told me,' Molly said, who was now curious to find out more.

'He should have done, since the Chiesa di Santa Maria was very much part of her story.'

'Seriously? I would love to meet her, Maria… How old is she?' Molly asked.

'Well into her nineties now… But she still has her wits. I will arrange for you to meet her. I warn you, she won't stop talking once she starts… But first things first… We need to go to the Uffizi to examine the Mantegna.' Maria put her foot down as the car sped back to town.

PART 8

FLORENCE
SEPTEMBER 8TH 1943

I

Francesca Vannini opened up her green painted newspaper kiosk, as she did daily, that was located on the south side of the Arno at the corner of the Lungarno Soderini facing the Ponte Alla Carraia. Francesca cut a diminutive figure at five feet two inches. She rarely made an effort with her appearance, and yet unknowingly, she effortlessly caught people's attention. She always had low self esteem about her looks when in reality she was a very attractive young woman. She had short dark brown hair, always brushed to the side. With large green eyes, a perfect mouth which was overshadowed by a larger than normal sized nose that perversely seemed to be in perfect proportion to her face, she had no shortage of male admirers.

It was 6:30 in the morning when she laid out all the newspapers on the shelves and counter of the stall. Although it was the most beautiful sun-lit September morning without a cloud in the sky, she had never really got used to waking up early since her husband had died after losing his battle against influenza two years previously. His passing away in the small family flat on the Borgo San Frediano, a stone's throw away from the kiosk, meant that Francesca's life had dramatically changed.

She had got married when she was only seventeen years old. Falling in love to a boy named David Vannini who was in the year above her whilst at school, led to them both taking risks.

Unfortunately they took one too many and Francesca became pregnant with twin boys. David immediately knew that he had little choice but to do the honourable thing and marry her. Although not being religious, abortion was clearly out of the question in early twentieth century Catholic Florence. It was not that they did not want to marry; indeed they were very much in love, but both of them would have obviously preferred to have waited until they were older.

David had no real family after both of his parents had died when he was very young, and was looked after by foster parents who were not now interested in him. Francesca's parents were very much alive, but disowned her when she became pregnant. However, despite being abandoned by their families, and neither having siblings, David refused to give up and worked hard in casual labour jobs, saving money as he went along, before seizing an opportunity whilst working as a delivery boy for a newspaper. He became friendly with the old kiosk owner by the Carraia Bridge who had mentioned that he wanted to retire and sell up. He took a liking to the young lad, and wanted to help, having heard of the young couple's predicament. David managed to persuade the old man that the best way of helping him and Francesca was to sell the kiosk to him. The old man was hesitant, but after David had offered him a small deposit which in fact amounted to his entire life savings, he finally agreed to the sale.

David took over the kiosk and after one year he had managed to pay off his debt to the old man. In the following year, he was able to make a small down payment on an apartment in the nearby San Borgo neighbourhood. This meant that the couple, with their twin babies, could leave the hopelessly inadequate rented accommodation, and were now able begin a new life together. From a desperate start, the young Vanninis could look forward to a bright future together. Despite the turmoil that was happening elsewhere in Europe, Francesca felt that the second and third years of her marriage were the happiest of her life. The happiness however was radically cut short by the sudden death of David.

His passing away had left an enormous vacuum in Francesca's life. They had only been married for three years, and had been in the flat for less than two of them. The boys needed looking after and Francesca feared that she would not be able to care for them as well as run the kiosk. However, with the help of some friends and her cousin Carla, she began to find her feet and slowly came to terms with her situation. Indeed a year after David had died Francesca had changed the kiosk, not only in relation to its display, there were many more magazines than before, but she also expanded the variety of its contents. She now sold cigarettes, lighters, scarves and handkerchiefs, as well as souvenirs. The latter were particularly of interest to young soldiers, away from their families, who were stationed there briefly.

As a single mother, with twin boys who were now seven years old, Ludovico and Giovanni, she knew she still faced an uphill battle in survival despite the equilibrium she had recently discovered in her life. The future was bleak. She believed that the war was not going to end any time soon, and that Italy's position had now become an extremely insecure one. Despite the desperate fighting elsewhere in Europe, Italians had hitherto continued their lives with relatively limited interruption up until the summer of 1943. Being a member of the Axis, along with Germany and Japan, there had been no fighting on Italian soil during the previous four years.

However all that had changed in the July two months previous, when the Allies invaded Sicily, and had bombed Rome. This had led to a chain of events that followed each other with breathtaking speed. The king, Victor Emmanuel III, dismissed Mussolini as prime minister and then formed a new government with General Badoglio. This then led to a secret armistice with the Allies, signed on September 3rd at Fairfield Camp in Sicily. The news of which was about to become public.

2

Francesca always read the headlines as she laid out all the newspapers in their various positions on the shelves and shutters. Indeed during the day she would read all the papers and was arguably the most well informed woman in Florence. Normally she was unphased by what she read given that everyday something dramatic was happening all around war torn Europe. However that morning it was impossible not to have ignored the headline. *Armistice signed. Mussolini dismissed. Allies Reach Mainland.* Francesca stood still as she read about Italy's volte face in the war. Although a young woman of only twenty-one, she was mature well beyond her years. She knew immediately what this would mean to her country. The situation would undoubtedly lead to civil war, which would involve violent partisan resistance to an inevitable occupation by the German Army. This in turn would mean the end to a relatively peaceful life enjoyed by most Italians during the first four years of the war.

There was a strange unease felt throughout the city that morning. Francesca, sitting on her chair next to the kiosk observed passers by, as they went about their business as best they could, not knowing what to do, or how to behave. She noticed a change in attitude in some. Normally friendly customers were less talkative, whilst some of her regulars would not stop talking, asking her whether she had heard anything.

Fear gripped the people of Florence, as they waited for events to take hold. It would not be long before their freedom was taken out of their hands. Swiftly the Germans demobilised Italian units, only keeping those soldiers willing to fight for the Wehrmacht. Others were deported to German slave camps or simply sent home. Within weeks General Field Marshal Albert Kesselring, who was in command of all German forces in Italy ordered his Tenth Army to immediately take control of the country.

Italy, in a matter of weeks, would become an occupied country. And just as Francesca had thought, when reading the newspaper headline that early September morning, the Resistanza Italiana rapidly became active. Although at first there were many independent groups of partisans, the movement unified under the leadership of Committee of National Liberation, or better known as the CLN. More active in the countryside and the mountains, the CLN still managed to set up a vast network of safe houses in the cities. She, like many other citizens of Florence, at first was unsure over what to do. She knew the difference between right and wrong, and that the German occupiers represented an evil that she wanted nothing to do with. And yet she felt helpless. Her children were the priority. She believed that by staying out of the situation and not becoming involved, would be the best course of action. She was not proud of herself in adopting this position, but if anything happened to the twins, her life would not be worth living.

It was not an easy decision. Francesca had remained friendly with many of her old school friends, and had seen how choices could destroy lives and relationships. Some had joined the Resistance from the outset, but a large number had also thrown their lot in with the Fascists. Francesca had walked a tightrope, always explaining that her children meant everything to her, saying that she preferred to just get on with her life, selling newspapers and being a caring mother. She knew it was morally wrong not to be a patriot, but she reconciled herself with the fact that as a mother, her children came first, second and third. Her friends who had joined the CLN did not agree. They also had children, but had chosen to resist. They accused her of collaboration, since selling goods to the Germans was just the same as being a collaborator. This accusation hurt her. She was desperate to show her support and sympathy, but felt that her hands were tied.

Everybody had to adapt, and indeed adapt very quickly to the new situation. Grey uniformed soldiers were ubiquitous throughout the city. The first thing that Francesca noticed was the different atmosphere regarding Florence's three thousand Jews. Although, she was unaware of the extent of the atrocities that were being carried out in the rest of Europe, she did know that the lives of the Jewish people in Italy were not happy ones either under Mussolini's reign. She had not come across any Jews in Florence, but this did not assuage her disgust at the racial laws, which were introduced against them as early as 1938. These decrees amongst others meant that intermarriage was illegal and that Jews were not eligible for military service. Jews were barred from state employment and prohibited from owning a business. In 1939 a law was introduced that made it impossible for Jews to practise as doctors, lawyers, accountants, teachers or even as journalists. Further prohibitions were activated restricting their lives to the extent of them not being able to enter public buildings.

Life for the Jewish population as a result of these laws was very difficult in Italy even before the German occupation. A quarter of its population before 1943 had either emigrated or converted. And yet perversely, Mussolini's racial laws were less effective because the Italian psyche, during that period, did not embrace the institutionalized anti-Semitism that was now in place. Francesca Vannini was no exception in this respect. She was appalled at their treatment, but like many she did nothing. Whatever the injustices behind these events, they were subsumed behind her desire for her children's wellbeing. But before the Occupation, it was easy to make that choice, since the vast majority of the population did very little. She didn't really have to justify her behaviour during that time.

With the arrival of the Wehrmacht, and with it, the Gestapo and SS, conditions for the Jewish population of occupied Florence rapidly deteriorated. Their plight was now much more visible to the Florentine citizens. It was no longer so easy to ignore what was happening in the streets. Despite the increasing tensions, Francesca kept to her decision and remained uninvolved, detached from the reality of the situation. She avoided any areas where there might be disturbances, and just tried to carry on, undisturbed by the increasing violence in the city. This meant selling cigarettes and newspapers to German soldiers, being polite to the officers, and minding her own business when local disorders broke out.

3

This contrived detachment was always going to come under threat if she was confronted by an act of barbarity. And indeed it did come to an abrupt end one afternoon in November 1943. Allied major offensives had failed to break through the defensive German positions on the Winter Line, and any hope of an early liberation had almost disappeared. There was an air of desperation amongst the city's Jews, when on the 6th November the first round up for deportation took place. Francesca had just finished her shopping, when she was unexpectedly pushed to the side of the pavement by a patrol of German soldiers. This time she could not avoid the violence. Held back against the walls of the buildings, she saw a group of well dressed people, with suitcases being marched across the square to the Santa Maria Novella rail station. Unbeknown to her these wretched souls would be sent by train to Fossoli di Carpi Transit Camp and then on to Auschwitz Concentration Camp.

Francesca had heard from some of her friends who had joined the Resistance, wild stories about the fate of the Jews in Eastern Europe but had chosen not to believe them. They were too terrible to take seriously. But now seeing a group of innocent people; men, women and children being frog marched out of their houses to a place unknown, brought home to her for the first time the tragedy that was befalling the Jewish community. Maybe her friends were telling the truth after all, and that the terrible stories she had heard about huge death factories in the east really did exist. She now knew she could no longer remain on the side-lines whilst this tragedy was being played out in front of her. She needed to help these people. She had a duty, not only for them, but also to herself in doing the right thing. Suddenly her children's safety temporarily receded from the forefront of her mind.

She struggled and wrestled free from the guards and rushed out onto the street, running after the procession of deportees. Oblivious to the dogs barking and the cacophony of whistles blowing, she continued to run until she was grabbed and brought down to the ground by a forty-year-old man. He hauled her up and dragged her back into the crowds, and then out of sight from Gestapo officers who had been alerted to the disturbance.

Marching her into a nearby café on the Via del Corso, his hand holding Francesca's arm in an uncomfortable grip, he pushed her onto a seat, and then sat opposite her.

'What the hell were you trying to do?' he asked angrily.

'Who are you? How dare you manhandle me in this way... I must leave.' Francesca stood up to leave, but the man grabbed her again, and forced her back down.

'Wait... Please listen to what I have to say. You cannot act in that way. You have no idea what these people can do to you... If the Gestapo don't get you... The Banda Carita will.'

'Who are they?' Francesca asked.

'It's a Fascist squad here in Florence led by Mario Carita... An Italian whose brutality is worse than the torture delivered by the SS... Francesca, you have no idea what you are doing. You could be in so much danger. You have to be careful... We need you.'

She paused whilst she stared at him. 'How did you know my name?'

'I was a close friend to David, your husband.'

'What? That's ridiculous. David never mentioned anyone

like you. He told me everything… I don't believe you. What are talking about? How do I know you're telling the truth?'

'Because…' He sighed and paused. 'You have to believe me. We have been watching you since the German Tanks rolled into the city… Francesca, the lives of hundreds of people could be in your hands.'

'I don't understand…' Francesca felt the tears roll down her cheeks. She was overwhelmed by the situation.

'Waiter! Can I have two brandies as soon as possible.' The man saw that Francesca would benefit from a large slug of alcohol. He then continued.

'David was part of a group of us, who opposed the Fascist regime here in Italy. We formed a group to attack the party, intellectually. You probably knew the Rosselli brothers… Or even Piero Calamandrei… There were others of course…' He waited for some form of acknowledgement from Francesca. She nodded in bewilderment. The drinks arrived, and Francesca who was not used to drinking, knocked back the cognac in one gulp. The effect was almost immediate. She felt a warm sensation rush through her veins, and a peaceful feeling take over her body.

'Some of our publications… He helped us sell at the kiosk. He was incredibly helpful in our clandestine campaign against Mussolini. And now, the opposition is more open and stronger… The Committee of National Liberation, CLN has taken control of all the anti Fascist parties. It's openly forming a Provisional Government. All of our previous work, including David's is now reaping rewards.'

'I knew David was very anti-Mussolini, and had sympathetic leanings to helping the opposition… But I thought only in a peripheral way… I had no idea he was so committed.' Francesca felt rising resentment, as she tried to grapple with the fact that she was unaware of her husband's political work.

'He was… But his real commitment was to my people.'

'Who are your people?'

He leaned forward, and said in a quiet voice. 'Francesca, my name is Giorgio Nissim... I am a Jew.'

Francesca sat back in her chair and stared at Nissim. She tried to think back, and remember her husband during the year before he died. She could not recollect anything suspicious in his behaviour.

'Why didn't he tell me about all of this?' She said softly. 'He could have done... I would have helped.'

'Perhaps he was trying to protect you... And of course the boys. He loved you very much. He frequently talked about you and the twins. Don't feel upset about his secret life helping us. It was very dangerous... And even more so now. Believe me... Francesca, you meant everything to him.'

4

For the next two hours Giorgio Nissim explained his role in the current situation facing Florence. He explained that he was a member of the, now illegal, Delasem organisation. Set up in December 1939, with the authorisation of the Fascist government, the 'Delegation for Assistance of Emigrant Jews' was the most important group to help Jews in Italy, and to facilitate their migration. Nissim watched Francesca's growing interest and admiration when he described how successful the organisation had been in helping thousands of Italian Jews leave the country.

'But Francesca... Now... In this year, with the German occupation, Delasem has become illegal. We are faced with different challenges... The extermination of Italy's Jewish citizens... We have to now adapt to this new era.' He stopped speaking, and drank the remaining cognac from his glass. 'I am from Pisa, but all of Delasem's work in Tuscany is under the control of Raffaele Cantoni. He has instructed me to concentrate on the Florentine community, which appears completely unprepared for what is happening.'

'Yes but what can I do? I'm not Jewish...'

'I know... That really doesn't matter. There are many gentiles who have helped us. You've obviously heard of Gino Bartali?'

'The cyclist... Of course I have heard of him! He won the Tour de France!' Francesca laughed.

'Bartali has been helping us for years. He's acted as a courier, carrying photographs, false visas and travel documents, saving countless Jews in the process. He is currently on his way now to Lucca with counterfeit identity documents for a certain family. He is a remarkable man... A saviour to us... And now, Francesca, we come to you... Your help is urgently needed.'

'But how... Why... What can I do?'

'David told me that his... Your family own an old derelict church, the Chiesa di Santa Maria, between the Lungarno Soderini and the Borgo San Frediano, near the Ponte alla Carraia.'

'Well... Yes... That old building has been in his family's ownership for generations. It wasn't actually the Vannini family's building, it's just that the keys have always remained in the family. He never really paid much attention to it. We certainly never believed in the legends attached to it... About hidden frescos and treasures. In fact the only worry he had was that the roof was very unstable and that he might one day have to replace it. The problem would then be that he never had the money to pay for it. He used to say to me, that he should give the building to the city... But he was quite nostalgic so he kept control.'

'Well, It's lucky that he didn't give it to the city to look after. Francesca, our organisation needs it. We can hide Jewish families there, before moving them out into the country. It will be an excellent temporary hiding place... Indeed a vital one.'

'I don't know... If I want to get involved, Signor...'

'You can call me Giorgio... Please,' Nissim interrupted.

'I am not sure if I even know where the keys are... David had always kept them in the same place in his study... God I can't believe this is happening to me. I always wanted to stay out of this war. I am very sorry for your people, but I have my own children... I can't endanger them... You must understand.'

'Francesca, of course I understand, but we need you. Things are getting desperate. I know you are in your heart one of us… Your behaviour this morning showed me that you understand how cruel and merciless the Nazis are. Innocent families are being marched away to their deaths.'

'But how do you know that?'

'We have reports… The Jews are taken to a temporary camp here, and then on to Auschwitz. Have you heard of this name?'

'No… Should I have done?'

'I suppose not. It's a camp of death. We believe that trains go to a place called Birkenau, which is part of the Auschwitz complex, where the people are herded off the trains like cattle. They are then split into two groups. Those who are strong enough to work are taken away for slave labour. The rest… The old, the infirm, the young children… They are then led to enormous gas chambers where they are killed. I know it's unbelievable, but they are killing Jews on an industrial scale. I can see…'

'I don't believe you… I don't believe you! I have heard rumours about this… But it can't be true!' Francesca tried to leave again, but was held back by Nissim.

'I know Francesca it is impossible to believe. When we heard the information… from our sources… and even recently events were recorded on the BBC… it was still hard for us to take it all in. But if you need to be convinced, just ring this top number.' Nissim gave Francesca a note with two local numbers. 'If you are ready to help after speaking to this contact.' Nissim pointed to the top number. 'Then ring me by calling the second number.' Nissim then let Francesca go.

Francesca bolted out of the café, and ran towards the city centre. She wandered around the Duomo and the Baptistry trying to gather her thoughts. She was desperate not to get involved. She had two very young boys, who needed their mother. And yet, if it were true, how could she let these innocent people be led to their death? It was a question she had to answer.

She glanced at her watch. She needed to get back home to relieve the carer, her cousin Carla, who was babysitting Ludovico and Giovanni. She turned around, and started to walk briskly south back over the Arno towards her home in Borgo San Frediano.

5

During the next forty-eight hours, Francesca continued with her normal daily routine. However, her thoughts were preoccupied with Giorgio Nissim and the Jewish citizens of Florence. She was still taken aback by her late husband's involvement with the anti Fascists. She at first resented the fact that she had not known about the extent of David's Resistance work but her anger subsided, and was later replaced with an admiration for his quiet bravery. She searched David's office for the large set of iron keys, which she eventually found at the back of one of the draws of her husband's desk. She sat down and held the keys tightly, knowing that they could determine the difference between life and death for many people. At that moment she realised that she no longer had the luxury to stay out of the war. She had to honour her husband, and continue his work. She decided to ring the number that Giorgio Nissim had given her.

'Hello... who is this?' the softly spoken male voice asked.

'My name is Francesca Vannini... I have been given your number by Giorgio Nissim. He told me that you might be able to help.'

'Ah... Francesca. I have been expecting your call. My name is Don Leto Cassini. I am a parish priest from Varlungo, on the eastern edge of town. I was a friend of your husband David. He loved you very much, but he was very clear that he didn't want you, at that time, to get involved. Your twin babies were his main concern. But times are now desperate, Francesca. I have been working with Nissim, and the Delasem since the war began. I can assure you Francesca that everything Giorgio has told you is sadly true.' He then continued in detail of what was, or had happened to European Jewry over the previous four years. After ten minutes of describing the catastrophe that was befalling the Jewish people in Eastern Europe, he paused. 'So you can see, we really need your help.'

'But how can it be?' Francesca asked. She could not believe that innocent families were being sent to this factory of death.

'It's worse than you can possibly imagine. The reports are that there are actually five other killing centres where hundreds of thousands are being killed... And it's not just Jews... Homosexuals, gypsies, and political opponents are being massacred. However, the vast majority are Jewish, and we can save them.'

'How can we save them?' Who do I need to see?' Francesca, from being scared and uncertain, had now become more convinced that she had to help.

'We need the use of your church. You don't need to do much. Just make sure that we can have access, and keep us informed of any suspicious activity.'

'Yes I understand... I have the keys... Do I give them to you?'

'Next week we are having a meeting with the Delasem at 6pm in the Via Pucci... Number 9. I think you should come. You will meet the necessary people then.'

'All right then, Father, I will see you... Father?'

'Yes, Francesca?'

'I have twin boys... I have to be there for them.'

'Don't worry, Francesca, I will make sure that you and your boys will remain safe.'

The phone went dead, and Francesca placed the receiver down. She looked at the keys again, and smiled, remembering how David always hated this family responsibility. He always used to say to her how he feared the roof falling in, or the building collapsing, killing people in the process. It was an albatross around his neck. The irony now, was that this derelict old building would not be a danger to human life. On the contrary it actually could save hundreds of people. She walked back to the phone, and rang the second number on the note.

'Giorgio?' she asked.

'Yes, who is this?'

'It's Francesca…' There was a silent pause. 'I will see you next week at Via Pucci,' she said quietly.

'God bless you Francesca.' He placed the receiver down and hung up.

6

In that fourth week of November Theodore Dannecker and his SS Einsatzkommando was going from city to city in Tuscany, rounding up Jews for deportation to Auschwitz. Pressure on the Jewish population was made even more intense when the Italian Interior Ministry issued instructions to the local provincial chiefs stating that all Jews should be treated as foreign aliens and placed in concentration camps, and that all of their property be confiscated. The proclamation was broadcast on the radio, and sent shivers down Francesca's spine. It was also a signal for even the most unlikely of people to become involved in protecting, and in some cases, hiding Jewish families. Gerhard Wolf, the German consul in Florence, was one of these unlikely heroes. He had been in the city since 1940, and was a great admirer of Florence and its art treasures. It was he who warned the local population of the increased SS activity, and ensured that the art historian Bernard Berenson was taken away and hidden for his own safety.

The tension in the city became unbearable with the arrival of Karl Wolff. Not to be confused with Gerhard; indeed he could not have been more different to the latter. The SS Obergruppenfuhrer of the Waffen SS, was overall commander of all SS forces in Italy. With many German commanders beginning to leave the city, Wolff's position as supreme police leader, meant that he became de facto military commander of

Italy. He and Dannecker were free to step up their operations and continue their task in cleansing Tuscany of its Jewish population.

It was in this febrile atmosphere that the meeting of Delasem leaders and their network of contacts in Via Pucci at the end of November took place. It was just one of many that were taking place all over Tuscany. Francesca met Giorgio Nissim in the café in Via Corso, and walked the short distance to Via Pucci. They entered the building, and were given a lit candle so that they could find their way to the room on the top floor.

'Don't be frightened... You are safe with me,' Nissim reassured her.

'You say that, but I heard only a few days ago, a convent was stormed by the SS, and all of the nuns were captured and deported.'

'I know... Collaborators were responsible for that outrage... But there are very few people who know about this meeting, and we have taken every precaution.' He opened the door and led Francesca to the table where the meeting had already begun.

7

'We have to move quickly... Ah Giorgio, come and sit down.'

'Thank you, Nathan... Please let me introduce you to Francesca Vannini. She is the woman I told you about... You know, she owns the Chiesa di Santa Maria, on the south side of the city near the Ponte alla Carraia.'

'Of course... Welcome to our meeting, Francesca. My name is Nathan Cassuto. I am Chief Rabbi of Florence,' Cassuto said with a smile. He exuded charm and a gentleness that immediately comforted Francesca. 'Are you feeling all right. You look slightly pale... Fetch some water for her.' He leant over to Francesca and whispered, 'For my sins, I am also a doctor. You'll be fine.'

'Thank you... Yes I am very scared.' She looked around the room. 'Are you all Jewish here?' she asked innocently.

'No... Of course not. We are all friends, sharing the same ideals, but there are a number of us here who are not Jewish. Sitting over there is Father Cipriano, and there is Don Leto Cassini, who I believe you have already spoken to. And over there is Father Meneghello, the Archbishop's secretary, and next to him Professor Giogio Pira. Also we normally have Gino Bartali here, our cycling champion, but he is carrying out a delivery for us. They have all, like you, agreed to help us. The rest of us here are Jewish, including my wife Anna, opposite me, and our driving force behind Delasem, Raffaele Cantoni... Here next to me.'

'Thank you,' she said quietly, bewildered at the number

of important people in the room. 'You mentioned Father Meneghello... Does that mean the Archbishop himself is involved?'

'Cardinal Elia Angela Dalla Costa, who you know as the Archbishop of Florence, is more than involved, Francesca. He has instructed the clergy here to help us find safe houses in the city. He is an inspiration to us all.' If Francesca had any doubts about what to do, they were finally dispelled. Despite being comforted by the doctor, and reassured by the number of notables in the room, she however remained very frightened.

'I have the keys to the church... please take them. I can then leave you to your plans,' Francesca said, standing up, thrusting the large set of iron keys in front of Cassuto. She was shaking. She now just wanted to get out as fast as she could. She was happy to give them the keys, indeed the church, and by doing so she would discharge her duties as she promised she would. Surely that was all they wanted. She was wrong.

'Thank you, Francesca, but we need more from you. We cannot have the keys. You see, if one of us is captured with those keys, what do we do then. It is vital that you remain in charge of your church. Opening it and closing it. Allowing our families to stay there for short periods before being taken to the countryside where they can hide.'

'But... I thought... How will I know when to do all this? I am so frightened.'

'Of course you are... It is natural to feel this way. However we have vast networks being set up. There are... Or were until very recently three thousand Jews living in Florence. We are determined to keep them alive.' He pushed the keys back across the table and placed them into her hands. His touch sent a warm reassurance through her body. 'Now listen, we will be in touch in the next two days with specific instructions.' He looked across to Giorgio Nissim. 'Take her home, Nissim... The poor woman needs time to take all this in.'

Nissim took Francesca through the back door. Before leaving, Nathan Cassuto called out. 'Francesca, it goes without saying how thankful we are to you. We will never forget this act of bravery and charity.'

Francesca nodded and left with Nissim, who took her home.

'Do you think she will do it?' Raffaelle asked.

'Yes I do,' Cassuto replied. He looked behind him towards the window, where there was a sudden disturbance outside. Within seconds the door of the meeting room had been forced open.

8

The group, just like at the convent a week earlier, had been betrayed by collaborators and was rounded up, and immediately imprisoned. Within days the Jewish members of Delasem who had been captured were deported to Auschwitz. Francesca would never see Nathan Casutto again. He died at Auschwitz. Raffaele Cantoni, however, miraculously escaped, and fled to Switzerland. The others in that group, managed to regain their freedom. Don Leto Cassini, in particular owed his release due to the direct intervention of the Archbishop. The effectiveness of Delasem in Florence had been seriously compromised by the loss of its two leaders in the city. It was now dependent on Giorgio Nissim and Don Leto Cassini to coordinate operations, with help from the Archbishop and his network of priests and Monsignors.

Francesca learnt of what had happened to the Delasem leaders a week later when Giorgio Nissim contacted her. She could not comprehend how close she came from being captured.

'You told me that it was safe...'

'I know, Francesca, but we were betrayed... We believe by one of our own... Yes, it's a harsh reality that there are Jewish collaborators out there.'

'Well... Do you still want me to help, or have the operations stopped.'

'Of course we still need your help. There are plenty of us,

including the priests who are willing to assist us. Your job is simply to be at the Chiesa di Santa Maria at seven o'clock tomorrow evening. The only thing you have to provide is access and some torches and candles. I will ensure that there is enough food and water. I will also make sure there will be blankets and extra clothing. They will be there for a short time... A day or two.'

'How many people will be coming?'

There will be two families... My job is to produce false identity cards, visas and ration coupons. Bartali will get these for me within twenty four hours. The Germans think that his training regime is most unusual... Daily hundred kilometre trips around the same roads of Tuscany! I will then come to the church at nine o'clock the following night, and we will them get them out of the city.'

'Alright then... Seven o'clock tomorrow night... And then you will contact me to open up the following evening at nine.'

'That's right... Oh and Francesca, do not tell anyone... Not even Carla who looks after your boys.'

'No of course not... I'll think of something... I don't know what... She knows my whole routine. But wait Giorgio. How did you know that my cousin's name is Carla?'

'We do our work... We know everything... We have to know everything.' Giorgio walked off and disappeared into the cold night air.

9

Carla Martini was a second cousin of Francesca. She was ten years younger than the Francesca, and had just finished school. Since David's death she had been an invaluable help to Francesca in looking after the twins, whilst the latter earned a living running the newspaper kiosk. Carla loved Ludovico and Giovanni, and they in turn loved her as a second mother. Unlike a lot of her friends, and more like her elder cousin Francesca, Carla at first was not interested in joining any of the resistance movements in the city, whether it was Group of Patriotic Action, the Communist Party, or the Florentine Party of Action. She wanted to lead a life outside the terror of war. She was desperately scared of the Germans, but also feared the violence of the Italian resistance. Not being a part of the war alienated her from many of her school friends.

Finding solace in looking after Giovanni and Ludovico, she managed to continue living a life that was removed from the horrors of what was going on all around her. Francesca was extremely grateful to Carla, without whom it would have been impossible for her to continue running the newspaper kiosk. Apart from agreeing on staying out of the war, the two of them became very close following David's death, and told each other everything about their current lives. When Francesca left Giorgio that afternoon, she felt a sharp tension in her chest. Francesca had already told Carla about the Delasem meeting that she had attended the previous week, and had also informed her of what she had been asked to do. Carla's reaction was one of extreme anxiety, especially for the twins. She might not have been involved in any wartime resistance, but she knew how dangerous it was. She felt anger at Francesca, and begged her to stay away from any activity. It would put the whole family at risk.

Francesca certainly wasn't going to let Giorgio know of her indiscretion, but what was she going to say to Carla now. To tell her that she was going on a date was not only stretching credibility too far, but also sounded preposterous. Carla's reaction would have been hysterical. Francesca was nervous about telling her anything more about her clandestine operations. And yet she knew she had little choice when returning to her apartment.

'I have to do this Carla... I cannot just sit around and watch people be marched away to their death.'

'You believe all of those stories? Really Francesca? There is so little proof.'

'I do believe them... And what proof do you need Carla? Nobody comes back. Their houses and all of their possessions are confiscated... I can help. You must understand.'

'But Ludovico and Giovanni... What about them? You are their mother... You have responsibilities. What about the safety of their lives? Don't you think they're more important than these Jews?'

'Carla... My boys are not in real danger. They are not being led off to be gassed. I have been promised that if we are silent on all of this, they will not be at risk.'

'They will be if you get caught.' Carla began to cry.

'I will not get caught, but you have to remain quiet about all of this.' She walked over and put her arms around her. 'You know, Carla... I, like you, had always wanted to stay out of the terror, the violence... Nobody loves my boys like I do, and the last thing I want to do is put them at risk... But I can't back out now. It's the right thing to do... You know that, don't you?'

Carla although unconvinced, nodded and whispered, 'Yes... I suppose so.'

10

Francesca shut the Kiosk for lunch the next day, and walked the short distance to the Chiesa di Santa Maria. She bought with her three torches and five candles, no easy task given the rations facing the city. The location of the church had always been a quiet one, slightly hidden away from the north, and not easily accessible unless approached from the Carraia. Very few people at this time of the year visited the city, let alone this particular quarter. She waited and looked around to see that no one was looking, and then opened the doors for the first time. Turning on one of the torches, she entered the empty building. She walked around, looking at the damaged east wall where, unbeknown to her, Denon and his assistants had tried to remove Uccello's work.

She then moved towards the large southern wall. The torch failed to give off enough light for her to notice at first glance anything different about the façade. She could smell the stale damp aroma pervading the church, and the mould that had accumulated in various parts of the building. She looked up and saw that the central part of the roof was obviously in desperate need of repair given the puddles of rain water that had formed directly below it. She smiled to herself thinking about her late husband's reaction if he saw the precariousness of the structure above. She quietly continued walking around pondering about the history of the building.

She couldn't help wondering why David had not talked more about the chapel, or why he hadn't taken her here. She knew that he worried about it falling down and injuring people, but he always casually dismissed these concerns by changing the conversation. David, like herself, was an only child, and having lost his parents at such an early age, had no one to talk to about this legacy. Francesca had found no documents of ownership since his death, and could only rely on what David had told her about the Vannini's historical attachment to the church. One of the legends told of a beautiful fresco, but Francesca could find no evidence of its existing inside.

She knew that for people to stay here, even for twenty four hours, she would have to bring some basic provisions. In her mind she visualised tables and chairs, rugs, blankets and mattresses. Most of it could be placed against the southern façade, an area that appeared to be the least affected by the water. She then looked more closely at the wall, which covered Masaccio's fresco. She noticed that the wall was darker than the other walls. She placed her hand, and felt that the texture was different. Although it was clearly in a more advantageous position in regard to weather damage, the wall had aged badly and had succumbed to the pollution far worse than the stone walls surrounding it. Whilst questioning this strange difference, and beginning to think that there might be some truth in the old legends, she heard a sudden noise from outside. She immediately turned off her torch and walked slowly towards the doors, where a thin shaft of light provided guidance. She opened the doors slowly, and saw nobody.

Although a false alarm, it encouraged her to leave. She locked up the church, having left the torches and candles as promised. She walked briskly back, continually looking behind and around her. It was a very short distance from the church, along the Arno to the Ponte alla Carraia where the newspaper kiosk stood, yet she still had to be careful. As she made that short walk she now realised that she was part of the resistance movement. She was doing something that would save lives, and be a benefit to humanity. Francesca Vannini felt a sense of pride for the first time since her husband had died. At the same time, she had forgotten about that strangeness of the southern façade. Denon's secret had survived its first interrogation.

II

Francesca waited for them outside the church at seven o'clock, but there was no sign of Nissim or his party. She was worried. It was freezing cold and she wanted to return to her apartment to put the boys to bed. After an hour she walked towards the river, thinking that she would leave, when she saw a small group led by Nissim walking towards her along the bank of the Arno. There were four people behind him, two adults and two young children.

'Giorgio... Where have you been?' Francesca said in a desperate loud whisper.

'Francesca, nothing happens to clockwork when doing this type of work. Guards change their routines, incidents occur all the time... Rarely do things happen to schedule. Patience is vital.' He smiled, and stroked her cheek. 'Come, take me inside the church.' He smiled, finding her inexperience refreshing.

Francesca led the party into the church. The building, which had barely been used for hundreds of years, was now going to be constantly occupied over the next eight months. It would act as a sanctuary, safe house, refuge, and hiding place for hundreds of souls. It would become an operating church, in an unconventional, and indeed broadest sense for the first time in its history. The irony lay in that the Chiesa di Santa Maria was built by, and for God fearing Christians. Its founders would have been astonished if they had known that the only people it

271

would save would be those of a faith that they themselves had persecuted for over a thousand years.

'Perfect Francesca... We will have to get some tables and chairs. Maybe some rugs, and some basic furniture. Also we need some heaters...'

'Yes I agree... We should put them against the south wall... Over there. It's not so damp there.' Francesca pointed towards the wall where Masaccio's fresco lay hidden behind Denon's false wall.

'What happened to the roof? Everything else looks to be watertight,' he asked, pointing to the makeshift ceiling Denon had constructed during the fiasco one hundred and forty years earlier.

'I don't really know... But it's not in good shape. I'm amazed its still there... The water appears to only collect in the main area.' She indicated the central part of the nave. 'That is why the resting place must be next to the south wall where it's dry,' Francesca told him.

'Yes I agree... I will deal with it this week... Oh Francesca, let me introduce you to the Continis. They are from Fiesole. We are taking them out tomorrow evening to a family in the countryside near Arezzo, who have agreed to protect them.' He paused. 'You look surprised... Don't be... There are hundreds like you who are helping thousands like us.'

'I know, Giorgio.' She nodded, and then turned to the Contini family. 'It's nice to meet you. Have you got anything to drink or eat? I'm sorry there is nothing here.' She felt desolate for them. She suddenly asked herself why had she had not got anything during the afternoon... Rations were scarce, but she could have bought some milk at the very least.

'Oh... Don't worry. We have... Please you have done enough. We cannot thank you enough.' The father replied grasping her hand with both of his. His expression was filled with thanks.

Francesca looked at the little boys; they could not have been older than five years old. 'What are your names?' she asked.

'Luigi,' said one. 'Gianfranco,' said the other.

'I am very proud to have met you!' She removed her hand from the father's tight clasp, and put her arms around them, and held them tightly as if they were her own.'

'Come Francesca... Your job is now done... Return at nine o'clock tomorrow night, so that you can lead us out.'

'But what about you, Giorgio? Where are you now going? Don't you think you should stay with them?'

'Don't worry Francesca... The Continis know what to do. I have other families I need to deal with... Come, let's go... Everything will be fine. I promise.' Giorgio signalled good bye to the Continis, and departed, leaving Francesca to close the doors and lock up.

Francesca left the church, and walked back to her apartment. She felt a mixture of both elation and fear. The one thing she did not feel was doubt. On the contrary she never felt more certain in her life that what she was doing was right. She ran up the two flights of stairs, and opened the front door. Giovanni and Ludovico ran to greet her. She crouched down, and hugged them, silently thanking God that she was not Jewish. She looked up and saw Carla who wore a disapproving look, and had her arms crossed standing behind them. Francesca could sense her displeasure. Over the following months there would be a nagging insecurity, which ate away at Francesca, knowing that Carla could break and betray them. Not because she was a Fascist, or that she morally disapproved of what she was doing. It was just that her cousin feared that the boys might be put in danger.

12

Francesca opened the doors at 8:45. She was eager to see how her adopted family were faring. For twenty four hours her anxiety over the Continis gnawed away at her stomach. After a sleepless night, she could hardly hold herself back from leaving the kiosk during the day and checking that everything was alright. But she was under strict instructions not to visit the church under any circumstances. There were informers everywhere, and anything out of the ordinary could be reported. Visiting the derelict Chiesa di Santa Maria during the day would have certainly attracted enough suspicion.

As she opened the doors, winter's first snowflakes began to descend on Florence. She looked up at the snow falling on Europe's most beautiful skyline, and immediately recognised the juxtaposition of such aesthetic beauty against the brutal ugliness that pervaded Florence at that time.

'Hello… Are you all alright?' she called out.

'Ah! Francesca… Yes, yes we are all fine. Giorgio brought us some blankets, and although it is freezing, we have been fine,' Alano Contini, the father, replied.

'Oh, I'm glad… What about food and water?' she asked.

'We have our own food. We would not have been able to eat anything that is not Kosher, so don't worry about not having any! I wanted to reassure you last night, but I was so emotional at your generosity I couldn't really express myself.'

'Oh...' It hadn't entered Francesca's mind that these people had dietary requirements. 'Just as well that I didn't bring some salami then!' She laughed, making light of the situation. 'Giorgio should be here soon.' At which point there was a familiar rehearsed knock on the door. One that Giorgio and Francesca had practiced in order to identify each other.

'Giorgio?' Francesca whispered.

'Yes it's me.' She opened the door. 'I am glad you're here a little early, Francesca.' He looked across at the Continis. 'Come, we have to go now... The Germans have changed their timings at certain lookout points. If we leave now... Its our best chance.'

They gathered up their scant belongings and hurried out of the church, leaving Francesca to tidy up and lock up..

'What do I do now?' She asked Giorgio, grabbing his arm.

'You wait until I contact you again... It might be tomorrow... It might be next week. I just don't know.' He smiled. 'You have done a great job... Thank you.' He turned around to walk off. Suddenly he stopped, and reached for his pocket, and took out a scrap of paper with a telephone number. He pressed it into her palm. 'Call this number... He will provide you with some basic furniture... And heaters. His name is Antonio... Don't forget.'

'I won't,' she replied.

Giorgio and the Continis then scurried away in the snow. Francesca turned back inside the church and tidied up. The following day she rang Antonio who indeed supplied and delivered all the necessary furniture and appliances, as Giorgio had promised. The delivery took place in the middle of the night, when the boys were fast asleep.

'Thank you, Signora Vannini... Your help is invaluable,' Antonio said, turning to leave.

'Oh... Its no problem at all... Be careful not to be seen out there,' she said. He laughed as he turned around and left. Francesca felt a little stupid warning him having immediately realised by his laugh, that Antonio had been involved much longer than her in the fight against fascism. However, there was now no doubting her commitment to the cause, and her fully fledged status as a member of the Resistanza.

13

The Allied advance into Italy in the early months of 1944 was painfully slow. The strength of the Winter line, coupled with snow blizzards leading at times to zero visibility meant that the Germans were still in control. However, after four major offences, the Allies finally broke though, and in May were advancing at a relatively rapid pace. Very limited resistance was met, but as a result of General Clark's bizarre decision for the US Army to enter Rome and not destroy the German Tenth Army, meant that the latter survived with few casualties. Kesselring now ordered the army to tactically retreat, and base its defence on the Gothic Line, a fortified position running from the coast, north of Pisa along the Apennines between Florence and Bologna, and towards the Adriatic coast. It was only a matter of time before Florence would fall.

All of this was not lost on Karl Wolff, the supreme SS leader and his enforcer, Theodore Dannecker, the SS Hauptsturmfuhrer. The latter's Einsatzgruppen were continuing at a ferocious pace sweeping up Jewish victims around northern Italy. During those opening months the atmosphere throughout Florence was one of unbearable fear combined with excruciating tension. Betrayal became a common currency with which everybody would come into contact. It infected mothers who feared for their young ones, fathers for their livelihood, and children to report any suspicious acts of their parents' friends to the men in grey uniform. It was an inhuman time, and some people behaved accordingly.

Francesca Vannini continued working with Giorgio Nissim during these tortuous months. The Allied bombs that now rained on the Florence, which until recently had been off limits due to it being a 'Category One' city and only to be attacked under specific instructions due to its historical importance, were meant for the rail stations. Notoriously inaccurate, the bombing raids managed to find Florence, but not the railway stations, damaging two hospitals instead and leaving hundreds of Florentines dead. However the progress of the Allied advance, coupled with their air raids on the city in the spring raised expectations among the Resistanza.

'How long, Giorgio? When do you think they will reach Florence?' Francesca asked him at the kiosk on one of their rare meetings away from the church.

'I don't know, Francesca... But the Delasem in Rome are confident that German defeat is palpably close. We must keep going. The Fascists are intensifying their operations. They have more informants than ever... You must trust nobody.'

'I understand... I heard that Carita's men infiltrated a Resistance hideout and found a huge stockpile of its weapons... Of all the people to seize them.'

'I know, Francesca. It was a few weeks ago. A number of our friends were captured and shot. It was a very low point and the movement nearly collapsed, but it has recovered, and thankfully the network survived. But it's more dangerous out there than ever.'

'How many more escapes can we arrange, Giorgio?

'I don't know... We might have to double our numbers if things get worse.' He looked at her face. He could see she was upset. 'I know Francesca... Things are getting better, with the war ending soon, and yet at the same time they are so much worse here.'

'I can't stand it, Giorgio… All those families… I hope they are still safe. I hope the world will realise what has happened.'

'They are all safe… And yes… The world will find out. The Russians are advancing on the Eastern Front… And they will reach the death camps in Poland. The intelligence I hear, says that there are six of them, but the Nazis have already destroyed two of them, making sure that there is no evidence of the mass slaughter. It's just too unbelievable to take in…' He paused, almost breaking down.

'Who do we have tonight?' she asked, seeing Nissim's emotional distress, and getting back to concentrate on the business at hand.

14

At the beginning of July, what remained of the Wehrmacht in Florence bore no resemblance to the fighting force that invaded Poland and Western Europe four years earlier. Knowing that they were about to leave, the soldiers became ruthless. Scrambling for food and stealing from supply centres that were initially meant for the Florentine citizens, became daily occurrences. Atrocities were committed at such regularity that people became blasé about death and torture. And it wasn't just food that was in desperate demand. The threat of the water being cut off, or gas supplies being terminated, hung over the city. People queued for hours for fruit and vegetables. Meat was now so scarce that the prices were exorbitant and thus unaffordable for the local population.

Activity on both sides polarised. Carita, and his Fascists suddenly left the city. Many Republicans also decided to vacate the city since the inevitably of its fall to the allies was imminent now that Sienna had fallen only thirty-five kilometres away. However this left a vacuum that General Wolff knew had to be filled. The formation of the Black Brigades by Alessandro Pavolini some months earlier fitted the bill perfectly, and were a much more terrifying proposition than Carita's thugs. Indeed Pavolini's own personal guard, the Bir el Gobi, were an additional frightening adjunct to the Fascist action squads.

Pavolini, seeing that there was a great deal to be gained

from such a vacuum in the city, set himself up in the Excelsior hotel, and conducted his terror operations from there. He was helped by the new arrival of Colonel Fuchs and his highly trained parachutists. It seemed that the Germans were making final preparations for violent street battles, regardless of their situation. Roaming the streets, armed soldiers posed a constant threat to the civilian population. It was at this point that the Republicans who had remained decided not to negotiate, and that only an insurrection against the German occupiers would bring them liberty.

Francesca knew that her activities would have to come to an end. It would be impossible to continue under these violent conditions and without being seen. Round ups were incessant, now focusing on the Republican resistance as well the Jewish population. She was even more vigilant than ever, as the terror inexorably increased. The last transport occurred over a week previously, and although one was planned for the next day, 29th July, she imagined it would be cancelled. The Allies were now approaching and the risks of being caught, with salvation being so close, would be too great. As she sat at the kiosk that afternoon she saw Nissim walking hurriedly towards her.

'Giorgio... Are we still going ahead with tomorrow's plans? Has it been cancelled? If it hasn't, surely it must be our last one?' She asked as he pretended to browse through the magazines.

'Francesca... You have to leave the city... You are now suspected of helping us. You are on a 'wanted' list.'

'But how... Nobody knows what I do. I'm so careful. It's impossible that I have been watched... I have been so vigilant,' she said in a fearful tone.

'You were betrayed... Tomorrow's transport... Indeed all future transports are now abandoned. It's over. You must leave with your two boys... Tonight,' he said, clutching both her hands.

'But what about those who are still here… We can't just leave them…' Francesca replied, not quite understanding the danger she was now in.

'You must understand… You have been betrayed, Francesca. You have done more than enough. Safety is around the corner for most of us. I have to leave as well. You will probably never see me again. Francesca, you have been a saint, and our people will never forget what you have done here.' Nissim looked around, and seeing that nobody was watching, he took out from his pocket a gold necklace. 'It was my mother's. I want you to have it.' He let go of her hands and slowly walked away.

'Wait Giorgio… Wait!' she cried, walking after him. But he quickened his pace, and gestured for her stay. Francesca managed to regain some composure, realising that if she chased after him, it would undoubtedly give rise to suspicion. She walked back to the kiosk, desperately trying to make sense of what had suddenly happened.

Francesca looked on, not quite believing what had just occurred. She opened her hand and saw the simple piece of jewellery. She stood staring at the necklace. The gravity of the situation began to dawn on her as she began to shake with fear. She put the gold necklace on around her collar, fumbling with the clasp. Finally letting the jewellery hang from her neck, she began to feel the chain with her fingers. She breathed in a deep breath, and then turned around and closed the kiosk. Realising that if she had indeed been betrayed, she had to go to her boys immediately and leave the city as quickly as possible.

15

The short walk that Francesca took back to the apartment from her kiosk felt very different. Normally it was a walk she made either first thing in the morning, or well after sunset. Over the last few months, she had rarely walked the streets during broad daylight. She was so immersed in her activities that she never had time to take in and see the deprivation that had swept through Florence. The streets had now become more crowded with the advance of the Allies. People were coming to the city from the countryside to escape the brutal behaviour of the Germans. Mass slaughters and looting were rife as the Wehrmacht forces retreated. Francesca noticed for the first time unburied corpses in the street, the smell of sickness and death that now permeated the city's atmosphere.

She reached the apartment and opened the door. 'Ludovico? Giovanni? Mama's home…' she shouted as she placed her bag on the kitchen table. She turned around and stopped in her tracks, as two black uniformed young men confronted her. 'Who are you? Get out of my flat… Who let you in?… Oh God where are my boys? Carla… What have you done?' she screamed.

'Your boys are fine… They are with your cousin Carla, who was worried about you. She felt that the boys needed… How do I say… More privileges… More food, than you could provide them. They now have a much more comfortable life in a calmer part of the city.' The man spoke in an educated voice.

'What did she tell you? I don't believe she would say anything... My boys were fine. Look what's happening out there. We are about to be liberated. Why would she suddenly take from you after all this time.' Francesca refused to believe that Carla had betrayed her.

'Carla Martini was caught two weeks ago stealing meat from a nearby butcher. She begged for her to be released when held by our guards... You know the punishment for such crimes don't you, Francesca?'

Francesca stared in disbelief, as she suddenly realised what had happened.

'Anyway,' the man continued, 'We dragged her across the road out of the public gaze. She was very amenable to giving us information that more than paid for the meat. Indeed, your boys have been benefitting from our generous provisions over the last fortnight. I am surprised you were not suspicious.'

'I had no idea... But Carla must have been lying... Whatever she told you... They are lies.' Tears welled up, as she tried to break free. Every day during that period Francesca had dreaded that something like this might happen. This was what she had been fearing for the last nine months.

'Please don't struggle, Francesca... Carlo, look in her bag and see if there are an old set of keys. Take them, and then together we can walk along to the Chiesa di Santa Maria, and see what is inside.'

'Please... My boys... What are you going to do with my boys?

'That depends on what we find in the church, Francesca,' he said coldly as the two brigade members marched her out of the door.

16

Led out onto the streets, Francesca was pushed and jostled along the narrow Borgo San Frediano towards the Chiesa di Santa Maria. There was commotion that early evening as people saw posters being nailed to the walls ordering them to evacuate all areas around the bridges of the Arno. It was clear to the Nazis that the Allies would enter the city and would need the bridges for access. Notwithstanding the declaration of Florence being an 'open city', Colonel Fuchs did not want to repeat the mistake made in Rome where the city remained open and the bridges, being left intact, meant that thousands of German troops would be vulnerable to the Allied onslaught.

The panic in the streets around the south bank, near the Ponte alla Carraia was palpable, which made the short journey for Francesca and Pavolini's brigade men an arduous one. Matters were made even worse by the thousands of leaflets dropped by the RAF encouraging the Florentines to stand united and not let the occupiers destroy their city. Given only a few hours to gather all their belongings, and with no transport of any kind available, people were becoming desperate. Despite Cardinal della Costa's pleas, even the hospitals in the area of evacuation were closed.

They reached the church, where Francesca was given her keys to open its doors.

'Leave it open… Put that stone there,' Federico told Carlo,

his junior. 'I need the light for the time being.' The latter moved the large stone block, and forced the heavy wooden Renaissance door to stay open.

'Ah... Tables... Chairs... And look... Matrasses and pillows. It must have been very comfortable for your Jews.' Federico walked around the old church, and stopped by one of the tables. 'Tell me, Francesca... You still deny you weren't keeping Jews here?' He held a Jewish prayer book in one hand and an old Torah scroll in the other.

'I don't want to say anything to you.'

'Oh... I think you will, Francesca. We are quite happy to actually let you go... And then you can see your boys. But we want names... And all of the names of the Resistanza who you were dealing with. You must know everyone involved with Delasem. We haven't got long to sort this out. The British are near... And we have to get out of here. We need names. If you don't cooperate we will kill your boys. It's simple. Now then... We know about some... But we know there are many more.' He lit the remaining candles that had been left in the church from the Delasem's previous operations. He now indicated to Carlo to shut the door.

Francesca remained silent. Federico looked at Carlo, and nodded. The subordinate walked over to Francesca, and struck her across the face, forcing her to fall onto the ground. She momentarily lost consciousness, but was aware seconds later that she was being pulled up and thrown onto the chair. She was bound so tightly to the seat that the rope tying her arms behind the chair cut into her wrists. She could no longer feel her fingers, as the blood supply was to her hands was severely restricted. She now suddenly realised for the first time that her clothes were wet. Sweat from the suffocating heat, and urine due to the terrifying fear she now felt, were the reasons for the humiliating sensation. She had lost control of herself through the distress that she was going through.

286

She was then subjected to interrogation of the most brutal kind. Each question was either similar, or the same as the one that preceded it. Each one, if not answered was followed by a punch or a kick. It continued through the night. There was no one there to help since by the following morning many of the previous night's hoards had managed to evacuate the area. She was awake through most of the night, screaming from the pain that was inflicted on her. Slowly her screams and wails faded; her larynx was exhausted. Her tears dried up; her eyes had no moisture left in them.

She finally did lose consciousness, and woke up as she was being unbound and forced to stand against the south wall. Her face, bloated by the swellings from her beatings, was pressed against Denon's false wall. Her legs were kicked apart, as Federico ripped her skirt down, and forced himself inside her. Pounding inside her without respite, the pain Francesca felt was like none other she had ever felt before. When he had finished, he instructed Carlo to do the same. Francesca was left lifeless, leaning face up against the wall, as she felt blood trickle down her thighs, as the brutality of the rapes took their toll.

She collapsed onto the floor. She could not move. Her sense of repugnance and revulsion heightened by the feeling of their seed inside her.

'Just the names… We only want the names, Francesca… Who are behind these operations to get Jews out of the city?' Federico shouted. 'Look you have been here for thirty-six hours… I promise you… We will kill you and your boys unless we have those names.' He was screaming into her face as he crouched down next to her. He stood up, and then took of his belt. He wrapped the leather strap around his hand, and prepared to unleash its buckle end across her face and body. He lifted his arm, and said in a cold voice…'Names!' He then screamed at the top of his voice, sensing his failure in finding out what he needed to know. He realised that Francesca was close to death.

She would not be able to survive much more violence. This was the last time he could use it. 'Names! Francesca... Come on...!' he screamed again.

'What names would you like?' A calm voice was heard from the door way.

Federico and Carlo turned around suddenly and saw the dark silhouette of a young man set against the bright sunlight behind him, armed with a gun pointing at them.

'Who the hell are you?'

'My name is Enzo Rossini... I am a member of the Resistance... You want names... I can give you one name... Giorgio Nissim. And by the way... He sends his regards.' He then discharged his weapon, killing both Federico and Carlo instantly. They both fell next to their raped and tortured victim. He rushed over to Francesca, and covered her with a sheet. He pulled a bottle of water from his pocket, and placed it against, her bruised and bloodied lips.

17

They sat there resting against the south wall of the Santa di Maria. The horrors that had taken place in the church were in cruel contrast to the compassionate beauty of Masaccio's *Madonna and her Son with Angels* hidden within the structure of the building. The cruel irony of such compassion being just a plaster's width away from such brutality was lost that stifling afternoon in the Chiesa di Santa Maria. After an hour of resting, and recovering just enough to be able to walk, Enzo lifted Francesca up and put her arm around his neck to provide her with support.

'Come on... We have to go... Listen... you hear that?' He was referring the increasing hum of approaching aircraft. 'That's the RAF... They are carrying out more air raids now, sporadically, on strategic sites. We have to be careful... The accuracy of Bomber Command has not been great recently,' he said with a sense of black humour and understatement.

'I can hear,' Francesca muttered. 'I must find my children... Do you know where they are? Please...'

'Yes I do, and I am going to take you to them now, but we must leave now Francesca. It is not safe here. We are too close to the river and rumours are rife that the Germans will blow up the bridges. This is going to happen regardless of them declaring the city being open. If they do, here... This part of the city will be on its own... Completely cut off... Take this... You'll need it.' Enzo gave Francesca a handkerchief to cover her face. The stench of rotting corpses and disease had become overwhelming outside, in the summer heat.

Enzo slowly managed to carry Francesca away from the church. As they walked away from the church, they could hear the Allied planes coming over the city, and then saw areas being bombed. The accuracy was indeed questionable, and yet the effect on Fuchs' parachutists defending the city was demoralising. At that point, there was a sudden loud explosion behind them. Enzo stopped and turned around. A bomb had landed on the top of the Chiesa di Santa Maria, and had exploded, blowing the roof completely away. Incredibly, just as it happened one hundred and thirty years previously, the walls remained intact, but the structure was now severely weakened. Francesca said nothing, not feeling any emotion, too exhausted to really comprehend anything at that moment.

18

They continued walking away from the church, arriving at the Pitti Palace, where thousands of Florentines were seeking refuge. Although south of the Arno, the old Ducal residence was considered far enough away from the area of perceived danger. Entire families had arrived at the palace, now a museum, with all their belongings. There they could live in relative comfort, and even wash and bathe in the famous fountains of the Boboli gardens. The place resembled a refugee camp, with people sleeping and eating in makeshift areas, all located in the most beautiful rooms in the palace. Although comforted that they were now safe, the evacuees were also terribly worried about the fate of the city.

Enzo was indeed right in that, although no public declaration had been made, it was a certainty that the bridges would be blown up. Dr Gerhard Wolf the German Consul since 1940, who although mixing with the most corrupt and evil individuals, had acted with honour when it came to saving Jews in the city, knew that Fuchs was determined to destroy any access that the Allies might need. Being highly cultured and an art connoisseur, he wanted Florence's treasures protected from the barbaric acts of the Wehrmacht. The bridges were sacrosanct in Wolf's belief. He begged the general of the Engineering Corps to prevent the bombings, particularly Bartolomeo Ammannati's exquisite Ponte Santa Trinita. It was to no avail, and only the Ponte Vecchio would be saved. Wolf was exasperated by the Nazis' decision, but he could do no more. To save the Vecchio and not the Santa Trinita was for him an absurdity since the latter was culturally so much more important. Whatever happened, Wolf knew that the bombings were a catastrophe for European culture.

Written orders from Kesselring to Fuchs' Parachutists were given on 31st July for Operation Feuerzauber, which laid out instructions for the destruction of the bridges and all buildings next to them. This would make it impossible for the Allies to enter the city. Three days later the Germans ordered everybody off the streets. The penalty for not abiding by this curfew was death. The effect of the order resulted in Florence becoming a ghost town, littered with corpses strewn across the streets. Boxes full of explosives were lined up along all of the bridges, including the Ponte alla Carraia, a stone throw from the Chiesa di Santa Maria. The final act of detonating the bombs would be carried out in the very near future.

19

Francesca's painful recovery at the Pitti Palace was slower than she would have wanted. Tended to by doctors, and volunteer nurses, she eventually began to think and feel like a human being again. Whenever she tried to find out where her boys were, the response was either not to worry, or that she would see them soon. On August 3rd, three days after she had been rescued, she managed to get out of her bed unaided for the first time. She wandered over to the window and saw in the distance children splashing and playing in the fountains of the Boboli gardens. Her eyes became blurred as she strained to identify two of the smaller ones frolicking around.

'Ludovico... Giovanni... You're alive...' she whispered. She wanted to scream, but she had no voice. She wanted to cry, but she had no tears. She banged on the windows with her fists, and then tried to open them. It was useless. They were too far away to be heard even if the window could have been opened. She turned around, desperate to see them, but she fell to the ground. She was far too weak to run, and the distance to the fountains was too great for her to cover unaided.

'Francesca, what are you doing?'

'I want to see my boys... You! You are the man who saved me? Who are you? How did you know about me? Where have you been?' She uttered the words so hoarsely that she could barely be understood.

'Francesca, here... Come and sit down and I will tell you everything.' He sat her down at the foot of the bed. 'My name is Enzo Rossini, I am a member of the Resistance. The Delasem had warned us that you were being watched. Giorgio Nissim immediately informed us that you were in real danger and that you might be taken by the Nazis... And if not them, then Pavolini's men. He told us of your work... Francesca, you are a heroine. Giorgio had to leave the city that afternoon... But we couldn't get to you immediately due to the commotion of the evacuation orders. I finally managed to escape the attention of Pavolini's brigades, and found you. I am so sorry for what you went through.'

'Is Giorgio alright?'

'As far as we know... Yes.' He paused, and then walked towards her placing his hands gently on her shoulders. 'You are safe now. We think either the South Africans or the New Zealanders will be the first of the Allies to liberate us. The big problem at the moment is that the city is completely sealed off... According to the Swiss consul, Carlo Steinhauslin, all of the bridges have bombs attached to them, ready to be detonated, apart from the Ponte Vecchio. So much for Kesselring's open city.' He smiled as he walked away from the bed. 'It won't be forgotten you know,' he said, looking out of the window.

'What?' she asked.

'The heroic efforts you made... and the people you saved.'

'Well... I think my husband would have been proud of me.' She smiled, remembering his young face that she loved so much. 'Can I now see my boys?'

'Of course, I will bring them to you right away. They have been asking after you since you arrived, but we couldn't let them see you in the state you were in.'

'What about Carla... What happened to her?'... Carla Martini... The carer... My cousin.'

'She was shot... As a collaborator,' Enzo said coldly. He looked at her calmly.

'Oh my God! Why? Why? She was so young... And frightened. She only did it for my children... She was so good to them. You should not have murdered her.' Francesca stood up and walked up to Enzo. 'She did it for my kids... For God's sake she was so young.' Francesca started sob, but again no sound or tears were produced, as she fell into Enzo's arms. He put his arms around her.

'I feel responsible for her...'

'You were almost killed because of her actions, Francesca.'

'I know that... But Carla was a good person... She didn't betray me out of evil intent. She wasn't a collaborator in that sense.' She was speaking, but she was barely now audible.

'It's war, Francesca. My people do not have time for sentimentality... It's an extravagance. They have no time for forgiveness. Too many of our parents, siblings and friends have been killed due to the actions of people like Carla. I'm sorry for your loss... But I am not sorry for her. I simply can't afford the luxury of those feelings that you still have... Now please stay silent, and rest your voice for your boys!'

20

Francesca spent that afternoon with Ludovico and Giovanni. It was the first time she had felt like a mother since the day she had met Giorgio Nissim, the previous autumn. She embraced them, breathed in their smell, kissed them, and played with them for hours. She hadn't realised how much she had missed being a mother. For nine months her maternal instincts had deserted her whilst she had devoted herself to saving the lives of the unfortunate Jewish families endangered in the city. In days, when the Allies would enter the city, the Jews would be safe again, and all of her efforts would not have been in vain. Her innocent joy at being with her twins was suddenly brought crashing down to earth that evening when Enzo returned to her room.

'Francesca… Let the children go to sleep. I want you to come with me to the roof of the palace.'

'Come, both of you… Lie down here, and try and get some sleep. I will be back soon,' Francesca said, coaxing the boys onto their mattresses.

'Mummy… When is your voice going to be normal again?' Ludovico asked.

'Soon my darling… Very soon.' She stroked his forehead. She kissed both of them as they fell asleep almost immediately before their mother could even wish them a good night.

'What do you want me to see, Enzo?' she whispered.

'The calm before the storm… The destruction of our city is about to take place. Come quickly.' He took her hand, and led her to the stairs to the attic.

The evening of August 3rd was suffocatingly hot. Enzo and Francesca stood, with hundreds of others seeking refuge at the Pitti Palace, on the roof, looking out across the silent city. There was not a soul to be seen, as almost everyone had obeyed the German curfew. Suddenly at ten minutes to ten there were series of massive explosions that reverberated all around them. The windows of the palace shattered, and the glass below them rained down everywhere. Terror gripped everyone as the bombs continued to be detonated throughout that night, while bridge after bridge collapsed into the Arno. All of them, with the exception of the Ponte Vecchio fell into the river, disarming Florence of its Renaissance history. The last bridge to fall was the Ponte Santa Trinita. The destiny of the bridge that was considered the most beautiful of them all, given its perfect symmetry and harmony, finally fell at the very end. There was an irony in that it was so well constructed that it took more than three blasts for it to finally fall. Wolf's desperate requests for its redemption had come to no avail, much to the cost of cultural civilization.

'My God… It's like the whole city is burning,' Francesca cried watching the destruction. 'It looks like they're bombing around the bridges as well. It will be impossible for anyone to get through,' she uttered, gazing at the apocalyptic vision below her.

'That's why they are doing this… Look the Ponte alla Carraia no longer exists… I don't have much confidence in the Chiesa di Santa Maria surviving,' Enzo replied, turning around to look at her.

Francesca did not respond, as she looked at the devastation in front of her. Much of mediaeval and Renaissance Florence had either vanished, or had been damaged in the space of seven hours.

21

The next morning Francesca, had an overwhelming desire to see what had happened to the Chiesa di Santa Maria during the bombing. It seemed strange that she would want to risk her life yet again, especially having now been reunited with her boys. However having been through so much, she felt a certain indestructability about herself. Despite the obvious danger, she decided to walk out of the palace towards the church ignoring all the obvious risks. She had retrieved the keys to the church from Enzo, who had tried to convince her not to step outside because of the curfew in place in the city. She replied that she had to go back one more time to see what had happened.

Retracing the footsteps of both Napoleon and Denon, the distance being less than half a mile, she knew it would not take long. The perils that lay around her could be heard and seen. Sniper shots rang out at intermittent periods. People lay dead in the street having been shot for breaking the curfew. And yet some people had also ignored the situation. They were desperate to try and find food and water to feed and nourish their families. Others wanted to see what damage had been done to their homes, which they had left during the evacuation.

Meanwhile the situation in the city became worse by the hour. The water shortage was critical, made more severe by the unbearable August heat. The sanitary conditions were a disaster with the stench of dead bodies mixed with the garbage becoming intolerable. Despite this catastrophic scenario, where disease was as much a risk as a sniper's bullet, Francesca made her way to the church without attracting much attention. Walking down the Via Maggio, she immediately saw that the destruction was enormously extensive. Looking straight ahead over the river, she saw that although the spans of the Ponte Santa Trinita no longer existed its support bases were still intact. Turning left along the Lungarno Guicciardini which, led into the Lungarno Soderini, she noticed that the Ponte alla Carraia had completely disappeared from the city landscape of Florence. All around her was debris. The demolition of the city's properties around the bridges was far worse than she initially thought.

She stopped at the point where the Ponte alla Carraia met the Lungarno Soderini, the very place where the Vannini newspaper kiosk had stood for fifteen years. The stand where her husband had worked for ten years, and she for five years thereafter, which had provided a living for their family, no longer existed. There were two wooden planks lying at the curb, which she recognised by the green paint, but they were the only remnants that were left. After a while reminiscing, she continued her walk through the rubble which lay along the Lugarno Soderino.

As she got closer, her steps slowed down dramatically. There standing out from the destruction that lay all around it, stood the Chiesa di Santa Maria. Such was the perfection of its design, it appeared that not only had it survived Denon's earlier attempts, but also the German's Army's best efforts, to destroy it. Similar to the Ponte Santa Trinita, which had also been perfectly constructed, the structure proved to be resilient to total destruction. Amazingly the church was the only building that still had a semblance of being a building on the south bank of the Arno that morning. Francesca however was approaching the church from the south, and from where she was looking, it appeared that the church walls had survived intact. As she got nearer the reality of its condition became clearer.

The north and south walls together with the western façade had indeed survived the bombs. An achievement in its own right. The east wall however had been obliterated, and with it, any unlikely vestiges of Uccello's work that might have partially survived the damage of Denon's folly and the decay of the dirt and pollution that had accumulated over the centuries. From one side, the church appeared ready for a service. From another, it resembled just another war damaged building site.

It was hard for her to think clearly about the church. She knew very little about it whilst her husband was alive. But for the last year it had become the centre of her life, simultaneously providing life for others. And yet it was also a place where she had been tortured, and subjected to brutality. As she walked around it, the goodness that emanated from the structure drowned the unspeakable atrocity that she suffered. After a while, she left the church and tried to approach the Borgo San Frediano in order to return to her apartment. However access was impossible, and so she decided to walk back to the Pitti Palace.

She took a detour back around the church to the river bank, retracing her own steps. She stopped at the river, and then threw the old set of keys into the water. There was no point in having them anymore. She would not be able to afford to repair the church, and its upkeep would be prohibitive if she had responsibility over it. She certainly did not want to have to recount her experiences of torture to anyone, particularly to her boys, after the war was over. Despite being a heroine, she was happier for the time being to remain anonymous. The direct family responsibility, if not the family connection, that the Vanninis had for the Chiesa di Santa Maria ended at ten o'clock in the morning on August 4th. Ludovico and Giovanni would only know of the family link with the church many years later. Only when their mother told them about her rescue attempts, and the horrors she endured in that church, did they find out about their connection with a church that was now only a derelict site with three walls.

22

Lieutenant J Adamson led the Kimberly Regiment that was part of the South African Sixth Armoured Division through the southern parts of the city early on the same morning as Francesca was making her way to the church from the Pitti palace. The Germans had fought a strong rear guard action, and had delayed the Allies long enough so as to enable them to bomb the bridges. This was crucial since when the South Africans arrived at the Arno, closely followed by the New Zealanders, they found not only the bridges destroyed, but access to them impossible. The Ponte Vecchio remained, but nobody could cross it such was the debris that blocked the way.

Greeted with wine and flowers by the Florentines, the Allies remained south of the river, not attempting to cross, in case the city became a war zone. It was not until the 31st August that the city was finally secured and liberated. During those weeks in August, despite the conditions being alleviated by food distributions from the Allies, the situation in the city was desperate. An insurrection by the partisans was met with bitter resistance by the remnants of the German Army that had remained. The fighting was savage, but during the last two weeks the Allies and the partisans fought side by side. German cannon located on the hills continued to bombard the Renaissance city. It was a miracle that the Duomo survived intact. However the damage was extensive making the German promise of Florence being an open city an empty one.

Francesca and her two boys went back to the apartment, and slowly returned to a more normal life. The city provided her with the funds to establish a new kiosk from which to sell her papers, magazines and cigarettes. Ludovico and Giovanni went back to school and being so young, were not at all scarred by the events of the that year. Francesca remained silent about her wartime activities until one day in 1965, when she received an unexpected telephone call from someone unknown to her. It meant that her secret about her wartime heroism could no longer be contained.

23

'Hello... Who is this?' she asked, early one morning before going out to shop.

'Is that Francesca Vannini?' the foreign voice asked.

'Yes... It is... But who is this?'

'My name is Paul Reidenbach... I work for Yad Vashem... You might not have heard of us... Or about what we do.'

'No, you're right. I have never heard about your organisation. Where are you from?'

'I am from Israel... And I work for my country's official memorial to the victims of the Holocaust.'

'Ah... that is interesting,' Francesca replied slowly, at a loss over what to say.

'Mrs Vannini, the memorial was established some twelve years ago, but for the past two years we have been remembering not just the victims, but also those who helped save the victims... Gentiles who put their lives at risk to save Jewish people during the war... In a more specific way.'

'Why would you do that? It's been such a long time... Over twenty years now. Surely nobody is interested anymore,' Francesca replied, a little concerned at the way the conversation was leading, and immediately sensing that her privacy might be invaded.

'We think it is very important to remember those who put their own lives at risk... We now plant a tree, with a plaque, to represent each hero or heroine, along a road. It is called the

'Avenue of the Righteous Among Nations'. The 'Righteous Ones' who are selected, are carefully investigated to ensure that their bravery, which meant risking their own lives in the act of saving our people from going to the camps, is correctly represented… You, Mrs Vannini, have been chosen as a 'Righteous Among Nations'. I hope that you will come to Yad Vashem, in Jerusalem for the ceremony.'

'But how did you know? Who told you about me?' Francesca asked in a raised tone.

'There are many people who owe their lives to you, Mrs Vannini. We have over fifty people who have written to us telling us of your bravery.' Paul was unsurprised by her reaction. Indeed these great people were almost always incredibly modest about their wartime acts of courage when being told that they were to be honoured.

'Well, I'm very flattered, Mr Reidenbach. But how did you know who to contact?'

'Do you remember a gentleman called Giorgio Nissim?'

'Yes of course I remember him… He's still alive?' Francesca paused, and touched the gold necklace that she wore around her neck. It was the same necklace that Giorgio Nissim had given her before he left Florence.

'Yes he is,' Reidenbach replied. There was a pause whilst Francesca fully digested the information she had been given. 'Giorgio was alive,' she said quietly to herself. During the last twenty years she had always wondered what happened to Giorgio Nissim. She had never made any attempts to find out because she was scared about his fate. At the time, if she had discovered that he had been killed, she would not have been able to cope with such a terrible loss after what she had gone through with him. As time went on, she preferred the comfort of not knowing, hoping that he had survived and was living a full life. That fear had now been extinguished, and the joy that she felt was scarcely containable.

'I am so happy, Mr Reidenbach… Overwhelmed. Will I be able to see him?' Francesca had a lump in a throat, and her voice was beginning to crack under the emotion.

'Of course you will be able to see him. He will be at the ceremony, and will be speaking on your behalf… Actually it was Mr Nissim who was behind your nomination… And might I say that his recommendation not only carries weight given his wartime exploits but also, has been fully justified given the letters we have received about you.'

'How wonderful… When will this ceremony take place? Will I know anyone there?'

'Don't worry we will take care of all your needs.'

'Thank you,' she replied, realising that she would have to finally inform people, including her boys, of her actions during the war. The only person she had kept in contact with over the last twenty years, who really knew the extent of her bravery, was Gino Bartali, now that the Archbishop, Cardinal Elia Angela Dalla Costa had died two years earlier. Bartali, like Francesca, kept his involvement a secret, and it remained that way until after he had died in 2000. Both Bartali and Della Costa were later named 'Righteous Among Nations' in 2012 and 2013. Others from Florence, who were at that fateful Delasem meeting in November 1943 including Don Leto Cassini, professor Giorgio Pira, Father Giacomo Meneghello, would also be honoured for their bravery, but Francesca had lost contact with them now.

After placing the telephone receiver down, and finishing her conversation with Paul Reidenbach of Yad Vashem, she immediately called Ludovico, to come to her flat with his young wife Maria, and his twin brother Giovanni. She needed to see them to explain her role in the resistance, her torture and rape when caught, and why she had remained silent for all these years. She also wanted all of the to come to Jerusalem with her for the ceremony. She fell into her large armchair, and began to think about her life. She was now forty-six years old, and with the money saved from the newspaper kiosk coupled with a state pension that she would receive, her life would continue to be relatively comfortable. Giovanni had taken over the kiosk, whilst Ludovico was a bus driver. The latter's wife, Maria, far cleverer than both her sons put together, had finished her masters, and was now employed by the Uffizi as an art restorer.

24

Having arrived at their mother's apartment on Borgo San Frediano, the twins and Maria sat down in the sitting room. It was the very same room that in twenty years' time, the young Gianni Vannini with his father and uncle would watch that World Cup thriller between Italy and Brazil. The three of them heard Francesca relate the entire story of her wartime experiences. Ludovico and Giovanni, now in their twenties were stunned by what they heard.

'Why did you not tell us, Mama?'

'The horrors of what I went through… You know Ludovico, even notwithstanding that terrible afternoon on July 31st, none of us… I mean my comrades, have ever discussed our actions. Maybe we just feel that we should look forward and not hark on about the past. I feel proud now about what I did… But I also carry some guilt for Carla, who was just a young simple twenty year old looking after you two boys… Who made a simple mistake.'

'I vaguely remember her… but we were only eight at the end of the war,' Ludovico mused.

'I understand, Mama… But you were a heroine. I must say… Seeing Jerusalem will be very exciting.' Giovanni loved to travel, and had little opportunity so far to do so.

'Well, you… And you, Maria… Are all coming,' Francesca said smiling.

'I can't wait...' Maria replied. 'There is so much to see... The theology I have had to study over the years will take on a new meaning when actually I see the sites there... I mean the Holy Sepulchre... Calvary... We can go to Bethlehem and Nazareth... My God it will be fantastic to see everything.'

'What about the church... Is it ours?' Giovanni asked, not very interested in his sister in law's desire to see Christian theology's birthplace.

'We never owned it. We just, somehow, over the hundreds of years looked after it. Your father told me that it all started with the stonemason who was in charge of building the structure.' She smiled, remembering her late husband. 'Anyway... What church... It's just a derelict site with three walls. Funnily enough, after the war, they performed salvage work, managing to retrieve a lot of the original stonework of the bridges, including the Santa Trinita and Carraia. But they also found the large Renaissance keys that I threw in the water. They published the find in the newspapers, and I went to the city council and explained the story, and how the keys ended up in the river. The officials were happy to keep them... Indeed they are actually on permanent show in the Palazzo Vecchio.' She looked at her boys, who remained silent.

'It is... Or was... Definitely a Renaissance building,' Maria said. 'You can see from the design. I wished the city paid more attention to that site. I'm sure it has a significant architectural value. Its typical of this city to let something like that go to ruin.'

'You are right, Maria... There is something fascinating about the structure, but I'm not sure it will stand for much longer. It looks like the walls are going to collapse on their own!' Maybe for health and safety reasons the city council should clear the place, and build some apartments overlooking the Arno.... But anyway... The point is... The connection between the Vanninis and the old Chiesa di Santa Maria is over!' Francesca declared, not realising then, that very soon in the future an event would take place that would once again draw the Vannini family back towards the Chiesa di Santa Maria. Francesca got up and walked into the kitchen to make some tea. The Vannini household remained quiet, taking in the unbelievable story they had just been told.

PART 9

PRESENT DAY FLORENCE

I

Maria and Molly, having left the convent and raced back to the city, arrived at the Uffizi late afternoon. 'I'm going to take you down to the basement where I work on all the museum's Renaissance restoration. You are really in for a treat, Molly!'

'Are you sure that's ok? I don't want to cause you any problems with the staff,' Molly said apologetically, hardly containing her excitement.

'Molly... I am in charge. They have no choice. Anyway they won't mind. They're quite a nice bunch of people actually! Just terribly serious.' Maria smiled at Molly as she took the brief case out of the boot of her car and took her down to the basement where the restoration work was carried out. As they descended down towards the bowels of the building Molly became even more excited. For her, this was the holy grail. Paintings not on show to the public, being restored to a likeness of their original state, were things that Molly only dreamed of seeing as a doctoral student.

'Buon giorno a tutti!' Maria exclaimed as she entered the offices. 'Can I introduce you all to Molly. She is a graduate studying Neo-Platonism for her PhD. She also works as a part time guide at the Museo di Santa Maria. Please make her feel welcome... Come this way Molly... to my office.'

Molly followed Maria to her office, smiling at the various employees as she walked past them. They smiled back, removing any unwanted feelings of suspicion that she might have felt on her arrival. As they entered her office, Maria placed the brief case on her desk, and carefully took the Mantegna drawing, which was now protected by a transparent plastic cover. Maria unzipped the plastic, and shined a light on the image. 'Well then… It looks even more beautiful here in the light than when we saw it at the convent, Molly.'

'I know… The body of Christ is so lifeless, and yet it exudes such power… and look at Mary and John… The sadness in their eyes. It's amazing, and it's only a drawing. He was a real master,' Molly replied looking up at Maria, who had now walked towards the door.

'Allegra? Please come in,' Maria called out. Immediately a leggy brunette in her late twenties, dressed in a white T shirt, tight jeans and trainers walked towards the office.

'Hi… I'm Allegra Bianchi. Pleased to meet you.' She nodded at Molly, who returned the gesture.

'Look at this Allegra… Don't turn the drawing over. Tell me what you think.' Maria asked, almost as if she was showing off her staff and basking in the reflected glory of their brilliance.

'I think it needs a lot of restoring at the edges… The image itself is in excellent condition. It needs a good clean Doctore don't you think!' She laughed, as did her boss.

'Who drew it do you think?' Maria repeated the question.

'Andrea…' She did not look up, but continued to inspect the drawing. 'Mantegna.' She looked at Maria and Molly waiting for a response. Maria smiled and looked across at Molly.

'Yes… Well done… Molly found the drawing up at the convent in Fiesole. Astonishing that these places remain repositories for these treasures Allegra.' Maria nudged Allegra to one side and resumed looking at the image herself.

'I know… Congratulations Molly. It really is a beautiful

discovery. We will be able to restore this image in a number of weeks.'

'Thank you Allegra,' Molly replied, astonished at the assistant's ability to know the artist who drew the image in literally two minutes.

'Can it go upstairs, or do we have to return it?' Allegra asked Maria.

'Upstairs I think. We will certainly be able to exhibit it for a period of time. It's in the national interest... But I have to do some negotiating still, and I will have to talk to the director. However I am sure it will stay here. You should alert the press office of what we have found, so that we can arrange a special exhibition highlighting our new find.' Maria looked at her watch.

'Christ, I'm late. I have a meeting to go to. Allegra, will you show Molly around?' Maria kissed Molly on both cheeks, whispering, 'Enjoy yourself... Allegra is dazzlingly brilliant and will explain to you what we do here. I will contact you soon... Don't forget to speak to my mother in law Francesca... You'll be amazed at her story.'

'I won't. I promise,' Molly whispered back, before Maria left.

'Shall we?' Allegra ushered Molly ahead of her, out of Maria's office.

2

Allegra took Molly around the Restoration Department, showing her masterpieces that were about to be restored, those undergoing restoration, and those that had been restored and were about to go back on show. Molly was beguiled by the splendour of the works, and took a particular interest in those that were of the period she was studying. Allegra explained to Molly all about the techniques they used, and how practises had developed over the last sixty years.

'The big game changer in this field came with the floods of 1966,' Allegra said, walking in front of Molly.

'How was that? I mean I know about the disaster, and the extraordinary work that was carried out by the Florentines in saving the city's treasures… What were they called again?' Molly asked.

'The Angeli del Fango… The Mud Angels… They performed miracles. But they weren't all from Florence. People from all over the world, including celebrities came to the city to help. The power of art…'

'Yes, I know… I have read newspaper articles about what happened, but I hadn't realised that the floods had such an impact on restoration techniques.'

'Are you joking, Molly? The impact was enormous. The most important change was the establishment of the Opificio delle Pietre Dure. An institute devoted to research on restoration.

But there were other influences such as people like Ugo Procacci, Umberto Baldini, Luisa Becherucci here in Florence, and Americans like Peter Waters who set new techniques and standards which were then followed everywhere in the world. It is impossible to overestimate the impact that the floods had on our particular field.'

'Was Maria around at that time?'

'Yes of course. She was very young at that time... In her early twenties. She had graduated top of her class, and had completed her post graduate studies a year before that November disaster. She worked directly for Baldini and Becherucci. She is revered here... She has legendary status for being there at the time of the floods, and being part of the ensuing redemption.'

'Wow... I really am walking in the shadow of greatness! I wonder what it was like back then when the flood hit the city. It must have been such a traumatic experience.'

'It was, Molly... People lost their lives... Much of the city was irreparably damaged... An enormous amount of art was lost forever, particularly the manuscripts from the library at Santa Croce. Ironically there are lots of books on the disaster... I think we have a number here. Doctore Vannini often delves into them, reminiscing about the past!'

'Do you mind if I borrow some of them. I would love to read about it.'

'Of course... The boss won't mind... In fact she would be delighted. It will give you something else to talk to her about! She loves reminiscing around that day in November of 1966.'

PART 10

FLORENCE
NOVEMBER 3RD 1966

I

Ludovico Vannini left his flat in the Via San Spirito early that morning with a noticeable spring in his step. He had found out the previous night that his wife Maria was pregnant with their first child. He walked down the Borgo San Frediano, where his mother's apartment was located, and then left towards the Ponte alla Carraia where his brother, Giovanni ran the family's newspaper kiosk. His brother was laying out the newspapers in almost exactly the same fashion as his mother had done twenty-five years previously. Each morning the twins would meet up at this time usually to discuss the failings of the city's football team Fiorentina, before Ludovico would then walk on to the bus station. However this time, the Viola would not come up in the conversation.

'Giovanni... Good morning... I tried calling you last night, but the phones were not working properly. It must be the weather. I've never seen so much rain fall in the last few weeks.'

'I know... The newspapers are full of it... Look, there's a report somewhere in one of them... Hold on... Ah here it is... Seventeen inches fell yesterday on Monte Falerona! That must be some kind of a record. Anyway... The weather is terrible for business... The papers become soaked as soon as I put them out even though they're under cover. Nobody is walking... I mean only a madman would come out in this.' Giovanni looked at his twin brother who had a broad grin on his face. 'Why the smile, Ludovico?'

'Well I thought you should know... Maria is pregnant!' Ludovico shouted, embracing his brother.

'Oh my God, that is fantastic, Ludovico... I can't believe it. I mean I didn't even know that you were trying. How is Maria?'

' We weren't... It was a surprise to both of us... She's fine... And very excited. The problem of course is her job. She's very busy with the restoration work at the Uffizi... And she is due a promotion. It's a bit of a problem... We need the money... But I'm sure things will work out. Listen, I haven't told Mama yet. Maria was adamant that I didn't tell anyone for the time being. It's too early, so keep this to yourself for God's sake,' Ludovico said laughing, unable to contain his joy.

'Of course not... Now speaking of work... Isn't it time that you should get going? The whole point, Ludovico, of public transport is that it operates on time... Not only are you going to be late, but you're now getting soaked.' Giovanni pushed his brother away jokingly, pointing to his watch. Ludovico nodded in agreement, and briskly walked through the rain over the Ponte alla Carraia towards the bus station.

Arriving at the via Santa Caterina da Siena, next to the Stazione Santa Maria Novella at nine, fifteen minutes later than scheduled, he clocked in his card and reported to the main inspector in charge.

'Pietro... Am I driving today? Or are we cancelling the public buses today. I wouldn't be surprised if all the roads become flooded later on if it doesn't stop raining. The Arno is already high.'

'No Ludovico... we are keeping the buses running as usual. We are receiving reports that in some villages... Figline Valdarno and in Montevarchi for instance, the flooding is getting really bad. But we are not expecting things to get too treacherous here... Anyway you're late, Ludovico!' Pietro

Rivera, the bus inspector walked towards Ludovico, and stood over his friend and employee. He was six feet six inches tall and was in charge of the city's bus service. He was however a gentle giant who would find it difficult to intimidate a flea, let alone Ludovico Vannini, with whom he went to school.

'My wife is pregnant... What do you want from me!' he blurted out, completely forgetting his promise to Maria to keep the news a secret. He waited for Pietro's expression to change.

'Really?' Pietro Rivera immediately showed surprise, knowing that his wife was very young, and extremely ambitious.

'Yes its true... I promise. Listen, it's a little soon for Maria, but we are both really happy.'

'Well... I'm thrilled, Ludovico... Congratulations then... Lets have a drink later when you get back!' He laughed, slightly bewildered by the news, and embraced his friend. He then paused and patted him on the back. 'Now go... And try and make up the lost time.' Pietro smiled.

The relationship between the Riveras and the Vanninis had lasted for many generations, both families living in the city and in close proximity. When the boys were at school, Pietro was bullied not only over his height, but also about his weight. He resembled a bean pole, and the other school children were merciless in teasing him. Ludovico, and indeed Giovanni, had been his protectors and fought many a playground battle defending him, for which Pietro would always be grateful.

Both Ludovico and Giovanni loved fighting at school. Thick set, and very strong, they were both feared and respected by the other children as they grew up. They could never be called bullies, since most of the scraps they got involved in, related to protecting the weaker children who were picked on. Pietro was not an exception. As the twins grew up, they became less pugnacious, and could even be described as being described as gentle. Ludovico, in particular, changed a great deal in early adulthood when he lost his job at the print works.

His relationship with Pietro had become diametrically opposite to what it had been at school when Ludovico was struggling to find a job. Pietro, who had attained a senior position in the public transport system wanted to repay his debt to his old friend by persuading the council to employ him over the other candidates, who were older and more qualified to drive the buses. Although successful, and Ludovico was extremely grateful, there was of course the continuing issue of controlling the new employee at work, which became increasingly problematic for Pietro. He had tried to tell Ludovico on a number of occasions that he had to comply with regulations, and not to take any liberties. These included him not wearing the uniform, turning up late, and most importantly being too familiar with his superiors. And yet there was a charm about Ludovico that managed to extricate him from getting into serious trouble. His sense of humour made him the most popular driver in the terminal, even with the bosses, and Pietro could do little to discipline him.

Sacking him was out of the question, so Pietro was resigned to having constantly, but gently, reprimanding him on his lack of professionalism. Ludovico used to react with expressions of surprise, and feigned innocence, but he knew the score, and as long as he didn't push things too far, he knew he would always get away with his behaviour. Life was too short for him to stick to the letter of the law, and Pietro knew that. Generally, the latter was happy to have his friend there, despite his public appearance. It did make work more fun. However, it was not about fun that morning and the tall inspector felt a real sense of relief when Ludovico had finally shown up, and had subsequently driven off. Only three out of the ten drivers reported for work that morning. Pietro was obviously aware of the weather, but had not fully appreciated the dire situation people were already facing out of town.

2

Being two hundred and forty kilometres in length the Arno is the longest and largest river in Tuscany. Originating on Mount Falterona in the Apennines as a gentle stream, it gathers pace in a southerly direction and then weaves westward towards Arezzo, and through Florence to Pisa, finally flowing into the Ligurian Sea at Marina Di Pisa. It is normally a relatively calm river, and yet historically it had acted in an unpredictable and sometimes malevolent way. It was no coincidence that Dante Alighieri had called it 'La maladetta e sventurata fossa', the cursed and unlucky ditch.

Between 1177 and 1761 the river flooded on fifty-four occasions, thirty of which were considered to be very serious events. The chronicler Villani was a witness to three of these floods, in 1269, 1288 and 1333, the latter auspiciously occurring on November 4th. On that occasion the Old, Carraia and Santa Trinita bridges were washed away as the river swept into the city unchecked, destroying many of the buildings. Over three metres of water drowned the city centre. The river then seemed to have retreated as quickly as it arrived, leaving the city's shops and underground vaults full of water, reeking with rotten scum and mud. The numerous tragic flooding events in the mid Sixteenth Century, described by the chroniclers Segni, Adriani and Ammirato, were of a similar nature. They tell of the river becoming a torrent, flowing unimpeded into the city, frightening the inhabitants, and causing death and destruction. The ancient Ponte di Santa Trinita was once again one of its victims in 1557, which led to the building of Ammannati's beautiful new bridge that Gerhard Wolf had tried so desperately hard to save, but failed, in 1944.

On November 3rd 1844, the most recent major flood to date, was yet another warning to the Florentines that the Arno was a capricious river and one that would continue to threaten the city. On that occasion it was reported, without exaggeration that inhabitants rowed in boats along the Via Maggio to reach their destinations. The authorities did a great deal to help and alleviate the anguish of the people, including Duke Leopold II who provided food, clothes and shelter. Indeed he even allowed some people to reside in his royal estate.

Decades after this great flood, a programme was developed to ensure that future floods would have limited impact. Between 1865 and 1870, when Florence was temporarily the capital of Italy, architects and designers planned to reconstruct the city centre. They made efforts to create buildings that were less vulnerable to flooding, as well straightening the course of the Arno at certain points. The riverbank walls were also reinforced. Memories of 1844 in time began to fade as the threat of a future flood had seemingly been resolved.

The history of the Arno was therefore, if not at the forefront of their minds, well known to the people of Florence. They were aware of its behaviour, and yet on that November 3rd morning, after two months of unseasonal rainfall, and more immediately after three days of torrential downpours, nobody appeared to be that concerned about the situation. Ludovico drove his bus as usual, stopping at all the bus stops on the Via De Cerretani, around the Piazza Del Duomo, along the Via Del Proconsul, and finally down the Borgo Dei Greci, just before Piazza Santa Croce. However the trip that morning took him almost two hours instead of the normal one. Here, at the Santa Croce, where the bus finished its outward route before returning to the Piazza Santa Maria Novella, he saw that the flooding was beginning to take a sinister hold on the city.

3

Ludovico stepped off the bus outside the Santa Croce church and looked around him. This was the site of the lowest lying part of the city, most vulnerable to flooding. People were still going about their business despite water starting to pool over the square and along the gutters. The drains were clearly full, since none of the water was being drained away. He hurried across into the church to see his old friend, Father Gustavo Cocci, and saw the frenzied activity that was taking hold of some of the administrators who looked after the historic building. Father Cocci, who was responsible for the church, the museum and the Capella Dei Pazzi at the back of the complex of Santa Croce, tried to calm the growing hysteria by maintaining an appearance of authority and calmness.

'The cellars are flooding... Go down there now... We have to start moving things quickly!' he told one of the monks who was panicking by the door.

'Ludovico! I haven't got time to chat I'm afraid... You can see it's all a bit of a panic here. The water in the basement is beginning to flood. Maybe you can help us?' he asked, looking at Ludovico. The old Father, had been close to the Vannini family for years. He had baptised both Giovanni and Ludovico, and remained good friends with their mother.

'Yes of course, Father. You know you don't need to ask.' Ludovico then followed Father Cocci down the stairs to the cellars. There he saw the growing crisis that was happening in front of his very own eyes. The water level was at least a foot high, and rising quickly. Everything seemed to be happening at an accelerated pace. People were shouting and screaming at each other as they tried to move art objects hundreds of years old, to places of greater safety. Concern was also now rising for the Biblioteca Nazionale, located next door where hundreds of thousands of books and manuscripts were vulnerable to the rising water.

Ludovico, after helping for two hours, by which time the water had reached their waists, left to return to the bus. As he left the church the growing threat of a catastrophe was becoming a reality. Manhole covers were being thrown from their positions by powerful jets of water that had nowhere else to go except into the air and onto the streets due to the failure of the drainage system. People in the area however appeared unconcerned, and were taking shelter or going home where they would either wait until the rain stopped, or simply stay there for the extended weekend. The following day was a national holiday, the Giorno delle Forzo Armate, where the country celebrated the ceasefire between Italy and the Austro Hungarian Empire. He quickly made his way to a public telephone box.

'Pietro? Can you hear me? It's a bad line? Hello?'

'Yes I can hear you, Ludovico... Where are you? You should have been back hours ago.'

'I'm at Santa Croce... Its terrible here... The water is rising... The drains are blocked and water is being sprayed on to the streets... The cellars and basements are flooding.'

'I've heard it's very bad, but why haven't you returned? There are people waiting for transport back.'

'Forgive me Pietro. I needed to help Father Cocci. I will come back as soon as possible.'

'It's going to get a lot worse, Ludovico. People need to get home. Engineers have reported to us that the Levane and Penna Dams in Valdarno are discharging vast amounts of water towards Florence. I know Santa Croce at the moment is very bad, but even where you live in the San Frediano area there are problems at the basement level... All the low lying areas of the city are in danger of flooding.'

'God, my mother is there now... I have to see if she's all right.'

'I know, Ludovico, just get the bus back here as soon as possible... And then you should go home... The city will hopefully suspend all bus transportation in one hour... If they don't, I will... Even in this part of town where at the moment it's not so badly affected.'

Ludovico ran back to the bus. He suddenly noticed for the first time that his trousers were soaked up to his waist. He had been so involved in helping Father Cocci that he had not noticed. He climbed into the bus and drove it as quickly as he could to the station. Stopping at all the stops, the bus was jam packed as he arrived back at the terminus.

'The roads are really dangerous, Pietro, but there are people still driving seemingly not realising the dire situation.'

'I know, Ludovico... But there are warnings everywhere. Listen, it's up to them... If they want to ignore the radio and television, and indeed ourselves, then it's their risk... You should go home as quickly as possible.' Pietro turned away, and walked towards the other drivers who had just arrived at the station. Ludovico set off towards his neighbourhood.

The twenty-five foot walls that stood on the banks of the river gave the Florentines a false sense of security, notwithstanding the height of the river already being considerably above its normal levels. By now it was mid afternoon, and he had three concerns on his mind. His mother's safety living in a first floor flat on the Borgo San Frediano, his wife's well being given that she was working in the basement of the Uffizi where the art restoration work usually took place, and Giovanni's security at the newspaper kiosk which was vulnerable being on the corner of the Lungarno Soderini and the Ponte alla Carraia.

4

Ludovico crossed the Carraia, surprised like Pietro at the number of people still going about their business in the normal way. Arriving at the kiosk, Giovanni was closing up.

'Thank God it's a holiday tomorrow... The rain shows no sign of stopping, and I can't sell a packet of cigarettes let alone a newspaper,' Giovanni said, bolting the shutters closed.

'I hear bad things Giovanni. Both the dams at the Valdarno are under strain, releasing tons of uncontrolled water. They're under pressure to open them... And if they do, God knows what will happen. Nobody here seems to be that worried, apart from Pietro at the bus station who suspended the transport for the day,' Ludovico said, looking out to the river. 'Look how high it's getting.' He pointed to the menacing level of the Arno that afternoon.

'I can see... Where are you going now?' Giovanni asked, putting the umbrella over both of them.

'To see Mama... She's at home, but I couldn't get hold of her. I just want to see if she's ok, and she has enough food for the long weekend.'

'I'll come with you.'

The twins walked briskly down the Lungarno Soderini, reaching the old remains of the three sided Chiesa di Santa Maria. Ludovico told his brother about his morning, and the events at Santa Croce. Passing through into the Borgo San

Frediano, they reached the building where Francesca Vannini lived.

'Ludovico, you go up to the flat, and I will pick up some food and other necessities, and I will see you up there in half an hour.'

Giovanni bought enough food for a week. Some of the shops were closing early, not because of the weather, but because of the holiday. Many shopkeepers were moaning that their basements were starting to flood, and some were bringing stock up to the shop floor to protect the produce. His final visit was to the off licence, next door to his mother's flat.

'I'll take six bottles of Aqua Panna, and six San Pellegrino please Carlo. I'll also have a crate of the Chianti.'

'No problem, Giovanni... Having a party then tomorrow?' the shopkeeper asked.

'My mother is having us over for lunch to celebrate the Arms Forces Day... I wish the weather would improve though.'

'Tell me about it... Look over there.' He pointed towards the back door where crates of bottles were stacked up. 'They're from the cellar... The flooding is quite bad this time.'

'Aren't you a bit worried? My brother tells me that at Santa Croce, the water is up to their wastes in the basements.'

'No... The rain will stop soon. Listen, the river can't breach its banks... Those walls were specifically built for this type of problem.'

'I'm not so sure...' Giovanni replied.

'Well, we are... We have to be... Have a good weekend, Giovanni' He paused as Giovanni turned and left the shop in a resigned fashion. 'Hey!' he shouted at his customer. 'And stop worrying.' The shopkeeper laughed as Giovanni disappeared. He then stopped smiling, and started to think about what Giovanni had said. He turned around, and shouted to his young assistants. 'Go downstairs and bring everything upstairs... Not just the drinks... Everything!'

Giovanni left the shop. It was now early evening and the rain continued to pour down relentlessly on the Renaissance city. He saw what his brother saw in Santa Croce. The drains were not functioning, being full to capacity, and unable to take in any more water. The gutters were full of gushing water, beginning to resemble small streams. If Ludovico was right, and the dams at Levane and La Penna did breach, then there could be a disaster. He looked down the Borgo towards the Chiesa di Santa Maria, just being able to see through the murkiness, the outline of the southern wall standing proud in the rain. A thought immediately crossed his mind, if the river did burst its banks, that the church might be a central point for the flood waters. It could finally be susceptible to collapse if the water weakened the foundations of the walls.

5

Maria Russo was considered the brightest star in a galaxy of talent in the Department of Restoration at the Uffizi Gallery. Her career path had been an accelerated one, and at the age of twenty-four, she was already considered one of the leading experts in the museum on Renaissance art restoration. Her life up until this point had been one of uninterrupted success. Top at school in all her exams she gained a scholarship, a year early, to study Italian Literature at the University of Bologna. After completing her degree she embarked on a Masters in Conservation and Restoration.

She returned to Florence, still only twenty-two, where there was no shortage of job offers waiting for her. Her parents, both doctors at the Santa Maria Nuova Hospital, persuaded Maria, without too much difficulty, into taking an offer from the Uffizi. There she would be allowed to pursue a doctorate in Art Conservation and Restoration part time, as well as work under the renowned experts of the age including Procacci, Baldini and Becherucci. After attaining her doctorate a year early, she impressed her employers, to such an extent that she received an immediate promotion in the following year. Her parents pride at their daughter's success was threatened by her sudden interest in a certain young bus driver, Ludovico Vannini.

She had met him when taking a ride home one afternoon. Maria had rushed from work, needing to be back for dinner, and joined the back of a queue waiting to get on the newly arrived bus. Ludovico was in one of his more jovial moods and told her that there was no room on the bus just as she had reached the open doors. She looked across through the windows and saw that the vehicle had plenty of vacant seats. She was about to launch a verbal attack on the driver, before realising that he was only joking. He then beckoned her on. He was attracted to her, but immediately sensed that she might be out of his league, both socially and indeed intellectually.

'Come on then... I haven't all day... Some of us have timetables to keep to.'

'I was about to launch into a tirade... What kind of driver are you?' she asked giving him her money.

'A humorous one... Well I try and be funny,' he replied seeing there was very little empathy.

'Well... I don't find you at all amusing.' She took her change and walked to the back of the bus, now smiling but not letting him see.

Since Ludovico drove the same route most days, the two met quite often. He tried to make her laugh whenever the opportunity arose. One trick he played, which was particularly frustrating for Maria, would be where he pretended to drive away just as she had arrived at the bus stop. It was during one of these pranks that the relationship took on a different dimension from one that simply depended on her taking his bus. Maria was, as usual late going home and raced across to the stop. She then saw Ludovico drive past her. She waved frantically, but in so doing fell over on to the pavement.

Ludovico pulled the bus over, jumped out of his seat, and raced to Maria, who was by now gingerly brushing herself down.

'Are you all right?'

'Yes I'm fine.' She looked up at Ludovico. 'Don't tell me that you have actually stopped the bus for me!'

'Well... Yes of course... I wanted to make sure you were ok... Are you?'

'Yes I'm fine.' Maria replied smiling. She looked at him differently. No longer in the bus, he was no longer simply the man who drove it. He became a different person in her eyes, and she saw something in him that she liked.

'Come on... I can't be late otherwise my boss, Pietro will go crazy.' He ushered her on the bus, and sat her down near the front. From that moment they developed a relationship which in turn became a romance that eventually led to marriage. This was something that Maria's parents were unhappy about. Ludovico, despite being a charming, perfectly amiable young man, fell short of their expectations for their only daughter. However Maria was determined to marry him, and convinced her parents that he was the right man for her. Francesca conversely was obviously delighted with the match. She knew that her elder twin son could do no better and privately agreed with her new in laws that Ludovico was a lucky man.

6

Maria had mixed feelings about being pregnant. She walked through the rain that morning flooded with thoughts on how she could best combine her work with having a baby. Initially, when finding out, she wanted to have an abortion. Although strictly forbidden, she really didn't care what the Pope thought. Unknown to her, Francesca, her mother in law, had faced a similar dilemma thirty years earlier and also had questioned what to do. However in those days Francesca had even less choice than Maria now faced. The latter felt that her work was far too important, and her career much too precious to be raising a family. She also believed that she was too young. Yet after seeing Ludovico's reaction to the news, she knew that she had little option, and made the same decision as Francesca had done, albeit for different reasons.

She marched through the Ponte Vecchio, towards the museum deciding that she would remain quiet about her condition for the time being. Entering the Gallery's side entrance, she checked through the minimal security, and went downstairs to the basement where some of the finest artworks lay. Her work at that moment was restoring *The Coronation of the Virgin* by Filippo Lippi. A single panel divided into three sections, the main one depicting a throng of various biblical figures, angels and saints. Christ and the kneeling Madonna dominate the image, painted in perspective in front of a blue striped sky symbolizing paradise. It was one of the great treasures of the Uffizi. To be given responsibility over such a work was proof in itself on how highly regarded she had become in the museum.

'Good morning Maria… How are you this wet morning?' Umberto Baldini, the head of the department asked her as she arrived.

'Wet, Signor Baldini… Very wet!' She laughed as she took off her raincoat and hung it on the coat rail.

'I know… God only knows when it's going to stop. How are you getting on with *The Coronation of the Virgin?*'

'I'm very happy so far. Its painfully slow… But I think we should have it ready for display in the summer… Why? Is there any problem?'

'No… Not at all.' Baldini paused for a moment. 'The basement here at the Uffizi is extremely vulnerable to flooding, Maria. If things continue like this tomorrow, I might have to ask you to come in, and help move the art upstairs. I'm not suggesting that such a catastrophe might happen, but just in case there's a problem, I want you to be aware.'

'I understand completely,' Maria replied, slightly bemused. She never considered the possibility of a flood, even after noticing that the level of the Arno was extremely high, and that it had not stopped raining for days.

During the day Maria worked on the Lippi's *Coronation,* barely stopping for lunch. She could hear the rain incessantly fall, tapping on the window panes above her, without respite. The words of Baldini that morning kept repeating themselves in her mind. Questions raced through her mind. What if the basements did flood? What would we do? She looked around her, at the other restorers who were working on masterpieces such as Masaccio's *Madonna St Juvenal,* Giotto's *Badi* polyptich, Botticelli's *Coronation,* and two Simone Martinis from the Berenson collection. She understood that everything on the basement and mezzanine levels were vulnerable and could easily get damaged. What she didn't realise at the time was that those masterpieces located on the ground floor as well would become vulnerable too.

7

Maria arrived home, early in the evening at their apartment in Via San Spirito and seeing that Ludovico was not in, rang his mother, who always knew where her son was.

'Yes he's here... He was worried about me. Maria, you're so lucky to have married him... He's such a caring man,' Francesca replied, mischievously knowing how irritated her daughter would get hearing her sing his praises.

'Yes... I agree... He is simply adorable. Can I speak to him?' Maria immediately felt relief that Ludovico had obviously not told his mother of the pregnancy, otherwise she would not have stopped talking to her and giving advice.

'Hello... Maria?'

'Ah... Nice of you to be waiting at home for me, Ludovico... I've had to walk across the city in the pouring rain... I thought you might have picked me up?'

'Oh... I'm sorry... But I thought it might be too dangerous to drive.'

'You are a bus driver, Ludovico... Its only rain for God's sake.'

'The buses were suspended this afternoon... And I thought if it was too dangerous to drive them... Then maybe I shouldn't dive the Cinquecento.'

'Unbelievable... I trust that you haven't told your mother about...'

'No... Of course not. I haven't told a soul... I promise.' Ludovico immediately felt a sinking feeling in his stomach. Giovanni was not the most discreet of brothers despite being warned, and Pietro had not been told that it was still a secret.

'Good... Now then... Shall I come straight to your mother's?'

'Yes... Good idea. Come over now. I have tickets for the cinema tonight... *Who's afraid of Virginia Wolf* is showing.'

'Oh Good... I've been wanting to see that since the summer. I will see you in a minute.' She replaced the receiver, and walked over to the window. It was pitch black outside, but she could hear the rain fall. She wandered into her bedroom where she turned on the radio. The mayor, Piero Bargellini, was being interviewed about tomorrow, Armed Forces Day, and was expressing his concern that the rain would play an unwelcome part in the day's events. Banners and flags were under strain from the wind and the water, and were unlikely to remain fixed if the weather did not improve. Maria laughed. 'How absurd to be worried about flags, when the greatest creations by mankind were at risk all around the city,' she said out loud, before turning off the radio and going out to her mother in law.

8

As Maria arrived at the front door of Francesca's apartment block, Giovanni was returning from the supermarket with bags of food and drink for his mother. When he saw Maria, he hurriedly put down the bags and opened his arms to greet her in a warm hug. Maria immediately suspected that Giovanni had been told of the pregnancy.

'Oh! Giovanni… I saw you only last night! Why the warm embrace?'

'Ludovico told me the wonderful news… I'm so happy for you…'

'So he told you then… So much for keeping things a secret. He was meant to keep it to himself for another six weeks. I knew it was too much to ask.'

'Don't blame him… He's only told me… And I won't tell anyone… Not even Mama.' Giovanni smiled. He had an enduring charm that never left him. It was extremely hard to ever become angry at the younger of the twins.

'Giovanni, I swear, if it wasn't for you, I would have killed your brother at least ten times since we got married!' She laughed. 'Do you need a hand with those?' Maria looked at the carrier bags that were now drenched in water.

'No, no… just take the keys and open the door. The old lift is still working… I can manage.' Giovanni gave the keys to Maria, and she opened the door.

Arriving in the flat, Ludovico was horrified that Giovanni had come in with his wife. It was inevitable that his brother had congratulated her, and he had no time to repair the damage. Maria marched in and pulled her husband gently to one side.

'Is there anyone else that you have told?'

'No one I swear, Maria... Not even my mother,' Ludovico said quietly.

'Are you sure... You don't want me to find out that there is someone else who knows... You understand, Ludovico?'

'Absolutely darling... But I swear that there is not a soul who knows, apart from me... And Giovanni, of course,' Ludovico said in a rather unconvincing manner. Maria's fiery temper was not something one would want to play with. He knew that if he had told her that Pietro was aware of her pregnancy, he would have had the full force of her fury vented at him.

'Are you all ready?' Francesca asked, putting on her raincoat ready to leave.

'Yes... Yes, we are of course... Come along, Maria, we mustn't miss the start... You know my mother is a slow walker.' Ludovico said leading the way.

The four Vanninis left the apartment and walked slowly through the sheets of rain down the Borgo San Frediano towards the cinema located in the Via Del Leone. As always they stopped briefly at the Chiesa di Santa Maria when passing by the church. Standing under three umbrellas, Maria and Francesca shared one making it easier for the latter to hold on to her daughter in law whilst walking, they looked at the decrepit structure. The three walls clung grimly to their foundations. There was something magnificent about the old structure still standing, undefeated by the vicissitudes of war and weather.

'I don't know why nobody in the council hasn't knocked the old church down... I mean why do they ignore it?' Giovanni said in a melancholic tone.

'We have this discussion every time we stop here. It's a

Renaissance building… Well what left of it is… the museum has spoken to the council, telling them they should look at restoring the walls rather than knock them down. We get the same response…'No money!' Maria replied.

'I find it strange that the southern wall is slightly thicker than the others… Look.' Ludovico pointed to the wall that contained Masaccio's fresco protected by Denon's additional skin.

'Yes… You know I noticed that during the war, and completely forgot about it. Your father once told me an old wive's tale about there being a magnificent fresco that adorned one of the walls… But the French took it during the Napoleonic wars.' Francesca paused and stood still remembering, always remembering, what she went through and what she endured whilst pushed against that same southern wall. 'Come… we will be late.' Francesca tugged Maria's arm, as the four made their way to the cinema, once again pushing the question of why the south wall was thicker than the others, to the back of their minds.

9

The cinemas across the city were full that night. This was normal given that the following day was a national holiday. Nobody in the audiences had any idea of the amount of water that was falling down on Florence that evening. Unremittingly pouring, the rain showed no sign of abating. The film ended at 10:30, and Giovanni Vannini, after leaving both his mother and brother at their apartments in San Frediano and San Spirito, walked to his own home on the Via Guicciardini. It was around eleven when he walked up the stairs leading to his front door. However, before finding his keys he was interrupted by the sound of footsteps coming down the stairs.

'What's going on? Where are you going?' Giovanni asked, surprised at seeing his upstairs neighbours, with two suitcases, running past him.

'I can't talk, Giovanni. I've been tipped off by one of our watchmen at the Ponte Vecchio that the water is only a meter below the tops of the arches. I have to get my stock out of the shop before it floods,' Umberto Cesare replied. He was one of the jewellers who had a store on the bridge. A number of these shop owners, particularly the jewellers and goldsmiths, paid for watchmen to see if there were any problems in the city at night. Usually they were meant to guard against burglaries but tonight was different. Clearly the height of the river caused enough concern for one of these watchmen to start warning the shop owners.

'That sounds very high... Are you sure he said that?' Giovanni replied disbelievingly.

'I'm not taking any chances... I will see you when I get back.'

Giovanni shrugged, and turned towards his front door, and promptly poured himself a large whisky. He sat back, and turned on the radio, and gently fell into a deep sleep. His slumber was rudely disturbed by the noise from outside his front door. He got up, and opened it to find both Umberto Cesare and his wife Luciana, shouting at each other, hauling three suitcases up the stairs to their own apartment.

'Well? What happened?' Giovanni asked.

'It's a total catastrophe out there, Giovanni. We arrived at the bridge. It was blocked by gangs of youths, threatening us, hoping to take advantage of the situation. The Carabinieri were not at all helpful. We managed to pass through the thugs... There was a lot of pushing and shoving... And opened the shop. We grabbed what we could... But it wasn't everything. God what we have left there...'

'Was it really necessary... Is the water that high? Is the bridge in danger?' Giovanni asked incredulously.

'The whole bridge was shaking... We could hear the water gushing underneath us... Tree branches, heavy ones were charging across the bridge smashing into the shop fronts. There were bloated carcasses of animals being thrown about. The water was everywhere.'

'My God... What about the Carabinieri? They must have done something.'

'They were just screaming at us to get off the bridge... But they were not under any orders... They just kept saying...'We have no orders; it's on your heads!'...'

Giovanni helped them with one of the suitcases up to the next floor. He looked at his watch as he left them. It was four o'clock in the morning. For the first time that night he realised that there was a possibility that his newspaper kiosk, located on the corner of the Lugarno Soderini and the Ponte alla Carraia, was in danger of being washed away if the rain continued. In reality, it was not a possibility, but almost a certainty. Unbeknown to him at this time the E.N.E.L, the hydroelectric authority, to relieve the pressure had ordered both the La Penna Dam, and then further south, the Levane Dam at Valdarno to be opened. As a result, up to five thousand cubic meters of water per second was discharged towards Florence at a speed of sixty kilometres per hour. The amount of water heading down the Arno that would eventually drown the Renaissance city would be estimated at a mind boggling four hundred million cubic metres. Florence was now doomed.

10

The phone rang waking both Ludovico and Maria from their slumber. It was 6:45, and it was still pitch black outside.

'Hello… Who is it?' Ludovico asked, worried that something had happened to his mother.

'It's me… Giovanni.'

'It's quarter to seven and it's a holiday, for God's sake… What is it? Is Mama all right?' he asked.

'Yes… I assume she's fine but… Have you looked outside… The city is going under… Literally.' His brother said in a cold tone.

'What are you talking about, Giovanni…' Ludovico took the phone with its extension, and walked into the sitting room, over to its window and pulled back the curtain. It was too dark to discern anything. However he could hear, if not see, the water. The sound was not one of tapping rain on the pavement, but one of a torrent gushing through the city streets. It was the noise of the Arno, mixed with torrential rain, already breaching the Lungarno Guicciardini and threatening to swallow the Ponte Santa Trinita.

'My God… The Kiosk… Giovanni, you better leave and see what you can salvage. I'll get dressed and meet you… Wait… I'm going to move the car away from the river.'

'Ok I will see you at your block in thirty minutes.' Giovanni replaced the receiver, fearing that something catastrophic was about to happen.

Ludovico returned to the bedroom and saw that Maria was already up and in the bathroom.

'What are you doing... You are meant to be in bed. It's a national holiday... Come Maria... You need some rest. In your condition.'

'Ludovico, for goodness sake... I'm only eight weeks pregnant. I feel fine. But I want to get up and see what's happening. Can you hear that noise?'

'I'm going to move the car and then help Giovanni with the kiosk... It might not survive, and we should try and salvage what we can.'

'I agree... Come on then.' Maria was not going to return to bed.

At that moment, the phone rang again and Maria, this time was first to the phone.

'Hello... Maria Vannini speaking.'

'Maria, it's Luisa Becherucci here.' There was a pause. Maria breathed in deeply. She had never spoken to the director of the museum before, and she immediately knew that whatever it was, something serious was developing at the museum.

'Oh hello... How can I help?'

'Maria, I'm sorry to disturb you so early, and on a national holiday, but we have a very serious problem here. I am ringing you to see if you can come in with the other restorers to help move the art from the basement and mezzanine to higher floors. Indeed we might have to move works from the ground floor.'

'Of course... I will come... How bad is it?'

'Well Ugo and Umberto have told me that water is already coming into the basement which is rare indeed. It's going to get worse. The mayor's office and the civil engineering department have told us that they are expecting severe flooding across the city.'

'I will be there within the hour, Signora Becherucci.' Maria put the phone down. She took a deep breath. If Ugo Procacci, the superintendent of fine arts, and Umberto Baldini, not to mention the director of the Uffizi herself, were already at the museum, the situation must be critical. She looked at her husband.

'It's really bad... They've called me to the museum. Everyone is worrying about the basements... There's so much art there that's vulnerable to water damage.'

'Do you want to go straight there, or do you want to come with me first, check on my mother and then help Giovanni secure the kiosk?'

'I'll come with you, but I won't have time to help with the kiosk. I will go over the Carraia and back along the Lungarno Corsini. It will give me a chance to see how bad things are in the city.'

Ludovico glanced at his watch... It was seven-twenty. 'Quickly then... I still have to move the car, and Giovanni will be waiting outside. Hurry up Maria. 'I'm going downstairs.' At that moment the phone rang for a third time.

'Hello... Pietro, what is it?'

'Ludovico... Things are getting critical. All transport has been suspended until further notice. The national holiday events will not be taking place. You know, one man has already died at the Alconella water plant. The water is rising rapidly... We are not even sure that the Vecchio will survive. If you want to help... Go to your friend, Father Cocci, at Santa Croce. I believe the church complex is in a critical state.'

'I'm on my way to help my brother at the kiosk. After we have dealt with that, we will go there together... What's it like at Santa Maria Novella?'

'The river here is going to break its banks at any minute... I fear the worse,' Pietro said in a desperate tone.

Ludovico was about to respond, but the phone went dead. Power in the city that morning suddenly shut down and Florence was alone at the mercy of the Arno. It was seven twenty six.

11

Ludovico raced downstairs, and ran through the blanket of rain to his car that was parked next to the riverbank. Already the rain was forming streams in the gutters that were washing around the wheels of the parked cars. He got into his Cinquecento and drove it four hundred yards to park on slightly higher ground near the Pitti Palace. He then rushed back to his block, meeting Giovanni and Maria outside, before wading down the Via Santa Spirito. The water was rapidly rising, already reaching their ankles. After checking on Francesca, and telling her not to leave her first floor flat on the Borgo San Frediano under any circumstances, they proceeded back via the Chiesa di Santa Maria towards the Ponte alla Carraia where Giovanni's kiosk was located. The church appeared through the gloom as they approached. Standing strong, the three walls were already collecting debris which had been washed up into the semi enclosed space.

'God... Look there are bicycles and tables... Remains of tree trunks... It's already unbelievable,' Ludovico said, looking at the debris that was already piling up against the walls.

'Yes... It might be quite protective for the Borgo San Frediano... The old church walls might act as a defence against big objects... Even cars... Being thrown down the street,' Giovanni said. 'Come on... we have to get to the kiosk.'

They arrived at Giovanni's stall, which surprisingly was

not flooded. Located on the slope of the bridge and Lungarno Soderini, it was relatively undamaged. Indeed stacks of La Nazionale newspapers had been left by the kiosk. Giovanni picked them up. He read out the headline to his brother and sister in law. "*L'Arno Staripa a Firenze*"... It's already predicting what's going to happen... that The Arno will overflow in Florence. The water is already streaming over the embankments... This was already at five o'clock this morning.'

'Carry on Giovanni... What else does it say?' Maria asked impatiently.

'It says that the river burst its banks at Rovezzano and Compiobbi at one o'clock this morning... The Via Villamagna and the Alconella water plant is already under water... At 4:30 the military were ordered to stand by.'

'When did they print this?' Ludovico asked, astonished that the news was so quick and recent.

'La Nazionale has just moved into brand new offices with state of the art printing presses... The most advanced in Europe. They can get the papers out now in hours but the machinery is all located in the basement... They'll also be ruined,' Giovanni said as he put the papers inside the kiosk.

'There is not much we can do here, Giovanni. It looks like the kiosk will be ok... Make sure its locked up and securely fastened. I'm going to Santa Croce to help... Maria, I will walk you to the Uffizi, on the way.'

'I will meet you there at Santa Croce... I'm going to take the more valuable periodicals, and tourist souvenirs and take them to Mama's flat,' Giovanni said.

Ludovico took Maria over the Ponte alla Carraia. The river had become a torrent roaring through the arches. The bridge was passable, but the water was so high that it was crashing over the top. The Lungarno Corsini was a different matter; it was completely submerged so they took a detour through the Piazza san Giovanni and the Piazza del Duomo.

It was now approaching nine, and although the areas around the Duomo and the Baptistry, and the Piazza della Signoria were still dry it would not be long before the waters reached there.

12

Maria arrived at the Uffizi to be greeted by Umberto Baldini. There were twelve restorers who had managed to turn up for work that morning. They began the rescue attempt immediately working from the bottom of the building and moving upwards. Once in the basement, Maria immediately realised that the crisis was far worse than she thought. The water had damaged the central heating tanks all over the city. The city had still got its electricity from these oil tanks that were located under the buildings. The Uffizi was no exception. The greasy black oil mixed with the mud and other pollutants became a deadly concoction. The water everywhere began to turn from a brown muddy colour to a thick red-grey fast-moving slick.

'Signor Baldini, where do we start?' she asked.

'We have to move the most important works first... There are over three hundred paintings down here. And... It's not just water damage... Look!' He thrust his hand out at her showing the oil droplets that clung to her palms and fingers.

'My God, everything will be destroyed,' she cried.

'I know... I know... Listen, the Masaccio, the Botticelli and the Giotto... And of course the Lippi which you are cleaning... Must go up straight away.' Baldini spoke with authority. He had been working there for some time that morning, and was soaked to the skin. Wrapped in blankets, he and Maria worked tirelessly throughout the morning and early afternoon. Luisa Becherucci, the director, was working mainly on the mezzanine and ground floors. She had been there all night saving the artwork, strictly adhering to her policy of saving the most important first.

The Uffizi operation provided a mirror image of what was happening in many museums around the city. It was reported that Maria Luisa Bonelli, the curator of the Museo della Scienza, walked outside along the second floor ledge, smashing through the window, where the water level was rapidly rising to, and grabbed Galileo's telescope, bringing it to safety along with other extremely valuable objects. However the miracles being performed by these extraordinary people could not be replicated everywhere.

At ten o'clock the water, thick with mud and covered by the dark scum of oil, overran the Piazza san Giovanni and Piazza del Duomo. It became a torrential deluge, similar to an urban Congo. As in the basement of the Uffizi, the colour of the water had turned to a sinister grey-red confluent. There was no one who could stop the five panels from Ghiberti's *Gates of Paradise* being ripped off the doors. The very same panels that Ghiberti and his brilliant workshop, had designed and created five hundred and twenty years earlier. Now, *The Creation of Adam and Eve, Original Sin, The Story of Esau,* and *Jacob and Joseph* were reduced to sunken bronze slabs drifting somewhere under the black water.

And it wasn't just Ghiberti's bronze wonders that were damaged. Pisano's South door lost three panels and its frame. The level of the water was now approaching three feet, and the flooding of the Baptistry itself meant that Donatello's wooden statue of Mary Magdalene was destroyed. The Museo dell'Opera del Duomo was also a major casualty, with Brunelleschi's famous wooden model for the Cupola of Santa Maria del Fiore being lost forever.

However, it was the low lying areas of Florence that would be most severely affected. Ludovico now joined by Giovanni, arrived at one of the lowest areas, Santa Croce, at around the same time as the Ghiberti's bronze panels were being ripped away from their Renaissance doors. The brothers looked across the piazza, and immediately realised that they could not make it to the entrance of the church. Almost twenty feet above the pavement, the polluted water, laced with nafta, Florentine heating oil, was roaring around the area. The whole Santa Croce area had become a foul and fetid lake with upturned cars, motor cycles floating and dead animal carcases floating on the surface.

Crossing the street before the piazza, Ludovico noticed a furniture shop where the door and windows were shattered. He climbed in and took a table top that was trapped in the store. It was large enough for both of them. The two brothers got on the 'raft', and paddled feverishly through the piazza to the church. The doors of the church were wide open, and the two brothers careered into the church at speed. There they saw a situation that was almost unsalvageable. The water level was sixteen feet high in the church. The sarcophagi of Machiavelli, Michelangelo and Galileo were now submerged in water. They called out for Father Cocci, but there was no reply. It was impossible to see much, and the sound from the gushing water was deafening. The church resembled an apocalyptic vision.

13

The two brothers made their way towards Cappella dei Pazzi, an exquisite chapel located at the back of the Santa Croce complex constructed by Arnolfo di Cambio and Filippo Brunelleschi. There they saw thousands of dark blue bundles bobbing up and down. These were manuscripts that had floated through the broken doors of the Biblioteca Nazionale next door. At that time they had no idea of the extent of the damage to hundreds of thousands of books in the library itself. The irony of the catastrophe that destroyed these books was that the library was built on the river bank as a precaution against a potential fire.

They finally saw the Father. He was crouched in a rubber dingy he had taken from the sports shop, and like the Vanninis, was using it as a raft to navigate the church.

'Come with me, boys... I need you over here.' Father Cocci was relieved to see the Vannini brothers arrive. He was fighting a losing battle to save anything. 'There is nothing you can do here. The books and manuscripts are lost for ever. There's much more at stake elsewhere. We have to go next door to the museum... Quickly!' he shouted desperately. The old refectory that was now the Museo dell'Opera di Santa Croce, had doors that were over fourteen feet high. The waters covered the frame. It was impossible to get in.

'What now, Father?' Giovanni asked.

'We have to wait until the water recedes... My God there

are masterpieces in there that need to be rescued. Some of them are downstairs waiting to be hung in the chapel... Cimabue's crucifix is one of them.' He then tried to squeeze through the entry but there was no way he could do that at the present time. As they waited there for three hours they were joined by a number of monks shivering, trapped in a dark room filled with polluted water and flotsam. They all knew that the damage would be disastrous to the collection that was being held in the adjacent museum.

Finally by mid afternoon, the water, although not receding, had calmed down somewhat, and Father Cocci now felt that he could attempt to gain entry into the Museum. The old cleric, together with his senior priests, were the first in, and what he saw confirmed his greatest fears. The gigantic painted crucifix by Cimabue, the father of Florentine painting and Giotto's predecessor, was one of the crucial works of the early Italian Renaissance. The tortured head and the vulnerable body of Christ on the crucifix had been exposed to the water and oil, which meant that large sections of the image were no longer there. More importantly the gesso that Cimabue used to bond the plaster and paint to the wood was being dissolved by the toxic water. As the water receded, the plaster and paint were coming off and were floating in the water.

'I will be back... I have to get a fishing net. I don't know much about conservation, but if we can retrieve some of the gesso, and the scraps of painted plaster, it will help. Try not to disturb the water too much.' He turned around, and paddled as fast as he could back to the shop to find a net.

Ludovico and Giovanni, with the help of the monks, kept the massive wooden crucifix steady and upright. A number of them started to collect the fragments. When father Gustavo returned with his fishing net, they had already salvaged quite a lot, and had placed the pieces of gesso, and fragments of paint and plaster on a dirty china plate they had found. It was a herculean effort by all but to little avail. Seventy percent of the masterpiece was destroyed, and would be the single greatest loss, in artistic terms, from the floods. It proved impossible to move the giant crucifix that day since the waters were still too high. It would be another forty-eight hours until the crucifix would be lifted to safety.

Exhausted and freezing cold Ludovico and Giovanni left Father Cocci and the monks when there was little more that could be done that late afternoon. Leaving the Santa Croce, they slowly made their way to the Uffizi, observing the enormous catastrophe that was unfolding in the city, to pick up Maria. It had stopped raining, and the height of the flood was now past them. However the Lungarno di Grazie leading to Corsini was still impassable. They entered the museum, and called for Maria.

'What happened?' she shouted as she saw the two shaking bodies of her husband and his brother.

'You have no idea... Santa Croce was under six meters of water... It was like a war zone. Poor Father Cocci... He was unbelievable today. Without him the cross would be totally destroyed...'

'What cross... Not Cimabue's *Crucifix*?'

'Yes... What about here?' Ludovico asked, but Maria was momentarily speechless at the loss of the cross. She knew that Cimabue's *Crucifix* was an enormously important masterpiece. It represented a link between the mediaeval and modern worlds. The representation of Christ was a complete break from the past, and was one of the fuses that lit the Italian Renaissance. To lose it would be a massive blow to not only Florence, but to the history of art.

'We are ok here, but we have heard that the Baptistry Doors, both Ghiberti's and Pisano's have been damaged. Uccello's *Creation and Fall* at Chiostro Verde in Santa Maria Novella has also been a casualty as has Ghirlandaio's *Saint Jerome* and

Botticelli's *Saint Augustine* at The Church of the Ognissanti.' She paused, and suddenly realising the state the men were in, shouted, 'Come we have blankets and some heaters. You need to get dry before we go home.'

14

Francesca had spent the entire day in her apartment, listening to the news and updates on the radio. It was late in the afternoon, and there was little light left in the day. She was desperate to walk outside to see how bad things were. She tried calling people but there were very few telephone lines working. She felt that she was missing out on the excitement of events around her. Not fully appreciating the danger that existed in the oil polluted water flowing down the Borgo San Frediano, she put her boots on, and took her heavy raincoat off the peg. Armed with an umbrella, she walked down the stairs to the ground floor.

The water, which was covered in a dark black scum, the nafta, and now reeked of oil, had risen up to the fourth stair, and was quite calm. This reassured Francesca, who thought that the conditions would not be so bad outside. What she had not calculated on was the effectiveness of the block's front door, a relatively modern and thickly built door that had been effective in keeping out more water than the surrounding buildings. As she carefully made her way to the entrance, she slowly opened the door. As she did so, she was confronted by the torrent of the water, that initially pushed her backwards, before taking her out onto the Borgo.

She had no chance of regaining control, as the water, mixed with the deadly oil that contaminated its flow, forced her down the street at twenty kilometres an hour. Her feet never touched the ground, as she was propelled towards the Chiesa di Santa Maria. The three-walled, old derelict structure became more visible in the gloom as Francesca suddenly realised that she was going to be swept into its gathering arms. She closed her eyes expecting the worst as she closed in on the church. How strange, she fleetingly thought, to be killed in the place that had saved so many lives, and where she herself had escaped death by a hair's breadth twenty one years' earlier.

However, as she approached the piazza, the water slowed down as it climbed the gentle incline to where the church was located. She had never really noticed the ever so slight slope that the church rested on. But now, that incline saved her life, as the gushing torrent less than a hundred yards away, miraculously became a gentle stream. Far from killing her, the Chiesa di Santa Maria welcomed her with open arms as a resting place. Francesca managed to stand up and take a few steps. She slowly regained her composure and finally looked up in front of her. What she saw shocked her to the bone.

Earlier that day, despite being situated on slightly higher ground the Arno had ignored the slope and smashed its way into the three walls of the church. It stood firm, and acted as a protector to the surrounding area. This was particularly true by mid morning, as the water at first brought with it, thousands of bottles of chianti, tens of thousands of cans of food, and then hundreds of chairs, café tables and bicycles. Later, by midday, Cinquecentos by the dozen piled up against the battered walls, yet still the latter stood firm. The church had collected the city's debris and had saved the surrounding area from even more damage.

Francesca made her way towards the church. It was hard to believe what she saw. She started to climb on top of the rubble. Most of it had piled up against the southern wall. The *Madonna and her Son with Angels*, protected by Denon's false wall, remained hidden from the public gaze. The Frenchman's jealous concealment over a hundred and fifty years ago had meant that Masaccio's masterpiece had not only been saved from the Nazis' brutality, but also from the Arno's capriciousness. Francesca, now in her late forties and unfit, slowly climbed the pile of debris, which had built up during the day in a paradoxical chaotic order. As she climbed higher she began to see the devastation that lay around her.

She looked across towards the Arno and to her left where the Ponte Vespucci was still completely under water. The top of the Ponte alla Carraia was clear, and looking down river, the Ponte Santa Trinita and Ponte Vecchio were both above water. She could see both sides of the river banks were completely breached and submerged. Entire areas of the city were under water, including San Niccolo and Santa Croce, San Giovanni and Santa Spirito, Santa Maria Novella and her own Borgo San Frediano. Flood waters, were flowing through the streets and piazzas turning Florence into a Venice of the Arno.

However this was no picture postcard. The torrents that raged through the Tuscan capital were not exquisite canals gently passing through historic buildings. This was a city besieged by foul smelling, oil ridden water filled with flotsam and all kinds of debris. Uprooted trees, dead animals, and cars coupled with furniture and household goods raced along the submerged Lungarnos, and smashed against the houses and palaces, doing untold damage. People were standing on the roofs of their houses, some literally hanging on to ledges. Thousands of acres of land were submerged, making it impossible to discern the Arno itself. The widespread damage would only truly reveal itself the next day when the waters subsided. 'Thank God it was a public holiday today,' she muttered under her breath, realising that if it had been a normal work day, thousands more would have undoubtedly been killed.

Francesca remained seated on a chair at the top of the pile of debris looking out onto the city. Suddenly she noticed that her old newspaper kiosk that now belonged to Giovanni, no longer stood at the corner of the Ponte alla Carraia. Obviously swept away from its position by the torrents, she looked around to see if there were any remnants in the church area. Out of the corner of her eye she spotted, ten feet away, green boards, which were unmistakably part of the kiosk. She smiled. It reminded her of a similar situation twenty one years earlier, after the Nazis had destroyed the bridges that August evening. They were the same wooden green planks that had been discarded then. How flimsy the kiosk had been in comparison to the mighty church walls of the Chiesa di Santa Maria. The city will now have to pay for a new one, just like it had done after the war. She had been telling Giovanni for years that the wood was rotten and he should ask the city to change it… It would now no longer be the subject of an argument!

Although soaking wet and tired, she felt quite comfortable. It had stopped raining and it was relatively mild. Besides, the sight before her was so extraordinary, she found it hard to leave. The thought of climbing down was a concern, but she knew there was still at least thirty minutes of daylight left before she needed to go down. She laughed, thinking what a strange sight she herself must be. An old woman, on her own, perched on top of a rubbish pile in a derelict old church. It was at that moment she heard screams from the Ponte alla Carraia.

15

Ludovico, Giovanni and Maria left the Uffizi that afternoon. With the rain abating, they waded through the Piazza della Signoria up through Via Calzaiuoli and onto the Piazza San Giovanni. Maria, for the first time, saw the damage that had been inflicted on the Baptistry doors. It sickened her to the stomach, to see one of the greatest art treasures had been ripped apart by the torrent. Pushing away capsized cars, mopeds and bicycles, they managed to pass through the Via Campidoglio, and reach the inundated Santa Maria Novella quarter. This low lying part of Florence had become a virtual lake, but since Ludovico had been working in the area at the bus station for the last six years, he knew the safest route to take, and led them to the Via del Sole and Via del Fossi, before finally reaching the gentle incline leading to Ponte alla Carraia.

The Ponte alla Carraia had just about managed to remain dry throughout the day, its spans managing to stay above the river. The three Vanninis crossed the bridge, but stopped for a moment to look across at the city. The water was so high that it almost seemed that Florence had become two separate cities, immersed in a vast water expanse. It was an extraordinary site. Both roads on the banks of the river, the Lungarnos Grazie, Corsini and Vespucci on the north, and Torrigiani, Guicciardini and Soderini on the south were not visible. They then continued down towards the San Frediano district.

'It's gone, Ludovico… Look!' Giovanni said, pointing to the place where his newspaper kiosk had stood that very morning.

'I can see, Giovanni… I'm sorry, but you can't be surprised,' he said, putting his arm around his brother.

'Mama will be pleased… She said I should have got the council to replace kiosk wood. It was rotten. I just never got around to it… They'll have to compensate me now and build a new one!'

Just make sure that you keep that site. Its worth a lot of money. You don't want them trying to put you elsewhere in an exchange for a new kiosk,' Ludovico warned his brother. He knew that council officers could make life difficult when all this was over.

'I bet we see some of the debris near the Santa Maria di Chiesa… Look at it… It looks like a huge dumping site. The floods must have washed anything that wasn't attached into that three-walled area.' Giovanni was now looking at the Chiesa.

'What on earth is that on top of all the cars and flotsam?' Maria asked, pointing across from the bridge towards the church.

'It looks like a person is sitting on a chair looking out over the city… How strange,' Ludovico commented and then began to laugh. 'What an idiot… Who would do such a stupid thing like that… It's so dangerous.

'It looks like a woman,' Giovanni replied, laughing as they edged closer.

'It looks like your mother…' Maria interjected, when they suddenly stopped.

'IT IS MAMA… MAMA! MAMA! MAMA!' Ludovico and Giovanni screamed as the three of them ran down the bridge and onto the flooded Lungarno Soderini.

They reached the Chiesa di Santa Maria moments later to find their mother sitting on a broken chair on top of a twenty foot pile of cars and debris.

'What on earth are you doing? How did you get there?' Giovanni asked.

'I climbed… It was very easy. I'm only a woman in her late forties you know… I'm not a geriatric! Anyway, stop fussing all of you. I am coming down… Its very easy,' she replied calmly.

'No you're not… You stay exactly where you are, and we will get you.'

'All right… All right… Whatever you want, but I got up here on my own, I can certainly come down,' she replied.

The twins and Maria began to climb over the debris, reaching the top of the pile in a matter of minutes. At that moment, a groaning noise began to be heard. The four of them remained still, paralysed with fear. The groan became louder as the whole area began to shake.

'Oh my God… We are going to die… I'm so sorry for bringing you here… Please forgive me.' Francesca held her hands out to her sons, not knowing what was happening.

'It's an earthquake!' shouted Giovanni. 'The whole thing is moving… Just try and remain calm… It won't last long,' he tried to reassure everyone, but to little avail, as the noise became deafening.

'It's not an earthquake!' screamed Maria. 'Look!' She pointed towards the western wall that was crumbling in front of their eyes. The collapse of the façade, that had finally given in to the weakened foundations, created instability over the whole site. As it came crushing down, for a moment there was fear that the north and south walls would follow. However, after the collapse, the tremors subsided, and the two remaining walls remained upright. The Vanninis remained at the top of the pile of debris for a few more minutes before they finally climbed down.

It was now getting dark, the time approaching 6:30 in the evening. The floods were not yet receding, but the atmosphere had completely changed. They looked at the Chiesa, which resembled a bomb site, and wondered how many more blows could it take before completely collapsing. And yet the two walls that remained appeared as strong as ever, as if they were showing that nothing would bring them down. They would remain untouched for another fourteen years before they became the centre of attention again. And when the Chiesa di Santa Maria finally did reveal its hidden treasure, it wasn't to a mad engineering folly, a bomb or an artillery barrage, or even to an apocalyptic flood. No, the south wall of the Chiesa crumbled to a soft leather football beautifully struck by a gifted teenage footballer.

As they waded through the waters back down the Borgo San Frediano they realised that the worse was now over. At eight o'clock the waters began to ebb away. The entire Vannini family stayed at Francesca's flat that night. There was so little information available, that they decided to remain together. By morning the flood waters had completely receded, and the Arno was back to its normal level. The bright sunshine that greeted the city on the 5th November contrasted with the utter devastation that had been inflicted on the city. Nobody quite realised how much had been lost and destroyed.

As Francesca had said whilst sitting on top of the pile of debris, being a national holiday meant that only thirty people were reported to have had died in the flood. However the tragedy had resulted in fifty thousand families being made homeless, fifteen thousand cars destroyed, six thousand shops going bankrupt, and fifteen hundred works of art being damaged of which eight hundred and fifty needed immediate restoration. At the Biblioteca Nazionale one million three hundred thousand items, including the Palatina and Magliabechi collections, were lost in the mud in the Santa Croce quarter.

All around the city there are plaques that act as a permanent reminder to inhabitants and visitors alike showing how high the flood waters reached that day. To this day there are still pieces of rice paper on some of the masterpieces indicating where restoration is yet to be completed. It was a catastrophe that would not be forgotten.

PART II

PRESENT DAY FLORENCE

I

Molly woke up realising that today was a special day. The Uffizi had made an announcement the previous week that a new drawing by Andrea Mantegna would go on show to the public for the first time. The local press had picked up the story, and Molly had been mentioned as the person who first found the work at the convent. Maria had given most of the interviews, but gave Molly all the credit for the discovery. The unveiling of the image was at six o'clock that evening, and a number of dignitaries had been invited to a preview that night.

However there were other reasons why this day was a special one for her. Molly's nine months in the Tuscan capital had been the most enjoyable period of her life. She realised that she wanted to live in Florence after she completed her doctorate. She had made a life here, making friends, and was sure that she would find a job, either in the arts or educational sectors with her qualifications, not to mention her bilingual talent. She obviously had to talk to her father, and since he was arriving that afternoon to attend the unveiling, she believed this was the occasion to raise the issue of her leaving London.

And yet, despite the fact that she would be seeing her father for the first time in nine months, the thing that most excited Molly that morning was her meeting with the ninety year old Francesca Vannini. The latter had been waiting for her call ever since Maria had told her about Molly's work at the Museo di

Santa Maria, and her interest in the history of the museum. Francesca in her final years, and no longer embarrassed by her heroic achievements during the war, enjoyed talking about her exploits to fresh ears. Someone as engaged as Molly was a real treat.

Likewise Molly herself was intrigued by the Vannini connection to the old church. Having heard briefly about the activities of both Francesca and Maria during the war and the floods, she was extremely keen to meet the old lady who now lived in the ground floor flat on the Borgo San Frediano. Arriving at her address that morning she rang the buzzer and waited to be let in. After five minutes of standing outside and wondering whether she had the right address, she was eventually greeted by Francesca herself.

'I'm sorry about the wait, dear... I was in the bathroom when you rang.'

'That's quite all right,' Molly replied with an air of reverence to the fragile diminutive woman.

'Hold on!' A shout came from behind Molly in the street. 'Wait... Molly hold the door open.'

'Who is that?' Francesca said, nudging Molly aside and looking on to the street.'

'I think it sounds like Maria... It is Maria... Look,' Molly replied, both excited and surprised that she was coming.

'Ah... Yes so it is... Come on then,' Francesca called out to her daughter in law, who was walking as fast as she could. Although twenty-four years younger than Francesca, Maria was a woman of over seventy.

'Hello you two... I thought I would join you both for your chat. I mean it all links in rather nicely with your wartime stories, the 1966 floods... And of course my Gianni's football game in 1982,' Maria said as they all walked into the apartment.

'What links in?' Francesca asked, slightly bemused.

'The Vannini family connection with the Santa Maria... We

374

were all involved… Some more than others of course,' Maria quickly added, seeing Francesca's mild irritation.

'Well I think Molly will want to hear about the war first, and then we can go on to talk about the floods, and then you can describe Gianni's football game.'

'I actually know all about 1982… The story is part of my job as a guide… But Mrs Vannini, I would…'

'Please call me Francesca.' The old lady sat in her chair, whilst Maria went into the kitchen to make some tea.

'Sorry… Of course. Anyway please tell me about your experiences during the German Occupation. Maria told me that you were a heroine.'

'Oh… She exaggerates.' She waved her hand away in mock modesty. 'I didn't do that much.'

Maria stood at the door frame of the kitchen, shaking her head, and smiling at Molly. Her mother in law loved to underscore her role in the war, only to be flattered by her listeners.

2

Francesca spoke for an hour without pausing to drink her tea. Molly was suitably impressed, and Maria, despite having heard the story many times, never ceased to admire her mother in law when hearing about her heroism.

'So going back to the start... You never really knew much about the connection between your husband's ancestors and the church?' Molly asked.

'No... Not really. There are all sorts of legends... One, is that the keys were originally given to the chief builder as payment for the work when the patron ran out funds... But there is nothing written,' Francesca said, smiling at her young inquisitive guest.

'It's amazing that nobody knows about the family who were originally behind the building of the church, or the architect who designed it. It's also unbelievable that such a beautiful fresco could be forgotten. It makes you wonder what else is out there.'

'Ah well that is a different story,' Maria interjected. 'It seems that the Vanninis had the keys to the building, and certainly guarded and protected it. We assume they kept the fresco a secret from prying eyes, so that people would forget about it. The family did not want the city authorities to take it away from them. They had no idea of the value of the fresco during those years. It all changed when the French arrived.'

'How do we know that?' Molly asked.

'Well, we know Napoleon and his Arts Commission were very active in stealing art from all over Europe. A man called Denon, who you might have heard of, stole an enormous amount of treasures from Florence. There are legends that if he could not remove the frescos from the walls, he would try and transport them, away from their buildings, back to the Louvre!'

'Really? That sounds unbelievable!'

'Well, they transported the horses from San Marco in Venice, so nothing is impossible... What we understand from the tests that were carried out on the materials left from the wall after Gianni shattered it with his football, showed us that they dated from the early nineteenth century. This was precisely the time when the Frenchman ordered his sweep of paintings from Northern Italy destined for Paris. We think... and of course this is all guesswork, that he tried to take the fresco, but having failed, covered it up with a false wall so that he could return sometime in the future and try to steal it again without people knowing of its existence.'

'But was the church used again? What did the Vanninis do with it?'

'They left it... But were always worried about the repair obligations if they finally claimed ownership.'

'That's right,' Francesca said. 'My husband always used to fret that the church would fall down and kill someone. He was, I think on the brink of telling the authorities that they should take over the building.'

'So after the wartime bombing, the church had three walls still standing... And of course no roof.' Molly was still trying to put all the pieces together.

'Yes... The western wall collapsed during the floods of 1966.' Maria replied.

'And that's where you come in, Maria... Allegra told me about your exploits during that November morning,' Molly said nodding her head understanding the sequence of events.

At that moment the buzzer rang. Maria went to the intercom.

'Ah... It's you. Very well timed. Come in.' She pressed the buzzer. 'It's my husband Ludovico. He can tell you about the flood better than I can. I was locked up most of the day in the basement of the Uffizi trying to save its art. He was out in the streets seeing events unfold.' Maria opened the apartment door.

3

By the time Ludovico had finished telling Molly the extraordinary story of the flood, Molly was hypnotised by what had happened. 'So you and your brother actually saved Cimabue's crucifix.'

'Well… With others. Father Cocci was the real hero of Santa Croce that day.'

'And Giovanni still runs the kiosk today? The one where I buy my newspaper from, on the corner of the Carraia.'

'Yes… He will die selling newspapers… He will never retire!'

'That is so funny… I never knew he was a Vannini, and your brother by the way… He has been really helpful to me, in particular getting old periodicals from various sources.'

'Molly, you must come to us for dinner before you return to London,' Maria said.

'You can then meet Giovanni properly, rather than just as a shopper buying papers… He has his own stories on the flood. He was the one who really alerted us to the catastrophe since his neighbours nearly got killed on the Vecchio that night. They saw the catastrophic flooding first,' Ludovico said, lighting a cigarette.

'Put it out… For Gods sake, Ludovico,' Maria scolded her husband. She hated him smoking. She looked at her watch. 'Christ, I must get back to work. I have a speech to prepare for tonight's reception… I saw on the guest list two Cavendishes.' She looked at Molly.

'Yes... My father is coming tonight. We haven't seen each other for nine months... I never thought he would actually come and see me here... But he has surprised me... When he heard about the discovery, he said he would come to the unveiling. I have to go to the airport to meet him this afternoon.'

'Well then... We shall see you at the Uffizi,' Ludovico said, standing up and finally stubbing out his cigarette. 'Mama, I will come back this afternoon... Do you need a lift anywhere?' he asked Molly.

'No, I'm fine... I am going to walk back to my flat. I feel so exhilarated by all of your stories. I also feel, for the first time, that I really know the history of the Museo di Santa Maria! A bit silly since I have been a guide there for the last nine months.'

'Nonsense... What matters is your knowledge on Masaccio... And I know you possess that!' Maria replied, leaving.

Molly walked back to her flat on the Via Martelli. Arriving at the Piazza San Giovanni, she slowed down almost to a standstill. She allowed herself the luxury of walking round the Baptistry and the Duomo. Reflecting on the story of the Chiesa di Santa Maria, she strolled over to Pisano's gates and then towards Ghiberti's two sets of bronze doors. These magnificent masterpieces were being sculpted and created presumably at the same time as the Chiesa di Santa Maria. She wondered whether any of them were involved in the latter's building, given that Masaccio had painted the fresco. After all they all knew each other at that time. Without realising the truth, she thought how wonderful would it have been if someone like Brunelleschi had been part of the history of the Chiesa di Santa Maria.

Seeing the doors so often, and indeed studying them, sometimes meant that she would miss their aesthetic beauty and greatness. Today she simply looked at them without trying to intellectualise them. To see them as tourists, and indeed as Florentines themselves saw them. She then paused and wondered why Vivant Denon had not simply removed the doors and had them sent to Paris. After all, he supposedly could transport anything. Or for that matter why had the Nazis not stolen them for Berlin. The floods had done their best to take them away, and yet even they could not swallow them up into oblivion. Admittedly the original ones were temporarily being restored in the Museo dell'Opera del Duomo, but the replacements seemed just as real, and still evoked a magical sense of beauty. Most importantly the doors remained as gates to the exquisite octagonal eleventh- century Romanesque building, named by Dante as 'the beautiful St John'.

Molly walked away from the Baptistry and strolled around the whole piazza, looking up at Giotto's Campanile, Cambio's Duomo, and Brunelleschi's dome. She stopped, and wondered how many tourists from the seventeenth century onwards, have come to this square and have thought themselves to be in the very cradle of western art. She smiled to herself realising how lucky she was to be here. Nothing was going to stop her from returning and living there. She then quietly walked back towards the Via Martelli, to her flat before her father arrived.

4

Molly waited for her father at the crowded arrivals terminal in Florence airport, craning her head around the throng of people looking out for the appearances of their loved ones. She felt unusually excited about seeing her father. It had been nine months since she had last seen him, and although they had been in regular contact through the phone and emails, she suddenly realised that she had indeed missed him more than she cared to admit. Feeling confused by these emotions, she suddenly felt a wave of anxiety sweep through her. She wanted to get some air, but knew that she couldn't. She turned around, and moved through the people to the back where there was more space, and where she could breathe more easily. Her introspection was interrupted by the reality of the situation.

'Molly! Molly!'

'Dad!' she shouted, waving at him. 'How are you? I'm so happy that you're here.' Molly walked quickly over to him and embraced him like she had never done before.

'Molly... Are you ok?' her father whispered in her ear, surprised by the sudden warmth and emotion that his daughter was showing.

'Yes... I'm more than ok, Dad... I'm happy... It's been a long time.' Molly started to cry in her father's arms. All the pent up emotion, the frustrated love that she had felt for her father were suddenly unleashed in that one embrace. She had always felt that her father was to blame for the lack of emotional warmth between the two of them, but now she realised that maybe she herself had not given enough to the relationship. 'I'm really pleased you're here now.' She let go of him. 'Come on, let's go to the hotel where you're staying… It's a nice Pensione on the Via de Pucci, a few hundred yards away from my flat.'

As they made their way to the hotel, Molly and her father talked like they had never done before. It was as if their entire relationship, which had been so stunted emotionally, had been unchained through the absence of not seeing each other for such a long time. Her father talked about the work he was doing for the parish, and how the church was now flourishing with new young congregants who were moving into the area. Molly spoke about her life in Florence, the stories she had heard about the Vannini family, and of course her discovery of the Mantegna drawing. There was hardly time for both of them to draw breath before they reached the hotel.

'Right… The reception at the Uffizi is at 6pm. If I come back here at 5.30, we can then walk together,' Molly said having seen the room that she had reserved for him.

'No, no… I would rather come to your flat. You know… See where you live… And all that.'

'Really? No, I think it would be better if I come here.' Molly replied knowing how untidy the flat was, and remembering how her father hated her mess.

'No, I insist… Now give me the address.' He smiled.

Molly scribbled the address on a pad, which was lying on the table next to the bed. 'Here… But don't be late!' she said, turning around and walking out.

'Molly,' he said, before she closed the door behind her.

'Yes, Dad?'

'I'm so proud of you… I mean, discovering such a treasure, being in the local press… It really is so wonderful.'

'Thank you,' Molly replied, feeling her throat yet again

swelling, and tears forming in her eyes. She then left before bursting out crying again. This was becoming a little too much for her. The entire day had been emotionally draining. With the Vannini family stories in the morning and the sudden dramatic warmth that permeated her feelings for her father, she was a little concerned how she was ever going to handle being feted at the reception that evening.

5

The buzzer downstairs rang at exactly 5.30. Her father had always been a stickler for punctuality and that evening was no exception.

'Hi... Come up.' Molly replaced the receiver, and looked around the flat. She had tidied it up pretty well given that it had looked like a bombsite an hour before. Her achievement was made more remarkable in that she had also managed to shower and change at the same time.

As her father entered the studio apartment, he was quietly impressed that everything did appear to be neat and ordered.

'God, Molly, you must have really made an effort... I bet you've thrown everything in the cupboards, or under the bed!' he said smiling. 'Don't worry, I'm not going to check.'

'That's lucky then!' Molly laughed. 'Now that you've seen it, are you ready to go? I'm a little nervous, and want to get there early.'

'What's this?' Her father picked up the photocopy of Pico della Mirandola's writing, which was lying on the desk next to her files.

'That is a copy of the parchment I found at the convent in Fiesole. I'm still working on that... It's really important for my thesis, but it's taken far longer for me to decipher than it should have done. I've had so many distractions over the last couple of weeks that my studies have slowed down just when I needed them to speed up!' Molly said, picking her bag up and walking to the door.

'This is extremely difficult to read... My Italian is so rusty these days.'

'Dad... Nonsense, your Italian is perfectly good... It's not as if you live here and need it.'

'Well, whenever I come here, I think back to when I first met your mother. I fell in love with her, and I fell in love with the city. Now I'm back, it's just as I had remembered it.'

'I understand... I'm coming back to London in three months, and then hope to finish my doctorate in the following year... And then after that...'

'Molly, before you go on, I need to tell you something,' her father interrupted Molly in full flow.

'What is it?' She asked putting her bag back on the table. There was still plenty of time for them to make the reception before any formalities began.

'I wasn't going to tell you this now, but since I feel more open with you than I've ever felt before, I want to.' He paused. 'The church has offered me retirement next year... five years early, but on a full pension. I have accepted it... I was surprised how easy it was to make the decision. I had devoted myself to the community for such a large part of my working life... I just felt that it was the right time. With you being away so much, I really started to miss you... I know I am not the most emotional of men, but you do know that I love you with all of my heart.'

Molly stood transfixed, looking at a man who she hardly recognised as her cold, undemonstrative, and emotionally reserved father.

'Yes... But, Dad, I was going to say that I plan on moving here after I complete my PhD... For good. I was going to look for either teaching or research posts in Florence next year. What will you do?'

'Would you mind if I came with you? You'll have to help me brush up my Italian… Because I will need it!'

'My God, nothing would make me happier.' She laughed. She picked up her bag again, and then stretched her hand out to him, as they left.

6

There were many people who came to the reception that evening at the Uffizi. As Molly entered the gallery where the guests were congregated, she felt a sudden flutter of butterflies swarm inside her stomach.

'God, I don't know anybody here,' she said quietly to her father. 'Do you want a drink... Because I need one.' She continued, as she reached over to take two glasses of champagne from a silver tray being held by a waiter.

'Thank you... Is that the drawing?' her father asked pointing towards the now framed picture being photographed by a number of cameramen.

'Yes... And there's Maria Vannini. Come with me, and let me introduce you to her. She's an incredible woman.' They walked through the crowd towards Maria, who was now being interviewed by the press.

'Maria!'

'Ah, Molly, you are a little late. Please come, I want to introduce you to the press, and also have our picture taken.'

'Thank you... Where do I stand?' Molly asked, feeling distinctly out of her depth.

'Anywhere, except in front of the drawing!' Maria replied, laughing. The flashes from the cameras made Molly momentarily feel like a film star, but they were over before she could blink.

'Thank you, gentlemen.' Maria turned to Molly. 'I've given

a number of interviews, and you have not been forgotten. Your part in the discovery has been fully explained. You should be very proud.'

'I am, but Maria, you don't have to keep promoting me... I'm just happy to be part of the whole unfolding story of the Florentine Renaissance.'

'I know... But it's important for your career to get the credit you deserve... Academic acknowledgement is vital, particularly when you finish your doctorate, you might be working at the Uffizi. You see, we need young research fellows here. There's so much to be done on the literature side. Would you be interested?'

'Interested? I can't believe it... Of course!' Molly was completely shell shocked by the offer, which was now so timely given what she had told her father earlier.

'Well then, we can discuss it in more detail later... Is this your father?' Maria asked, looking at the silver haired man next to Molly.

'What? Oh! I'm sorry... I was so taken aback by the offer, I forgot where I was. Sorry, Dad... Maria, this is my father, Simon Cavendish.' Molly continued to speak in Italian, pressurising her father to speak in the native tongue.

'Very pleased to meet you Mr... I mean, Father Cavendish.'

'It's a pleasure... I have heard a great deal about you... Molly thinks so highly of you... And it now appears, from the offer you have just made, the feeling is mutual.' Simon Cavendish was surprised how easily his Italian was coming back to him.

'It is... Really, your daughter is brilliant, and we want her here. Now please relax and enjoy yourselves. The museum remains open for another hour, so you can wander around the other galleries.'

'Thank you so much,' he replied, turning to Molly.

'Is the rest of your family here? I would like my father to meet them,' Molly asked.

'Yes... They're over there in the other gallery. Francesca is sitting on the chair, and the others are milling around.'

Molly took her father into the other gallery where the Vannini clan were congregated.

'Molly... Have you enjoyed your moment in the sun?' Ludovico asked.

'Yes... Very much... Particularly as your wife has offered me a job after I finish my PhD.'

'Wow... Mother must really think highly of you. Getting a job here is so difficult.' Gianni responded. 'Is this your dad?'

'Yes... But I want to introduce him to your grandmother first.' She looked at Gianni who felt a little disappointed. 'Don't worry... I will introduce him to all of you. I have fully briefed him about all of your achievements!' she said, laughing, knowing how extraordinary the existing generations of Vanninis were.

She walked her father to the matriarch of the family, who was seated on a chair usually reserved for the security guards.

'Dad this is Francesca Vannini, a member of the Righteous Among Nations.'

AUTHOR'S NOTE

Although this is a work of fiction, it has obviously been set in an historical context. All the incidents and dialogue amongst the main characters relating to the story are products of my imagination. Many of the characters in the novel are well known historical figures, but their dialogues are entirely fictional. The Chiesa di Santa Maria, and the main characters of the Vannini/Cavendish storyline are all fictional. In all other respects any resemblance to actual persons, living or dead, events within the storyline, or locations is coincidental.

The sources I have used in my research are as follows (* signifies source used extensively):

Wikipedia has been used for general facts and information on all sections.

Renaissance Florence

1) Vincent Cronin, *The Florentine Renaissance*, Pimlico, 1967.
2) George Elliot, *Romola*, Penguin Classics, Penguin Books, 1996.
3) Laura Jacobus, *Giotto and the Arena Chapel*, Brepolis, 2008.
4) Ross King, *Brunelleschi's Dome, How a Renaissance Artist Reinvented Architecture*, Bloomsbury, 2000.*
5) Thomas Mueller, *Brunelleschi's Dome*, National Geographic, February 2014.
6) Giorgio Vasari, *The Lives of the Artists*, World's Classics, OUP, 1991.*
7) Web site, *brunelleschisdome.com*

The Napoleonic Wars

1) Peter Brooks, *Napoleon's eyes*, New York Review of Books Review November 19th 2009. Reviewing the following: *
a) Dominique Vivant Denon, *L'oeil du Napoleon*, Exhibition.
b) Vivant Denon, *No Tomorrow*.
c) Andrew McClellan, *Inventing the Louvre*.
2) David G. Chandler, *The Campaigns of Napoleon. The Mind and Method of History's Greatest Soldier*, Patrick Stevens Ltd, 1977.
3) Anka Muhlstein, Trans. By Adriana Hunter, *Painters and Writers: When Something New Happens*, New York Review of Books, January 19th 2017.

4) Judith Nowinski, *Baron Dominique, Hedonist and Scholar in a Period of Transition*, Farley Dickinson University Press, 1975.*

5) Andrew Roberts, *Napoleon the Great*, Penguin Books, 2015.*

Florence in the Second World war

1) Maria de Blasio Wilhelm, *Other Italy, The Italian Resistance in World War II*, W.W. Norton & Company, 1998.*

2) Tom Behan, *The Italian resistance. Fascists, Guerrillas and Allies*, Pluto Press, 2009. *

3) Thomas R. Brooks, *The War North of Rome: June 1944–May 1945*, De Capo Press, 3rd Edition 2003. *

4) Illaria Dagnini Brey, *Florence in Mourning: Remembering the Nazi destruction*, August 3, 2014.

5) Raul Hilberg, *The Destruction of European Jewry*, Yale University Press, 3rd Edition, 2005.18)

6) James Holland, *Italy's Sorrow. A Year of War 1944–1945*, Harper Press, 2009.

7) Richard Overy, *The Bombing war, Europe 1939–1945*, Penguin Books, 2014.

8) Joshua Zimmerman, *Jews in Italy Under Fascist Rule and Nazi Rule*, Cambridge University press, 2005.

The 1966 Flood in Florence

1) BBC Radio 4 Podcast, Sarah Dunant, *Florence Under Water*, 29th April 2016.

2) Robert Hughes, *The Spectacle of Skill. New and Selected writings*, Alfred A Knoff, November, 2014.

3) Katherine Kressman Taylor, *Florence: Ordeal by Water*, Hamish Hamilton, London, 1967.

4) Sweitlan Nicholas Kraczyna, Ed. Dorothea Barrett, *The Great Flood of Florence*, 1966, A photographic essay, Syracuse University Press.

5) David Lees, For Life Magazine, *Triumph from Tragedy*, I Giorni dell'alluvione, Edizioni Polistampa, 2006.

6) Franco Nencini, Enrico Mattei (Preface), *Florence: The days of the Flood*, George Allen & Unwin Ltd, 1967. *

7) Eugenio Pucci, Timothy Paterson (Translation), Agenzia Gieffe and Photo Locchi (Photography) *The Flood in Florence*, Bonechi Editore, Edizione Il Tourismo, 1966. *

8) Paul Salsini, *Dino's Story*, (A Tuscan Trilogy), I universe, 2010.

9) Ken Shulman, '*Thirty years later, Florence warily watches the Arno*', New York Times: 9th February 1997.

10) A Tuscan Travellers Tales, *The 1966 Florence Flood*, Tuscantraveller.com, 31st October 2014.